LOVE'S MASQUERADE

Elizabeth laughed gleefully when Damon, dressed as a dashing pirate, asked her to dance. As Damon guided her across the floor, she relished his arms about her, sweeping her around to the music. The lights were whirling above, the melody was soaring—and then the dance was over.

Suddenly, the lights went out. Everyone oohed and aahed, as if they didn't know that tradition provided this opportunity for the gentlemen to kiss their partners.

Elizabeth raised her face to meet Damon's. She could feel his breath hot and quick as his lips paused before her own in a moment of indecision. And in that moment, the lights came on—their chance was gone.

High fun and hilarity surrounded Damon and Elizabeth. But they removed their masks very slowly. Damon looked down at her, his face reflecting a wonder which went as deep as his soul.

Perhaps, there was still a chance after all. . . .

EXCITING BESTSELLERS FROM ZEBRA

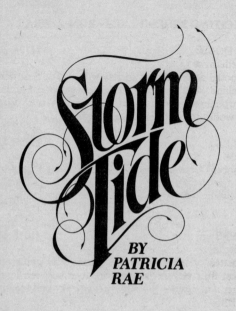

Storm Tide

BY
PATRICIA
RAE

ZEBRA BOOKS
KENSINGTON PUBLISHING CORP.

ZEBRA BOOKS

are published by

KENSINGTON PUBLISHING CORP.
475 Park Avenue South
New York, N.Y. 10016

Printed in the United States of America

To Pauline, Jeanne, Sis, Bud, and Jim

ACKNOWLEDGEMENTS

I wish to express my thanks to Mr. Larry Wygant, Associate Director for History of Medicine and Archives at the Moody Medical Library on the campus of the University of Texas Medical Branch at Galveston, and to my son, David, for helping me authenticate the background of UTMB during the years covered in this book. Also my thanks to Mr. Michael Wilson, former archivist at the Rosenberg Public Library of Galveston, for his assistance in my search of Galveston history, particularly that of the hurricane of 1900.

Author's Note

The facts concerning the University of Texas Medical Branch and the Galveston hurricane of 1900 are presented in this story as accurately as possible in accordance with historical data gathered in the archives of the Rosenberg Library in Galveston, Texas, and in the Moody Library on the campus of the University of Texas Medical Branch at Galveston. The faculty members of the medical school as characterized herein are based on actual faculty members living at the time, their academic achievements and character traits portrayed in accordance with a UTMB history, and taken from articles written and addresses made by the faculty members themselves.

For instance: the doctor who was the chemistry and toxicology professor during the period of time covered in this book did indeed operate the first x-ray machine in Galveston—one of the first in the country—and actually owned the first automobile in Galveston; the pathology professor did discover the *Necator americanus,* the hookworm larvae; the anatomy professor did experiment with and develop the formalin method of embalming and preservation which is still used today; and the professor of surgery was the first physician to specialize in surgery in the state of Texas.

Though the professional lives of the faculty members and other historic characters presented in this novel are based on fact, their private lives as depicted herein are purely fictional. Their names have been changed to protect the privacy of their descendants. Only the historically significant Galveston names of founder Meynard, the pirate Jean Lafitte, meteorologist Dr. Isaac Cline, his wife Cora Mae, Police Chief Ed Ketchum, the Ohioan Mr. Fayling, intern Zachery Scott, and architect Nicholas Clayton have not been changed. All other characters in this book have materialized entirely from the author's imagination, and any resemblance to actual persons living in the time span covered in this story is coincidental.

Prologue

It's ironic that I must leave the city of my birth, my youth, and my profession to go to another place more specialized in curing my particular disease, though I have spent my entire life involved one way or another in the medical complex here in Galveston, first as the son of one of the original members of the faculty of the medical school, and as a physician and faculty member myself for over forty years. The real irony, though, is that the place to which I have chosen to go—and probably to die—is Houston. Because my own physicians claim the cancer hospital there is the best in the South and I, like most of my predecessors, want to live. And if the best chance for me is there, then I choose to take it. Father would approve; because, even despite his immense loyalty to the medical branch here, he was first and foremost a practical man.

Standing as I am now at the top floor of Galveston's only skyscraper while my son sits waiting below in his newest Mercedes, I don't feel alone. I've never felt alone in this town, because it is a part of me. Perhaps it is all of me.

Looking down upon the city I'm amazed at the exactness with which each block is laid out, the straightness of the streets, the precise rows of houses almost identical in appearance from this height; tall, square or rectangular with gray-green roofs. They remind me of—what is it?—the little wooden houses and hotels of a Monopoly set. Ah yes, how appropriate.

To the east, the University of Texas Medical Branch is spread out into an enormous medical complex where there's always construction going on these days. I can count six huge cranes from where I stand, and four new buildings going up. To the south, the Gulf stretches blue and misty toward a horizon too hazy to discern, and nearer by on the north, the bay and the ship channel alive with shrimpers and small craft and one long, red steamer being slowly towed by a tug into port.

Galveston. Why do my eyes tear to think of leaving her perhaps forever?

A lady novelist—I forget her name, because I forget so much these days—once wrote of Galveston's ghostly charm, that she seemed built of ashes, and called her gray, shrouded and crumbling. The novelist is correct to say the city has ghostly charm, for she does, and that she seems built of ashes is true. But Galveston is no longer crumbling. Not since the beginning of the last decade when we began to restore the Strand and the old houses, trying to remember our golden age, a past that is my heritage and which was the vivid *present* to my mother and my father and to a seafaring uncle I never knew.

Galveston is haunted. Yes, by mostly friendly ghosts, I think. I have felt them while strolling down the Strand and while riding down Broadway, or bicycling through the old residential streets, and even as I stood beside the seawall gazing out over the Gulf. I suppose the feeling comes because of what happened here in 1900.

I've felt the ghosts as I've paced down the musty, dusty, crumbling halls of the old medical school building, now called "Old Red," where my father spent the early years of his profession, and in the family house on Avenue I. I've felt those friendly spirits on the beaches as the sand melted under my bare feet when the waves washed over them; and I've felt them while crossing the bay.

Sometimes it's almost as if I could shut my eyes and when I open them, the medical complex has vanished and only Old Red is there, and horse-drawn carriages ply the shell-paved streets, and square-rigged schooners navigate the waters of the bay. My mother sits at her dressing table winding her long, red hair round and round her hand to pile on top of her head in a shiny copper toddle, and father sits in the old, burgundy horsehair rocker in the back parlor smoking a pipe and reading the *Galveston News*.

But I open my eyes and it is still 1981, and I'm eighty years old and decaying inside.

It's sad to think that a century ago Galveston was destined to become the seaport of the west. As the oldest and largest town in Texas, Galveston was the Queen City of the Gulf, the New York of Texas; and Strand Street was the Wall Street of the Southwest. That she did not reach her manifest destiny still remains a mystery, shrouded in theory and speculation. She *is* great, but she isn't what she could have been. Some say it's because Houston dug the ship channel and stole her shipping trade; some say that it's because her seignioral citizens desired her to remain as she was, unravaged by the destructive influences of progressive urbanism. Most say—and I must agree with them—that she never fully recovered from the storm.

The storm. Appalling! That giant maelstrom slamming into peaceful, thriving, cosmopolitan Galveston, wreaking demoniac devastation so—how *dare* it choose this fair island to spend its fury! And why was this city, so beloved by my parents, the target of the greatest natural disaster in the history of North America?

And why am I dwelling on that now? Why does the thought of it still disturb me so? Why does my head ache to think of it even to this day, of what it did to this city and to my parents? God knows, from what I have read of it and the tales I have heard told, it must have been an *incredible* nightmare. . . .

Part One

One

These pallid, bloodless deaths were no nightmare fantasy . . . bloodless because the blood was staunched by salt and cold before it ever began to flow. And corpses do not bleed. What was happening to them, to him, was real.

Beth. Even in the roar of wind and water, the surge and threat of raging flood, with the blood from the wound on his head running into his face mixing with the salt of the seas gone suddenly mad, persisted the image of Beth.

Richard held onto the branch of an unidentifiable tree—and to his image of Elizabeth, his feet touching shifting sand beneath the water only every third or fourth step. But mostly they tread against the threatening currents. The roar of wind and sea deafened him. He was not certain which stung his face worse, the driven torrents of rain or the debris. Victims of the hurricane swept past, thudded against his side or lay sprawled on some disintegrating raft in death, or clinging, and he had no strength to help them. Not any more.

Beth. He should never have brought her here, to this island. He should never have yielded to his desire to speak to that blithe spirit the day he first saw her on the Strand. But he had, and now he wondered painfully if she had been swept away also into the waters of the Gulf, the sea. Oh Lord, not into the raging sea. . . .

. . . She huddled with Melissa and Joe Bob in the upper hallway. The demon outside shook the house and beat its fist malevolently against the roof, and surely there must be water upon the veranda now. It must be her wicker veranda furniture that pounded so heavily against the house, or one of her beloved palm trees.

Elizabeth watched Shad for a time, standing at the bedroom window where he had carried a lantern and placed it, watching for Richard just in case he came home in the dark. But surely Richard would have stayed at the hospital in its brick and stone safety. *Oh dear Lord,* she thought as a gust caused the house to creak and groan—and did it just now sway? For a moment she experienced resentment again because the house was not built of brick, for surely brick walls would be more secure against the wind. Yet these people, all these people had chosen the Morrison house in which to take refuge. All these people.

This was not the Galveston she knew, these scores of people huddled together in the second floor hallway whimpering. Where had their spirit gone, their bravery, their sense of pride? That was not Galveston outside either, the raging wind, the dark, threatening skies, the surge of seawater in the streets. Galveston was bright with promise and secure in its destiny; it was sunny and blooming and gay like that first day on Strand Street, that balmy May day—only three years ago?—when her heart was light and her future was so full of expectancy . . . expectancy. . . .

May, 1897

Buffalo Gal won'tcha come out tonight,
Come out tonight, come out tonight?
Buffalo Gal won'tcha come out tonight
And we'll dance by the light of the moon . . .

This wasn't the first medicine show Elizabeth had ever seen, but it was certainly the most colorful. The medicine man had drawn the attention of everybody on Strand Street by driving his huge yellow coach down the street while a real live Indian in full headdress sat stoically beating on a drum on the wagon seat beside him. Once Texas Pete had pulled the rig to a stop in front of J.F. SMITH & BRO, he leaped from the seat, and with the help of the Indian, flung open the two large doors in the side of the coach and hauled out a folding platform from within. A Negro dressed in a purple suit appeared from inside and pushed a small harpsichord onto the platform, then had sat down at the instrument and produced from

17

it a fast, reedy rendition of "Buffalo Gal," while fixing a piano-keyboard grin upon his audience.

By the time Elizabeth had gathered her skirts and made her way down the street to where the coach had stopped, there was already a small gathering there of gawking youths and small boys, being joined quickly by gentlemen and ladies smiling and nudging each other to show they knew what nonsense was about to follow the entertainment, and to cover the embarrassment of their own curiosity. Because the purpose of "Texas Pete's" appearance on the busiest street in Galveston was clearly advertised in the garish, red curlicue lettering on the side of his coach:

TEXAS PETE'S INDIANROOT
PATENT LIVER ELIXIR

After the Negro had completed several renderings of "Buffalo Gal," the Indian sitting upon the platform, began to beat the drum he held between his knees and the gray mares harnessed to the coach lowered their heads to settle themselves for a long *siesta*.

Texas Pete began his discourse by addressing the growing crowd as "most gracious ladies and distinguished gentlemen of the Queen City of the Gulf, the fair city of the treasure isle," and then proceeded to use the ultimate tactic to gain their attention, that of telling disparaging jokes about Galveston's crude, uncultured rival to the north, the city of Houston. It was not until he had gained their full attention and a measure of respect besides, that he explained in a sing-song chant that the true fountain-head of health and well-being lay within their own breasts, in a dark-red organ, located just under the lower right rib cage, called the liver.

"Yes indeedy, folks. Right next to the heart," he assured the crowd, smiting his breast.

Dressed in a jade-green suit and canary-yellow vest, Texas Pete sported a straw hat with a red band, and sweeping brown mustaches. He tossed from one hand to the other a long, bamboo cane while he discoursed, pushing his hat back off his forehead with the back of the cane, or pulling it down with the crook—whatever it took to keep the eyes of the crowd upon him. And one could almost believe the tall tales he was expounding because of his persuasive oratory and his self-assured manner. Indeed, he had captured everyone's attention as skillfully as any traveling evangelist who was adept at spreading the news that the rapture was at hand. But Texas Pete was preaching no such nonsense as doomsday; what he had to sell was much more earthy than that.

He began by telling a story that was as predictable to everyone as the product he was preparing to sell. He said that he was only a poor west-Texas country boy who was riding cross-country one day on is mule and came upon a friendly Indian village. He was sick at the time from some obscure illness and was given a miraculous elixir made by the Indians which cured him in less than twenty-four hours. The elixir was discovered centuries ago by the ancestors of Indian Joe, the Indian they saw sitting right there on the platform this minute. He took a sample of Indian Joe's elixir to a world-famous chemist who had pronounced it a remarkable concoction of all sorts of herbs and roots, and the chemist assured him that the elixir goes straight from the stomach to the liver and retards sluffing of the liver, the cause of all illnesses, in less than four hours.

Piffle, Elizabeth thought. But skeptical as she was, she was still glad the medicine show had come along, because it was fascinating to watch the medicine man's attempt to seduce the crowd by claiming to be a poor old farmboy from west Texas—with an unmistakable down-easter accent.

Smiling, Elizabeth looked around her. *These wonderful people!* she enthused. Their demeanor was euphoric, their gentility genuine. She supposed they were typical southerners yet unique in the prosperity of their own tropical island. She was so very glad she had agreed to accompany her father on his long journey south!

She and her father had crossed Galveston Bay by train only last evening. They had taken a series of Pullman coaches traveling from Chicago through Illinois, Missouri, the mesquite-covered wilderness of Oklahoma, and the wide plains of Texas, and drew near the end of their journey so physically exhausted that surely their weariness must have contributed to the phenomenon they beheld when they saw the city of Galveston for the first time.

Just as the train rattled onto the railroad bridge crossing the bay from mainland Texas, the city seemed to rise up out of the bay—of a sudden—was simply there—becoming visible through a transparent blue haze, a fairyland-like vision of shimmering white houses before which triangular sails drifted suspended just above the

blue-green waters of the bay. Nor did her enchantment
become dimmed when the Santa Fe train clattered off the
bay bridge onto the island, nor when its engine hissed and
puffed and clamored into the yellow-painted depot of the
city itself.

To the left, through the windows of the coach, they
had been able to glimpse warehouses and wharves on the
bay front, the giant masts of sailing ships, and the smaller
masts of yachts and shrimpers piercing the sky above the
warehouses, and of a single steamer in port. Fifteen
minutes later they had glimpsed the Strand, which Papa
had said was the center of the city's business district, as
they made their way to the Tremont Hotel where he had
made reservations by long-distance telephone. Since the
depot was located at the foot of Tremont Street, they had
only four blocks to ride in the cab, and had seen little of
the rest of Galveston that evening.

In the lobby of the elegantly southern Tremont Hotel,
Elizabeth became acquainted with her first palm trees,
potted and flourishing, as Papa signed the registry and
they became official visitors of Galveston, Texas for the
first time.

After sleeping the night in lavishly appointed rooms
they had breakfasted that morning in the Tremont's
dining room. It was there she first heard the Galveston
citizens' conversant drawl, gentlemen discussing business, ladies listening indulgently or not, sipping tea from
china trade cups beneath slow-turning electric ceiling
fans. There she noted the difference between the townspeople of cosmopolitan Galveston and those of the rustic
prairie towns of the interior.

Then Papa had left her to attend to the business for which they had come to the city, and she had strolled down Tremont Street to Strand.

The street was shell-paved, gleaming white except where carriages and wagons had woven deep, yellow ruts in the middle. Buildings on both sides exhibited curious ornamented facades of fancy brickwork and huge windows encased in iron. Buggies, hansoms, and coaches crunched along between rows of telephone poles and under a music staff canopy of whispering electric lines. And mule-drawn drays trundled up and down the street hauling their loads of freight to and from the docks.

There were few ladies on the walks under the arcades, this being the business district's main street where men sketched the building of empires and planned the acquisition of fortunes, admitting no need for feminine influence in the ventures, a facade as real as the ironwork on the building fronts and not nearly as formidable.

Now as her attention returned to Texas Pete again, she discovered that his oratory had not slackened, nor had the whoppers he was telling diminished in ingenuity.

"By many persuasions and various arguments," he was saying, "I persuaded Indian Joe to travel along with me to help make this miracle elixir available to good people everywhere. I have sold Texas Pete's Indianroot Patent Liver Elixir all over the United States, ladies and gentlemen, and patients have claimed cures within the body and out. It cures stomach aches, headaches . . . and *heart aches*, ladies. Rheumatism, vaporism, and Republicanism." As the crowd laughed, Texas Pete went on, "Poison Ivy, yellow fever, slow fever, intermittent fever, dengue fever, hay fever. Apply it to the scalp to cure fallen hair. Bleaches freckles and makes warts disappear. Yes indeedy. And . . ." he grinned winking, "it's been known that when the elixir is introduced into a cup of tea, the gentleman who drinks it becomes romantically inclined toward the first lady he sees."

The crowd chuckled at that.

"Now I tell ya what I'm gonna do," he continued, his oratory swinging into a hypnotic rhythm. "This beautiful Queen City of the Gulf has stolen this pore ol' Texas country boy's heart, ladies and gentlemen, so I tell ya what I'm gonna do. Gonna sell this fine elixir at *half price*. Yes indeedy, at half the cost I sold it in Houston just last week. You heard me there, brother. Gonna sell it at half price. Two dollars for a pint bottle of Texas Pete's Indianroot Patent Liver Elixir made by yours truly from an old recipe handed down to Indian Joe!"

Indian Joe stoically began to beat his drum again and the Negro to play a lilting arhythmic song on his harpsichord. Elizabeth instantly recognized the style of the music he played from last summer's music festival in Chicago. It was something new, rumored to have begun in the brothels of New Orleans, actually. What was it called? Ah yes. *Jazz!* The piano version of it called . . . jazztime? No, *ragtime*. And to its unorthodox nonrhythm Texas Pete began his seduction of the crowd.

"Step right up and place your two dollars in the basket by Shadrack's harpsichord. Yes indeedy who's going to be first to purchase Texas Pete's Indianroot Elixir?"

A well-dressed lady standing next to Elizabeth leaned toward her and said, "Do you think there's anything to it?"

Elizabeth shook her head no.

"Step right up, folks, who'll be the first?" sang Texas Pete.

A man stepped forward and dropped two coins into the basket, and Texas Pete handed over the first bottle of elixir. From then on he enjoyed a steady stream of customers—sailors, businessmen, ladies—yes indeeding his way through a continuous harangue while many in the crowd stood by pooh-poohing the whole thing, and a few still fluctuated between shrugging the thing off and going forward to purchase a pint, just for a lark.

"I forgot to tell you ladies," continued the medicine man, "Texas Pete's Indianroot Patent Liver Elixir causes the yellow to leave your skin, bleaches it smooth and white and blemishless. Brings a delicate blush to the cheeks and kisses the lips with a touch of wine!"

The lady next to Elizabeth said to her, "Now, I declare. That's going a bit too far, suggesting that such a thing can be a love potion and turn one into a beauty. You don't believe all that either . . . do you?"

Smiling, Elizabeth replied, "No I don't think it can do all that. In fact, the elixir is probably nothing more than a mixture of oil and spirits and has no more medicinal value than a cup of tea."

"As a matter of fact, there is *some* therapeutic value in this stuff," came a voice at Elizbeth's other side.

Turning, she found herself face to face with a blue-eyed gentleman in oxford-gray holding a bottle of the elixir up for her to see. "Any oil rubbed on the feet is bound to be soothing. And if rubbed into the muscles is apt to take away some of the ache," he said.

"And put enough of it in a gentleman's cup of tea," added another voice from behind her, "and he won't care if the lady looks like a frog or not."

Flushing now, Elizabeth turned just enough to see the gentleman who had spoken behind her. He looked so much like the first that she decided in a flash of reason that the two must be related. But the second one was younger and his skin much more deeply tanned.

"But to whiten and make the skin of the lady fair?" said the first as he held the elixir up to study its contents. "I doubt that." Smiling, he looked at her again. "Because if Texas Pete had made such a discovery, he wouldn't have to traipse all over the country in a coach, touting a Chinese coolie as an Indian chief, and keeping a drunken Negro piano player for entertainment."

Even though she had only moments before piffled Texas Pete's elixir, Elizabeth inexplicably bridled on his behalf. The first was speaking as if he were an authority on the matter, and the second as a careless skeptic—like herself. Suppressing a smile, she squinted at the gentleman beside her and said, "Just what makes you so certain that the elixir isn't what the medicine man says it is?"

"It's all the same. I've analyzed similar patent medicines before. They're all a hoax. But even hoaxes aren't all bad," said he. "Because if a person believes in a medicine strongly enough it can cure nine-tenths of what ails him."

"Or her," offered the gentleman behind her.

Pretending to be offended, Elizabeth turned to him

and said, "Your friend says he's analyzed the medicine. On what basis do you form *your* opinions, sir?"

He shrugged and spread his arms wide. "I guess on common sense to begin with, ma'am. And then my brother's word second." Then smiling broadly he added, "Besides, I've tasted the stuff." And shook his head, saying, "Nasty."

Vapors. Electricity. Or perhaps it was the air here in Galveston, but cool as she tried to be to these two strangers in order to show proper breeding, she became suddenly light-headed, flushed—and had to smile in spite of herself.

Curiosity (or was it mischief?) danced in the eyes of the suntanned stranger as he said, "I gather from your speech that you're a stranger in Galveston and I'll wager that you come from up north. Let me guess. Chicago." When Elizabeth's expression registered surprise, he went on, "I'm Captain Damon Morrison and this is my brother, Dr. John Richard Morrison. At your service, ma'am."

Generally, Elizabeth's affability influenced her behavior more than the conventions of society and this instance was no exception. She offered her gloved hand to Captain Morrison and said, "I'm Elizabeth Harbour." She gave her hand to the doctor, saying, "Your brother is correct, Dr. Morrison. My father and I *are* from Chicago."

"On business?" asked the doctor.

"Papa is in the textile industry and we've come to . . ." Elizabeth paused, hesitating to reveal too much, undecided whether these two could be trusted as much as she wanted them to be. She had been taught that it wasn't wise to speak to strangers, and yet, these two were not strangers somehow; and besides, she was curious. Why had the doctor purchased the medicine man's elixir? And why—

"Your father has come to deal with the cotton exchange," the doctor suggested.

She glanced in surprise at the captain, who said, "And I'll wager he's also come to negotiate lower shipping rates with Ingram and Sturgeon shipping company too."

Startled, Elizabeth said, "Why, what makes you think that?"

The captain did not answer directly, but looked up at the sky as if it were a habit of his, and she was inexplicably struck by the strength of his jaw, the muscles of his neck rippling under his deeply tanned skin. Then he looked down at her again, squinting a little and said, "And Galveston itself, have you seen much of it yet, ma'am?"

She must not let her guard down just because she was intrigued by these two brothers; the captain was too full of questions, too probing. But she looked at the doctor, who seemed so genteel and harmless that it caused her to reply, "No," recklessly, and dropping her defenses entirely she rushed on, "What I've seen is fascinating and lovely. Very lovely. And so different. There's something enchanting about the city isn't there? We will see it, all of it. That is, provided Papa can tear himself away from the stodgy old shipping agent in time. For you see, we leave the city tomorrow."

Captain Morrison smiled. "I'll take care of the stodgy

old shipping agent," he said.

She raised her brows.

"I'll see that your father gets away from him in time to take you on a carriage ride through Galveston. With two of the best tour guides possible. Free."

Puzzled, she looked to the doctor and he indicated his brother with a wave of his hand. *"He's* the stodgy old shipping agent today, Miss Harbour."

Elizabeth laughed and put her hands on her hips. "Ah! Now I understand why you guessed so much about my father and me. You were expecting us!"

"I was expecting your father. *You* have taken me by surprise, *quite* by surprise," replied the captain.

"Quite," she thought she heard the doctor say softly.

The captain was explaining, "I'm only acting as agent because both my employers Ingram and Sturgeon and their own agent have gone to New York on business and have asked me to act in their stead. They had informed me of the purpose of your father's visit before they left. Ah—I'm afraid . . . that what I'll have to say may make your father angry, Miss Harbour. But I hope that won't keep us from having dinner together, the four of us, so that I can explain at length the shipping company's position. Then, with your permission, ma'am, we could conclude the evening with a carriage ride and tour of the city."

Deep down inside this was exactly what she wanted, and it had happened so smoothly, so naturally. However, she returned demurely, "That will be up to my father, Captain."

"Then it will be our pleasure to see you again at dinner?"

"Only if my father agrees." She was not so naive as to think the captain's interest in including her in a business dinner was for the pleasure of seeing her again. No indeed! She suspected that the captain was attempting to bribe her in favor of the shipping company. It was an old game all businessmen played; to wine and dine and then to design, to influence the father through the daughter or wife by playing the charming gentleman. Had she not played the game in reverse many times herself? Besides, the captain's self-assurance in the game annoyed her and caused her to reply, "Before you meet my father, Captain, I think I'd better warn you. Papa is a shrewd man, and his temper isn't to be trifled with. I also should warn you that he won't be compromised. Or cheated."

The captain laughed shortly, incredulously. "Miss Harbour, we've no intention of cheating your father, believe me."

"No? From what Papa has told me, the Galveston Wharf Company charges such exorbitant wharfage rates that he can't pay the shipping costs anymore which such wharfage rates are ultimately costing him. Harbour Mills has traded through your company for twenty years but you're on the verge of losing his trade unless you lower your rates." She paused, tilted her head, frowned and said, "Just why do Galveston shipping companies feel they are immune to competition, Captain? Is the city unaware of the building of the railroads, both transcontinental and intrastate? That shipping by rail costs half what shipping by steamer does? That even other steamship lines charge less than Galveston shippers? You're rather arrogant in your pride as a shipping port, it seems to me. With the rates you charge, I wonder that you have any business these days at all."

The captain was staring at her, partly delighted, partly perturbed. He turned to his brother. "The lady thinks I'm dishonest, Richard. I'm afraid I'm undone. Should I argue about wharfage fees with a lady? I—I confess I'm not used to discussing business with a lady; at least one so well-informed. Should I acquiesce?"

Dr. Morrison's face had somehow undergone a change during the discussion; he was amused, but he was charmed too. As he continued to smile at her, he said softly to his brother, "I'd acquiesce."

The captain shrugged, spread his arms wide and said, "So be it then, Miss Harbour."

She was suddenly aware that Texas Pete's harangue was accelerating, that Indian Joe was already pouring a groaning basket of silver coins into a tin box on the platform, that the Negro jazz-player was grinning and playing another ragtime tune, and that the crowd was milling, laughing, purchasing the elixir, or explaining to others why they weren't. Meanwhile, a dray rattled by on the street with a load of lumber and a little organ grinder came strolling down the boardwalk, grinding out a tune as tinny as the cup he held out to passersby. A hansom crunched by on the part of the street where the shell paving was the thickest, and a pot-bellied man with a peg leg came hobbling along under the arcade clutching a bundle of newspapers under his arm, holding one out to passersby and calling in a monotone, "Dabey Naw. Dabey Naw."

"At five o'clock," Captain Morrison said as she focused her attention back to him. "In the dining room of the Tremont."

Her eyes twinkled back at him in spite of herself. "That is for my father to say," she said.

It was just as he'd thought, sarsaparilla, iron rust, and rhubarb pulp in a suspension of castor oil and corn liquor. And no trace of the snakeroot to which Texas Pete had obliquely referred. If one were to rub the warm, oily elixir on sore muscles, the heat would penetrate the skin and probably ease the ache. Dab it on an open wound and the alcohol content would disinfect it. A perfectly harmless elixir, unless one drank too much of it, in which case one would spend the better part of three days—and nights—enthroned in the privy.

Dr. Richard Morrison turned off the bunsen burners, picked up his pipe again and sat down in a nearby chair to resume smoking. Nothing in the elixir to necessitate inviting Texas Pete and his troupe to vacate the city. Ed Ketchum had asked him to analyze this last quack's elixir in case it proved harmful to the public. As police chief, it was Ed's duty to protect the citizens of Galveston from just such bunko artists. In this case, Texas Pete's cure-all—if not all that he claimed—at least was harmless. It was too bad the responsibility of extricating medical swindlers from the city fell solely upon the police. Each town and city's law enforcement agency had to decide for itself whether or not to allow such hucksters to peddle their patent medicines within the city limits. The American Medical Association had tried to convince Congress for several years now that the constitution did *not* guarantee the right of cure-all hucksters to deceive the public. But to no avail.

Richard puffed languidly on his pipe, sending miniature aromatic clouds into the airless basement room of the medical school's laboratory. Another year was done and the graduating class of 1897 had departed the medical hall forever. The rest of the students had either gone home for the summer, or were employed as orderlies at St. Mary's Infirmary or next door at John Sealy Hospital. Tourists were already thronging the beaches. And here he sat in the dank basement with its sand and concrete floor, enjoying a brief moment of blissful solitude after a harried day at the office. He should be making house calls now, but the picture of the charming Elizabeth Harbour in her tailored, blue suit and her rather absurd hat, kept intruding upon his mind and blanking out all other thoughts, like the sun was apt to do on a warm, spring day. He kept wondering most of all, what color of hair nature would have given a girl with skin so fair. Not black, surely. Maybe brown. Probably not, though, for her eyes were . . . blue. Yes, decidedly blue.

He rose from the chair, the pipe still clamped between his teeth, and went to the tin sink and turned the water into it, rinsing the test tubes and beakers thoroughly, leaving them to dry upside down in their racks, thinking that when he'd dirtied enough of them, he would boil them and store them away for the summer. But right now, he had to pay a call to old man Cunningham. And

Cully Swift had mumps, he should look in on him too. He took out his pocket watch, flipped open the case with his thumb, took note of the time, snapped the case shut, and tucked the piece inside the watch pocket of his trousers. Just enough time to see Mr. Cunningham and Cully and to go back home to clean up and change his shirt for dinner. Because, if he knew Damon, and nobody knew that rogue better than he, they would certainly begin the evening as Damon had said, dining at the Tremont at five.

Yes, he thought as he made his way up the stairs from the basement laboratory, he was curious about the color of her hair.

But Mr. Cunningham and Cully would have to wait another hour. For as Richard emerged from the stairs onto the first floor, he saw Will Kelly charging toward him down the corridor, trailing a stream of foul-smelling cigar smoke.

"Richard," he exclaimed, capturing the chemistry professor's arm, "you've got to come see me prize. Come, now. I'll show ye a speciment that'll strike envy in your heart and thrill the marrow in your bones. *Three days old and fresh as a daisy!*" Not waiting for Richard's reply, Dr. Kelly propelled him into the electric elevator, clattered the door shut, and commenced to nauseate him with the odor of his cigar as the elevator began its groaning ascent. "It's formalin, God's gift to pathologists and anatomy professors," said Kelly. "And thanks to you, Richard, for suggesting the original formula. Three years, and I've perfected the procedure. Beats alcohol, gas, aluminum salts and bichloride of mercury all to heaven."

33

Will Kelly's eyes were ice-blue and his gaze very pene-trating. His hair and beard were red, and still after six years, he spoke with a thick Scottish brogue. Kelly was unique among the "Old Guard" of the University of Texas Medical School in that he had studied art in Europe and was probably as good an artist as he was a lecturer. He nudged Richard now in the side and said, "He went to his eternal reward three days ago and on a hot spring day." He threw the lever that stopped the elevator just as Richard remembered his pipe and decided to manufacture his own smoke; because shortly, he was sure to need it. For whether there was a cadaver on hand or not, Kelly's dissecting lab always smelled the same, the sweet, putrid odor of decay having seeped into every crack in the floor, every pore in the plaster walls.

"Come, come," Kelly urged gleefully, blue eyes gleam-ing.

Richard followed him into the dissecting lab and stood for a moment just inside the door, while Kelly flipped on the electric lights. The architect who had designed the building seven years ago had also designed many of Galveston's most beautiful and monumental structures. In Richard's opinion, his artistic ability as an architect was unsurpassed. Before the architect designed the medical building, he had asked the Board of Regents for permission to visit other medical schools in the north and east in order to determine what the latest vogue was in the architectural design of such schools, and he was granted permission. The result of his tour and of his artistic skill was a great red structure of the latest Romanesque design, with colossal arches, turreted buttresses, protruding pilasters of red sandstone and Texas red granite, set into a facade of intricate brickwork, and with arcades of windows in the circular wings and in the main front.

Inside, the rooms were large. The dissecting room where Kelly was rushing ahead of him was some thirty by eighty feet and at least twenty feet high. The only thing wrong with it was that it was too dark. Where the architect excelled in artistic imagination, he lacked medical know-how. In this, the dissecting room, where delicate dissecting of tissues and organs was performed, light was needed and plenty of it. A skylight would have been appropriate in the ceiling here, a fact which Kelly had made known to the school's Board of Regents in each of its yearly sessions, and which it yearly ignored.

"Come, come," admonished the anatomy professor now, his Scottish brogue thickening with eagerness.

Richard knew, of course, what lay beneath the canvas sheet on the slate table, and he puffed avidly as he drew near it.

Kelly balanced his cigar on the edge of a table, whisked the sheet away, and Richard beheld the stony face of a gray-white male cadaver, eyes closed, patiently resting in eternal expectation.

"What do you observe, now, Richard?" Kelly demanded.

Richard puffed his pipe, slowly running his eyes over the anatomy while Kelly's piercing gaze sought to penetrate his thoughts.

"Come, come, what do you notice?"

He saw nothing but a perfect cadaver with a Y-shaped

35

incision, each branch of the Y extending at an angle from each clavical downward across the chest to join at the sternum, and from there extending down over the abdomen to the pubic bone. "I see a cadaver in excellent shape, which you have just begun to dissect," Richard said.

Kelly chuckled, and suddenly he was bending over the cadaver and spreading open the incision with a retractor. Behold, the inner workings of man; the small intestine coiled in the center, the pale-pink large intestine surrounding it, a healthy liver to the right, mostly hidden by the rib cage and diaphragm. Kelly's fingers probed into the abdominal cavity and with one twist of scalpel, came up with a kidney for Richard to see. "One," Kelly chuckled.

Richard continued smoking his pipe without comment.

Kelly dug down again grinning and came up with another kidney and placed it with the other on the butcher's scale at the foot of the table. "Two," he said. And now, chuckling, he dug down into the cadaver again and came up with yet another kidney. "Three," he chortled triumphantly. Then turning to Richard, he again pinned him with his intense ice-blue stare. "Three kidneys," he said holding up three damp fingers.

Remarkable, of course, for a cadaver to have three kidneys, but hardly an occasion for such delight in a man of Kelly's experience. "That explains why the liver was displaced slightly to the right," Richard offered mildly.

Kelly laughed gleefully. "But you've missed it, Richard. You didn't even notice!"

36

Richard studied the entrails again, saw nothing amiss, looked up, and squinted through the smoke at Kelly, waiting for an explanation.

"The smell," the Scottsman chortled. "The smell is absent. And you didn't even notice."

The devil! It was true! The odor of putrefaction so common to a three-day old cadaver was missing. And instead, there was another pungent odor—formalin. And perhaps alcohol.

"Formalin," Kelly shouted. "A mixture of formalin and alcohol mainly, infused into the circulatory system by none other than yours very truly, Richard. It's a revolutionary discovery, I tell you, and I can't express how ecstatic this makes me. Soon we can have a whole *room* full of cadavers ready and waiting for the students. I tell you, Richard, once we work out a cheap manufacturing process for this formalin solution, this will revolutionize the undertaking business, and pathology as well. Behold!" Kelly took a jar of solution from a nearby shelf, unscrewed the lid, and the stench of formalin stung the nostrils of both men as he dropped the kidneys one by one into the jar and screwed the lid back on. "They are in perfect condition from the infusion and will remain fresh as daisies for decades," he chuckled. Reverently, he placed the jar on a shelf with four other floating specimens; a brain, a liver, a stomach, a spleen, then turned and began to let water into a basin where he commenced to wash his hands, saying, "I'll develop a whole museum of specimens, Richard, for the students. No longer will we be in need of specimens!"

Richard covered the cadaver again with the sheet

saying, "What did this patient die of?"

By now Kelly was scrubbing his hands vigorously with lye soap. "It was a sudden death, so methinks it was his heart. But just in case, Richard, you best wash your hands too. Now that we know of such things as bacteria, we can at least *drown* the little beasties so as not to carry them to our patients." He turned and leaned against a chair while he dried his hands on a towel. "We know that decaying flesh is the most advantageous host for every dread disease in man; and that, Richard, is why God gave it such a *mean* odor, so that living mortals would bury it deep before it offended their olefactory senses, man not knowing until recently that the burying was also preventing the spread of disease. But now, with formalin, there's no need to use our cadavers within twenty-four hours after death. Thanks to Dr. William Kelly with the able early assistance of Dr. Richard Morrison, we can now store cadavers like *cheeses*."

Richard picked up the bar of soap and began to scrub his hands while Kelly asked, "Going to the concert tonight?"

"Nope."

"Going to play chess with Rob Tate?"

"Nope."

"Then you must have a lady in labor."

"Not yet."

His curiosity now aroused because of Richard's evasiveness, Kelly picked up what was left of his creosote-smelling cigar, eyed him keenly, and said in a husky whisper, *"What* then, ye damn Texan?"

Intending to let Kelly suffer a bit with his insatiable

inquisitiveness, Richard dried his hands slowly, picked up his pipe, then leaning toward the Scotsman in a conspiratorial manner said, "I hope to be taking a carriage ride, Will." And satisfied with his friend's disappointment, he clamped the pipe between his teeth and puffed a moment before he added, "With a lovely lady," just to make him suffer a little bit more.

Two

Strand Street—or "The Strand," as the Morrison brothers called it—which was paved with crushed sea shells, changed from an iridescent white to yellow in the early evening sun. The hooves of the horse pulling the surrey did not clop or thump as they might have on a macadam or dirt street; rather the sound they made was *spat-spat-spat*, as he pulled the surrey down the street.

Captain Morrison was driving, with Elizabeth sitting in the forward seat beside him, and Dr. Morrison and her father, Randal Harbour, sitting "abaft," as the captain had put it.

"There," Elizabeth said pointing. "On the corner. That building. You see what I mean, Captain? There's an occasional one that is somewhat different from the others. I noticed that yesterday. You see, don't you? There are pediments and extra pilasters and intricate brickwork the others don't seem to have."

The captain threw her an approving glance. "Yes. I

see. And you're probably noticing the work of Nicholas Clayton, one of Galveston's architects. He's been quite active here as you'll see."

The Strand was really not much different than other streets in other business districts in other towns she had seen, but it excited her more. Perhaps that was because the ship channel was just two blocks away with its huge steamers and square-rigged sailing ships in port, discharging seamen and cargo from distant ports. Or perhaps it was because of the handsome sea captain sitting beside her, acting as their guide.

The surrey turned right and the captain pointed across the street. "How do you like that one? That building houses a real-estate firm, another Clayton masterpiece."

The structure was narrow and tall, sandwiched in between two others, but there was that venturesome architecture again, the extra scrolls of stone, carvings in granite, ornamented windows, and boggling brickwork in various shades of pink and red.

"It's lovely."

The sea breeze of the Gulf of Mexico was blowing up the street from the south cooling her face, and it was so strong that she had to hold onto her hat. Oh, she was enjoying herself so! And to think Papa had almost spoiled the whole evening.

She and Papa had come down from their rooms at the hotel that evening and were met by the captain who stood tall and handsome, dressed in a navy, double-breasted suit made of fine wool. He had removed his square crowned hat as they approached and inclined his head toward her. "Miss Harbour." Then to her father he extended his hand. "Mr. Harbour, good to see you again, sir."

"I doubt that it will be for long, my good man, if the evening is only a continuation of this afternoon," Randal Harbour had quipped, and gripped the captain's hand just long enough to be civil.

The captain ignored his barb. "Dr. Morrison hasn't arrived yet and I think he'll probably be late. But we can go to the dining room for tea while we wait for him, if you like."

"We'd like that very much," Elizabeth said and took the arm he offered her.

She knew at the time that her father's appointments with the representatives of the various shipping companies had not gone well, though she hadn't time to discuss it with him when he'd come back to the hotel rooms after the meetings. But as they talked over tea in the Tremont's dining room, the situation had become plain.

Captain Morrison had been instructed by his employers, Ingram and Sturgeon, not to reduce the rates which they were charging the Harbour Mills for shipping compressed cotton up the Mississippi to Chicago, nor the import rates of raw silk from the orient, nor the export rates of finished products to the west coast, the West Indies, and western Europe.

The situation was grim from a business standpoint. Harbour Mills was located on the south bank of the Chicago River, and Ingram and Sturgeon Shipping Company had, for twenty years, shipped compressed cotton to the mills from the interior of Texas and Louisiana. They also imported for the mills raw silk, wool, and flax from seven foreign ports, and this was shipped out of Galveston in steam packets, past the port of New Orleans, up the Mississippi River, and through the Illinois Michigan canal to Lake Michigan. During the previous summer, Harbour Mills had begun the experimental production of chemically man-made fibers in two of its mills at great expense, forcing the board of directors to seek to cut as many production costs as possible. When they first looked toward labor as a source of cutting costs, Elizabeth, one of Chicago's popular socialites, and a rather radical young lady who believed that women should have the right to vote, interceded in behalf of the laborers by reminding her father and the other board members of labor's growing unrest all over the country, influencing them to look elsewhere for ways to cut production costs.

One of the places to which the board looked for cutting costs was shipping. Upon fierce investigation, it was discovered that Harbour Mills paid almost triple the shipping costs of both raw material and finished textiles as did the big textile mills on the east coast. So Randal Harbour decided to speak with the steamship agents in Galveston in person and brought with him to the city his daughter, Elizabeth.

After having spent a day speaking with the various steamship agents in Galveston, Randal Harbour began to realize that he was in a truly befuddling predicament. He would not—could not—pay the shipping company's exorbitant rates, and the Ingram and Sturgeon Shipping Company would not cut costs. For though they held a controlling interest in the Galveston Wharf Company because of their large stock holdings, they were nevertheless shippers and had to pay the same exorbitant wharfage rates as everybody else, and if they cut their own shipping costs while having to pay the high wharfage fees, their margin of profit would be extremely narrowed. Even to the point of threatening bankruptcy, Captain Morrison had explained. Harbour had discovered during the frustrating course of the day that he could do no better with any of Galveston's other lines either. Because, whether they were members of the wharf company or not, they still had to pay the same wharfage rates. It seemed to Harbour that the shipping companies who were members in the wharf company—and that was most of them—were cutting their own throats, which made no sense to him at all.

Elizabeth suggested that perhaps Harbour Mills could ship the raw cotton to Chicago by rail.

Harbour said, "That would help. But trains can't carry goods across the Atlantic."

"But you could cut some of the costs," she persisted, "by shipping the raw material that comes into the port of Galveston, by railroad rather than by steam packets up the river."

"But not much, Miss Harbour," said the captain, "though I have to agree that it would be some cheaper to do that. I suppose it *is* worth checking into."

"I'll *have* to check into it, Captain Morrison. I have no damned choice," Harbour said morosely.

Randal Harbour was a short man in his late fifties with brown mutton chop whiskers, whom Elizabeth adored but found necessary to rule over with a soft, insistent persuasion, because he was often tactless and brusque. He had been a fierce abolitionist during the war and distrusted "Southern Rebels," so it had always irked him to have to do business with them. However, he often said he'd do business with the devil himself if it proved cheaper to do so. Because, in spite of the high wharfage rates at Galveston, the transportation of both domestic and imported raw materials up the Mississippi from the Gulf had, until recently, been cheaper than shipping goods from the eastern ports by rail. Too, Galveston was located in south Texas where the cotton industry was flourishing, Texas alone producing three million bales of cotton a year; whereas the cotton industry in the southeast was even yet struggling to recover from the ravages of the war—was also further away—making the prices of shipping cotton by rail to the midwest somewhat higher.

At some point in the conversation, Dr. Morrison had finally made his appearance, dressed immaculately in the same gray suit and square crowned hat he'd worn earlier in the day, but with a fresh linen shirt. Captain Morrison rose and introduced him to Mr. Harbour, and the doctor nodded to Elizabeth and extended his hand to her father. "Miss Harbour, Mr. Harbour, sir. My apologies for being late. I had two house calls to make."

"Quite alright, Dr. Morrison," Randal Harbour muttered into his beard, unable to recover from his present gloom.

The doctor sat down at the round table, and the captain called for the waiter.

The seafood dinner had gone well, with the captain

telling seafaring tales at Elizabeth's prompting, and this was interspersed with occasional barbs from her father who she feared would finally anger the captain and spoil the entire evening. However, either the captain side-stepped Randal Harbour's thrusts, or she quieted him momentarily with her warning glance, or the mild-mannered doctor changed the subject.

Though Elizabeth was totally involved in the conversation at the table, with a Morrison brother on either side of her, she was conscious at the same time of the townspeople sitting around them in the dining room having dinner. The gentlemen were dressed with excellent taste in wool worsted suits, and the ladies in silk shirt-waists or afternoon frocks of exquisite crepon cloth, muslin, and lawn, fabrics of much lighter weight than one would find in Chicago that time of year. Their soft southern drawl contrasted genially with her father's own clipped, midwestern cant; but there was an occasional boisterous fellow among them dressed in coarse wool and run-down-at-the-heel boots, whom she decided must have come from the interior of Texas—perhaps from Dallas or Houston.

At last the conversation had turned to Galveston and its exciting history which she recalled as the shiny, black surrey rattled down one of the business district's less attractive streets.

The Morrison brothers had told about the European explorers coming to Galveston island and finding it inhabited by the cannibalistic Karankawa Indians; later the handsome and dashing pirate Jean Lafitte, had established his commune and built his residence at the east

end of the island. Years later the site of the city of
Galveston was purchased by a Mr. Menard whose mansion they would drive by later, Captain Morrison had
said, and which was now occupied by Ed Ketchum, an apt
name for the city's chief of police. Galveston grew and
became a port of entry and by 1857 a railroad had connected Galveston with the interior of Texas.

Galveston enterprise was disturbed very little by the
Civil War, growing rapidly, and the many and varied
business transactions carried on behind the cast iron
fronts of the buildings on the Strand gained the city the
reputation of being the New York of the Gulf, and Strand
Street, the Wall Street of the Southwest.

"And even then the Galveston Wharf Company had
gained the reputation of being the Octopus of the Gulf,"
Randal Harbour had groused at that point in the conversation.

Now the surrey turned onto a wide street—oh so
wide—with a broad, grassy boulevard down the center
which nurtured giant live oaks and tall rustling palm
trees; and the shrubbery burgeoning with pink and red
blossoms were called oleanders, and others were crepe
myrtles, Dr. Morrison explained from the rear seat of the
surrey.

"Broadway," said Captain Morrison with a gesture
that encompassed the length and breadth of the street,
"the avenue of kings, the elite, the aristocracy!"

"Members of the Galveston Wharf Company," came
Randal Harbour's jibe from the rear seat.

Elizabeth turned halfway around and silenced him
with a glare.

47

The street was bordered by a tapestry of high gabled mansions in brick and stone, turreted castles beyond black, ironwork fences, flourishing gardens, hedges, and towering palms. Elizabeth had seen houses like these before; Romanesque, Gothic; doorways guarded by granite griffins and gaping lions of marble, statues in the gardens, wrought iron settees under brooding oaks. But there was still that certain magic here. Perhaps it was the semi-tropical vegetation, or the salty sea breeze touching her skin with its soothing lotion, or the honeysuckle scent of spring in the air. Or the handsome sea captain in the carriage beside her.

The captain turned left off Broadway to a neighborhood where the houses were smaller and frame, painted the dazzling white one saw shimmering when one approached the island from the bay. Occasionally Dr. Morrison would point out a residence built by the same architect who had designed the more picturesque buildings in the business district, and it was not long until Elizabeth could recognize one of Nicholas Clayton's houses before the doctor could call her attention to it. His houses were like intricate needlework trimmed in lace; yet not one was overdone. The neighborhood was charming with its smaller yards and color-splashed gardens. And now they were near the bay.

Captain Morrison drew the carriage to a halt before an imposing structure, a red fortress in brick and granite, almost oval in shape and some three to four stories high, with mosquelike turrets reaching like bejeweled fingers to the sky.

"This is the Medical School Building," Dr. Morrison

said. "Six years old. The University of Texas Medical School. Guess who designed it, Miss—"

"Mr. Clayton," Elizabeth said clasping her hands like a child. "And is this where you teach, Doctor?"

"Yes. I lecture in Chemistry and Toxicology."

"And you have your own private practice as well?" asked Randal Harbour.

"Yes."

The captain glanced at Harbour in the rear seat. "John Richard was one of the top ten in his graduating class at Columbia School of Medicine, Mr. Harbour."

"There, that building adjacent the medical school," said the doctor, changing the subject, "is John Sealy Hospital where our students do some of their training. And behind the medical school, the building you see there was the old city hospital which is now the Negro hospital."

"Well, my Lord!" exclaimed Harbour. "You southerners have even separated the Negroes from the whites in your hospitals!"

Elizabeth quickly turned about. "Papa!" she scolded furiously.

"Southern hospitality," he muttered into his whiskers.

Captain Morrison quickly shook the reins, clucked to the horse, and the surrey began to roll down the street again.

They were quiet now, Dr. Morrison having been put in his place as well as the captain, with Mr. Harbour sulking in the rear seat and Elizabeth embarrassed in the front.

But the sudden sight of the Gulf of Mexico appearing blue-green and vast before them, opened up new avenues of conversation, and immediately transported Elizabeth into an ecstacy of awe.

Captain Morrison guided the surrey onto the beach road along which the white, sandy beach stretched as far as the eye could see, dotted with a few lingering bathers playing in the surf or sunning on the sand, or walking down by the water. There were giant beach houses built on piers of creosoted pilings stretching out over the water; and the beach road itself, busy with carriages carrying the city's citizens out for an evening's drive, was embellished on either side by colorful shanties and concessions selling frankfurters, ice cream, saltwater taffy, varieties of candies, lemonade, dolls, trinkets, post cards—a midway of modest mercenary enterprise. To the right, landward, she could see blocks of white houses, tall and narrow, facing the Gulf.

As the surrey crunched along the shell-paved beach road, passengers in other carriages meeting them occasionally called to the captain or the doctor, and gave Elizabeth a chance to smile and nod and pretend that she was a regular part of the scene; and it pleased her that young men plodding along the road paused to stare as they went by—at her—a thing Captain Morrison seemed oblivious to.

The surrey passed a mule-drawn electric trolley car and a young man stuck his head out a window and called, "Hey, Dr. Morrison!"

And then they saw ahead, and finally came abreast of, the most magnificent structure they had seen yet, an enormous beach hotel, a glamorous, mauve palace constructed rather like three luxurious pavilions joined together, with candy-striped roofs in red and white, and a brilliant, octagonal dome rising many feet into the air and topped by a flagstaff and weather vane.

"Nicholas Clayton designed that," said the captain. Which surprised Elizabeth. For the structure was unworthy of Mr. Clayton.

Gawdy. She did not like it. And liked it less when the Morrison brothers told of Texans coming from near and far to stay at the hotel to enjoy the beach—and extramarital affairs; it was a place that inspired gossip and intrigue.

"If the city continues to construct and develop tourist accommodations and attractions such as that hotel represents," said Elizabeth in a huff, "the entire island will soon be a paradise for brothel owners, saloon keepers and gamblers." And she thought she heard Dr. Morrison cough from the rear seat.

But the hotel was soon behind them and now to the left the beach stretched and the sea rolled with the sun just above the water in the southwest, causing her to shade her eyes with her hand in spite of the surrey's fringed top.

"Captain," she said suddenly, "oh, do let's park the surrey and go down to the beach." She turned to her father. "May we, Papa? It's only a short stroll."

The captain happily did her bidding without her father's consent, and while he jumped down and tethered the horse to the post, Dr. Morrison helped her from the carriage. Her feet touched the soft sand and she went a little ahead of the others, down to the sea beyond the concessions, and to where the indigo surf rolled in and

51

washed the white sand, turning it to glass.

The captain fell in step beside her, hat in hand, the straight, dark locks of his hair blowing across his forehead.

She had worn the forest-green fitted suit with the skirt that did *not* have a train—for which she was thankful—and a small, straw hat with pale green and gold flowers, to protect her complexion on the ride, and because it was fashionable. But oh, she longed now to pull the thing off, to be free of it, to feel the ocean breeze in her hair. She glanced at the congenial captain strolling beside her, at her father discoursing to Dr. Morrison behind them.

"So you really are a sea captain," she said to the one at her side.

"Yes ma'am."

"On any particular ship? Or do you sail on any that's available?"

"Any ship. I started out with the square-riggers, Miss Harbour, but now sail mostly the steamer *Arundel*. She's in dry dock now, though, having her bi-yearly scraping and some engine repairs done."

"You didn't wreck her!"

He laughed. "No. It's the engines. Much to my dislike, I've had to push her unmercifully to meet the schedules the company has set for her. Her engines have broken down so often this past year, I've hoisted sail more than I've used steam."

"Is she a paddle wheeler?"

"No ma'am. She's screw driven. Her engines turn drive shafts that turn the propellers, which is what propels her in the water."

"I see. Sort of like a paddle wheel, only it's *under* the water entirely, *behind* the boat, and turns *sideways*."

The captain started to laugh at her, thought better of it, contemplated her explanation, and finally nodded saying, "As a matter of fact, Miss Harbour, that's absolutely correct." His eyes took on a faraway look as he looked out over the Gulf and said, "The propellor is driven by a reciprocal steam engine, an 'up-and-downer,' we call it. A powerful engine but subject to so many breakdowns that—" He came to himself and glanced at her. "Anyway, the *Arundel* will be in dry dock for six months."

"And where do you sail?"

"Up the east coast, or to the West Indies, and down the east coast, around the horn, and up to San Francisco. Sometimes even to Europe. Not on the same voyage, of course."

"May I ask a personal question, Captain?"

"Of course."

"Why did Ingram and Sturgeon ask you, a sea captain, to act as agent for them in dealing with my father?"

"As I explained before, they and their agent are in New York and have left the business in my hands. Eric Ingram thinks I've a sort of genius for ships and shipping. But he's wrong. You can't equate genius with plain old practical experience." He bent down and picked up a shell, examined it briefly, then cast it out into the surf.

"Does that apply to women as well as ships?"

He smiled. "Why should such a thing as my experience with ships—or women—interest a lady of your obvious gentility, Miss Harbour?"

53

She shrugged, something her mother had once taught her not to do because it was unladylike. "It doesn't. Only I think it must be hard for the girls to resist your attentions, Captain. I mean, when you wear your uniform."

He grinned. "I don't wear a uniform, but if I did and that were the case, I'd wear it all the time."

They walked in silence for a moment while her heart seemed to fill her entire breast; for she was keenly aware that she was strolling on a beautiful beach with a handsome sea captain, that she was still young, and there was still a world of things she did not know and had not experienced; and she was suddenly enamored by the thrill of adventure. Under the circumstances, however, all she could do about the latter was to untie the scarf under her chin and *remove her hat!* Then, looking up at the sky, at the gulls swooping and shrieking and soaring white against the darkening sky, she asked, "Do you have a girl, Captain?"

"Do you have a beau, Miss Harbour?"

"I asked for that, didn't I?" she laughed.

"I think I might have asked it anyway."

This time it was she who bent down to pick up a seashell and toss it out to sea. "I know who your lady is, Captain," she said, and when he glanced sideways at her, she said, "It's the sea. Like all the sea captains one reads about, married to the sea."

"The sea is not a lady; it's neuter. But you're right, I'm bound to it. But that doesn't mean I love it."

"Not love the sea?"

"I hate the sea."

"Then why are you bound to it?"

"It's not the sea I love, it's the legacy of wealth. Because of it, men have discovered continents, built empires, established fortunes. I understand the sea. I know its habits good and bad. And from it someday I intend to build my own fortune."

"Why do you hate it then?"

They paused and the captain, looking out over the Gulf for a moment, said, "It's devious, unpredictable. It's a murderer. It's as vicious as it is seductive." He seemed to brood for a moment, then began walking again. "It changes, you know, with every wind that blows."

"You talk as if it's alive."

"It is."

"Piffle."

"You'll see, Miss Harbour."

She studied the fine profile a moment before she replied, "I'll see?"

"Yes. Somehow, I know you will."

She started to ask how or what he meant, but his hand shot out suddenly and caught her arm and they stopped walking abruptly. "Portugese Man O' War," he said, pointing to a wet, pinkish lump lying on the beach just at the water's edge. "One more step and you would have stepped on him; or I should say, *them*. They're a colony."

She shuddered and turned her steps aside, casting a glance back to see Dr. Morrison and her father avoiding the thing also. She went ahead and when the captain did not fall into step beside her, she paused and looked back.

He was standing still, hat in hand watching her. And spreading his arms wide, he said, "It just occurred to me, Miss Harbour, your hair is the color of the sunset."

All four of them turned then to see the sun, an orange-red disc sinking beneath the dark-blue horizon, which was Gulf water as far as they could see. The sky itself was bright-orange near the giant orb, and faded outward slowly to gold and then to pink.

His face seemed dark and somber as he said, "I think we should be getting back to the carriage before dark."

They joined the doctor and her father, and the four of them retraced their steps to the surrey, discussing as they went the new fad of bathing in the sea. In the surrey going back, the men talked about how all the houses in the city were built up on high foundations to protect them from any storm tides that might come. They passed down a street lined with brooding old oaks and saw the old Menard house, a Greek Revival mansion hidden in a tangle of trees and vines; and other mansions among small forests of blooming oleanders.

And then it was time to say goodbye. That she was in love with a time and a place did not surprise her. Nor did she want this splendid dream to ever end. Was it possible, she thought as they drew near the hotel in the sweet-scented dusk, that she would never see this city again? Never see Damon Morrison or his amiable brother, Richard? If the whole day was but a magnificent dream, then how does one *will* oneself not to awaken in the morning?

They said goodbye outside the lobby of the hotel. The captain in his double-breasted suit and top hat, bowed. The doctor in his oxford-gray inclined his head to her and offered her father his hand. "If we can be of any further assistance to you, sir—"

"You can, Doctor," her father interrupted. "You and the captain can advise me as to what you would do if *you* were in my place, unable and unwilling to pay the Galveston shipping companies' shipping rates, sir."

Wide-eyed and speechless because of this unprecedented concession on her father's part, Elizabeth looked at the captain whose eyes were shining with the answer, but whose lips could not utter the words of mutiny.

"If I were you, sir, I'd forget Galveston as a port and ship my goods from the port of New Orleans."

She saw a sense of relief pass over the face of the captain; it had not been necessary after all to betray the trust of his employers.

For it was his brother who had answered.

Three

The summer was hot and muggy in Chicago that year, which helped to perpetuate the city's favorite sport, that of yachting on Lake Michigan. The discussions among the educated youth that season, mainly among the college students home for the summer, included the latest novelists such as Mark Twain, Henry James, Hamlin Garland, Stephen Crane—*one must read his* The Red Badge Of Courage—and the newest rage in painting, the Impressionistic works of Manet, Monet, Renoir and Degas—*strictly dreamlike, one must possess a bit of romanticism to appreciate it, you know.* Young and old alike attended open air concerts enjoying the orchestral renderings of some of the newest masters, Strauss, Brahms, and Tchaikovsky. The names of architects who appeared occasionally in the newspapers included Louis Sullivan, Henry Richardson, and the newcomer, Frank Lloyd Wright. And among the hit songs of the year were, "The Band Played On," "Kentucky Babe," "Sweet Rosie

O'Grady," and the hilarious, "You're Not The Only Pebble On The Beach."

There were enthusiastic arguments at every garden party and on every picnic over the Cuban revolt against Spain and whether or not America should intervene. President McKinley's name was batted about like a tennis ball—he was spineless, roared one faction, he was simply being cautious argued the other.

The Women's Suffrage movement was gaining momentum in the states. If Wyoming and Utah could confer on women the right to vote in national elections, then so could the state of Illinois, argued certain progressive ladies in Elizabeth's crowd. If an uneducated Negro could vote, so could an educated woman, they insisted. Elizabeth participated in the rallies of the Women's Suffrage movement, but not in those of the Temperance movement, which was very vigorous that year in Chicago. Randal Harbour was not a heavy drinker, but he did like his wine at dinner and his toddy at night. Since he and his daughter frequently entertained and were entertained by a clique of Chicago's elite industrialists and merchants— occasions on which liquor flowed as freely as the Chicago River—such participation in temperance rallies by his daughter would not be prudent either from a business standpoint or from a social one.

Since her mother had died four years earlier when Elizabeth was twenty-one, the pleasant task of planning and executing all the social occasions at the Harbour's thirteen-room Georgian house near Lake Shore Drive fell to her. And she loved every minute of it. Yet, that summer, all the brilliant luster of the balls, dinner parties, picnics in the country, tennis on the lawns, garden parties had become dull and tarnished for her. The excitement of the June weddings palled. None of her lady friends were interesting anymore, and her several beaus had become but fumbling youths hedging about trying to gather up courage to try for a bit of serious courting.

Life was not the same for her after Galveston. She hadn't yet quite relinquished the dreamlike memories of her visit to that enchanted southern island in the Gulf of Mexico. *And it was enchanted; it beckoned even in her dreams.* The sunset over the roof tops of Lake Shore Drive was not the same as that she'd seen over the rolling surf of the Gulf, nor did the beauty of Lake Michigan compare with that of the Gulf itself. Even the humidity of Chicago was found wanting that summer, it was not like the soothing rose-water balm of Galveston.

But Elizabeth was not one to spend her hours day-dreaming, sulking, or brooding. She was occupied with her social and cultural activities as always. Outwardly, nothing had changed. Except, perhaps, her attitude toward her father's teasing. For four years or so he'd teased her about her gentlemen friends. "That Charles is coming around rather often, Elizabeth. Is he trying to garner up the courage to ask for your hand? Eh?" Or, "When's Hensley going to pop the question, Elizabeth? You could do worse, you know." But just let one of her beaus show too much inclination toward her, and Randal Harbour became uncomfortable and went about the house puffed up like a balloon saying things about pompous young asses, bumbling young fools, and mountebanks—which was his favorite word for scoundrel—wanting to put her in gilded cages. She used to laugh at him. Now she gently said, "Please, Papa. There's no need to worry."

No need to worry at all.

In moments of solitude, her mind did go back to that day they left Galveston, the Galveston-Houston-Henderson coach rattling over the rails of the bay bridge, the shrimpers plying the bay waters followed by clouds of eager gulls, the early morning sun casting a billion diamonds upon the surface of the water. A copy of *The Love Letters of Elizabeth and Robert Browning* lay in her lap, but she had not been able to concentrate on it. Her father was reading the *Galveston Daily News*, purchased from the same peg-legged peddler she'd seen on the Strand the day before, who cried sonorously, "Dabey Naw. Dabey Naw," which they decided was only a worn, weathered, and weary corruption of *Daily News.*

She had not been able to see Galveston receding into the distance behind her but once, and then she saw it only briefly, a geometric block of white against a canvas of blue sky above and blue-green bay below. That last glimpse. . . .

. . . Aha. Just as I thought. This gentleman suffers from occasional bouts of sluffing of the liver. . . . As a matter of fact, there is some therapeutic value in this stuff. . . . The lady thinks I'm dishonest, Richard, I fear I'm undone. . . . I hate the sea . . . it's devious, unpredictable . . . you'll see . . . somehow I know you will. . . . It just occurred to me, Miss Harbour, your hair is the color of the sunset. . . . If we can be of any further assistance to you, sir. . . . I'd forget Galves-

ton as a port and ship my goods from the port of New Orleans. . . .

"I know why you're so quiet lately, daughter," Randal Harbour said at the dinner table one day in July. "You've set your cap for that sea captain in Galveston. No, don't deny it. I've never seen you so pensive, and it's been since we left Galveston last May."

"Papa, it's the city I've set my cap for."

"The city, eh? Well, one doesn't marry a city, my girl. No, nor would I be favorable to my daughter marrying a sea captain. Or a doctor either, for that matter. Those fellows are never home. It would amount to nothing but his putting you in a gilded cage—"

"Oh, Papa!"

"I'll amend that statement. In the case of those two gentlemen, the cage wouldn't even be gilded. It would be *bamboo.*"

"Papa!" She scolded him fondly, but she did not deny or confirm his surmise. After all, how do you explain to someone who's never experienced it, that you're in love with a dream?

Does a mosquito bite a Negro?

That's what the subject of the monthly faculty meeting had digressed to. And how does the secretary of the faculty record such a subject for posterity? In one sentence; "The subject of the etiology and source of malaria was discussed by the faculty, with the question of the possibility of immunity of the Negro race to malaria being introduced by Dr. Cross." Richard Morrison leaned back a moment in the golden oak chair to rest his spine.

The faculty members were lounging in the large, bright boardroom around a conference table proceeding with their meeting in spite of the heat. Faculty meetings were always vigorous and animated, though little good ever came of them, except for the planning of curriculum, changing of curriculum, and arguing over curriculum, which actually wasn't in the faculty's power to plan or change in the first place. But it was in their power to argue over it, which they did. The intentions of their meetings were always more noble than that, however, and a theme for the improvement of the school or the betterment of the city in which the school was located was always introduced for discussion.

Richard himself had introduced the theme for today's meeting only minutes earlier, stating that he and Rob Tate, the dean of the medical school, had done a study on the water from some of Galveston's cisterns. When the medical school had opened six years earlier, all of Galveston's water supply came from unscreened overhead, or shallow underground cisterns—rain water collected from pigeon-infested roofs. But when the artesian water was finally put through pipes across the bay from the interior, the city physician caused a city ordinance to be passed making it mandatory that all cisterns be screened or covered.

Faculty members murmured their own recollections of those recent years when Richard paused in his discourse. He went on to say that there were some cisterns in the city yet unscreened, but what bothered him and Rob most was that many of Galveston's citizens still used cistern water for drinking, or at least for washing and cleaning. The water samples they had taken were full of wiggletails and other specimens necessitating the straining of the water to separate an incredible amount of impurities, most of which were very much *alive*.

Dr. Mason interrupted, wondering aloud that they were still so primitive. Rob Tate spoke up and explained that the wiggletails were mostly mosquito larvae, and if the theory was true that malaria and other tropical diseases were caused by mosquitos, then the exposed cisterns throughout the city were definitely more a health hazard than they first thought. And what concerned them as much as the breeding of tropical fevers was the possibility that such contaminated water could cause typhoid.

Richard and Rob's investigation of the water supply was inspired by the concern of the faculty members over the fact that the previous winter had been unusually rainy and mild, and that the possibility of an epidemic of malaria, yellow fever, or typhoid was very real. Concerned as the medical doctors of the city were, however, Galveston citizens remained blissfully ignorant of the danger. They saw that their streets were watered daily to keep the dust down and took great pride in their fine homes, but their streets and vacant lots still pooled with stagnant water, and in many of their carefully-kept back yard gardens stood privies.

The problems of the city's apathy when it came to public safety had been discussed by the doctors many times. As Dr. Cline, professor of climatology at the medical school, who was also Galveston's meteorologist, once said, "The island seems to cast a spell of euphoria upon its people; the climate is an opiate that renders them insensible to the dangers of sea, sickness, and satan."

But now the discussion had moved to the cause of tropical diseases and from thence to why Negros seldom contracted them.

Dr. Grimes had suggested that the Negro skin was too tough 'for the mosquito to penetrate. Dr. Jackson, professor of surgery, had challenged Grimes, saying the Negro skin was no such thing.

Dr. Cross interrupted saying he'd proven cases of malaria in the Negro both at the bedside and microscopically but had to admit that such cases were not frequent among Negroes. He wondered if the race, which originated in malarial climates, had developed an immunity to it and had handed the immunity down to its progeny.

It was a pause for thought indeed. And all wondered exactly what immunity *was*. Richard had once postulated the theory that immunity was the body's own bacteria—or other organisms—fighting the invading disease-causing bacteria. Since a few years back when Pasteur discovered that microorganisms caused fermentation and disease and Lister had reduced the dangers of infection in surgical wounds by using antiseptics, the subject of bacteria was a much-discussed one among Richard's colleagues, because nobody knew much about it. At the moment though, his mind left his colleagues and his eyes drifted to the window and fixed on the grove of cottonwoods shimmering and quaking outside the building in the gentle Gulf breeze. . . . *Oh, do let's park the surrey and go down to the beach. . . .*

"Richard," said Will Kelly. Which brought him out of his musing. For somewhere between the discussion concerning immunity and the present moment, Richard had been woolgathering.

"I'm sorry, what did you ask?" he said looking pleasantly guilty.

The doctors laughed and Dr. Jackson replied, "I say, Richard, I've mentioned that what we need to do is inform the people through the newspapers that the custom of keeping outdoor privies can be the source of an epidemic, that the installation of indoor water closets and the elimination of outdoor privies should be encouraged."

Rob Tate said, "So we wondered who among us should approach the newspapers with the idea, and who can do a good write-up on it. Will suggested you."

All eyes were upon him hoping he would take the responsibility, and Will Kelly nudged Richard in the side with his elbow. "You can begin your article by telling how you're installing a water closet in your *own* new house. Eh? Show the citizens of Galveston how it's done. Eh?"

"Will you write the article?" Dr. Tate asked. "You're the logical one, Richard.

"I will," he agreed.

"Good. In that case, our meeting has amounted to something for once," Tate said. "Next month we'll discuss schedules for the new term. Have you examining doctors finished grading the entrance exams?"

Drs. Cross, Smart, and Morrison nodded.

"Then I believe our business is concluded. Do I hear a motion this meeting adjourn?"

"Make the motion."

"Second."

"All in favor say 'aye.' Meeting's adjourned," Dr. Tate said, and picked up his papers.

Chairs scooted back from the table and the doctors began talking among themselves as they left the conference room, all except Drs. Kelly and Morrison. Kelly said to Richard, who was still recording the last minutes of the meeting, "Ye didn't hear two words of the last part of the meeting today, Richard, and knowin' your recent frame of mind as I do, I'll wager 'twasn't the installation of a water closet in your new house that's occupyin' your mind, is it? No. It's the installation into it of one of the world's oldest household commodities—a woman."

Richard only smiled and kept writing.

"Ah yes. And I think I know which one," Kelly said. He nudged Richard again in the side. "From your description of her that day, Richard, I have to approve, you know." He stroked his beard and said gently, "Ah, remember this, Richard my friend. There's no *way* you can go wrong if it's the lady with the red hair that you chose."

The twentieth day of August was the last day of the Collegiate Summer Music Festival. When it was over, Elizabeth, as refreshment coordinator, came home tired and hot and glad the whole thing was over. After greeting her father in the parlor, she went up the stairs, and once

67

in the privacy of her own room, fell across her bed face up with her arms over her head.

Thomas rose from the pillow beside her, yawned luxuriously, and regarded his mistress fondly for a moment before he made up his mind to rub his face against her cheek, which caused her to laugh and take him in her arms where he commenced to purr contentedly. "Thomas, you old rogue," she said stroking him, "when are you going to learn not to sleep on the beds and sit on the furniture? Elsa will catch you some day and you'll be put out of the house forever."

At this prospect, Thomas decided to get down off the bed—for it was too warm a day to be cuddled anyway— and go downstairs to check his bowl just in case the maid had put something in it earlier than usual.

Elizabeth rolled over on her stomach and rested her cheek on her arm. For a while she forced her mind to go over the events of the day, checking off things she should have done, and concluded at last that she had done her job well. Then it was that she let her thoughts go to Galveston—and to Captain Morrison. She had just finished reading *Two Years Before The Mast* the night before, and during the reading of it could not help but imagine Captain Damon Morrison in the place of young Dana. Captain Morrison himself was young, certainly not older than twenty-eight. And his brother, the older of the two, no more than thirty. It was curious that neither had married yet, but understandable. Both were extremely busy men. Lucky for her. *Elizabeth!* Thinking like a schoolgirl, daydreaming, fantasizing like a silly child! Still, it was fun to have something or someone to dream about. And about time too, she supposed. Most of the friends she had gone through school with were married now. And here she was, already almost an old maid—not from lack of beaus, but from the lack of . . . the *quality* of beaus. *Elizabeth, how snobbish.* What did she consider as quality in a gentleman, anyway? In her entourage of friends there were good-looking ones, rich ones, educated ones—

A knock on her door interrupted her thoughts, and in one motion she rolled over and sat up calling, "Come in, Elsa."

The maid came in and went directly to the counterpane-covered pillows on her bed where the imprint of Thomas betrayed his latest travesty, and began brushing them off vigorously saying, "I'll svare! Dot Tom cat, Elizabeth! If I catch him on dis bed—"

"You will do what?" laughed Elizabeth. "Elsa, your great, Swedish heart's mush. Admit that you've gotten fond of Thomas."

It was Elsa's custom to appear stern, even when she didn't feel like it, and when she put on airs of being angry, she was merely comical. She hurried to Elizabeth's vanity table and began to straighten things on its top, and remembering her mission, said, "Your father sent me up to tell you to come down, because he has a visitor and got called to dat awful telephone ting before dey more dan lit dere obnoxious pipes. De call was business and likely to occupy him awhile. Elizabeth, are you listening?"

"Yes. But I can't go down. I'm a mess."

"You can smooth back your hair. And I'll help you into de little blue muslin," Elsa said and opened up the armoire.

"But I smell. I've sweat so."

Elsa brought the dress out of the armoire and came to the bed where she laid it across the counterpane saying, "Nonsense. No lady smells. Dey svett, but dey don't smell."

Chuckling, Elizabeth stood up and turned her back so that the maid could unbutton her shirtwaist, then shrugged out of it, stepped out of her skirt, and stood in her camisole and silk petticoats wishing she could shed the rest of it, especially the corset. Elsa handed her a damp washcloth from the wash basin and she rinsed her face, arms, and neck. Then she puffed talcum all over and let Elsa pull the dress over her head. She then took her brush and hastily smoothed up the loose wisps of her hair into the bun on top of her head, which she had called a "toddle" since she was very small and had watched her mother at her dressing table do her hair much the same way.

"Papa say who the fellow is?" she asked as she pushed the tortoise shell hairpins into the toddle. "It's not McMurphy, is it, the one who keeps talking to him about hiring more Irish immigrants for the mills?"

"No, no, Elizabeth," said Elsa, draping the frock she had just shed over her arm. "Dis is some gentleman, rather young. Which the two of you met in dat Texas town on the Gulf Coast last May."

Elizabeth turned quickly from the mirror and stared at the maid, not believing for a moment what she had heard; and blushing she asked softly, "Did . . . did you happen to hear his name?"

70

Elsa shut the doors to the armoire. "Morrison. I believe his name was Morrison."

Elizabeth clasped the back of her vanity chair with one hand, and the other went to the bow at her bosom. "Did he say . . . *Captain* Morrison? Or *Dr.* Morrison?"

"Don't know as I caught his title. But he's a nice-looking gentleman. And very proper. Are you ready to go down now?"

"Tell him . . . tell him I'll be down shortly, please."

When the maid had left, Elizabeth in a fever began to pinch her cheeks to make them pink, bite her lips to make them red, and pinch her eyelashes between her fingernail and thumb to make them curl. Then she splashed toilet water on her neck, and would have done a dozen other silly things girls did when beaus came calling, but there was no time for it.

She took one look at herself sideways in the mirror, checked her figure, straightened her bow, and with heart pounding, hurried from her room and descended the stairs. In the foyer she paused and made an effort to control her breathing before she went into the parlor, lest it appear that she had rushed. How silly, she kept telling herself, exactly the kind of behavior one would expect of a schoolgirl.

He was sitting on the parlor sofa in the same oxford-gray suit he'd worn both times she had seen him in Galveston, pipe in hand, studiously blowing a stream of smoke into Thomas's face, who was sitting on the arm of the sofa managing to maintain his feline dignity in spite of it.

Her heart fell like a deflated dirigible. And with it all

her fondest hopes.

Still, he was the brother and she was immensely glad that he, at least, had come.

"That's very unhealthy, Dr. Morrison," she said pleasantly, coming into the parlor. "Didn't you know cats are subject to respiratory problems which tobacco smoke can complicate?"

By then he was on his feet smiling sheepishly like a small boy caught stealing. He spread his arms in a supplicating gesture—reminding her so much of his brother— and said, "Miss Harbour, I just hope before this day is done, that I've caused more complications in your life than you thought possible."

And in that moment, Elizabeth knew with absolute certainty that Dr. John Richard Morrison had come courting.

Four

Elizabeth was laughing. "Do sit down, Dr. Morrison," she said, indicating the sofa, and taking the chair opposite him. "And never mind Thomas. He has to inspect every guest who comes for a visit."

Richard was momentarily dumbstruck by her perfect poise, her patrician grace, yet her friendliness denied his apprehension that she might consider herself superior to him.

"I see Papa left it up to me to have tea brought, but Elsa will have brewed some already." She rang the crystal bell on the table beside her chair. "Or would you care for a glass of lemonade?"

He had sat down again carefully on the mauve, velvet sofa, having already observed the fine classic furnishings in the room, the heavy mauve draperies at the windows, so that he was painfully aware of how at home she was amid such tasteful elegance. His shirt collar was exceedingly tight all of a sudden, and he resisted the urge to hook his finger in it like a bumpkin and pull it away from his epiglottis so that he could breathe better, or at least swallow without his tie bobbing up and down. "Miss Harbour, I would be very grateful for a glass of ice cold lemonade," he said.

At that moment, the Harbour's maid, a tall, very correct woman, appeared, and Elizabeth gave her instructions to bring them both a glass of lemonade, ice cold, then turned her perceptive eyes upon him. "I must apologize for Papa. Without a telephone in the house, I'm sure Harbour Mills would go bankrupt."

Richard nodded. "Yes, telephones can be very useful," he managed eloquently, still holding his pipe like a pistol.

She smiled prettily. "And please resume smoking your pipe, Doctor. I'm used to it. I'm not one of those ladies who believes smoking should be limited to one's own parlor. Please. Father smokes both a pipe and a cigar, and I like it."

Greatly relieved, Richard said, "Thank you," and proceeded to puff. Sigmund Freud would undoubtedly conclude that his maturation had been arrested in infancy, that he was an oral individual, and that sucking on a pipe stem was a substitute for his mother's breast. And he would probably be right, because puffing the pipe did soothe his jangled nerves as nothing else could. Not usually so easily discomposed, Richard found that Miss Harbour was even lovelier than he remembered, livelier too, and this unnerved him somewhat.

"So," she began, trying to think of something to say to this gentleman whom she'd seen only once before, who appeared slightly ill at ease and with whom she sympathized. "You've come a long way from home, Dr. Morrison."

"Yes, it's been a long trip."

"Arrive just today?"

"Yes ma'am. By train."

"I know how exhausting that can be. Are you here on business?"

"Well . . . you can call it that, Miss Harbour."

"I see. Will you be staying long?"

"I hope not. That is . . . I'll have to conclude my business within five days or so, because I'll have to get back to the university to prepare for the next term."

Elizabeth had long ago discovered that there exists an invisible, mischievous urchin, an imp, who hovers around young couples in those first stages of courtship, and who seeks to stage embarrassing situations from which the couple cannot escape. That had to be why Thomas, normally a perfectly well-mannered cat, had elected to jump down from the arm of the sofa the minute she entered the room to begin a thorough washing of himself on the floor before them, exactly halfway between the sofa on which the doctor sat, and her chair. She pretended she did not see him, hoping . . . hoping . . . *please dear Lord, don't let him*—"Where are you staying, Doctor. Anywhere close?"

"At the Commodore Hotel. I have a room, and my luggage is there."

"Your brother, Dr. Morrison . . . how is he these days?" she asked looking somewhere beyond his left shoulder.

"Damon? He's taken a steamer to Liverpool by way of the West Indies and has been gone most of the summer."

"Oh. Liverpool! How delightful! And the West Indies! But isn't he a little afraid of being sunk or shot at by the Spanish in that part of the world? I mean with the difficulties in Cuba and all?"

"No. I'm afraid he's more concerned about West Indies hurricanes this time of year. Or—"

Thomas had washed every bit of himself now and had gracefully lifted his leg to wash, thoroughly, his under parts, necessitating that Elizabeth pick up her fan from the table beside her chair to cool her feverish face.

"Or—" What the devil was he saying? He had forgot. The damned cat was doing such a thorough job of cleaning under his tail. . . . "Well, you know the hurricane season is considered to begin the latter part of August and extend through October. They have their beginnings in the area of the West Indies, it seems."

To make matters worse, embarrassed as she was, Elizabeth had an overpowering urge to giggle which was absolutely the worst thing she could do. To put Thomas out of her peripheral vision, she ducked her head and pretended to pluck some lint or thread off her skirt while the doctor haltingly said things about one-hundred-mile-per-hour winds and torrential rains and how the cyclones picked up speed. And just before she lifted her head again, she saw him furtively nudge the cat with the toe of his shoe. "They pick up speed over water, you know, and die out over land," he said, his face a study in innocence.

There was a moment of tense silence in which Thomas stalked off indignantly, the doctor puffed furiously on his pipe, and Elizabeth fought desperately to keep from exploding with laughter.

But Elsa spared them by coming into the room at that moment with a tray of tall, sweating glasses of iced lemonade and a plate of gingerbread, so that by the time they had taken their lemonade, the embarrassment had lessened for them both.

"I suppose Galveston, being on the coast, has seen its share of hurricanes," Elizabeth said, smiling too brightly.

"It has."

"Sounds dreadful."

"Does it scare you?"

"Not really."

"Why not?"

"Because I don't live there," she answered and sipped her drink.

"But if you did?"

Still smiling, she answered, "Then I'd put the fear of it at the very back of my mind and enjoy the good days as they come."

He caught himself returning her smile just as Randal Harbour entered the room, loudly apologizing for the interruption of the telephone call, and took from them the ambivalent burden of conversation. In spite of her father's dominating the conversation from then on, Elizabeth was still able to invite Dr. Morrison for dinner, which he gratefully accepted, and at the mahogany, Duncan Phyfe dinner table in the dining room with its padded dining chairs upholstered in the same green velvet as the draperies, the doctor and her father discussed the chemical components and possibilities of man-made fibers.

To Randal Harbour's obvious delight, Dr. Morrison, being a chemist of sorts, knew a great deal about the scientific processes involved in turning cellulose into fibers, though he was skeptical that the Chardonnet procedure, being extremely expensive, was the best way. Rather, a new method developed only five years before, which turned cellulose into viscose, was more practical. And Dr. Morrison said that if it were he experimenting with cellulose in order to produce an imitation silk, he would choose the latter way. Her father was pleased, because that was exactly what he had concluded just a few weeks earlier, and hearing the doctor's pronouncement lifted his spirits even more than his best vintage wine.

Dr. Morrison discoursed on other new ideas too, during the dinner. "I've recently read a paper on an element similar to cellulose which is found in seaweed, alginic acid, which can be dissolved in solution, hardened into filaments basically the same way as cellulose and blended with other fibers such as cotton or wool and woven into a light-weight fabric of excellent quality. . . ."

Their gentlemen talk, their important, exclusively male discussion, extended into producing fibers made from chemicals derived from coal and oil, and into spinning and weaving, and by the time Elsa served dessert, had progressed to the reasons why certain natural fibers caused irritating effects upon the human skin.

Elizabeth listened with fascination as they talked. If Dr. Morrison had come calling on her with any romantic intent, as she had thought at first, he showed no inclination of it now. She was generally, if politely, excluded from the conversation. But she was accustomed to that. In fact, the exclusion of ladies from conversation by men at social occasions had always infuriated her. It made her angrier quicker than anything else that men could do. It was as if they believed women did not have the intelligence to fathom the depths of their superior intellect. All the more she was determined to listen and to comment occasionally just to remind them she was present and that she could follow the drift of their conversation. And when at last the men repaired to the parlor to have their after-dinner drink, a smoke, and a resumption of their chat, she took her embroidery and went too, though she wasn't invited.

After a few moments, inevitably, her father was called to the telephone again and Elizabeth was left sitting in the same Louis XVI chair she had occupied earlier, with Dr. Morrison on the sofa again smoking his pipe, just as if three hours had not lapsed since their first strained conversation.

Richard was aware that they both had relaxed a bit, however, conversation not nearly so strained between them, and he was glad she had not become so bored with the discussion that she'd left him alone with Randal Harbour. That gentleman was courteous and interesting to talk to, but Mr. Harbour was not whom he had come to visit.

"Tell me, Doctor," she began, her embroidery lying in her lap, her needle still poised between two delicate fingers above it, "what's been going on in Galveston since Papa and I were there?"

Richard considered the question a moment, wondering how one could answer it. That there had been an unusual infestation of mosquitos all summer? That they had several cases of malaria and a few of yellow fever, and an epidemic of dengue? That a toddler had drowned in an open, underground cistern? That his article about the possibility of an epidemic in the city had been published in the *News* and duly ignored? That the German band had played concerts in Central Park at least one night a week all summer, and that Will Kelly's wife had another baby girl in June? He was suddenly acutely aware of how very dull his life was. How dull it must be compared to Miss Harbour's. The discovery almost defeated him.

"Not much," he finally said. "The usual. Lots of tourists this year. The German band, an excellent home-town band, played open air concerts in Central Park every Friday evening. The anatomy professor's wife had a baby girl which I delivered because her own doctor wasn't back yet from his vacation."

"Oh, do you deliver many babies, Dr. Morrison?"

"On an average of one a month."

"How . . . fascinating."

"Yes, birth is."

"Yes, I'm *sure* it is."

Yes, how dull, Miss Harbour. How dull I must seem to you.

"Doctor, you say you came to Chicago on business?" she asked brightly.

"Yes."

"Does it have anything to do with the medical school?"

80

"Not directly."

"I see."

He met her direct and unflinching gaze and held it. A slow blush began at her lovely throat which was most charmingly revealed above the rounded neck of her bodice, and went into her cheeks. She bit her bottom lip for a moment, then dropping her gaze to her lap and lifting it back to his face again, asked softly, "Why did you *really* come to Chicago, Dr. Morrison?"

Her question caught him off guard. He studied her face, the perceptive blue eyes which he decided must see more than a travel-weary man come to Chicago on a business trip and who was spending more time calling on two mere acquaintances than was customary. But he had prepared a hackneyed answer to which, in his discomfort, he fled. "There's a seminar which. . . ." He paused and dropped his hand to the arm of the sofa. "No," he said, still meeting her gaze, so open, so honest, *and so damned wise.* "I was about to tell you a bloody lie, Miss Harbour." Her eyes never strayed from his. "I came to ask you to go back to Galveston with me, Miss Harbour. As my wife."

For a moment she did not move. Then, she lay aside her embroidery and folded her hands in her lap. "What makes you think," she began, gently incredulous, "that by the most extravagant . . . aggrandizement of the imagination I would consider such a . . . a proposal, Dr. Morrison?" The flush had not left her cheeks, nor the brightness from her eyes. "I hardly know you at all!"

He returned simply, "That puts us on equal ground."

"Well then?"

"How long does it take a person to discover that he or she would like to spend the rest of his or her life with someone? Is there a set number of days or weeks or months, Miss Harbour?"

"But—"

He spread his arms in that gesture that reminded her so much of his brother on the beach that evening. "I'd gladly pay court to you properly if you'll allow me, but it will have to be . . . *condensed*. Into three or four days. Or else from a distance of almost two thousand miles for a year or more."

"But a lady needs *time*."

"Does she?"

Elizabeth studied the gentleman in gray wool before her, his face now so ruddy with an inner tension that was not otherwise discernible.

"I agree," he said, "that there will be a sacrifice on your part. No time for preparations for a large wedding—"

"That's not important to me, Doctor. But what about—about affection, Dr. Morrison. You haven't said anything about any . . . affectionate regard."

He smiled gently and replied, "I'm quite certain that I love you, Miss Harbour, otherwise I wouldn't have come for you."

She felt her face flushing again as she said, "And what about me? Don't you expect affection in return?"

He pressed his lips together a moment, then said, "With everything else I've ask of you, Miss Harbour, that really *would* be asking too much on so short a notice, wouldn't it?"

She studied her hands in her lap. Marry this stable, genial man? Live in Galveston with him? The prospect was immediately far, far more exciting than anything she had ever known, and he a far more desirable candidate for a husband than she had known before. She thought of her infatuation with the captain, knowing that he had regarded her at least as a fetching woman. But *he* had not come for her; his brother had. There were dreams, and there were dreams. She looked up. "Dr. Morrison," she said, "I think . . . I think I should like to go with you to Galveston . . . as your wife. I think I should like that very much."

They sat looking at each other in a pleasant, exhilarating ambience. What do two strangers say to one another when they've so suddenly and so completely agreed to a union of a lifetime? They did not have to say anything at all; for at that moment, Randal Harbour blustered into the parlor again saying, "What's this? Marriage? What were you saying, Elizabeth?" He stood holding his smoking cigar, ashes falling onto the carpet, looking from one to the other and bellowing, "Now see here, you two. What are you saying? What makes you think such a thing is possible? You hardly know each other. Isn't this kind of nonsense a bit sudden? See here, Dr. Morrison. Suppose you explain your intentions regarding my daughter, sir!"

Candidly, Richard did.

During the next four whirlwind days with hurriedly purchased wedding gifts arriving from acquaintances, and hundreds of calls from friends, and frantic shopping trips, frenzied packing, dizzying instructions written for

Elsa about the things temporarily left behind which must be shipped, Randal Harbour paced about the house muttering about that brash, young mountebank carrying off his daughter to an arrogant city of pharisees, but reasoning at the same time that she at least had sense enough not to end up marrying one of the pompous young asses who would have only put her in a gilded cage. And to complicate things, *it* happened.

She tried to tell Richard, she really did. The day before their wedding she tried to tell him as they walked in the small, spent garden behind the house, a rare moment in which, during the four busy days that had passed since he proposed, that they were alone. They were walking beside the privet hedge under the giant old elm. Richard had come calling with a bouquet of greenhouse roses and had told her that he was unable to secure passage for them on any steamboat out of Chicago, or on the Illinois River at Moline, and that if they were to leave for Galveston when they'd planned, the best they could do was take a day coach on the express train from Chicago to St. Louis. She told him that was fine with her, and then she tried to tell him. "Richard, I have to speak to you about something. It's only fair that I tell you. . . . Well. . . ." She drew in her breath, reddening, and blurted, "That . . . that Aunt Martha has come to visit!"

He raised his brows. "That's nice," he said. "We can invite her to the wedding."

Invite her to the wedding indeed!

Then the next day in a private ceremony in the Episcopal Church with her father giving her away and the Reverend Grayson and his wife Mary present, she became Mrs. John Richard Morrison.

During their ten-hour ride by express train from Chicago to St. Louis that same day in the hot coach full of passengers young and old, they read the *Chicago Post*, and spoke haltingly, superficially about the weather, the countryside, the darling child held in its mother's arms across the narrow aisle from them. The coach rocked along, slowing at small terminals so that mail bags could be flung aboard the train, speeding up in open country, the whistle sounding short or long and always melancholy even on that bright and flawless August day. Sitting side by side, jostled against each other occasionally, they began to speak of other things, the medical school at Galveston, and of the summer music festival in which she had been refreshment coordinator. It was such a tedious, sticky, sooty, airy ride through fields of tall rustling corn disturbed by the rush of the train, flat, golden prairies, black pasturelands, and green-forested hills.

She was dressed in her new tailored suit of textured linen and silk dyed a soft, pastel peach. On her head she wore a tan dress-shaped hat with colorful velvet flowers and a small stuffed dove nestling among them. Her gloves were white kid, her shoes tan laceups with the new foxed heels. And Richard wore a brown worsted suit and a contrasting brown derby. She thought they made a handsome couple.

By dark they were comfortable in each other's company and soon the train gasped, clamored, and sighed at last into the hot St. Louis depot. A bumpy cab ride to the fine, overdecorated hotel and an electric elevator ride to the third floor, brought them at last to their suite of three rooms.

While Richard gave a tip to the two porters who had carried their valises and Elizabeth's trunk to the room, she went to the window of their bedroom and stood pulling off her gloves, gazing out over the shadowy tree-tops below. She had no idea what to expect from this man she had married, now that they were alone and she was his. One heard all sorts of awful stories, though she was certain she could expect nothing of Richard but the greatest gentility. He came to the window to stand beside her. "The porters told me that from this window you can see the river even at night," he said, gently touching her arm. "There, Elizabeth. Beyond the church spire to the right. I believe that's our boat in port. It's lit up so that you can see it."

The dark line of trees must follow the river, she thought, and there a quarter of a mile or so away she could see lights from the boat at the docks. "Yes, yes, I see." After a moment she moved away from the window, and from him, and went to her valise. Later, more crates and steamer trunks with more of her frocks and hats, linen and wedding gifts, and even a few pieces of furniture, would be sent after they arrived in Galveston. But for the trip downriver, she must live out of the valise and trunk which she had brought with her.

Richard picked up her valise and placed it on the bed for her. "Elizabeth?"

She looked up at him.

"I'll go down the hall to the public bath to wash up, and leave you to freshen up in the bath here. Then I can go down to the desk and order dinner brought up to the room, or we can go down to the dining room. Whichever you wish."

"We'll do as *you* wish, Richard."

"Ladies' choice tonight, Elizabeth."

"I'm not usually one to become so fatigued, but tonight I am rather tired and would rather not have to dress again. It's so late—"

"I understand," he said. He seemed to fumble a little as he picked up his own valise, and her heart went out to him, knowing that he too must be tense and fatigued from their journey.

And then she tried to tell him again. Before he became too—Before he anticipated too much of the impossible. "Richard?" She turned to face him and saw a softness settle upon his face which she recognized now as a reflection of his affection for her. "I . . . I have to tell you something. I tried before, but you didn't understand."

He waited, his eyes searching her face, and when she just *couldn't* go on for embarrassment, he said, "That you are having your monthly visitation?" He smiled warmly and placed his hands gently on her shoulders and made her look him in the face. "I know that, Elizabeth. And it doesn't matter." As she stood there speechless, he took her hands in his and said softly, "There are subtle ways to tell such a thing in some women, and I knew. But you must understand this, that the menstrual flow is not unclean, it's pure and the most natural phenomenon in the world."

"I'm so sorry it happened now, though, Richard. Please believe me," she said, hardly able to meet his eyes. "Otherwise I—"

"Elizabeth, it doesn't matter to me if it doesn't to you. But if you are hesitant or uncomfortable about it, then . . . I'll wait. I'll wait anyway until you're ready. I'll never demand from you what the vulgar call a man's 'conjugal rights.' Because the only real rights a man has over a woman are those agreed to and consummated by mutual consent."

Grateful for his gentleness, she touched his cheek with her hand. "Thank you, Richard," she whispered.

He straightened, and shifted his shoulders as if uncomfortable in his suit and said, "But rest assured, Elizabeth. As for desiring you, I do. Very much. So much so that I had quite lost my appetite."

Smiling, she dropped her gaze to the green Turkish carpet.

"And now," he added blithely, "it seems I have reason to get my appetite back." He bent down to pick up his valise again. "I'll be thirty minutes or so. You'll be alright?"

"Yes, thank you," she said and watched him as he left the room.

Later, alone in the cool bed with its soft, linen sheets, she felt awful. He'd chosen to sleep on the sofa for her sake. But she did not feel comfortable, nor did she have any peace of mind, hearing him sighing and tossing upon the lumpy sofa in the other room.

Not exactly his idea of a wedding night either, spending it on a lumpy sofa with a spring poking up right in the wrong place and his feet hanging off—with his bride in the other room. But that's what should be expected when one doesn't have time to give the lady her choice of wedding dates, he thought. She had sacrificed too, having to settle for a small wedding when, if she had had the time, she could have had an elaborate one befitting her social position. He had no right to ask her to marry him, to live on the three thousand dollars a year he made chairing the chemistry department and half that from his private practice.

He turned over again now, the springs of the sofa thudding and gonging like a dozen grandfather clocks going off at the same time, the broken one gouging his hip. He pulled the suit coat up over his shoulders. He was trying to sleep in his underwear and the damned things were binding him from top to bottom like a cocoon. But after a while, though feeling himself still riding in the coach, he at last drifted off into a fitful sleep.

And woke suddenly.

She was standing beside the sofa, an apparition in white, a lovely vision in the dim glow of the gaslight coming from the bedroom nearby. "Richard?"

He struggled to his feet, groggy, his vision fuzzy, the circulation rushing back into his left leg like a million nettles stinging. He grabbed his coat and held it up to cover himself.

"Oh, Richard," she said softly. "Do come to bed. I hate being alone tonight and you've been so wonderfully kind."

He was so shocked, he dropped the coat. "Elizabeth?"

"And please. I really don't mind . . . if you don't."

What was this thing about a woman that could turn a man into the same protoplasm from which he had come a hundred billion years ago? He didn't know. It was a phenomenon worthy of analysis, but this wasn't the time . . . in-depth research was needed first. Effortlessly he lifted her up into his arms. Research into the phenomenon was the most certain thing to him now as he carried her into the bedroom. The most certain thing in all the world.

Five

When Vicksburg fell to the Union during the war, Lincoln said of the Mississippi, "The Father of Waters flows unvexed to the sea." And indeed it did. Generally, the river reminded Richard of a slow, pleasant, half-witted old man, barely able to fetch his halt limbs forward enough to gain momentum, but determined to do so no matter the obstacles met. He knew that the river snaked and bent upon itself in horseshoe curves, meandering, overflowing, sometimes rushing but mostly sliding slowly and muddily toward the Gulf. He knew it had ravaged forests, eaten away at bordering farms, flooded valleys and wrecked boats, but had the river been a rapids or an ugly, flotsam-laden thing, he would have thought it beautiful because of the lovely Yankee bride at his side.

During their trip down the river on the *Jessie Day*, Elizabeth made him see beauty he would otherwise have been blind to, to feel emotions he would ordinarily not have experienced; to laugh, to tease, to muse eloquently, to be jealous, and to love. Into his placid, summer's twilight disposition she caused to explode a fireworks display of emotions, sights, sounds and sensations. She possessed a capacity for worshipping things, all sorts of things; the swirls on the face of the water, the forest-crested limestone bluffs along the banks of the river turning pink or gold in the early morning sun; the furrowed fields unfolding like giant fans, the grassy meadows studded with grazing cattle, the glimpse of deer in the woods, a broken W of geese winging southward above the river.

She loved the passengers and laughed privately at the captain who emerged from his cabin only in the evening like an owl at night, to participate in the festivities and strut before the ladies and spin yarns with the gentlemen.

A Dixieland band played every evening in the Natchez Room for those who wanted to dance, but their first evening on the riverboat Elizabeth and Richard spent leaning on the burnished brass railing of the cabin deck and watching the shadows of the Missouri shore grow longer and deeper, mirrored in the quiet surface of the river. They watched dusk creep stealthily up from the river to the forested hills, up to smother the giant orb of sun, and up to the gray-hazy sky turning it pink and indigo and purple, darkening until the stars appeared glittering. There was no moon.

That night she dreamed. The luxury of the St. Louis hotel in which they had spent the previous night, the quadruple-decked steamboat on which they had just spent the day with its elegantly furnished staterooms and dining halls, its superb cuisine and roaring engines, all meshed together in her dreams and became an ocean-going vessel the like of which the world had never seen. There were luxurious passenger liners to be sure, she reasoned in her dream, but none like this. It was enormous, screw-driven, capable of carrying not hundreds but thousands of passengers. The ship was absurdly long and wide and contained luxurious staterooms furnished with gilt Louis XV chairs, bombe chests, velvet chaise lounges. There were dining rooms with enormous chandeliers, bands, dancing, tennis, and other games on the decks, carpets, filigree—and at the helm stood Captain Damon Morrison squinting handsomely ahead, then turning smiling, and opening his arms and saying, "It just occurred to me, Miss Harbour—"

No! She must not think of him. She awoke in a fever when it was still dark, and rose quietly pulling on her wrapper, and went to the window between the beds. Richard was sleeping softly with his head thrown back upon his pillow, mouth slightly open, hair damp and stuck to his forehead. She pulled back the draperies and watched the dawning.

There was only a silent darkness at first. The inky silhouette of the forest against the dusky sky. Richard was suddenly behind her, smelling of soapy warmth and damp sleep; she leaned against his chest as he rested his chin on top of her head. The forest became slowly alive with a deafening tumult of bird sounds; ripples on the face of the river; the sky glowed awash with liquid gold. For the hundredth time since spring she now yearned to see Galveston again and thrilled to remember that that dream, at least, would soon come true.

They were five days on the river from St. Louis to New Orleans, stopping only at night to put into shore, or briefly to take on wood for the boiler room. The memory of their trip down the Father of Rivers would be forever printed into their minds, like an impressionist painting by Monet or Renoir done in pastel colors of landscapes, people, fashions, veiling mists, hazy shores, blushing sunsets. And at night their sharing one of the twin beds in their stateroom; Elizabeth always pleasantly, softly, hopefully receptive to his gentle love-making, reaching, almost reaching the same unbearable pleasure as he, but not quite. Not quite yet.

The air grew warmer, moister after they passed Vicksburg with its clay-pocked cliffs where he had learned that Elizabeth's Uncle Rupert had lost his life and Randal Harbour had been wounded during the siege, during the frantic battle of endurance and desperation between the Union and Confederate armies to gain control of the great North-South waterway.

Baton Rouge. Truly now they were in the South, for there were sugar plantations on either side of the river, green stretches of land for miles and miles, Greek Revival Mansions—once magnificent and white—now decaying and peeling; Negro shanties, wash flapping on the clotheslines, magnolia trees with shining green leaves, towering live oaks hung with gray-green Spanish Moss.

They reached New Orleans just at dusk on the fifth day, the waterfront lined with brick warehouses and wooden wharves, with sailing ships, barges, steamboats, and ocean-going steamers and square-riggers plying the waters of the port.

The *Jessie Day* put into port just after the electric lights came on in the city, a longshoreman hailed the captain and came aboard. The boat rocked back and forth at the wharf, waiting.

Then the captain sent a messenger around. New Orleans was experiencing a small epidemic of yellow fever, he said. As a courtesy to the passengers the captain advised those who were going on to Galveston not to go ashore that evening, but to stay on board the *Jessie Day* and board the shuttle boat to Galveston scheduled to leave promptly at seven the following morning. Richard agreed to stay aboard for the night. Most of the passengers disembarked. Those planning to go to Galveston remained on board, and at six the next morning, left the *Jessie Day*, boarded the smaller paddlewheeler, *Cougar*, and steamed out of the port of New Orleans at seven.

The *Cougar* was shabby, but she was swift. After the slow, steady twelve-hour progress from New Orleans through the channel and southwest pass, the Gulf of Mexico opened up before her just at dusk, vast, deep, wide, and hazy on the horizon. And the old steamer, billowing enormous dark clouds of smoke from her twin chimneys, shuddering with increasing speed, set her course westward into the setting sun.

At seven o'clock the next morning, she was well along her way across the Gulf, about five hours out of the port of Galveston, the captain told the breakfasting passengers. At ten, Elizabeth was leaning over the steel railing of the deck straining her eyes westward, anticipating her first glimpse of the fair city which was soon to be her home.

The entire trip had been sunny and hot and this momentus day was no different. Except there was a cool, misty haze over the water, and small, meaningless clouds drifted over the burning sun from time to time, casting down rays from the heavens to the rolling face of the sea, transparent rays into which birds soared. Every cloud was gilt-edged, every ray of sun golden, every bird silver-white.

Above the steamer white gulls appeared seemingly from the clouds, circling, calling, soaring upwards, dipping toward the boat. There. To the west-northwest upon the horizon. "Richard?" She pointed to something white lying parallel to the crest of the waves.

"Yes. I think that's it," Richard said squinting at the horizon.

A chill shuddered through her body and tears stung her eyes. "Yes, yes. Look," she said softly, her gloved hand going to her throat.

It was as she had remembered, only more dazzling white, rising higher above the water, suspended in space; one was almost uncertain that it was real.

Richard had not approached Galveston from the Gulf side before, had not experienced the illusion of the city suspended in space, seemingly hovering just above the water. He reasoned that the city appeared that way because the highest elevation of the island was only a little over eight feet above sea level. Yes, that was it.

He put his arm around his bride and felt a constriction in his throat, the sight of the city, his bringing to it his bride, stirred something deep inside of him. He wasn't an emotional man, but *coming home* had always affected him deeply, warming his insides, almost causing a mist of tears. He wanted to say, "I love you, Elizabeth." He wanted to tell her how proud of her he was, how hard he would work to make up for his mediocre income, how he would strive to make her happy forever and always. But instead, referring to the phenomenon of the suspended city to which they swiftly moved, he murmured, "Levitation. It's called levitation. A mystic type of phenomenon if it were real. However, it isn't. What it actually is, is an illusion."

She smiled. She could see two tug boats riding the soft waves to the west, a huge steamer seemingly parked in the Gulf, a square-rigged vessel with billowing sails to the north, and ahead the fairyland city shimmering white in the sun. "Yes," she said, "the sight is an illusion. But thank God, Richard, the city itself is real."

The next ten hours were filled with disembarking at the wharf and hiring a cab to take them and their luggage through the sleepy afternoon streets to the Lucas Terrace flats where he had been renting a flat now for seven years; with Elizabeth's gaiety at seeing her new city again, her delight at his bachelor dwelling, her concern over the potted plants he had bought in an attempt to brighten up the apartment and which were now dead from lack of water; her tossing her hat onto his—*their*—bed; with her raising the windows and opening her arms to embrace the Gulf breeze; her chatter, her feminine grace, her smile while he explained to the grim landlady at the door that the lady he had just brought in with him was indeed his wife; Elizabeth's turning her charm upon the landlady, of that mollified woman bringing over a pot of stew an hour later and a cake for their dinner; with Elizabeth's graciousness, her laughter, her bustling energy; and every movement of her body a sonnet from her soul.

That night she held him to her moaning for the first time in the ecstacy of his embrace, and they fell asleep in each other's arms with a special excitement dancing in their souls for tomorrow, and the many tomorrows yet to come.

Six

"Hello! Hello! Central? Hello! Yes, Central. Please ring the number for the Galveston Cab Company for me."

Elizabeth, coming suddenly awake, sat up swiftly, blinking. The window of their bedroom facing the Gulf was aglow with the light of dawn. Richard was not in the bed beside her, but she could hear him shouting from the entry.

"Hello. No, not the Wharf Company. I said the—I said the—Hello, Central? Yes, I said the Cab Company. Cab! Cab! Yes, thank you."

She smiled and threw back the sheets, the mosquito netting, and swung her feet to the side of the bed, wondering why it was necessary for her husband to shout; for evidently he was telephoning on this first morning of their life together in Galveston. He had said the evening before that he would hire a buggy so that they could take a drive early. As she pulled on her wrapper and ran a brush through her hair, she could still hear him shouting.

"Hello, Central? You connected me with the Galveston Brewery and I asked for the Cab Company. What? I say you gave me a wrong number, Miss. Yes, the Galveston Cab Company, please. Thank you."

She left their bedroom and as she came into the hallway, saw him clutching the telephone mouthpiece in one hand, the earpiece in the other, as if hanging on to the instrument for dear life; he was hunched over, his shoulders tense, his face a study in perplexity. But upon seeing her, he smiled briefly, then jerked to attention shouting, "Hello! Is this Mr. Vieira? Dr. Morrison here, sir. I would like to rent a carriage for the day. If you'll have your boy drive it over, sir, I'll be happy to pay extra."

She went into the kitchen, a small, dismal cell smelling strongly of sour milk and damp wood, and began rummaging in the pantry for flour with which to make biscuits. Presently Richard joined her in the kitchen as she was slicing the bacon he'd ordered the evening before from the grocery, and took her in his arms saying, "My dear wife, we'll have a carriage by eight so that we can go for our drive, because I have something special to show you which I hope you'll like." Then he kissed her lingeringly on the lips.

Laughing, she drew away from him. "Dr. Morrison, that isn't a go-driving kiss."

"No? Then maybe we should put off the drive till tomorrow."

But they didn't.

Shortly after eight, the Galveston Cab Company's carriage, drawn by a sprightly bay mare, was gliding through the tree-bordered, shell-paved streets. The air was still and sultry except for a light breeze from the Gulf which caught gently at her best cream-colored parasol. Dew still sparkled on the emerald lawns beyond the picket fences and the tall, narrow houses—built so close together that a carriage could not have passed between—exhibited little vignettes of Galveston's citizens awake and busy early; ladies in aprons sweeping their porches, watering potted plants on their banisters, children playing in the streets, and businessmen in derbies and vested suits leaving their drives and alleyways in carriages and hansoms for the day. Richard tipped his hat to ladies on the walk, Elizabeth inclined her head to them and to the gentlemen who were tipping their derbies to them from other carriages. No need to pretend she was part of the scene this time; for now she *was* a part of it. The warm, humid air touched her cheeks with its own special lotion as the carriage moved on northward down Sixth Street, then turned west on Avenue I.

"You don't seem weary from our trip from Chicago," Richard said.

"No. I'm seldom weary, especially when I've bathed in such luxury as the *Jessie Day*. She was so different from the riverboats Mark Twain wrote about."

"You've read Mark Twain? So have I and enjoyed reading him."

"You do read some then, Richard? I mean things besides your medical journals?"

"Some. As for reading medical material, I don't do

101

much of that, only the journals to keep up with new trends and discoveries. Medical books are too expensive. At the school we didn't even have a library at first. But gradually, we doctors have built it up. Almost no allowance was made for a library by the board of regents of the school in the beginning, nor recently either. So for every book we doctors buy for our personal libraries, we try to buy one for the medical library. We've slowly built a small one, nearly five hundred volumes now, and keep the books locked up in cabinets." He glanced at her. "At any rate, I do read the newspapers avidly and a book now and then. I enjoy reading Dickens and Hawthorne, and don't tell anybody, but I even enjoy reading the speeches of Abraham Lincoln."

Elizabeth laughed. She had a throaty laugh that was more a chuckle, a sort of bubbling up out of her like a spring from an underground stream. As she gazed around her she sighed with contentment, watching a small boy running down the street with a dog at his heels, a colored man spading a border along a wooden fence.

"Elizabeth?"

She looked at him as he stared ahead down the street somewhere. "Haven't you wondered why I haven't given you a wedding present? I mean besides your ruby wedding ring?"

She looked ahead again. "Yes, now that you brought it up, I have."

"Well, as a matter of fact, I have one for you which I'll show you very soon. Being a bachelor and working at two jobs for six years, I managed to accumulate a small sum. You know of course that my father died two years ago, and the estate was split up between Damon and I, which left me another small sum."

The street was newly paved. Here, the houses were further apart and larger, the yards a little wider. As the carriage began to slow, Elizabeth was surprised to see a great deal of activity in a yard ahead. Building. A house was being built—here where he drew the carriage to a halt.

The outside of the house was nearly finished, it seemed, standing tall, wider than those on either side of it; not nearly as large as the ones only one street over on Broadway, of course, and not brick either. Oh, but it was lovely anyway, ornate, frosted with its first coat of white paint. There was such fretwork, latticework, fancy carpentry, and jigsaw design. Very charming. In the yard there was such a mess of raw lumber, and piles of huge rectangular stone and brick for flues, and men carrying things. The smell of paint and new wood and. . . .

Suddenly she turned to look at Richard, saw his smile, his eyes intent upon her face. Her eyes widened, her mouth fell open.

"A house burned down here last fall," he said. "The owners put the lot up for sale. Probably another sacrifice you will have to make, Elizabeth, not being able to choose the plans of your own house."

She drew in her breath and turned to look again, both gloved hands now clutching the handle of her parasol. "Oh! Oh, *Richard!*"

"Of course, there's time to choose the wallpaper—"

But she was closing the parasol, and before he could get out of the buggy and help her out of it, she had already gotten down of her own accord, holding her skirts up out of the sawdust, shavings and sand, and was moving forward, her eyes fixed upon the house.

"Dr. Morrison," called a carpenter in overalls carrying a roll of papers. "A good mornin' to you, sor."

"Sorrenson," said Richard. "This is Mrs. Morrison, come to see the house. Elizabeth, the contractor in charge of building the house."

"A good mornin' ma'am," the ruddy-faced carpenter said, snatching off his cap.

She would never remember answering Mr. Sorrenson that day, or their brief, cursory conversation, or Richard's becoming engaged in a discussion with him about some matter concerning delayed materials; for her mind and her eyes were on her house, her residence, and later the memory of her first impressions of it would be mixed up with the embracing observations and conceptions of the architect himself, speaking with dignity, shyness, fierce, embarrassed pride. *Or had the house itself spoken of him?*

First she noticed how high it was raised. Eight feet above the ground on a foundation of red limestone. There was a full basement aboveground with arched windows. The wide steps leading to the veranda were flanked by an ornate balustrade shining with its first coat of white paint. On the left, a bay reached from the first floor veranda to the roof two stories above, where it was crowned with the most charming lacy turret; and the veranda above and below was a carpenter's sculpture of sawtoothed arches and fretwork; and a sort of wheel-in-a-wheel motif was repeated at the apex of each arch.

Within, the entry hall was long and narrow and she could smell the new plaster, new wood, new varnish, new *everything*. As she entered the front door, she knew that the large, bright room on her right must surely be Richard's study with its wall of shelves and its wide windows opening out onto the veranda; and to her left the front parlor with its lovely bay windows. And as she hurried in she saw that there was a pair of walnut doors which slid into the wall on either side of the wide doorway between the front parlor and the smaller back parlor beyond, and another pair of sliding doors between the back parlor and the dining room, so that when the two sets of doors between the three rooms were slid into the walls, they became one long room, a veritable reception room! Oh the parties she could have here!

The kitchen beyond the dining room was small but large enough for a table and chairs and a large cooking stove; and there were real china cupboards with shelves and glass doors. Beyond the kitchen was a small, glassed-in porch and a pantry fitted with shelves. And from the side of the pantry, a narrow stairway for the servants led to the upper floor.

Excitedly, Elizabeth rushed from the side of the kitchen to the entry hall and up, up, up the wide front stairway to a landing where a round, stained-glass window shone in reds, purples and greens; then turning to the right, the stairs went up onto the second floor. On the south facing the Gulf was the master bedroom with its bay windows overlooking the gallery and the bathroom behind that with its porcelain bathtub and water closet already installed. And there was a small room on the other side of the hallway, *the nursery,* and a guest room facing north. She could see the bay and the ships in port from its window. Out of breath she ran back to the hallway, heard Richard calling her from below, and rushed to the balustrade looking down upon the circular staircase.

"Here, Richard. I'm up here. Come and see!" she cried.

"I would advise you not to lean on the balustrade, madam, because it isn't yet fastened securely enough."

Startled, Elizabeth spun around to see who spoke, and before her stood a living likeness of—my Lord—Mark Twain!

"Oh," she said, "I'm sorry. I didn't see you!" When the gentleman did not reply, she stammered, "I—I'm Mrs. Morrison. Dr. Morrison's wife."

Then, the gentleman's blue eyes twinkled as he smiled. He was in his fifties, slightly stocky, dressed in a vested suit and a black, four-in-hand silk tie, and carrying a bowler. His hair, cut just below his ears, was steel gray like his mustache. He bowed with great dignity and when he straightened, said softly, "I was examining a piece of moulding in the—ah—water closet room and in your haste, you quite overlooked me. And your first impression of the house, Mrs. Morrison?"

In spite of her initial disappointment that her first residence would not be brick or located on Broadway, she was breathless with the realization that this house was hers; hers to keep, to decorate, to furnish, live in, to share. "It's lovely. Of course I can't see how the inside will look when it's painted and wallpapered, but it's already lovely because of the design, the architecture, and the carpentry work. It's truly a work of art. But I can't place the style."

The gentleman's smile widened. "Neither can I. It's revolutionary though, don't you think? Much like three or four others in the neighborhood. I think we can call it a transition between Gothic Renaissance, Queen Anne, and . . . contemporary."

She clasped her hands. "I'm pleased. I thought no one could build a house like Nicholas Clayton, but now I can boast that I have one every bit as beautiful as any of his. If not more so."

"Can you now?"

This twin brother of Mark Twain's had been studying her closely and now rocked back on his heels beaming amusedly at her. It suddenly occurred to her that she had just committed a *faux pas*. Flushing she said, "Oh dear, I'm sorry. It just occurred to me that you may be—"

"The architect?" He smiled. "I am. But don't be embarrassed, I am also Nicholas Clayton." He bowed again. "At your service, madam."

"Elizabeth?" Now Richard was beside her and began making introductions and explanations. Because she had admired Clayton's houses so, he had commissioned him for his own house, much to the furious jealousy of some of his medical school colleagues. "Well, Elizabeth? What do you think?" he asked.

What did she think? "Oh Richard, I'm truly speechless."

But Mr. Clayton, who was normally a quiet, conservative man, was *not*. For the next hour, he acted as tour guide, showing the couple through their own house, passionately embracing every architectural detail, painting vivid pictures of stained-glass windows yet to be installed in the upper portion of the bay windows in the parlor, moldings etched in gold, of brass and glass chandeliers, varnished, white-pine floors, woodwork, molded cornices, cherrywood mantels in all the rooms; twelve-foot ceilings throughout, all windows facing south wide and long to catch the Gulf breezes with corresponding windows on opposite walls to draw the breezes in.

The front door was a carved masterpiece in oak. The huge oval opening in the center was to have a clear glass window with an etched vase and fruit design installed, not yet arrived. "For it's being shipped from Italy," Clayton said. Out back there was a carriage house just being built, large enough for two carriages, two stalls, and an apartment above for the servants.

As he sculpted, painted, and conducted a symphonic tour through their lovely but average-sized house, enthused as if it were one of his magnificent cathedrals, Elizabeth became aware of Clayton the architect, sitting long hours far into the night at his drafting table, climbing over raw lumber dressed in vested suit and tie, wading through shavings and sawdust in black patent shoes, witnessing his eclectic visions becoming stone, brick, and wood realities.

On the lower veranda they stood at last with Clayton pointing to houses down the street which he had designed. He spoke of the pain it had caused him when he saw many of his residences burn in an enormous fire that swept from the waterfront to the Gulf twelve years before. He spoke of the agony of seeing the ruins of his beautiful Electric Pavilion which had burned before the great fire, and Elizabeth had glimpsed tears in his eyes which he did not try to conceal. In those moments she became aware that she stood in the presence of a great man whom the world would probably never know, a genius whom history would never recognize.

Later, driving back to their flat, Elizabeth and Richard had their first argument. It began when she told him, "I've made up my mind; we should take the money Papa gave us for a wedding gift and buy furniture for the house."

Richard shook his head. "No, Elizabeth. Your money should be put in the bank."

"It's not my money, dear, it's ours."

"It's yours and should be put in the bank."

"Alright then. It's mine so I'll do with it as I please."

He slapped the reins to urge the horse forward at a faster pace. "I think you should know, Elizabeth, that I spent most of the money I'd saved and all of my half of Father's estate on the house. I'm paying cash for the house, as a matter of fact."

Elizabeth had learned that Richard and Damon's father had once been a physician and small-time rancher near Austin, and that when his wife died some eighteen years ago, he sold his ranch and left his practice and moved to Galveston with his two sons. He had died only two years ago, had left his sons a considerable—though not tremendous—amount of cash and some shares of stock.

"We can get by nicely on what I make at the school and from my private practice, but to be wise and frugal, we should have a little in the bank in case we have bad luck," he explained.

"What bad luck?"

"A hurricane, damage to the house. Or illness."

"Piffle."

He glanced at her. "Or a baby."

"Mr. Clayton just spent an hour explaining about how almost hurricane-proof our house is. I've never been sick a day in my life and neither have you. And I assure you, John Richard, that I don't consider having a baby bad luck!" She turned her frown to a smile briefly as they met another buggy passing on the street. "Besides," she continued, "I have the monthly dividend coming in from my mother's trust fund for such things. And if you think I'm going to put our wedding money in a bank and let it just sit there useless, you're badly mistaken!" Her chin went up with a jerk, and her parasol spun furiously.

"It doesn't just sit," he said morosely. "It draws interest."

"Don't you understand that I'd become the laughing-stock of my new neighborhood if we move into a house with no furniture?"

"I was going to speak to you about that."

"Oh?"

He let the mare slow her pace a little as he explained, "I have a patient who is a widow. Her husband was captain of a cargo schooner and the ship was caught in a storm somewhere off the Florida coast three years ago, was wrecked, and the captain was lost. Hennesey is her name.

Quite well-off, though she owes me a considerable fee—"

"Really? Are sea captains that well-to-do?"

"Some of them are."

"What about—your brother?"

"Damon?"

"Of course, Damon. You always ask that as if you have another brother."

"And you always avoid using his name." Richard shook the reins again. "Damon's probably more well-to-do than most, because he's like me, saves his money or invests it; puts his in company stock, Ingram and Sturgeon stock. But back to Mrs. Hennesey—"

"Do you think he will approve of your marrying me?"

"Probably. He was much taken with you last May."

"Oh? He was? . . . How do you know?"

"Well, he said you were lovely. And that you were gracious. And he especially mentioned that you did not giggle or simper, but yet you weren't haughty either."

As they turned onto Sixth Street, Elizabeth had to hold onto her hat because of the south breeze blowing up the street from the Gulf. She was smiling to herself, glimpsing the Gulf as they neared the Lucas Terrace flats. She said, "Richard? Let's go down to the beach and watch the ships."

"The place to watch ships is the ship channel, Elizabeth. Besides, I can't. I have to check with Rob Tate who's been seeing my patients for me while I was gone. And tomorrow afternoon I'll have to go back to the office, and there's a faculty meeting—"

"And I intend to go shopping tomorrow for furniture."

He drew the reins and the buggy came to a halt outside the Lucas Flats. "That's what I was trying to speak to you about. Tomorrow I have an appointment with Mrs. Hennesey—"

"Then another day?"

"Elizabeth, please listen," he said as he got down from the carriage and began to tether the reins to a tree. "Mrs. Hennesey is moving away, selling most of her furniture. And knowing that I was building a new house, has offered to let me have first choice in purchasing some pieces." He paused and took her hand to help her down. "I've been in her house and the furniture is in excellent condition. They had no children."

She was looking disappointed as they went up the stairway of the flats to their apartment. Finally, as he opened the door of their flat for her he said, "Dear, I cannot as a man accept the use of your money to buy furniture. Not in good conscience. It just—isn't done. And used furniture is the best I can afford right now; because we'll soon need a horse and buggy too."

He usually rode a bicycle everywhere he went because he did not own a carriage for want of a place to keep one. Besides, bicycles didn't eat hay, require a stall, and demanded only a minimum of upkeep. But soon they would have their own carriage house, and when they did, he planned to go to Houston and purchase a horse and buggy, the best he could buy with the money he had left. Richard had few interests in anything not related to his profession, but carriages were his weakness. He loved them all; hansoms, surreys, cabriolets. In the meantime, rain or shine, he'd continue to pedal his bicycle to and from his office and on house calls. If he and Elizabeth decided to take a ride, then he'd have to hire a rig.

She stood within the entry pulling off her hat thoughtfully as he watched her expression. Then he began to follow her through the apartment toward the bedroom, noticing the changes that had taken place in it since they had arrived, less than twenty-four hours ago.

There was fancywork everywhere; covering the round table in front of the window under his reading lamp, on the table beside the Morris chair, covering the threadbare back of the sofa, on the seat of his favorite horsehair rocker by the window. And knickknacks sitting around; colored glass vases, little porcelain statues, a likeness of Randal Harbour staring severely from an oval frame over the side chair. There was a linen cloth on the dining table, wooden spoons in a crockery pitcher, a dough board; women's things all over. And he wondered how in the devil she got all of it in one trunk.

In the bedroom she had put a new counterpane on the bed, something puffy with a lacy design all over, and fancywork scarves on the dressing table. There she tossed her straw bonnet with its colorful flowers and gauzy scarf upon the counterpane and turned to him.

"Buying used furniture would be the wise thing to do, wouldn't it," she said wistfully.

"I think so," he said, doubting so for the first time.

"Then we'll go see Mrs. Hennesey," she said. And turning away from him she went to the window and looked out over the Gulf. He could see the breeze stirring wisps of her hair, the sun touching the top of her head setting it ablaze. "It's just that I want everything to be

113

really fine. And I want it to be good enough for anybody who sees it, even the socially elite."

Sadly he shook his head and tossed his own hat onto the bed. "Galveston's not Chicago, Elizabeth. In Chicago your father fraternized with the upper crust. Here, the upper echelon is a small social clique that rarely admits a newcomer. Besides," he said smiling, "you've three things against you already."

She turned toward him. "Against *me?* I don't understand."

"First you're a Yankee. Believe it or not, Galveston as a Southern town is still prejudiced against northerners. They fought a battle here against the Union during the war and they've never forgotten it. They're like barnacles hanging on to an old ship."

"What else?"

"You didn't marry into money, and you're an outsider."

"But I should think your professorship at the college and your profession as a physician should lend you a great deal of respect. That should give you a foot in the door."

"Respect maybe, and a foot is all I have in the door. But admittance, no. As a matter of fact, we doctors are in a social clique just below the elite, along with store owners, attorneys and some of the lesser-known real estate brokers."

"Piffle! Piffle! Piffle!" She turned back to the window and folded her arms across her breast. "I intend to know everybody in this town; every man, every woman, every child, and to make everybody welcome in my house; I don't care what clique he's in. *Under* the elite?" She turned back to him. "No, Richard. We'll *not* be under the elite, but a part of it. An *important* part of it, a *necessary* part of it. Just you wait and see. I *promise* you that."

He regarded her a moment in silence. And for a moment at least, thought that with her, just such a thing might possibly be—possible.

Seven

They moved into the house on November seventh, precisely five days after Mr. Sorrenson, the contractor, had said it would be finished, about the same time Richard said Damon was due back from his extended trip to Liverpool, Boston, and ports in between. Elizabeth had sensed there was a sort of mystery about Damon's extended stay in Liverpool, a mystery Richard chose not to share with her. Perhaps because it, very simply, was none of her business. Besides, they had had a more immediate concern after purchasing the furniture from Mrs. Hennesey—that of storing it for sixty days. Elizabeth's own furniture, heirloom pieces she had inherited from her mother's side of the family, had arrived in October and was crowded into their flat awaiting moving day.

After purchasing the furniture from the Widow Hennesey, as she was called, Richard, in his usual calm and precise manner, rented space in a warehouse near the wharfs and had the furniture stored there on a second floor under the driest conditions possible. Then, the day before moving day, he rented two farm wagons, and hired eight longshoremen off the docks.

Just after nine o'clock the next morning, while Richard was at the warehouse directing the loading of the furniture onto the wagons and Elizabeth was waiting alone in the empty house, the doorbell jingled and she opened the door to a tall, very slender lady about her own age who was holding the handle of an iron kettle with one hand, the bottom of the kettle with the other.

"Hello, I'm Melissa Swift from next door. You must be Elizabeth. I've brought you some lunch if you've a place yet to put it."

"Oh do come in, Melissa. Richard has mentioned that your husband and he and Damon are good friends, but I've missed meeting you somehow. Yes, I have a stove already installed."

Melissa bustled in with the kettle and she and Elizabeth hurried down the entry to the side door of the kitchen, with the neighbor saying, "So glad to meet you too. I've been visiting my parents in Missouri for the last two months and missed meeting you. Cully's bringing the cornbread later when our Sissy finishes baking it." She set the kettle on Elizabeth's Sears & Roebuck cooking stove, wiped her hands on her apron, and offered her hand. "Welcome to Galveston and the neighborhood, Elizabeth. We've known Damon and Richard for years. Two very unlikely bachelors, I must say. But I always thought Damon would marry first, somehow. To someone much like you. Richard was always so caught up in his practice and the school."

From the first moment their eyes met and their hands touched, Elizabeth knew that Melissa would be her best friend; and where before she was only full of excitement, now her exuberance overflowed. Meeting Melissa Swift for the first time was like meeting an old friend.

"If I won't be intruding, I'd like to help you, Elizabeth. Because you'll be needing help if you're to be in order for the housewarming tomorrow night."

Seeing that her neighbor truly wished to help, Elizabeth seized her hand again. "Oh, Melissa, I'd be so grateful. I've got to hang draperies yet and more furniture is arriving tomorrow, and Richard says the whole town will turn out for the housewarming. I've never been so excited in my entire life!"

And so as the parlor furniture arrived on the first two wagonloads, and as the longshoremen struggled with the pieces from wagon to house, sweating in the warm November sun, it was Melissa who answered the back door where other neighbors came calling to leave cakes and cookies; it was she who shooed stray dogs and curious neighborhood children from the house, and passed dippers of cool water and glasses of lemonade to the burly, smelly, tattooed longshoremen, while Elizabeth directed the traffic. As the front parlor pieces were being set in place, Elizabeth couldn't help but recall the day it was all purchased.

She and Richard had gone to the Widow Hennesey's house on Avenue G the third day after their arrival in Galveston. The exterior of the widow's house—which was badly in need of paint—had caused her a few

118

moments of apprehension as to the condition of the furniture within. But she need not have worried, for as she soon learned, Abigail Hennesey had the same excellent taste in furnishings as she had in her dress. She was a short, plump, partridge of a lady who perspired profusely and fanned constantly as she touched every piece of furniture in the rooms lovingly with fingers beladen with exotic rings. Because she was wearing a frock of the most exquisite silk, with french lace cuffs and jabbot, Elizabeth was certain indeed that the Widow Hennesey was well-to-do. There was an hour or so of polite haggling over prices as they selected and purchased their pieces, especially over the pianoforte which Elizabeth coveted and which Richard could not afford.

But now she covered her ears wincing briefly as the men carried in the rosewood dining table, having had to remove its six, huge, carved legs in order to get it through the doors, and stayed in the dining room until the legs were replaced, the table set upright, the chairs, sideboard, and curved glass china cabinet placed.

Just before noon, Primrose and Shadrack arrived with their trunks, which Shadrack and his friends carried to their apartment over the carriage house. Then he returned to help the longshoremen unload the wagons. Primrose joined in helping Melissa and Melissa's maid, Sissy, unpack the earthenware and kitchen pieces. In spite of having to dash from room to room directing the placement of the furniture, Elizabeth was able to note how much more efficient Primrose was than Melissa's maid at managing the kitchen during lunch, doling out stew and cornbread to the hungry longshoremen. She was still secretly marveling at how they had acquired Primrose and Shadrack as servants.

While still at Mrs. Hennesey's house, after Richard had discussed the transfer of funds from his account to the widow's, Mrs. Hennesey had pulled the bell cord above the piano and said, "Before you go, Dr. Morrison, I want you to hear something."

Within seconds, a tall, burly Negro appeared in the doorway between the parlor and dining room. "Yes, Miss Hensey?"

"Play us some of that New Aw-leens music, Shadrack, for Dr. and Mrs. Morrison."

"Yes, Miss Hensey." The man sat down on the tufted cushioned piano stool and looked up at the ceiling, causing Elizabeth and Richard to glance up too. But they did not see what he was seeing; they could not see the heavenly scores written on the music sheets of his mind. From his callused, stubby, black fingers came the plaintive, soaring strains of—Yes, again it was jazz—ragtime.

Ragtime, the unrhythmic rhythm said to have been born in the bawdy houses of New Orleans. Elizabeth and Richard had been trying to remember where they'd seen the man before, and once he began to play, both recognized him—the harpsichord player from Texas Pete's medicine show. Shadrack shook his head smiling with wonder at his own marvelous ingenuity as he played. He glanced at Elizabeth once, cast his eyes down, as she had seen many other Negro men do here in Galveston, but he had seen her smile and he grinned at the keyboard knowing she was pleased. Suddenly, he changed the mood of his rendition and fabricated a tune that

120

resembled what the jazz-players were calling the "blues."

The piano's tone was excellent, painfully so, and Elizabeth was only half aware of the conversation now ensuing between the widow and her husband.

"One hundred twenty-five for the piano," said Mrs. Hennesey to Richard.

"I'm more interested in how much you pay for help like Shadrack."

"That is none of your business, Dr. Morrison, unless you have intentions of employing Shadrack; for, you see, he'll be needing employment after I leave. And so will his wife, Primrose, which is actually why I brought him in, so that you could meet him in case you need a couple of servants. You see, I take good care of my help too."

"Live-in?"

"Of course. Primrose is an excellent maid and cook. Shadrack works as my groom, gardener, and handyman." She leaned over to Richard and whispered something behind her fan.

Elizabeth saw Richard shake his head. "Too bad."

The widow placed her hand on Richard's arm and said, "But he's reliable when he *isn't*."

"Ain't got no money," Shadrack was singing, "ain't got no gal. Ain't got no honey, and ah ain't got no pal. So I'm singin', singin', singin' the blues." He was singing the blues and enjoying every minute of it. Elizabeth smiled at Richard.

"Want to meet Primrose?" the widow asked Elizabeth.

She nodded, too engrossed in listening to Shadrack's blues to be much interested though.

"How much did you say you'd take for the piano?"

Richard asked.

"One hundred and not a cent less, Dr. Morrison," returned Mrs. Hennesey, yanking the bell pull over the piano again.

"So I'm gonna get a job in the riverboat saloon, an' make me some money and a little whoopee too," sang Shadrack as Elizabeth laughed. "'Cause I'm singin', singin', singin', the blues."

Primrose appeared then, a thin woman in her thirties, wiping her hands on her immaculate apron and soberly looking from Elizabeth to Richard, as Mrs. Hennesey introduced her. Elizabeth started to offer her hand as she always did to people, servants or not, but Richard had anticipated her move and took her hand in his while Mrs. Hennesey told Primrose that Mrs. Morrison was from Chicago, Illinois. "You know, up nawth? She and Dr. Morrison are newlyweds, isn't that nice?"

"Yes, ma'am," said Primrose solemnly.

"Primrose and Shadrack just got married too, last summer," the widow said. "He was employed with a traveling medicine show, met Primrose, who lost her husband to typhoid a couple of years ago, and quit his job to marry her and help me here at the house. I've had Primrose now for four years, Dr. Morrison, as you probably know; for you've seen her before when you made your house calls." Then to Primrose she said, "The Morrisons will be needing help and I'm going to give you and Shadrack a good recommendation in case they decide they'd like to employ you."

Primrose looked at Elizabeth, Elizabeth looked at Primrose, and Shadrack had quit playing and was sitting and watching. The girl gave no hint that she was pleased, neither did she show a flicker of displeasure. But there was something, something in her eyes that told Elizabeth she might like to consider the arrangement. Something had clicked between them that signaled them that such an arrangement might please all concerned. Of course everything had just been mentioned, and there was the problem of Shadrack's drinking and why he had been involved in Texas Pete's medicine show, things which needed to be investigated. But at least it was something to consider.

Richard had said then, "We'd best be leaving now, Elizabeth, and let Mrs. Hennesey get back to her business."

Elizabeth had thanked Shadrack for his entertainment, gave one last glance at the piano, and went with her husband to the door. Once she was out on the veranda and supposedly out of hearing so that his professional ethics were not compromised, she heard Richard say, "By the way, Mrs. Hennesey, about my fee—"

Elizabeth turned to see the widow as she gushed, "Oh Dr. Morrison. Dear me, I'd just started to mention that. How much do I owe you?"

"Fifty."

"Fifty! My, how things do add up." The widow laughed, "Ha, ha, ha," until she observed Richard's patient, sober expression and she caught her breath and said, "Add fifty dollars to what you're paying me for the furniture and you can consider the piano yours and your fee paid."

"Sold."

With legs removed the piano was the last piece delivered to the Morrison house. It took seven longshoremen to place the instrument where it exactly fit into the curved area in the bay, the three long, wide windows reflecting in its polished wood, the light displaying its carved cabinet to the best advantage.

It was nearing four in the afternoon when Richard paid the longshoremen for their work and Elizabeth thanked Melissa for her valuable help and bade her good evening. Then she almost collapsed onto the sofa in the back parlor, which was now furnished with their furniture from the flats, the soon-to-be reupholstered sofa and slipper chair, Richard's beloved black horsehair rocker, the round lamp table in the center, its marred top covered discreetly in fancy needlework, looking more than presentable now. She gazed around her, concluding that she had chosen the wallpaper well to coordinate with the carpets and draperies which they had bought from Mrs. Hennesey along with the furniture. She would hang the draperies tomorrow with Melissa, Sissy, Primrose, and Shadrack to help. Richard's desk would arrive in the morning along with his leather chair and lamps they had purchased for the library. The only piece in the library at present was the hideous steerhorn chair they had purchased from the widow and of which Richard seemed disproportionately fond.

It was all theirs, the house, the furnishings, even the servants. But she told Richard that her greatest treasure was Melissa and that little boy of hers whom she had hardly glimpsed that day, Cullen.

"Cully's a strange little boy, more like a wise old man

than a boy sometimes," Richard observed, lounging in his rocker and lighting his pipe exactly as he had done every evening since they had arrived in Galveston. "He worships Damon."

She was half lying on the sofa, smiling up at the ceiling, and she turned her face toward him. "Does he?"

Her eyes, shining with weary joy, reflected something else too in that moment. Richard was comfortable being married, and content, and extremely pleased with his life as it now was. Too pleased to become disturbed any by the memory of their walk on the beach that first evening, with Elizabeth and Damon falling so easily into conversation together while he had to be content with talking to Randal Harbour. Or of Damon's later remark as he smoked his cigar, "Lord, John Richard. I could fall for a girl like her. Too much exposure to such a fine thing could infect you, couldn't it? I mean, it could get into your blood, couldn't it?"

"Undoubtedly," Richard had replied, for already he had felt a fever rising in him and had begun to see red-headed spots before his eyes.

Now as he puffed contentedly on his pipe, he reached for the *Galveston News* which Shadrack had dutifully brought in, and shook it out. An editorial projected that McKinley would urge "war-hungry Americans to be patient with Spain in regards to Cuba, in the hopes that its new and liberal Premier Sagasta would modify its Cuban policy." Further on down the front page was an article describing a street brawl in Houston in which two men were gunned down in cold blood. And on the second page was a piece concerning a new book written by a

Captain Alfred Mahan entitled, *The Interest of America In Sea Power*, which theorized that if America was to aspire to greatness, she should wield superior naval power as an instrument of commercial expansion as did Great Britain; that if she did not, she was in danger of falling behind in the struggle for economic survival in this era of "aggressive restlessness."

With that subject in mind, Richard looked up from his paper to mention it to Elizabeth, to tell her that Damon was of the same opinion and had come up with a fascinating idea that could be revolutionary in the shipping industry. But seeing her contented expression and that she was apparently daydreaming as women seemed so often to do, he changed his mind. Better to see how far along Damon had come with his idea first anyway, and whether or not he had revealed it yet to the "powers that be."

"In theory it appears to be sound, Damon. In practice, I haven't seen it. What you've proposed takes time and money, even for a scale model. I have the time, you've got the money. I'm as curious as you are to see if it works, but I'm even more curious to see if Ingram and the board go along with the idea."

"It works, Joe Bob. It's been proven. Ingram wants faster ships for obvious reasons—he's up against tough competition. And faster ships means more trade, not to mention a better reputation among the merchants." Damon propped his booted foot on Joe Bob's drafting table, took out the only two Havanas he had left—being unable to purchase more because of the Cuban situation—

and offered one of them to his marine engineer friend. Joe Bob took it matter-of-factly as if it wasn't his last, got a match out of his pocket, struck it, and lit the cigar the same time Damon lit his.

"Ingram wants speed. Sturgeon wants economy. That's why we kept sails on our steamships so long, economy of fuel," Damon said after a couple of puffs on the cigar. He spit out a shred of tobacco and continued, "Besides, they didn't trust steam propulsion. But if you'll remember, they didn't trust steel either."

Joe Bob Swift puffed languidly and leaned back in his chair with his eyes shut. Damon looked out the engineer's office window at the shipyard across the channel. Even from here he could see the *Arundel* in dry dock having her hull scraped and painted while the mechanics tried to overhaul her engines for the sixth time.

Ingram and Sturgeon Shipping Company had begun operations in 1847 when the clipper ships, the fastest and most beautiful sailing ships in history, were developed for plying the seas in the China trade. Ingram had a fleet of them until the steam-driven sidewheelers proved so efficient that sailing ships could not compete; and although to this day Ingram and Sturgeon still maintained four square-riggers for trade around the Horn to California, they had scrapped the rest of their sailing ships and turned their monetary sights to steam-powered vessels, first acquiring steam-driven paddlewheelers for coastal trade, and later replacing them with screw-driven vessels, and iron hulls with steel. Changes in shipbuilding had been rapid and dramatic the last fifty years, competition being fierce among certain nations, with Great Britain leading the pack. The improvements were the direct results of changes in industry. Inventors like Bessemer, Watt, Edison, Alexander Graham Bell, all added their genius to the revolution, each invention changing industry, and industry in turn giving rise to new inventions.

The Industrial Revolution, as the economists were now calling it, had produced new vocations, like Joe Bob's. He was a mechanical engineer, adept at marine engineering. He understood compound expansion engines as if he were weaned on them, and the designing of ships was his special forte, though he did it merely as a sideline, not part of his regular job. But he was short-sighted, oddly enough, unable to grasp some abstract concepts; one had to demonstrate an idea to him or draw it up as accurately as possible as he had done with the diagram for the turbine engine. He had presented Joe Bob with a primitive drawing, primitive because he'd constructed it from the drunken ramblings of an English sea captain named Hodges, knowing that if Joe Bob could enlarge upon it and they could build the thing, and if it worked, Ingram and Sturgeon might lead the American Shipping Industry—and maybe the world—in producing the first turbine-driven cargo ship in history.

Damon had presented the concept and his infant drawing to Joe Bob back in June. However, when in Liverpool recently, he'd read that a man named Parsons, trying to sell the idea of the turbine engine to the British navy, had demonstrated the superiority of the engine in a yacht doing over thirty knots, outdistancing a pursuing

naval vessel at a naval review at Spithead. Damon had
been disappointed because he was not the first to demonstrate the engine's advantages, but encouraged by the
success of it nevertheless. Parsons had been having
trouble with what he called "cavitation" before he
perfected the relationship between propeller speed and
turbine speed, the article said, a concept which Damon
understood, and which had to be explained at length to
Joe Bob.

Now, if only he and Joe Bob could sell the idea to Eric
Ingram and Max Sturgeon, the board of directors would
go along with it. Joe Bob had studied the principle of the
discharge of steam as a result of impulse and reactionary
forces, which was simply a rotary-type engine, and had
drawn up a sophisticated sketch since he'd presented the
idea to him in June. Now on the drawing board it looked
good, and what was needed now was a scaled-down model
of the turbine in order to demonstrate the principle to
Ingram and Sturgeon and the board.

"As I recall," Joe Bob said, bringing Damon back from
his woolgathering, "it was you who got the old gentlemen and the board to convert to steam propulsion in the
first place when you were but a beardless youth, a bit of
strategy that won you their highest regard."

Damon put his other booted foot up on the first, both
now propped on the crossbar of the drafting table. "I did.
And somebody before me talked them into using steel
instead of iron in building hulls, and before that iron
instead of wood when *they* were but lads."

"And whoever it was, a man named Stinson, as I recall,
died a pauper while Ingram and Sturgeon grew rich."

"Stinson must have been an ass. And he wasn't Damon Morrison. I have a vested interest in Ingram and Sturgeon to begin with, and I have navigational know-how. Give a ship like the *Arundel* a turbine engine and she'll do twenty-six to thirty knots."

"Are you sure?"

"No. But I *am* sure about the principle."

"So I build the scale model of the turbine so we can demonstrate the principle to Ingram and the board. Is that all?"

"That's all. If we sell the idea to Ingram, he'll sell it to the board and we'll get her built, install a couple of them in the *Arundel*, I would go to England and see how she does on the long haul."

Joe Bob puffed three times. "How does this make you rich?"

"If it works, I'll demand a partnership with the old men."

"You should. Ingram can't scratch his behind unless he asks you first as it is."

"Now you've seen the difference between Stinson and Damon Morrison. If a company is to survive in this dog-eat-dog free enterprise system, somebody's got to do the brainwork, somebody's got to do the legwork, and somebody's got to know the trade." Damon squinted at Joe Bob through the smoke. "Somebody's got to anticipate the results of industrial expansion and the effect of the transcontinental railroads on shipping."

"What we need to fight the railroads is a canal in central America."

"We don't fight the railroads. We join them. You've

heard the talk about the shipping company buying up land for a railroad, combining the industries, a thing I & S should consider too. In time."

"Meantime it needs faster ships, bigger ships."

"With a smaller more powerful engine like the turbine."

"Okay. I'll build the model with your money and your help. But I've got reservations. The *Arundel* may not be the best ship to try the turbine engine on."

"Maybe not, but she's the one undergoing the complete overhaul. The condition in which I left her engines this time—Well, they're irreparable. So we need to strike while the fire's hot."

"Irreparable just in time to present the turbine principle. If I didn't know you better, Damon, I'd say you did that on purpose."

"Never."

"Besides, fire's always hot. The metaphor, I think, Damon, is to strike while the *iron* is hot. Isn't that it?"

Damon grinned. "Who knows? But that reminds me. Remember that young lady I mentioned to you last summer, the daughter of a textile manufacturer named Harbour?"

Joe Bob paused mid-puff and stared. "Indeed I do. So does Eric, since you lost the account for him."

"Never mind that. If Ingram buys the turbine engine idea, I'll be financially in good shape so that I've a good mind to go to Chicago and court that lovely lady and maybe even fetch her back to Galveston with me." He smiled. "That's one Harbour that would be mighty pleasant to come back to."

131

Joe Bob threw back his head laughing, got choked on smoke, and commenced coughing raucously for several minutes. When he recovered at last he said, "Damon, friend, you are too late." He coughed again and said, "Guess who my next door neighbor is?"

"I hate riddles."

"You remember the Harvey's house next door burned down last fall and old man Harvey put the lot up for sale?"

Damon nodded.

"Well, your brother bought the property right after you left last June, had it cleaned off and commissioned Nicholas Clayton, no less, to design him a house. Clayton hired Sorrenson and Sons to build it."

Damon stared. "You lie, Joe Bob."

"I don't."

"John Richard build a house? Part with his money to . . . *build a house?*"

"It's built."

"What the devil would he do that for?"

"Went to Chicago and fetched the same young lady you were just now contemplating."

Damon let his boots drop to the floor. "I don't believe you, Swift."

"He came home the latter part of August with her, about the time you were courting turbine engine ideas in Liverpool."

Damon leaned forward, eyes staring, almost bugged. "Pretty? Red hair?"

"Yep. Elizabeth Harbour. Now Mrs. John Richard Morrison. I haven't met her yet, but Melissa has.

Melissa's loco about her. You know how women are about people they like."

Damon stood up slowly, staring out the window. "That scoundrel," he breathed.

"Be truthful, Damon. You wouldn't have gone to Chicago to bring back a bride. You're just having bachelor fantasies. Besides, you'd be a helluva husband. Never home. She's not the kind of wife you go off and leave for months at a time. She's upper class."

"That blackguard," Damon said absently. Then he burst out laughing. "But you're right. I'd make a sorry husband. But—*John Richard married?*" He laughed again. "I can't believe it. This is rich. This is beautiful. My bachelor brother tethered and harnessed by the bonds of matrimony?" Cheerfully he looked at Joe Bob. "When did you say they moved into their house?"

"Yesterday. The doctors' wives, the medical auxiliary called the Happy Eighteen or something like that, is giving them a housewarming tonight, inviting the entire city of Galveston. They'll have a crowd too. You know Galveston—any excuse for a party."

Damon looked down at Joe Bob's sketch of the turbine engine on the drawing board. "I think I'll surprise them," he said. "They won't know the *Arundel*'s in port yet, so don't tell them."

"Don't worry about that. I'll be here all evening getting the plans ready to start building on the engine. When can I expect you to come and lend me your inventive brain power, not to mention your muscle power?"

"Tomorrow."

"Good. I need your presence if I'm to do this thing right. I can't ring you up to ask questions, because that telephone thing here isn't much good. Can't hear anything out of it, and people keep breaking in on the line."

"Well don't mention my engine into it, then. I don't want our plans to leak out to Moran or Mayfield or anybody else." Damon eyed the boxlike contraption on the wall near Joe Bob's desk. "It would have been a help if they'd perfected that thing before they foisted it on the public. If they keep working on it, though, I'll wager it'll be a convenience to own someday."

"I doubt that," said Joe Bob shaking his head. "It'll never replace the telegraph. It's like the gasoline buggies they're experimenting with up north with those internal combustion engines. Won't come to anything, Damon, I promise you that. Won't come to anything at all."

Eight

Every window at the Morrison house was aglow with a
festive warmth that promised gay camaraderie within,
while storm clouds billowed up in the west and a brisk
breeze from the northwest promised rain. If a house built
of such stuff as the Morrison's could bulge at its seams,
theirs would have done so at any hour between six and
ten that evening. For by eight o'clock, Shadrack had
counted almost two hundred persons in the house at
once, including the infants and toddlers upstairs, and the
old men spinning yarns on the veranda. The young
people had gravitated to the wide stairway where they sat
on the steps, taking their refreshments and making merry
with each other while having a gallery view of the guests
below.

The Jolly Sixteen, who were sponsoring the Morrison
housewarming, were busy serving in the dining room;
cakes, pies, cookies, and several varieties of punch. And
in washing and drying the used crystal and china in

the kitchen.

Richard was comfortably at home, both figuratively as well as literally; for he was among his medical school colleagues who spent a great deal of their time in the library during the evening, where they went to smoke and gossip. Elizabeth was aware, however, that the doctors had become particularly intense about their gossip tonight, and she was able to overhear some talk among them about dengue fever. She didn't know what dengue fever was, and at the time didn't care; for she too was in her natural element.

The invitations had been printed in each of the Galveston newspapers, announcing the housewarming and that everyone in the city was invited, provided they bring a gift for the "house or larder." The gifts were carried to the back porch because there was such a crowd, there was no room for opening the wrapped ones and no time for acknowledging them. For indeed it seemed the entire city had turned out for the housewarming.

The sliding doors between the parlors and dining room had disappeared into the walls, creating a long, hall-like room which, though full of people, seemed enormous to Elizabeth. There were people sitting, standing, and overflowing into the hallway, into the library, and upstairs, where Sissy and Prim, the official baby sitters, took care of the infants and toddlers in the spare rooms. Elizabeth was aware that this night would establish her and Richard in the community forever; for they were virtually on stage, in view of the entire town, and she had determined that their performance as host and hostess should win everlasting applause.

The first thing she had done to accomplish such an elusive distinction was to take stock of her resources in order to use them to the best advantage possible. Now as she stood in a group of five gentlemen and ladies, listening to one pompous fellow named Corkel—Corkel's Drugs and Sundry—tell of the great Galveston snow of 1895, she glanced at Shadrack, moving among the guests in the entry making sure each had registered; but not straying far from the front door he was in charge of answering. Shad had been the first asset she had drawn upon to their advantage. For in Shadrack she had seen a diamond in the rough, an unpolished gem. That morning after the telephone had been installed, she had rung up the Galveston Costume and Uniform Rental service, and rented him a suit of livery. Then she had set about to accomplish as much polishing as possible in the little time she had left before the housewarming. Shadrack had proved enthusiastically agreeable.

She taught him how he should answer the door, bow from the waist, and offer to take coats and hats. She recalled now, smiling to herself, that when she complimented him on how quick and well he learned the ritual, he had grinned, showing two rows of gold-capped teeth, and replied, "Miss Morrisey, please ma'am, it's not like I wasn't experienced *at all* in matters of greetin' folks kindly at the door."

When she and Richard had interviewed Primrose and Shadrack in their flat a week after they'd purchased Mrs. Hennesey's furnishings, and after reading the widow's flowery recommendations, it was Elizabeth who had stated the rules to which she would expect both servants

137

to adhere. Richard knew nothing about servants, having never had any of his own, and did not know what to expect of them. She had told Prim she expected neatness of person always, and outlined exactly what her duties were to be, and that if carried out with promptness and efficiency she could expect regular raises in her wages. She told Shadrack what his duties would be, then stated the wages she was willing to pay them both, and also when they could expect raises in pay. Then she had presented them with the "shalt nots."

"I would prefer that you not entertain your friends in the house or yard without special permission, and that you keep personal telephone calls from the house to a minimum; that you not repeat anything you might overhear or see in our house that's of a disparaging nature, whether it's said or done by our family or by guests. That you keep our financial and other personal matters in strictest confidence, and that neither of you drink to excess in public or in the house or yard." Then she had made a statement she was soon to regret—and to regret embarrassingly—for the rest of her life. "We expect people to drink occasionally, but we expect them to know their limits and abide by them, and will never tolerate drunkenness on our premises."

Primrose's background was simple and blemishless. Shadrack's was shadowy, though not spectacularly iniquitous. He humbly mentioned being raised in a New Orleans tavern which featured "ladies of the night, please Miss Morrisey," of having been converted by a street preacher, of "throwin' in" with Texas Pete— thinking he was honest, and later learning he was a fraud—and of his daily struggle with "the demon rum, please Dr. Morrisey." He told how he'd met Primrose at church, of marrying her, and of Mrs. Hennesey's kindness in trusting him enough to hire him.

And there he stood, black as midnight and as tall and suave as any English butler, in black coat and tails, opening the door, bowing, offering to take coats and hats, taking the gifts and handing them to one of the doctors' children who were designated throughout the evening to carry them to the back porch, indicating the way to the table, and enjoying every minute of it all.

When Grandfather's grandfather clock, standing sedately between the library door and the tapestry in the entry, gonged eight, she gave Shadrack his cue.

So bowing and nodding, he made his way to the piano in the parlor where a young lady, seeing his intent, vacated the piano stool. Shad flipped back the tails of his coat, sat down, stretched his arms, set his hands upon the keys, and suddenly the piano came alive; the crowd noise hushed momentarily as the "blues" drifted through the rooms like a fragrance, and the young people on the stairs vacated the steps and swarmed like colorful butterflies around the piano.

Within ten minutes, it was established that Dr. and Mrs. Morrison had not only hired a proficient servant, but a musician of the most versatile sort as well; for he could play the new blues, jazz, and popular things. He was an excellent entertainer besides enjoying himself tremendously in the meantime. Such ability to enjoy his own entertaining was contagious, and it wasn't long till the young people were singing "Kentucky Babe," "You

Aren't The Only Pebble On The Beach," "Sweet Rosie O'Grady," and other new popular tunes. The older folks continued their conversation, but with more gaiety, and the doctors went back to the library where they could continue their discussions and arguments without having to shout to be heard.

Elizabeth's second resource was herself. Because her best color was green, she had chosen a proper high-necked gown in emerald, had done her abundant hair up in huge curls pinned to the back of her head in glistening folds. She felt just beautiful and poised enough to elicit envy, but not jealousy—there was an important difference. She spoke to every person in the house, learned every name, and when her memory faltered, she faked it until she heard the person referred to by name or until she guessed it.

By now she was well-acquainted with each member of the Jolly Fifteen—or Sixteen, counting herself—because she had attended all three of their monthly meetings since her arrival in Galveston, and knew pretty well what each one was thinking.

They told each other how they were ecstatic at the turn-out tonight, each expressing delight, and suppressing a torpid envy; *they didn't turn out like this at OUR housewarming*, but consoled themselves with various reasons as to why; *ours wasn't as well-planned as this one; the doctor had already lived in the house for two years and it wasn't new; our house wasn't this nice, so people weren't as curious to see the inside*, and so on. They seemed torn between envying her and being glad she was such a charming and knowledgeable hostess; for didn't she—

and the house—not add a certain quality to the auxiliary? Well, if you want to equate God-given good looks and Nicholas Clayton architecture with quality. . . . Speaking of Nicholas Clayton, isn't that him over there in the corner talking to the mayor? Lord, I don't know, but somebody ought to offer the mayor a glass of punch because I think he just now came in. . . .

Elizabeth, still within earshot of the doctors' wives, pretended to listen to Mrs. Billingsley—Billingsley & Sons—extol the virtues of the latest fashions, while her eyes moved over the crowd. Every doctor in town had come to the housewarming, and every doctor's wife. Surprisingly Richard seemed to be the youngest doctor in town, even counting Galveston physicians who weren't on the staff at the medical college.

". . . Paris. But it's my prediction that they'll have to bring crinoline back again, though I say good riddance to the hoop skirt," Mrs. Billingsley was saying.

"Not me," put in birdlike Eva Parkins—Crown and Parkins Dry Goods—"If anyone can predict what they'll do next in Paris, then I predict the train will disappear and skirts will become shorter altogether."

"Heaven forbid," put in Mildred Crabtree, the Morrison's sanctimonious neighbor from across the street, "because when the skirts go up, morals go down."

The ladies tittered at that while poor Mildred stammered, "Why I didn't mean it like that. Oh dear, how embarrassing. What I meant was. . . ."

Yes, neighbors were here, the doctors, shopkeepers, lawyers, clerks, nurserymen, the mayor, the police chief, Mr. Clayton; all the people Richard had said would be

141

here and more. But the elite, the high society were absent. The bankers, ship-owners, the big merchants—absent. Why? *Why?* But so were the longshoremen, the sailors, the street peddlers. There were only a few from the Jewish community, a few from the German community, professional men all. But no Italians, no Negroes, no Mexicans. A place for everyone and everyone in his place, exactly as it was in every village, town, and city in the world. But that was *their* problem. Hers was acutely painful; for *she'd been snubbed by Galveston's aristocracy.*

"I say, Mrs. Morrison," Ed Ketchum said suddenly at her side. "Do you have any objections to the young people dancing on the carpet in your front parlor? Because they've started it. I'll go stop them for you if you like."

Elizabeth was burning with indignation now that she was aware the aristocrats of Broadway had not turned out for her and Richard's housewarming, and as she turned toward the police chief, she tried to give a lilt to her voice as she replied, "No, Mr. Ketchum, let them dance. From now on when there's a party at the house I'll roll up the carpets. But tonight, let them dance on it. Perhaps it'll bring us good luck."

Mr. Ketchum said, "Going to have lots of parties here, are you?"

She fixed her shining eyes fully upon him and replied, "Oh yes. Yes, indeed. Many parties." Then she asked, "Tell me, who in your opinion gives the most and the best parties in Galveston?"

He looked surprised and rocked back on his heels. "Why, I suppose the uncontested winner of that distinc-

142

tion is Emily Ingram. You know, of Ingram and Sturgeon Shipping Company."

She nodded delightedly, thoughtful. "Ah."

Ketchum laughed and swished the punch around in his glass. "Thinking of getting in with that crowd?"

She only smiled at his perceptive conclusion.

"It shouldn't be hard for you to be introduced to that circle," he said.

"Why?"

"Your husband's brother's in it."

She smiled wistfully. "Damon's no help. He's never home."

"But when he's here it's like—How does the saying go? He makes hay while the sun shines."

Elizabeth smiled again at that, but at the same time felt a stab of jealousy so painful that it made her face flush vividly. She wasn't sure exactly why.

Richard had not intended for the argument to get this heated. It had begun with Jud Mason stating that the cases of dengue fever which his patients had suffered the past summer were unusually severe, and that it was no wonder that if the other doctors in town had treated as many cases of it as he had, that Galveston was considered as having an epidemic of it. That was when Matt Cross spoke up, "I still contend the epidemic was not dengue, but yellow fever."

It was like digging up a spadeful of fat worms, the doctors hopping on the controversy like a flock of hungry sparrows. During the past summer physicians all along the entire coast had diagnosed enough cases of yellow fever to announce there was an epidemic of it, and indeed Galveston had her share of yellow fever cases also. But in the opinion of most of Galveston's doctors, both those on the staff of the medical school and those not, the epidemic here had been dengue, not yellow fever. Except for Matthew Cross, professor of principles and practices of medicine, who had contended from the beginning that it was yellow fever, a similar disease but more severe than dengue. To prove his point, Cross had somehow let the U.S. Public Health Service know about the controversy, and in September they had sent a yellow fever expert to Galveston, who studied some cases and ended up supporting Cross. This made all the other physicians in town look like fools, a predicament which they found somewhat embarrassing. So they all contended that the expert from the Public Health Service was only a damned Spaniard who knew nothing of tropical diseases.

Tonight, the argument had become heated early, with Cross not giving an inch—he had the U.S. Public Health Service behind him—and the others arguing for the sake of their pride. All evening the wave of contention flowed out of the library into the crowd in other parts of the house, and back again. By nine o'clock, Elizabeth had overheard parts of the argument and kept casting Richard questioning looks. He'd shrug just perceptibly enough for her to see; and once, when he came to stand beside her, said, "At least it hasn't come to blows yet."

Small comfort he was.

What was really bothering the doctors was that there was no foolproof way to distinguish dengue from yellow fever, and although the treatments for both diseases were similar, there was an element of danger in not being able to give a specific treatment for a specific disease. Because yellow fever was more severe and it involved the liver. Dengue did not. Rob Tate, as the pathology and bacteriology professor, said they needed to attempt to isolate the bacteria of dengue fever and yellow fever, to distinguish between them. It hadn't been done yet because the study of bacteria was new on the medical scene.

When the grandfather clock in the entry gonged nine o'clock, Richard and five of his colleagues were deep into the conversation of why the systematic study of tropical diseases was critical, with Rob Tate saying that it would take not only Dr. Cross, who was always writing *theoretical* papers for the medical journals, but himself and Richard as well.

Richard said, "Why me?"

Tate replied, "I need better chemical dyes to stain bacteria. The uptake of stain for each strain of bacteria is different. It's your job, Richard, to find the chemical stains that can make the different types of bacteria more visible under the microscope."

"That takes equipment I don't have," Richard said thoughtfully. "And chemistry is my field, not biochemistry."

"Bah," Bert Jackson, who chaired the surgery department, erupted. "It's all the same. Chemistry is chemistry."

"I'm afraid that's as unreasonable a comparison as saying one surgery is the same as another, Bert," Richard countered calmly, though feeling his ears beginning to burn. "And what of chemical surgery, which you teach?

Is that the same old chemistry as the rest?"

Now there were five doctors swelled up, but Elizabeth was suddenly there amongst them. "Talk, talk, talk," she laughed, taking Bert Jackson by the arm. "You doctors have had your mouths open so much this evening you're bound to be dried out. The ladies have just mixed up a new bowl of punch, and since most of the children have gone home to bed, they've added a little vodka this time. And there's some excellent cognac from France which I think Dr. Cross brought, didn't you Matt?"

Dr. Cross's popularity index took a sudden upward swing, for the time being, and Dr. Smart, who'd remained out of the controversy all evening because he chaired the obstetrics and gynecology department at the school and had no real interest in the yellow fever argument, clapped him on the back. "Come on, Matt. To the devil with dengue fever. What's this about cognac from France?"

"Not dengue," Cross chuckled as they turned to leave the library. "Yellow fever, yellow fever."

"Marcie will murder me if I take a drink," Rob Tate said, going through the front parlor with Richard. "We're Baptists and you know how that goes. . . ."

". . . curious as to why your grandfather located a textile mill in the Chicago area, Mrs. Morrison," Dr. Jackson was saying as he escorted Elizabeth—or rather, she escorted him—to the punch bowl.

"It was after they built the Erie Canal, which opened up a waterway to the eastern seaboard, Bert. He was hoping to corner the western market. . . ."

In ten minutes the arguments still existed, but on a lighter note; Bert Jackson's face was no longer red, nor

Richard's ears. Matthew Cross became capable of telling uproarious tales, and Dr. Kelly had cornered Nicholas Clayton, whom Elizabeth saw laugh for the first time all evening at a barrage of Kelly's Irish jokes.

She caught Richard's eye as he stood with a glass of punch in his hand. Her look said, "Don't you *dare* let another argument get started." And his expression replied, "You avoided a very unpleasant situation with a bit of successful strategy, my love." To which she smiled and tilted her head. And that's when he saw the smile freeze on her face.

The chatter of the lively crowd waned for an instant, then picked up again, causing Richard to turn to see what had caused Elizabeth to become suddenly so rigid.

Damon.

It was Damon, exactly as she remembered him, only taller, handsomer, standing just inside the entry handing Shadrack his hat, his eyes moving over the crowd until he saw her. And she was gliding toward him, hands outstretched. Damon, her lips said. He smiled and seized her hands.

"Captain Morrison," she said. "Oh, why didn't you ring us up and tell us you were in town?"

"I just got in this morning. And wanted to surprise you anyway." He released her hands and took his brother's in greeting. "Could it be I've been gone only five months, John Richard? Or is it that you work fast?" He bowed slightly to Elizabeth. "Miss Harbour—or I should say Mrs. Morrison—" He did not finish his sentence but addressed Richard again. "You surprise me, John Richard. I had no idea you were intelligent enough to

147

recognize such a prize as Miss Harbour."

"You're lying, Damon. You were aware of it, you just didn't believe I'd carry it through."

After both brothers had laughed and Richard released Damon's hand, he said, "Come join the festive board, Damon. I'm sure you'll find the punch to your liking.

As they moved among the guests in the front parlor, the captain said to Elizabeth at his side, "I've a wedding gift in the carriage outside, actually two. One for the house, one for John Richard's office." He looked up at the ceiling, at the furnishings, the draperies, and as she placed a glass of punch in his hand, he breathed to his brother at his side, "My Lord, John Richard, you must have increased your office fees considerably."

She had no idea Damon Morrison could still affect her so. *No idea.* She was drunk when she had tasted none of the punch, flushing when she wasn't warm, giddy and absurdly weak in the knees. But she managed to keep up appearances; "Another glass, Mr. Dosier?" "Do try the chocolate cake, Mrs. Frieze." "Have you ever tasted pistachio nuts, Dr. Tate? Try them. They came from California." "Come meet Richard's brother, Dr. Mueller."

"How long will you be in town, Damon?" she said sometime later. "Or do you know?"

He shrugged, smiling. "As long as it takes, Miss Har— Mrs. Morr—Can't I call you Elizabeth?"

"Cap'n Morrison! Cap'n Morrison!" came the shrill cry from the crowd just as she was about to answer. "Cap'n Morrison! Cap'n Morrison!" It was Cully Swift, Melissa's five-year-old, who flung himself into Damon's arms, causing him to spill the punch on the carpet.

Damon thrust the glass into Richard's hand and picked Cully up laughing.

"Put me down. Put me down. I'm not a baby anymore," Cully shrilled, but grinning once he was back on the floor said, "Shake hands instead."

Damon shook Cully's proffered hand. "Building any more ships?"

"I've built an entire fleet of twin engine steamers, Cap'n. And I'm trying 'em out in the street when it rains. See any whales this time out?"

Damon drew a crowd of amused listeners while he described the whales he'd seen. And porpoises too, and dolphins. Somebody said they thought porpoises and dolphins were the same mammal and Damon had to explain that they weren't. "There's a difference," he told Cully as he launched into the discussion.

Cully worships Damon, Richard had said.

Around ten o'clock the crowd began thinning rapidly, which occupied Elizabeth and Richard for a while, saying good evening and thank you and exchanging promises of get-togethers in the future. Damon, meanwhile, stood in the back parlor chatting with the doctors as their wives finished clearing away the punch bowls, crystal, and china from the dining table. Then they too left one-by-one.

After the guests were all gone, Elizabeth dismissed Shadrack and Primrose for the evening, leaving no one in the house now but the three of them; Richard and Damon sitting in the back parlor, Richard in his black horsehair rocker smoking his pipe, Damon in the mauve overstuffed chair smoking a cigar. The house was quiet,

149

but vibrating with an expectancy only Elizabeth felt. The clock in the entryhall struck eleven.

She sat down tiredly and quietly with her needlework in the little windsor rocker which once belonged to her mother, and had now been placed near the fireplace. Shadrack had lit the coal-burning stove, not needed when the guests were in the house, but which now added a cheery warmth to the parlor. This was not a gorgeous room like the front parlor, elegantly furnished in the rococo burgundy horsehair suite and the Louis XV slipper chairs purchased from Mrs. Hennesey. But it was comfortable with its empire sofa, clawfooted chippendale center table, the old organd lamp on top, Richard's rocker, the overstuffed chair—all antiques from Richard and Damon's family.

"The problem is this," Damon was saying, oblivious to her presence, "America is entering a new era as surely as she's entering a new century, with a complete revolution in industry. . . . What the steamship lines need is more efficient ships, faster ships which are more economical to operate. . . ." Once he tapped the ashes of his cigar into an ashtray, not even glancing at Elizabeth. That was the way it was when men talked. If a woman presumed to sit in on their conversations, she was duly ignored. No opinions, observations, or thoughts of hers counted; nothing she could offer could be of any consequence. She found herself pulling the stitches of her needlepoint too tight in her growing anger, causing the canvas to warp. She spread it on her knees and tried to smooth it flat again.

". . . I'm not a shipbuilder, but I have some ideas. I

intend to see that Ingram and Sturgeon builds bigger and better ships, expecially if—'' He glanced then at Elizabeth, hesitating to launch into some mysterious subject in her presence. She suspected that he wished she'd leave the room so that he could discuss it with Richard, but she had no intention of doing so. Primly, she continued stitching.

Richard, puffing contentedly on his pipe said, "I've got only one question. How are the Galveston shipping companies going to compete with Houston once its deep-water channel is finished?"

"That's years away."

Elizabeth looked up from her needlework. "Richard?"

Both men looked over at her as if seeing her for the first time.

"Excuse me for interrupting," she began with an edge to her voice, "but since I've been in Galveston, I keep hearing about Houston's ship channel. How can Houston, which is fifty miles inland, have a ship channel?"

Damon looked over at Richard as if surprised she had spoken, and would therefore let his brother take care of the matter. Richard never batted an eye. "It's just that Houston's located on a bayou as well as on the San Jacinto River. About fifty years ago they started dredging a channel to Galveston Bay. The channel's deep enough now to admit small schooners, but it's still in the process of being dredged deeper and wider for big ocean-going steamers."

"But that's absurd, when Galveston can already receive any kind of shipping," she said.

Damon spoke up, "It's not absurd, Elizabeth, when

you consider that now merchants have no choice but to deal with Galveston shipping companies and Houston sees an opportunity to establish its own seaport and attract the trade."

"But what happens to Galveston when Houston's channel is finished?" she asked.

This time it was Richard looking to Damon to answer. Damon said, "The wharfage company's not concerned, else it would reduce its rates. You see, the channel won't be deep enough to admit deep-draft ships for a couple of decades yet."

"But—But—"

He smiled at her. "Don't worry, Sister-in-law. Somebody'll do something to compete with Houston."

Richard said, "Will they?"

When both Elizabeth and Damon looked at him, he said, "It seems to me this city's bigwigs have all the real estate and money in Galveston tied up and are making a conscientious attempt to keep Galveston from growing. It's as if they want the city to stay like it is."

"That's what it looks like on the surface. But surely not," said Damon.

Elizabeth gave this a thought. "I can see their point. What if Galveston grew like New York or Chicago? What a shame that would be, to turn this beautiful island into a smelly, dirty, busy ol' city."

"You see?" Richard said to Damon as he pointed his pipe at his wife. "That's exactly the attitude I mean."

"I'd hate losing all that trade to Houston," Damon mused.

"Let them have it," she countered. "It's only a ramshackle, rowdy ol' frontier town anyhow, and they need all the help they can get."

Damon's brown eyes hardened a little as he looked at her for a moment. After all, Galveston shipping was the source of his livelihood. "You're an opinionated lady, aren't you?"

"Oh, indeed I am."

"Frankly," Richard said, taking his pipe out of his mouth, "*I* don't care one way or another, just as long as the Board of Regents at the university keeps the medical school here."

"I care, because it's my bread and butter, and hope later it'll be my beefsteak and wine. And for that to happen, Ingram and Sturgeon has to grow. I seem to be the only one in the company with any vision, which is odd. Both Eric Ingram and Max Sturgeon live in Galveston, whereas most of the other owners of the shipping companies live elsewhere. It seems to me Eric and Max would be in a better position to see what's happening concerning the Houston channel than the others."

"The Ingrams and the Sturgeons are among the several families here who like Galveston the way it is," Richard said.

"Well, I have ideas that will change that, I think."

Now Elizabeth plunged in. "Like what, Damon? What ideas?"

He glanced at Richard hesitating to answer.

"Oh don't be silly, Damon," she said. "I won't go around telling your secrets, no more than I discuss what few medical cases or school problems Richard confides to me. I can be trusted."

He studied her face a moment as if gauging whether he could trust her or not. Apparently he couldn't decide, because he leaned back in the chair, tapping the arm with his fingers, seemed to sidestep the primary issue he was on the verge of discussing, and launched into another instead. "I have an idea that concerns a cargo which presently is considered minor, but which *I* consider major, a cargo I believe will grow and grow and which will eventually take bigger, faster, more elaborate ocean-going ships. And any steamship company with vision enough to capture that trade will not only succeed, but will flourish."

Richard studied his pipe, then leaned forward and knocked out the ashes in the ashtray while Damon continued.

"The cargo, John Richard, is passengers," Damon said. *"People.* The Industrial Revolution has produced a society of rich people, the nouveu riche. With money so readily available I believe more and more people will be traveling, not just on riverboats or short-haul steamers up and down the coasts, but transoceanic—" He broke off and looked at Elizabeth, who was listening with fascination, her needle poised in midair above her needlework. "I'm sorry, Elizabeth. This must be boring you."

Amazed, she shook her head. "Not at all. In fact, when we were taking the riverboat from St. Louis—"

"Excuse me, but I expect you to keep this discussion in strictest confidence."

Her face flushed with anger. "I assure you, Damon, that I can keep *any* secret," she said tightly. "To eternity

154

if necessary."

Their eyes met, in a confusion of meanings which neither of them grasped. She put her needlework aside and stood up. "Now. If you'll excuse me, I'll be going up to bed, which is what you both would like me to do anyway, I'm sure," she said, smiling sweetly.

They shook their heads, surprised, denying her accusation; but their eyes told the truth. Yes, they'd appreciate it if she would leave them alone, two brothers with a lot of man-talk to do—and probably hoping to sip a drink or two also while they were at it, she suspected.

They rose and stood like gentlemen until she had left the room. And on the stairs she paused, hearing Damon say, "You realize you captured a prize in Elizabeth, John Richard? I didn't know you had it in you."

"She brings out the best in me, Damon."

"And all these years I thought it was *I* who was the romantic."

Smiling in spite of herself, she went up to the bathroom, then into their bedroom, finding both rooms a little littered with the evidence of ladies who'd come up to powder their noses and smooth their hair—and see the rest of the Morrison's house. Someone had sat on her precious feather mattress, leaving it lumpy and the counterpane rumpled. But after changing from her clothes into her nightgown and crawling between the cool, crisp sheets, she found the mattress soft as a cloud. Drowsily, she could hear rain on the roof and a shutter rattling loose on the house somewhere. Must remember to have Shad fix it in the morning. Though she could still hear the men talking downstairs, jovially now and a little loudly too, she soon drifted off to sleep.

But sometime in the night, groggy and befuddled heavily with sleep, she thought she heard them singing softly and laughing. And later when Richard came to bed, thought she heard a man singing outside in the rain, as a horse's hooves splashed away in the street below.

Nine

Chemistry lectures were the most boring that the medical students had to endure. Richard didn't blame them for dozing in his class. Still, a physician had to give and recommend hundreds of medicines, and had to have a basic understanding of the chemical compounds that made up the medicines, as well as their effects on the human mind and body. The freshmen needed to learn how to analyze milk and urine, and test for proteins, fats, carbohydrates, and common poisons; also acidemetry and alkalimetry. The sophomores needed to understand qualitative analysis and a bit of organic chemistry.

But today even the lecturer's mind was elsewhere. Ever since the housewarming in November, when the subject was brought up about what his role should be in helping to isolate the bacteria of tropical diseases, he'd been obtaining the necessary solutions it would take to experiment with certain strains. The trouble was, he didn't have the time to spare for it. He had to give an hour lecture a day in chemistry to the medical students, conduct lab twice a week, lecture to the nurses two hours a week, and conduct two one-hour lectures a week at the new school of pharmacy. Besides that he had to maintain his private practice and perform x-ray services besides.

He had finally told Elizabeth about having an x-ray machine, the only one in town. He had hesitated mentioning it at first, thinking she would probably be like her father, suspicious of any apparatus out of the ordinary that had to do with medical science. Because almost no one had heard of x-ray, it was difficult to explain to people about a machine, invented only three years ago, with light rays so powerful they could penetrate tissue and actually photograph the skeletal structures of the body.

When he had first heard about the invention of x-ray, he had learned the particulars, secured a Crooke's tube, and one night had demonstrated the thing to several of his medical school colleagues in a lab he'd set up in a room next to his office, by taking a picture with his monstrous machine of the bones of his own hand. The doctors were very impressed, and soon he, the first and only roentologist in town, was doing a considerable business, every physician in town sending all their fractures to his office for x-rays. The referrals of such patients to him for x-ray benefitted everyone; it not only benefitted the patients by confirming the diagnoses of the extent of the fractures—and consequently how the fractures should be set—but it showed the patients how very up-to-date their own physicians were. And the frequent arrival at Richard's office of patients by ambulance gave the impression to passersby that he was doing a considerable amount of accident practice. It was excellent advertising for his practice, which was one reason he offered the service free to his colleagues in spite of the expense to himself. Now that he was married, though, the x-ray practice had become a pain in the neck, because it required several hours to develop the plates. He had to mix his solutions, cool them with ice from the ice box in his office, then develop, fix, and wash each plate and set it up to dry. It took about three hours, sometimes more. But he supposed the time would come someday when that amount of time would be cut down to perhaps one hour. He could use the new improved tubes but couldn't spare the money for it. He had come to hope and pray each day that none of the other doctors in town would have patients with fractures, or suspected fractures, so that he could go home at five o'clock like his colleagues and every other businessman in town. And besides all that, he had the usual number of house calls. Even when he was home he had to seclude himself in the library and prepare the lectures for the next day.

Elizabeth could occupy herself during the day, but it was the evenings that were bad for her. Their nights weren't always free so that they could go calling, or to the concerts at the opera house or any other—

"Dr. Morrison, sir?"

Richard, startled from his musing, turned from the blackboard to face his class. Marvin Haversham on the second row was holding up his hand tentatively.

"Yes, Mr. Haversham?"

"Doctor, you're erasing the equation with your left

hand almost as fast as you're writing it with your other."

Richard glanced at the blackboard and saw that the student was right. He'd caught himself doing that before and had decided it was because he felt pressed for time. He noted that a student near the back of the class was dozing, and that another was woolgathering in spite of the incredible noise the switch engines were making in railyards below near the bay. "I beg your pardon, Mr. Haversham," he said. "Perhaps you should learn to write faster, sir."

Haversham glanced abashedly at his colleagues, who laughed uproariously, glad for any break in the monotony of Old Beaker's qualitative analytic monologue. Richard knew how they felt. Chemistry was a bore, but to impress on the students the importance of chemistry and toxicology to their profession, he feigned an indifference to their boredom, allowed no monkey business in class, no dozing or woolgathering either. Miss one equation in class and they'd be behind for the rest of the year.

Yet, the students knew, by some divination that only students were capable of, that his cold indifference was a facade. They knew they could go to him with a problem in chemistry and he'd sit with them, explaining and making them work the problem until they understood it, sometimes letting his patients wait in his private office for thirty minutes or more. Some of the students had even gone to his house with their problems, and some of the problems had been of a personal nature. At Ol As-a-matter-of-fact's house, they had discovered that his wife was an extraordinarily lovely lady not much older than themselves, who was very friendly and served them tea and cake and caused them to stumble into a misery of hopeless infatuation with her. And Richard was perceptive enough to suspect that a certain amount of the wool-gathering, by those particular students in his class, was actually fantasizing about his own wife.

Now he tossed the chalk onto the chalk rail and dusted off his hands, took out his pocket watch and noted the time . . . half past two. Too early to dismiss class, yet too late to begin a new equation. Stuffing the watch back into his pocket, he said, "Gentlemen, be sure you have memorized the basic equation by Monday's lab. And now if one of you can resurrect Mr. Jannock back there, and if Mr. Vance has managed to come back down out of the clouds to join the rest of us, you might be relieved to know that class is now dismissed."

Richard got his notes together as the students vacated the classroom. Provided there was no x-raying to do, he could go home about five, and he had half a mind to put a sign on the office door—CLOSED SATURDAY—so that he could spend the entire weekend at home. And unless a new case came up he was unaware of, he'd have no office calls to make for a change. He could take Elizabeth to the west end of town, not very pretty out there but different, and to Lafitte's grove where there was a little history to relate to her. And then there was Sunday Church and he believed it was their turn to have the Swifts and Damon over for Sunday dinner.

He hurried out of the classroom and down the wide stairs to the first floor, where Will Kelly was just coming out of the elevator with his sketchpad in his hand. Noting that Richard was frowning at his sketch of an enlarged uterus, trying to make sense out of it, Kelly said, "Richard. Out early? So am I." And falling into step beside him, he explained, "Today we studied the gravid uterus. Monday we'll dissect our first female cadaver which I suspect is pregnant. I hope so. Ah, how I love Fridays, and the weather's fair and Isaac Cline says there's no rain in the offing. I've a good mind to put a sign on my door that says CLOSED SATURDAY and take Flossy and the girls on a picnic."

"That's strange," Richard said as they were going out the big double doors into the bright sunlight. "I was just thinking the same thing, because I've been feeling guilty about not spending more time with Elizabeth."

"Were you now!" Will said as they hurried down the long steps. "Ah, but Richard, feelin' guilty, I've discovered, is a natural part of being married. Get used to it, because now you're like the rest of us here at the school, drinking of the same bitter-sweet waters of marital bliss."

"You're not very encouraging, Will."

"Well, I'll tell ye, Richard. I'm less encouraging than you think. Want to know why I let lecture out early?"

They'd reached the bottom of the steps by then and Richard looked up at the sky—blue and fair—the air was brisk but not cold for January, almost balmy, as a matter of fact. Excellent weather for a drive. "Why?" he said.

"I just got word that a patient of mine fell off a house, fractured his femur in several places and maybe his clavicle too. I don't know yet what all. Sorry to impose on you, Richard my friend, but he's going to need a heap of x-rays."

*　　　*　　　*

"Ain't never heard of light bread with corned beef and turnip greens," Primrose said for the third time that afternoon. She took one of the two irons off the top of the stove, dampened her finger with her tongue, tapped the flat side of the iron with it, and when it hissed, knew it was hot enough to finish Richard's shirt.

Elizabeth was testing too. Having taken the tin lid off the bread bowl on the countertop near the stove, she pushed two fingers into the yeast-fragrant mound of dough to see if the dents remained. They did, which meant the dough was ready to punch down. She took the bowl over to the round oak kitchen table where she would have more room to work, and pushed her fist into the center of the dough while Prim watched.

"Don't scorch the doctor's shirt, Prim, that's one of his best ones," she reminded the maid.

To Elizabeth there was a way to iron things well and a way to iron them better, and when it came to Richard's linen shirts with the attached collars and cuffs, the ones he wore daily, she expected the ironing to be perfect. She'd taught Prim how to starch collars and cuffs stiff, to iron them with a linen towel over them to prevent scorching, and to fold the shirts neatly, all buttons buttoned, sleeves folded so that they did not wrinkle. Prim at first had sulked about the extra trouble, not that she minded extra work if it was necessary; but she couldn't see how any of it was necessary if the doctor was only going to cover up the whole shirt with a coat. But one compliment from Richard proved to her that Miz Lizbeth was right. And now no gentleman's shirt in town looked neater than Richard's.

Elizabeth pulled the edges of the dough up and turned the ball of dough over, replaced the lid and put the bowl back near the warm stove so that it could have its second rising, aware all the while of Prim's sulking.

"If folks fix beef brisket with turnip greens, an' has corn bread as is proper, it don't take no risin', punchin', and waitin' all day," Prim said, still ironing.

Elizabeth knew what was bothering the maid. She was set in her ways. As far as she was concerned, light bread was for Sundays only. And just as important, the only acceptable entrees for Sunday dinners were roast beef or fried chicken. No other meat was proper. Any new Yankee dish Elizabeth showed her how to fix was looked on with grave suspicion until it proved itself. The way it proved itself was to receive compliments from the "gentamen." Shadrack did not count as a gentleman "'cause he can eat a dried up ol' corncob and think it's delicious," Prim had said.

The screen door on the porch slammed and Shadrack came in, hat in hand, just as Elizabeth was poking the beef brisket with a fork to check its tenderness. "Afternoon, Miss Lizbeth. Don't look like rain today, please ma'am."

"That's good. There's no place on earth gloomier than Galveston when it rains," she said sliding the brisket back into the oven. And shutting the oven door, she straightened and put her hands on her hips, smiling. "But when the sun shines, there's no place on earth brighter or prettier."

"Oh, yes ma'am."

Prim said, "You state your business, black man, and get out. 'Cause there's two of us in the kitchen with work to do, and three makes a crowd."

"I jus' wanted permission to shine the carriage if, please Miss Lizbeth, you ain't plannin' on takin' it out this afternoon," Shad said.

Elizabeth took three cups down from the cupboard. "No, I'll be staying home. Do as you like with the carriage."

"Dr. Richard says keep it shiny, for if the salt spray stays on it long, it rust quick, and he got it dirty goin' on the house call yesterday." Shad shook his head, smiling. "He's sure mighty proud o' that new buggy, Miss Lizbeth."

Elizabeth was pouring three cups of tea. At first Prim and Shad had been very uncomfortable drinking tea with Elizabeth in the kitchen on days when they had kitchen work to do, but it didn't take them long to get comfortable with the idea. "Dr. Richard never had a carriage before," she said. "Can you imagine anyone as fond of carriages as he never having had one of his own before? Sit down, Shad and have a cup of tea. Prim, are you ready to stop a while?"

"No, I got two more garments fore I'm through, Miss Lizbeth. So I'll jus' keep ironin' till I am."

Shadrack waited till Elizabeth sat down at the table, then he sat down slowly. "To tell the truth," he said, "Dr. Richard ain't never had no place to keep a buggy before. Only needed one when he went courtin'."

Elizabeth's cup paused halfway to her lips. "Oh? Did he tell you that?"

If a black man could blush, Shad did. He giggled, "Yes ma'am. But said he never in any way courted a lady the likes o' you, please Miss Lizbeth."

Amused, Elizabeth sipped her tea, her favorite; mint with just a touch of lemon. Contentedly she looked around her. Oh, it was such a fine, quiet day. Nobody had come calling today for once, and it was such a lovely day outside, and her kitchen so warm and bright with the fragrance of clean clothes, warm starch, roasting beef, and yeast-rising dough, mingling even yet with the faint smell of new wood and wallpaper and new paint.

A familiar rap sounded on the back screen door, and Primrose left her ironing to answer it while Shad and Elizabeth smiled at each other expectantly, listening for the familiar banter they knew would come from the porch. Elizabeth had broken Shad of casting his eyes down when he talked to her. She had noticed when she first arrived in Galveston that Negro men did that, cast their eyes down when they spoke to a white woman or stood in her presence. She'd said to him, "Don't ever cast your eyes down, Shad. If you're uncomfortable meeting someone's gaze, cast your eyes to the side, never down, because that's a left-over mannerism from the slave days. And you aren't a slave to *anyone*."

"Well you is, Cully Swift," came Prim's voice from the porch. "Now you go back home, cause Miss Lizbeth is busy and Shadrack's about to be."

Elizabeth called, "Let him come on in, Prim."

There was a slam of the screen door. Cully came marching to the table, and had pulled out a chair and sat down before the expected vociferation began outside. It began low like a moan and rose in crescendo up the scale. "Arrrroooo-oo-oo-oo . . ." Then came Prim's expected harangue from the back porch.

"Now, you git, you old mop dog! Go on! Git!"

Cully had folded both small hands on the tabletop and was watching Elizabeth solemnly. "Flop's feet are clean because we've been playing on the grass all afternoon," he said. "He won't get mud on your floor, Miss Lizbeth, if you decide to let him in."

Smiling, Elizabeth called, "Do let Flop in, Prim," aware that Prim did not approve of dogs in the house, but also knowing that as long as Cully was in the house, Flop would serenade them until he came out again. It was all routine, as familiar now as bacon and eggs for breakfast, or tea in the afternoon.

The screen door slammed again and the dog padded into the room and sat down beside Cully's chair panting happily, a pink tongue protruding from an invisible face.

Elizabeth smiled at Cully, the little boy whom Richard had said was like a wise old man, which was true only part of the time. At other times he was only a five-year-old boy bubbling over with innocent questions and childhood trivia. He was a befuddling combination; a bewildered child beset with unanswerable enigmas, and a sage charged with complicated solutions too numerous and weighty to endure.

"What can we do for you today, Cully?" Elizabeth asked, instinctively knowing that today Cully was perplexed with a problem, the solving of which required carefully executed strategy. He sat with his small brow knit with worry, though a lock of straight, dark hair had fallen exactly over his deepest frown line. *Melissa, Melissa, how lucky you are,* Elizabeth thought in that instant.

"Been engaging in a hit fight with Jason Crabtree again?" Shad asked smiling hugely. Cully was always an immense source of hilarity to Shad and never failed to elicit his best humor.

"No," Cully said.

Shad giggled. "Yo gal found another boy friend?"

Cully sighed. "No."

"What then, Mister Cully?"

Cully glanced at Elizabeth and sighed again. "I could think better," he said, "with a jelly bread."

"Come in here trackin' mud on my clean floor," muttered Primrose, already in the process of slicing a piece of bread off a fresh loaf. "Just mopped this mornin'. Have a good mind to dip that ol' dog in the bucket and mop with *him.*" She cast Flop a dour glance and said, "Looks more like the mop than the mop does."

After Prim handed him the jelly bread, Elizabeth said softly, "Can you think about your problem now, Cully?"

Cully paused. "The problem's big," he warned.

"That's just fine. We'll try to work it out anyway," she said.

Cully said to Elizabeth, "You know I collected all that leftover lumber when they built this house, Miss Lizabeth, and how I went around and picked up all the nails they left on the ground?"

She nodded.

"And you know I'm building one of the best ships I ever built? Well, I drawed it all out and sawed all the pieces and now it's time to nail the pieces together. And guess what?"

"What?"

"I can't find a hammer."

She said, "Cully, I'm sure your father has hammers somewhere."

"He does, but they're all locked up in the shed and he's got the key and he rang up my mother and said he'd be coming home late tonight because he's working late. So I won't get to build on my ship until tomorrow and you know what that means."

"What does it mean?"

"It means one more day is wasted. I don't have very many more days before I start to school."

Shad giggled and Elizabeth said, "But you don't have to go to school until next September, Cully."

"I know. But I figure it'll take that long to build the ship. I've got lots of carving on it to do."

"Well, I agree with you then. You do have a problem."

"You don't s'pose Dr. Richard would let be borry a hammer do you?"

She smiled. "I don't think Dr. Richard *has* a hammer."

"He does," said Shad grinning, "but I am the keeper o' that hammer, and I don't 'low nobody to borry it; but I 'lows them to rent it. Cost you a nickel a week, provided you return the hammer at the end o' each day."

"You have a deal," said the small boy, the new light in his eyes betraying his delight. "But I'll have to run home and shake it out of my bank."

"I recommend you keep the rent till you're through with the hammer. Then we'll figure what you owe. Come on then, Master Cully, an le's go fetch that hammer."

Elizabeth put her hand gently on Cully's arm to detain him. "Is Captain Morrison working late too? With your father?"

Cully nodded.

"Wonder what they're working on."

Cully shrugged. "I don't know for sure, but I think I got an idea. It's a secret though, and I don't tell secrets."

"Oh."

"Thanks for the jelly bread, Primrose," Cully said and he and Flop followed the giggling Shad to the porch and out the back door.

While Prim was taking the turnip greens out of the ice box a familiar voice at the back door called, "Knock, knock."

Brightening, Elizabeth called, "Come in, Mel."

Melissa came hurrying into the kitchen holding out two red somethings in her hands saying, "Beth, look. Just like I promised. There were four of them ripe today. That vine only rested two months and now it's producing again. *Tomatoes*."

Primrose, coming back into the kitchen, threw up her hands crying, "Oh Lord, Miss Lissa!"

Melissa put the tomatoes on the counter top. "Truly, Prim, they aren't poisonous, I promise. Ask Dr. Richard. He knows."

"That vine has produced cause it's the devil's fruit, Miss Lissa. *He* don't rest just cause it's winter."

"The vine is on the south side of the house, Prim, that's why it hasn't died, and it thinks it's spring." Melissa sat down at the table and sighed looking around her. "My there's some delicious smells in here."

Elizabeth told Prim to pour Mel a cup of tea, and thanked Mel for the tomatoes. Prim obeyed but not without grumbling, "T'weren't no apple the serpent tempted Eve with. No ma'am. 'Twas a tomato. 'Twas why God put a curse on it makin' it poison." She filled Elizabeth's cup again and continued to mutter to herself as the two friends took their tea and went through the dining room to the back parlor as they always did.

When they had sat down, Melissa said, "Are you feeling alright, Beth? You're awfully quiet today."

"I'm alright. It's just that I'm disappointed. Aunt Martha came to visit this morning."

"Oh, that's too bad. And you had hoped you were in the family way."

"I wonder if something is wrong with me. We've been married over four months and . . . nothing."

"Don't get discouraged. At least you have prospects of it. After Cully was born, Dr. Smart said I couldn't have any more children. Look, Beth, you're a healthy woman. It'll happen in God's own time."

Elizabeth nodded and they sipped their tea silently a moment before Elizabeth said, "Have you any idea what Joe Bob and Damon are working on? I'm so curious it's painful."

"Only a notion." Melissa shifted her weight in her chair. "You know Joe Bob subscribes to an English magazine called the *London Monthly?*"

"I think I've heard him mention it."

"Well, most of the time he doesn't have time to read it. But last night, he was reading the latest issue and

171

suddenly erupted with an oath loud enough to get my attention and Cully's too. Later, I heard him tell Damon into the telephone that the story about Parsons was in the *London Monthly*. Well, I thought he was talking about a preacher, so after he had gone to bed and I was through with my work, I looked through the magazine and the only Parsons I saw was an Englishman named Parsons who had experimented with a new kind of steam engine which he tried to sell to the British Navy, but which the Navy rejected. I think it was called a—a *turbine* engine. Yes, it was called a turbine engine because the ship which he actually demonstrated it with was called the *Turbina*."

"Aha!" Elizabeth said.

"Beth, you've got the look of the devil in your eye."

"May I borrow the magazine and any other copies of the *London Monthly* that you have, Mel?"

"Yes, Joe Bob saves them all. Keeps them in the basement. Terrible fire hazard. I can bring you over the last twelve months' issues if you want them."

"I'll send Shad over for them today."

"Well, I've been curious about what Joe Bob and Damon were up to myself. I think maybe they're trying to build one of those engines, or experiment with one or something. Now I know you can keep secrets, so don't tell them I mentioned it to you. And don't breathe a word of this to anybody else. Promise?"

"Word of honor."

"It's only a deduction I made and an assumption at the most. But I was so curious I just had to know." Melissa smiled. "I was hoping it wasn't another woman, you see."

They laughed then just as the doorbell jingled and Mildred Crabtree's parrot voice called through the front screen, "Yoo hoo. Anybody home?"

"Uh-oh. Present discussion terminated," Melissa said.

"Time to progress to the front parlor," Elizabeth said rising. "If I can help it, I try to keep her out of this room because she'll find ashes on the carpet or something. Come on, Mel. Bring your cup."

Mildred Crabtree, the Morrison's neighbor from across the street, was short, dumpy and endlessly bustling. In her younger days her fabricated bustle was extraordinarily emphatic because of the prominence of the natural one, giving her an unfair advantage over her contemporaries where that bit of fashion was concerned. She bustled into the entry saying, "Amy Halstead has out her wash. I say if you want to know what the weather's going to do, watch Amy's clothesline. She's Portugese, you know, and she knows when foul weather's—Oh, hello, Melissa—coming. I can only stay a second, but I wanted to—My, I'm out of breath from climbing all those veranda steps of yours, Elizabeth. That architect, Clay Nichols, is certainly an imaginative fellow isn't he? I'm still marveling at why he built this house so high. It isn't consistent with the rest of the neighborhood. It's like you're on a hill. And didn't Abigail Hennesey's furnishings go well in here? She goes to our church, you know. I see you're having tea."

Elizabeth tugged on the bell pull saying, "Have a seat, Mildred. How has your day been?"

"Very good," Mildred returned as she sat on one of the slipper chairs. "Brother Bill came calling, wants me to be

173

in charge of communion for the upcoming year. I considered sending him over to see you, Melissa. Have you and Joe Bob gone to church lately?"

Melissa, whose back had become rigid, said, "Not for several weeks. Cully was sick the last two Sundays."

"You'll get out of the habit if you don't watch out. That's what the devil wants us to do. Brother Bill says getting out of the habit is the devil's favorite way of keeping people out of church, even worse than illnesses. I've always been *afraid* to use Jason as an excuse not to go to church. And you know Cully needs to be in Sunday School."

"Yes. You're right," Melissa said.

"I've been meaning to speak to you about Cully. I'll tell you now because I'm sure Elizabeth won't mind."

Prim came into the parlor just then carrying the silver tea service, a fresh pot of tea, and a clean china cup and saucer, having heard Mildred's yoohoo and knowing why Elizabeth had signaled her with the bell.

After Elizabeth had poured them each a cup of tea and handed Mildred's to her, Melissa said, "What were you going to tell me about Cully?"

Mildred sipped her tea. "I was taking a walk Wednesday evening when I passed your house and caught sight of Cully—ah—with his privates out, watering your trumpet vine, Melissa. You know, the one that grows on your back trellis?"

Melissa stared a moment, then burst out laughing. "Is that all?"

"Well, it's enough. Suppose I had been a little girl."

Laughing, Melissa said, "I'm sure that if you'd been a

little girl, Mildred, you couldn't have been more shocked than you were as a grown woman."

"Another cup, Mildred?" Elizabeth piped up smiling brightly.

"No, thank you," she replied. Then to Melissa, "I wish Jason and Cully wouldn't fight. They should be friends. Cully could learn . . . what I mean is, they could have so much good, clean fun together. The only other child on the block is Julie Wineburger and I won't let Jason play with her. Those German girls are just-a-lit-tle-bit-too-*wise* in my opinion. Anyway, Cully should be in Sunday School. Even though you and Mr. Swift aren't Methodists, at least he'll be in Sunday School and any's better than none."

Melissa was an optimistic, naturally cheerful individual, and even Mildred Crabtree could not dampen her excellent spirits. While Elizabeth sought for a way to change the subject, Melissa replied calmly, "I should hope so; for I would hate to think Cully was wasting his time attending a *Presbyterian* Sunday School. However, I've noticed Cully carries the same Bible on Sunday morning that Jason does."

Mildred blanched and set her cup into her saucer with a clink. "Oh dear, Melissa, I didn't mean . . . well, now that I've put my foot in my mouth again, I must be going, for I need to start dinner. As I said, I only meant to stay a moment, and I'm so glad you girls are so understanding about things. I just feel that if I had any problems I could always confide in you both."

She rose and Elizabeth followed her to the door where she shooed flies as Mildred opened the scr_en door saying, "Well, ta ta you two. Thanks for the tea, Elizabeth. Be good now."

"Goodbye, Mildred. We'll try."

Elizabeth eased the screen door shut and went back into the parlor. She and Melissa stared at each other, then burst out laughing.

Melissa, rising from her place on the sofa, said, "Poor Mildred. I think she means well. And now I have to go too and hope Joe Bob doesn't stay too awfully late tonight."

"Well, good luck," Elizabeth said, going to the center table where she began to stack the cups and saucers onto the tray. Straightening, she gazed out the parlor window through the lace curtains, watching Mildred Crabtree bustle across the street. "I'm so glad this is Friday," she mused aloud. "Because Richard, thank goodness, will probably be home early."

But he called at four to say he'd be late. Again.

Ten

"Religion seems to be a purgative to Mildred Crabtree," Richard told Elizabeth in the buggy on their way to
church. "She's warned the Swifts more than once that if
they don't attend church more often they'll get out of the
habit."

Elizabeth smiled, holding onto her hat because there
was a stiffer breeze off the Gulf than usual. It was a lovely
day, though not as lovely as yesterday when they had
taken the buggy to Lafitte's grove and picnicked on the
sand, and where Richard had come very close to making
love to her right on the tablecloth until she made him
stop.

Then during the night, a shower had come up from the
south, leaving the island palms and oaks dripping and the
streets rutted and muddy. For the first time since she'd
come to Galveston, she could see what Richard meant
about "stagnant pools of water here and yon which
breeds every specie of mosquito." Such wasn't a danger

177

in January, but in summer there could certainly be a problem.

She was looking forward to early spring when she could plant her shrubs and trees and start her yard and garden. Melissa had said one could plant shrubs and trees any time during the winter in Galveston; but alas, funds in the Morrison household would be low until the first of March. Thinking of gardens and money reminded her of how delighted she was with the church she and Richard had chosen. Being an Episcopalian happened to have the potential for being a valuable social asset, because—

"Look, Beth. Max Sturgeon's new cabriolet. Look at that upholstery on the dashboard!" Richard exclaimed as he drew the reins and pulled their own buggy to a halt next to a shiny black rig, a large two-seater, very fancy indeed. Blitz, their own handsome sorrel, snorted at the Sturgeon's white mare, who regarded him with mild, aristocratic disdain, tossed her beautiful head and flowing mane, and cast her equine attention elsewhere.

Richard absentmindedly helped Elizabeth from the buggy, and she had to pull him away from the Sturgeon carriage, for they were almost late for the services already.

Trinity Episcopal was an ivy-covered, pinkish-brown brick structure with no particular distinction of design, in Elizabeth's opinion. Its uniqueness rested in the fact that its first rector had fallen dead while discharging his holy office at the altar and was now buried beneath the sanctuary near the altar. Nicholas Clayton had designed the chapel adjacent to it, a structure which Elizabeth thought was much more beautiful than the one which they were now entering.

With Elizabeth's gloved hand in the crook of Richard's elbow, they passed down the aisle to their designated pew halfway toward the front of the sanctuary. Heads turned to stare at Elizabeth in an elegant blue wool frock trimmed with satin, the latest dress-shaped velvetta hat adorned with feathers and ribbon to match the frock, her gloves snowy, her mother's cameo brooch at her throat, and at Richard in striped navy trousers and frock coat, carrying a new square crowned hat. They stepped into their pew and took up a hymnal to join the singing.

It was no accident that she had chosen Trinity Episcopal in which to place their membership. She'd had a set-to with her aspirations just before Christmas and had decided to go about this business of establishing herself and Richard socially, in a scientific manner, her first step being to decide where she could meet Galveston's elite on common ground. At city picnics in the park in the summer? Too long to wait. At the Christmas charity dance sponsored by the merchants in the ballroom of the beach hotel? They attended, but none of the *elite* were there. The opera house? Good to be seen there, but nothing of consequence was on the program there for another month or two. Church, where people were obliged to be friendly whether they liked it or not? Yes. Perfect. Mildred Crabtree had been right after all. She *did* need church. Especially Trinity Episcopal, where she had heard the Ingrams and the Sturgeons and several of the other important families were members.

Now standing beside her handsomely dressed husband, sharing a hymn book, she glanced to the side—

across the aisle Myrna and Abel Coffman. And near the front, Emily and Eric Ingram, Matilda and Max Sturgeon, and others, yes, several others she could not identify but whose importance was impressively obvious.

Suddenly someone moved into the pew beside her, and knowing it could be only one person who would presume to share their pew uninvited, she did not have to look. Damon. Nor did he look at her or Richard, just took up a hymn book, bellowing the hymn by memory, perfectly articulated, though the melody was imperfectly rendered. She had to smile and lost her place in the hymn book.

He bent down to her. "I told you I'd come," he whispered much too loudly. "But how did you ever get my brother here?"

She whispered, "It wasn't easy." And thought the hardest part had not been convincing Damon to attend church, because he often did when in town, but in convincing Richard that they should join the Episcopalians and not the Presbyterians, which was the church his family had attended for decades.

After four stanzas, the hymn was done and the congregation sat down. The rector rose in all his vestments, took his place at the chancel near which every member was conscious the former rector lay buried, adjusted the small, wire-framed spectacles on his nose, and began an intonation that at first flowed pleasantly into one of Elizabeth's delicate white ears and out the other. It wasn't that she was irreligious or irreverent, for she had always attended church regularly, but the presence of Damon so close to her side had upon her a disagreeably pleasant and disturbing effect, and she slipped her gloved

180

hand slowly into the crook of Richard's arm and left it there.

Then she became aware that the rector was reading out of the Bible.

". . . And God saw that the wickedness of man was great in the earth, and that every imagination of the thoughts of his heart was only evil continually. And it repented the Lord that he had made man on earth, and it grieved him at his heart. And the Lord said, I will destroy man whom I have created from the face of the earth; both man and beast, and the creeping thing, and the fowls of the air; for it repenteth me that I have made them. . . . And God said unto Noah, The end of all flesh is come before me; for the earth is filled with violence through them and, behold, I will destroy them with the earth. . . . And, behold, I, even I, do bring a flood of waters upon the earth, to destroy all flesh, wherein is the breath of life, from under heaven; and every thing that is in the earth shall die." The rector raised his eyes from the good book and looked out over his prosperous flock, dressed in their Sunday best and said, "In God we trust. That is our motto. America, founded upon Christian principles. Galveston, 1898. Our streets are lined with taverns and saloons. And brothels thrive within our confines. Gambling and drunkenness and debauchery defile the beauty of our isle, and city fathers serve the god of mammon instead of the God of Isaac and Jacob and Abraham, and of our Lord and Savior Jesus Christ. Galveston, the fourth largest city of our state, the fifth largest seaport in our nation, importing rum and tobacco. . . ."

Damon took a deep breath and let it out slowly. Richard's fingers, which were resting on his left knee, began a quiet tapping rhythm.

"God never destroys a city or a nation without ample warning. The people of the earth during Noah's time had probably one hundred twenty years to repent after God's warning of the flood, with Noah reminding them all along there would be a flood upon the earth. . . ."

Eric Ingram coughed into his glove once.

". . . Sodom and Gomorrah, he sent two angels. But did the citizens of those evil cities heed their warning? No, for they were too busy with thoughts of debauchery and perversions, and were only interested in getting to 'know' the men who came to warn them."

A gentleman near the front of the sanctuary honked into his handkerchief while his wife nudged him. Matilda Sturgeon sneezed an anemic, "Tssst. Tssst," into her fist.

The rector had stiffened his stance. "How many times has Galveston been warned, dear parishioners? The hurricane of 1842, the great fire of 1885. God warns. Will we take heed? We *cannot* but take heed lest we be destroyed by fire or flood or. . . ."

And Elizabeth was thinking, Not Galveston. This city isn't any more wicked than any other city. And does God condemn the wealthy only because of their prosperity? Aren't the city fathers here also liberal in giving their money to the building and betterment of the churches and city? The wealthy families in this very sanctuary at this very moment had funded entire hospitals, orphanages, built churches and parks and homes for the aged.

182

Besides, Galveston is beautiful, and Sodom and Gomorrah weren't. . . .

Damon was thinking, Galveston is more likely to be destroyed *financially* by exacting such exorbitant wharfage rates while Houston quietly absorbs all her commerce and trade. . . .

Richard thought, More like a plague or two, or a big typhoid epidemic. . . .

The entire sermon was morose, and left the rector more depressed than his congregation. Elizabeth was glad when it was done.

The organ thundered the postlude as the congregation filed out of their pews and into the crowded aisles, greeting each other and talking among themselves. The Morrisons, however, held back; for Elizabeth dropped a glove which had to be retrieved, then paused to speak to a couple in the pew behind them, and otherwise found reason to dally.

Emily and Eric Ingram, whom Elizabeth knew on sight but had never met, saw Damon just as they came, at last, even with the Morrison pew. "Damon," Emily said, "good to see you. Where have you been keeping yourself since the *Arundel* put into port?" Then her eyes fell, for the first time, upon Elizabeth.

Knowing well that Elizabeth desired to meet Emily, and suspecting that was why she had insisted he attend church while he was in town, Damon introduced Elizabeth to her as "Elizabeth Morrison, my new sister-in-law from Chicago," and to Eric Ingram as "Richard's wife whose father is Randal Harbour of Harbour Mills in Chicago."

"Enchanted, my dear," Ingram said interrupting his wife's mild how-do-you-do. "I'm afraid we lost Mr. Harbour's very valuable business. Yes, yes. He's indeed a fine gentleman and an astute businessman, Mrs. Morrison. I do hope you like Galveston better than your father did."

"And you've both met Richard, of course," Damon said.

"Oh yes, indeed. How are you, Doctor?"

Emily Ingram was a delicately pretty, middle-aged lady dressed in an elegant black-dyed, silk suit trimmed in black sable, with a waist-length cape and a small black hat with enormous feathers which Elizabeth thought was a little overdone. She offered her hand to Elizabeth saying, "I read about your arrival in Galveston in the *Tribune*, dear." A quick flicker of her eyes over Elizabeth's tasteful frock revealed the barest glint of envy. "And yes, I've met Dr. Morrison. I'm so delighted. You do look a bit like your brother, don't you?"

They were moving now along with the rest of the congregation down the aisles with Elizabeth saying, "Mrs. Ingram, I'm so glad I got to meet you, because one of the first things I saw in Galveston which attracted my attention was your house and your gorgeous gardens. I've wanted to ask your gardener how he manages to get those pomegranates to grow in this salt air, but I found out it was you who keep the side gardens and I must compliment you."

They paused and shook hands with the rector at the door and passed on out and down the steps with Emily saying, "Oh, thank you, dear. It just takes work and not being afraid to get your hands into the soil. And yes, the side gardens are my pride and joy."

Eric Ingram leaned toward Elizabeth and said, "She spends more time tending to them than to me."

Damon said, "It's no wonder. The gardens offer more promise."

Elizabeth said, "That sounds like envy to me," while she thought, I had no idea Damon was this close to Eric Ingram.

They laughed and from the corner of her eye Elizabeth saw the Sturgeons approaching, Matilda Sturgeon's expression revealing that she was bent on finding out who in the world those people were that Emily and Eric were speaking to. It was Emily who introduced them to Elizabeth, and how-do-you-do's were said.

Damon, knowing how to keep Matilda's interest in the conversation and the people involved, said the magic words, "How have you been feeling, Matilda?"

If Matilda had entertained any desire to hurry away from the group, she abandoned it now and said, "Oh . . . not so good, Damon. You know every time I get out in the fresh air my sneezing just gets worse and Max insisted last night that I take a ride in the cabriolet and now my cough is terrible."

Elizabeth turned to Maxwell Sturgeon and said, "I understand your cabriolet is new. I must say I've never seen such a large one before. How does it ride?"

If Max had entertained any desire to hurry away from the group, he abandoned it now and his face lit up like a gas light. "Ah, Mrs. Morrison, it has Bessemer steel elliptical springs and rides like a cloud. You know it has full-length side and back curtains? And the seats are upholstered in the best buffed leather. Matilda doesn't ride out in the fresh air often. It disturbs her breathing."

Elizabeth lay a gloved hand briefly on Matilda's arm and said with a great deal of concern, "Oh, I'm so sorry to hear that, Mrs. Sturgeon. Are you seeing a doctor?"

"Oh yes, dear. Dr. Fogle," she replied. "He's old as the hills but he's been our doctor for many years." She gave Richard an apologetic look.

Richard said, "He's . . . very experienced."

Elizabeth turned again to Maxwell Sturgeon, who was shifting from one foot to the other impatiently wanting to tell them more about the new cabriolet, and said, "I've seen these carriages in Chicago on Lake Shore Drive near where I lived, but I don't believe I've seen one quite this large. I believe the wheels are larger, or maybe they just seem to be larger because they're painted yellow. Richard is a carriage enthusiast also, but neither of us have ridden in one of *these*."

"Well, perhaps some evening I can come by for you and Dr. Morrison and take you for a drive," Sturgeon said with enthusiasm.

Matilda said, "Max will then bring you by for . . ." She glanced in the rector's direction. "Tea, Mrs. Morrison."

"I'm sure Richard would be delighted and so would I." Out of the corner of her eyes Elizabeth saw Emily Ingram's eyelids flicker. "There's so much in Galveston I haven't seen yet. . . ."

Emily put her hand on Elizabeth's arm. "When spring is here and my garden is at its peak, Elizabeth, you must come by for lemonade. We'll sit out in the gazebo and talk gardens."

"Oh, how delightful!"

There was a little more of this kind of tête-à-tête, a cursory word or two between Damon and his employers, a brief, avid discussion about carriages between Richard and Max Sturgeon, and they were in their buggy again and off onto Winnie Avenue, with Elizabeth smiling to herself.

They rode in silence, meeting many other carriages and passing them on the street as other churches discharged their congregations, with Elizabeth smiling and nodding at the ones they met. When at last Blitz paced himself along under the brooding live oaks lining Avenue I, Richard glanced at her and said, "When do you plan to run for President, Beth?"

Her smile grew. "I have no idea what you're talking about."

"Oh yes you do. Such campaigning I haven't seen since Senator Sawyer came here in 1894 giving speeches in Central Park. If William Jennings Bryan had half the maneuvering finesse you have, he'd be President now instead of McKinley."

"Hush. It's just ordinary social amenities."

"It's social imperialism. What amazes me is that you spotted the subtle rivalry between Emily Ingram and Matilda Sturgeon and exploited it to your own advantage without either of them knowing it. And you perceived Max Sturgeon's greatest weakness, carriages, and exploited that too."

"It's a woman's business to perceive such things and

exploit them."

"All this exploiting makes me think its not social imperialism after all, it's a regular *blitz*." At the sound of his own name, the horse tossed his head. "Ho boy," Richard crooned to him. Then to Elizabeth he said, "Now what's your next move, Mrs. Morrison? The attack?"

She tilted her chin up, smiling merrily ahead of her. "No. I wait. And if nothing happens, I have other ploys I shall try. Really, Richard, I wasn't even *trying* today."

"I shudder. What I'm puzzled about now is why women like you aren't the presidents, the commanders, and the generals of the world."

She glanced at him and said, "Just give us time, dear husband. Just give us a little more time."

Only a couple of months of it and already Sunday dinner with Richard and Elizabeth had become a habit. Such company was of the best quality; Richard as his special confidante and brother, and Elizabeth as a soft, sentimental touch, and a balm for bachelor-weary eyes besides. Add to that his business associate and longtime friend Joe Bob, and his cheerfully pleasant wife, Melissa, and Cully who reminded them all of their own childhood, and one could swear on a stack of Bibles ten feet high that life was eternally sweet. And for icing on the cake, so to speak, there was always roast beef or fried chicken, creamed potatoes, gravy, black-eye peas, some kind of canned vegetable, and one of the lady's exotic desserts.

The dining room in his brother's house was a picture straight out of *Godey's Lady's Book*; a long, rectangular table covered with a lace-edged linen cloth and set with

fine, cream-colored, floral-decorated china, crystal gob-
lets with an etched flower design, silver tableware, can-
delabras, and chafing dishes heaped with fluffy potatoes,
cut-glass serving dishes, sunlight filtering through lace
curtains at the two long windows, and a five-armed
chandelier with flower-shaped globes, dripping with
crystal prisms above.

Damon said, "Cully, so you went to Sunday School
this morning, did you?" Because they'd been discussing
politics and had left the boy out of the discussion altogether.

At the moment Cully was making a chore out of eating
his okra which he did not like, and glanced at Damon.
"Yeah."

"Yessir," Joe Bob reminded him.

"Yessir."

"Did you learn anything?" Elizabeth asked.

"No, ma'am."

Everybody at the table exchanged looks.

"What was the Sunday School lesson about, Cully?"
Joe Bob asked frowning.

"About the creation."

"You had learned all that before, is that it, Cully?"
Elizabeth suggested.

"Yes."

"Yes, ma'am," Melissa reminded him.

"Yes, ma'am," Cully said. "But that's not why I didn't
learn anything."

"Oh? Why then?" Melissa asked.

"Because the teacher showed us a picture of God
creating the world and I didn't like it. Because God

189

doesn't look like that."

Everybody paused in their eating and were silent a moment watching this precocious boy as he chased a piece of okra about his plate with a fork. When Cully noticed that the grown-ups were all looking at him, he said, "God isn't an old man with a long, white beard, dressed in a robe."

They exchanged looks again. Damon leaned toward him a little and said, "What do you think God is like, Cully?"

The boy looked up from his plate and said solemnly, "God is everything."

Another moment of silence and Elizabeth asked, "*Everything*, Cully?"

"Everything," he said.

The friends around the table resumed their eating thoughtfully, except for Richard, who said, "Even the *bad* things, Cully?"

The boy seemed to consider this a moment, then replied, "Even those."

Silence fell over the group, only the sounds of tableware against china and the soft snoring of Flop under Cully's chair could be heard in the room.

Damon was thinking, Yes, in the giant icebergs around the Horn, the northern lights, the ghostly corposant playing about the masts on an electric light, the billowing of sails on a sunny day, the mighty storm with its angry heave and swell of the seas, the massive body of the great sperm whale, the flight of the albatross. . . .

. . . The dust on a polished table, thought Elizabeth,

190

the hummingbird, the blossom of a flower, the chill of winter wind off Lake Michigan, a new kitten nuzzling his mother, searching for his first meal. . . .

. . . Death? Suffering? The horrors I've seen? Richard was thinking. Birth, that first gasp for air of the newborn infant, the healing of a wound, the tears in the eyes of a colleague who has just saved a life, the first dawning light of understanding upon the face of a student. . . .

"More potatoes, Joe Bob?" Elizabeth said.

"No, thank you, Elizabeth. I've had plenty."

"Damon?"

"Please. I can't seem to get enough of the vegetables, and I'm glad you saved Melissa's tomatoes for today."

"Provided Joe Bob is through with Damon's secret project, whatever it is, by summer," Melissa began, "I'd love to have a large garden this year. But it takes a man to do the plowing."

"My secret project has turned out to be Joe Bob's as well. My apologies, Melissa," Damon said. "And you can go ahead and plan your vegetable garden, because by summer, we'll be finished with the project."

"Provided the thing doesn't blow up," Joe Bob said. Then flinched as if he'd said something he hadn't intended to say.

There was quiet at the table for a moment until Elizabeth breathed, "Steam."

Everyone looked at her, which caused her to realize she had spoken aloud, and she smiled. "So much steam coming from the potatoes yet, it isn't necessary to put the lid on the chafing dish. More potatoes, Richard?"

"Everyone must remember that Sissy and I made pecan pies," Melissa said, nervously cheerful. "So save room."

And Elizabeth smiled inwardly, satisfied at last that she and Melissa had discovered the gentlemen's secret project, and she could hardly wait to let them know it.

She didn't have to wait long. Joe Bob and Melissa stayed an hour after dinner, then went home, leaving the Morrisons to relax in the back parlor, the men with their smoking and Elizabeth with her needlework. She saw Damon watching her and wasn't surprised when he spoke up. "I think the Ingrams and Sturgeons both were impressed with Elizabeth," he said to Richard. "Any time Emily and Matilda vie for someone's favor as they did today, you can be certain they'll follow through with the supreme test."

"Which is?" asked Richard.

"An invitation to a party. The first party is like an initiation. New candidates for the inner circle go through an initiation process which involves three things; *if, how,* and *what* the candidates add to a party.

"If they fail?"

"They just don't get invited to any more functions involving the inner circle."

Because the needlepoint was stretched now on a tapestry frame which was attached to a stand, Elizabeth had to sit on the edge of a straight chair, her back stiff and straight, her skirts draping in luxurious blue folds around her. She said, "Doesn't the social circle have anything at all to do with friendship?"

Damon tapped the ashes off his cigar into the ashtray on the center table. "Emily Ingram has few close friends, and Matilda Sturgeon, as far as I know, has none. I don't know about the others."

She looked up from her needlework, smiling, and said, "I would dearly love to become a friend to both, especially to Emily. And I can't think of anything more to *your* advantage, Damon."

Damon took the cigar out of his mouth and smiled amusedly. "Oh?"

Elizabeth drew a couple of half cross stitches into her canvas before she continued, "After all, someone has to prepare the ground before one can plant, if one expects the plants to produce the desired fruit successfully."

"*What?*"

"The board of directors for Ingram and Sturgeon. You shouldn't present the project to them or even to Eric Ingram out of the clear blue sky. That's what spading up the soil is all about, *softening*. And most of the time the softening begins with the wives."

Damon looked over at Richard, who shrugged and said, "I didn't tell her a thing, Damon. I swear to God."

"He's telling the truth," Elizabeth said, her eyes bent upon her work. "You silly men are as transparent as glass. Your project blow up? That can be only steam or gas. My guess is it's steam. A new steam engine. What's new about steam engines? They've been around for over a hundred years, providing power for looms, locomotives, steamships, and lately electricity. Now, some fellow has come up with an ingenious device he calls a turbine engine, powered by steam. One is yet to be produced in America, at least to our knowledge." She glanced at Damon who was frozen with his cigar halfway between the ashtray on the center table and his mouth, which had remained open to receive it since the beginning of her monologue. "Unless, of course, there is some innovative ship captain somewhere and a marine engineer who are working on one—in secret so that their competitors won't steal the idea from them. And, after the captain and the engineer have built their very own turbine engine, they must present it to the board of directors for approval before it can be tried. But first, the captain must approach the president of the board in private, the president in your case being Eric Ingram."

Richard, blank-faced, had resumed puffing on his pipe, and Damon's eyes had gone black, as the ashes of his cigar dropped harmlessly to the floor. "Damn Joe Bob."

She looked up from her needlework. "Don't. He hasn't breathed a word of your secret."

"Then I'll be damned."

"You needn't be." She smiled. "It's an old story, Damon. It's a part of the free enterprise game. It happens all the time. It happened when a young foreman presented the idea of steam-powered looms to my grandfather in Chicago. You men have scuttled about with your secrets for years and you haven't fooled us women. Who do you think the young foreman courted *first* with the idea of steam-powered looms in the Harbour Mill? My grandmother." She shook her head. "We women have always led you to believe that we aren't aware of your silly comings and goings." She paused and rested her hands on the tapestry frame. "And both of you listen to

194

me. This is my house too, and anything you have to discuss, you can discuss in my presence. I am not simple-minded, nor am I a child.''

Damon had leaned back in the chair by then, not yet having recovered fully from his shock, a peculiar look on his face. ''Not everything, Liz. We can't discuss . . . quite everything in your presence.''

''Everything that's proper,'' she said, her body tingling suddenly from head to toe.

Damon scratched his chin thoughtfully as he studied her. ''Very well, you know about the turbine engine. *How?*''

With a lift of her chin, she replied, ''Deductions, assumptions, and slips of the tongue.''

''What else do you know?''

''I know about the diesel engine too just developed in Germany. And frankly, Damon, from what I've read about both kinds, the turbine seems much more suitable for your passenger liner, and the diesel for cargo ships and men-o'-war. I don't understand the mechanics of either engine, for no one has explained it to me, but from what I've read, the turbine is smoother-running than the diesel.''

Damon made a gasping sound deep down in his throat. ''Where the devil did you get the idea that I was thinking of the turbine in relation to a passenger liner? I haven't even mentioned that to Joe Bob!''

''You mentioned just two months ago that any steamship company with vision enough to capture the passenger trade would not only succeed, but would flourish. You spoke of having two ideas. I put the two together, that's all."

Damon looked over at Richard who was still puffing, and clearly enjoying the exchange between his brother and his wife. Damon blew smoke through his nostrils. "Alright, Liz, you're right. I've planned to present to Ingram a scale model of the turbine engine, hoping to sell him on the idea and to build two for the *Arundel.* If it's successful, I want Ingram and Sturgeon to build several cargo ships installing the turbine in each."

"I wouldn't."

"Pray why not?"

"Don't put all your eggs in one basket, Damon. Since the turbine is new, wouldn't it be better to wait a year or two to see how it works out? You might want to experiment with the diesel too. Meanwhile, if the turbine engine is successful, put turbines in a couple of cargo ships and build your passenger liner installing the turbine. Build a liner larger than any that exists now. A transatlantic cruiser. Then, if the diesel proves successful too, you won't have exhausted all Ingram and Sturgeon's capital on one kind of engine, and you will have built your liner which will cost, I'm sure, a great deal more than a cargo ship."

"Do you really think there's a future in passenger trade?" he asked hopefully.

"No. Not unless some enterprising company sees that shuttling passengers back and forth across the ocean has no greater financial future than it enjoys at the present, and realizes that the ship *can* be more than just a luxurious way to travel." She paused in her stitching. "It must be not a ship, but a *romantic adventure, a floating city*, not like any liner that exists now and not like any so-called floating palace. But enormous, luxurious. It must give birth to the attraction of cruising itself, not just the means by which people reach a destination. It must *be* the destination."

Damon stretched his legs out before him. "Where did you get this . . . this fantastic idea, Liz," he asked softly.

"A dream," she said. "Of an enormous floating city carrying not hundreds but thousands of people. People dancing to bands in huge halls, dining in great rooms under crystal chandeliers, six or seven decks, luxuriously appointed state rooms, Louis XV chairs and settees, satin and damask draperies, gilt, and brass. Chairs upon sun decks, merchandise shops, a theater, a barber shop, a newsstand."

"A huge crew, porters, waiters, tailors, dressmakers. It would employ hundreds of people," he said.

"A circulating library, game rooms, tennis, baseball."

"Well," said Richard, "with that many people aboard, you'd have to have a medical clinic and a full staff of doctors and nurses. Just thought I'd get in on this . . . pipe dream."

Elizabeth looked across the center table at him. "Dreams like this are *made* of tobacco smoke, Richard, and sometimes from the vapors of a romantically inclined lady."

"The liner itself is the attraction . . ." mused Damon aloud. But he straightened up in his chair, for it wouldn't do to let them see that a woman's dream had suddenly caused his own vision to become clear. Even the dream of a woman like Liz.

Liz, who was no ordinary woman. He had known that from the beginning. Her beauty, her self-assuredness, her capacity for happiness—none of it was ordinary. But her practical reasoning powers, her business instincts were a continual surprise to him. They could not be interpreted as being representative of an intelligence equal to that of an educated man, however. Could they?

The front screen door slammed and Cully, who always knocked and waited for permission to enter, came huffing and puffing into the back parlor without permission and sat himself disgustedly down on the sofa, folding his arms with a jerk.

"Ahoy, mate," Damon said. "Beating up against a headwind, lad?"

Cully shook his head, pouting.

"Got a privateer bearing hard astern?"

But Cully refused to answer.

While the three adults sat in silence waiting for him to decide to speak, the telephone in the entry jangled and they heard Prim answer, "Hello, Dr. Morrison's residence." There was a pause. "Just a minute, ma'am." Then Prim came into the parlor giggling and said, "It's Miss Crabtree over the telephone and she says she saw Julie Wineburger kiss Cully, and she want to be informin' Miss Lissa so Miss Lissa can tell Julie's mama. But she says she tried to ring up Miss Lissa and nobody answer the telephone over there. I believe they is in the back yard. Want me to call them to the phone, Miss Lizabeth?"

Elizabeth rose and moved around the center table, her skirts rustling and brushing Damon's boot as she went.

"No, I'll speak to her, Prim," she said, and went on into the entry.

As her voice drifted softly to them from the entry, Damon and Richard quietly and soberly studied Cully, who was blushing furiously. They did not speak for a long moment. Then Damon said, "It's one of the hazards of being a man, Cully. All these women around. The world's full of them. Can't go anywhere where they aren't."

Cully looked over at Richard.

"It's true," Richard said, taking his pipe out of his mouth. "They're everywhere. A man's just got to learn some kind of self-defense. It's the only way."

"They ain't on ships," Cully said angrily. "I could get on a ship someday and go out to sea, and there'll be nobody on board but sailors, and sailors don't kiss you."

Damon nodded as he leaned forward to squash out the cigar stub in the ashtray. "Aye," he said as he ground the cigar into the tray. "Sailors don't kiss you. But as for women being out at sea . . . well, I'm afraid they're about to infiltrate the shipping industry too, my lad." He glanced toward the entry hall. "In fact, Cully," he said, "I'll wager it's already begun."

Eleven

"Oleanders iss no trouble, Miz Morrison. Vot you do iss take cuttings like dis in Octoper and root dem in sand in a pot in de basement all vinter, den by sprink you haf . . ." Mr. Ziegler held up a clay pot with a flourishing oleander plant. "Dis. A baby shrup. How many do you vont and vot colors?"

Mr. Ziegler lived just west of town on six acres of sandy soil on which he had erected a large hot-house of hundreds of panes of glass, installed two gas heaters, and all winter grew small plants from seed and cuttings to sell to Galveston's garden-conscious citizens.

The old German also cultivated four types of oaks, two kinds of palm trees, magnolias, chinese tallow, and eighteen varieties of shrubs. As Elizabeth gathered up her skirts and stepped gingerly upon the pecan-shell paths, following him among the rows, Mr. Ziegler extolled the virtues of his trees and shrubs. One of his legs was shorter than the other, some "congenital anomaly," Richard had explained, which caused him to rock grotesquely from side to side as he heaved his egg-shaped bulk between the rows, with one hand on his bad hip, the other waving to encompass all his acres, saying, "Dere you haf two kinds of palm trees, Miz Morrison. As a baby de fan palm iss lovely; as an adult, he iss ugly, unless he is planted among other shrubs and trees. Den he giffs de garden a stately visdom, like your Apraham Lincoln." And later he had held a small, potted geranium in his hand as delicately as one might hold a rare gem and said, "De geranium iss not an aristocrat among de flowers, Miz Morrison, bot it is like your hosband who iss my doc-tor, easy to get along vith and dependable . . . always dependable."

Mr. Ziegler sent the shrubbery and seedlings to the Morrison's house in two farm wagons by his dull-witted helper, Arthur, "who don't haf all de cogs in his machinery, Miz Morrison, bot he's a goot poy and vill follow simple instructions." Arthur unloaded the trees and shrubs into the yard and carried the seedlings into the basement where Shad had erected shelves of left-over lumber for storing canned goods.

"To make rich de soil in your yard, Miz Morrison, you should haf de doctor buy a load or two of . . . pardon me, Mizzus . . . manure from Mr. Svenson. You know him, he owns de dairy on down de road vest of here," Ziegler had advised, his watery blue eyes not meeting her gaze for embarrassment.

Richard hired a handyman named Coombs with wagon and team to deliver the manure, and Shad laboriously spread it around in the yard while Cully made a spectacle out of it by running around the house holding his nose and shouting, "Pew! Pew!" with Flop hard at his heels enjoying his master's extra burst of activity.

Somber Mr. Coombs came again and plowed up the yard with horse and harrow, the clattering and clanging of the trappings, and Mr. Coomb's often-crooned, "Hoo boy," causing Flop to stand on the Swift's front porch the better part of the day, barking at the strange man and horse, who he was convinced had no business in the Morrison's yard. Then Mr. Coombs was paid an extra two dollars to prune the fire-damaged limbs out of the two remaining live oaks in the yard, one in the front and one in back of the house.

The next day, Shad took a string and stakes and he and Elizabeth plotted the garden, taking up half the backyard, furrowing and planting rows of lettuce and cabbage, beans, peas, radishes, carrots, cucumbers, onions, turnips, spinach, collars, okra, and against Prim's grim protests, tomatoes.

Elizabeth was standing, her hands on her hips, dirt on her cheek, her hair loose in wisps about her face, and said smiling, "I spoke with Dr. Morrison last night, and we were wondering whether you might like to raise a few chickens out here."

Obviously Shad was delighted, because he grinned hugely and said, "Yes ma'am. 'Cause I got enough lumber behind the carriage house to build a chicken house, and with a little more, I can build a picket fence for the chicken yard. Can do it in two days."

Spring came early in Galveston. Spring had arrived in late February when the birds, which had wintered over there, began their nesting, when flocks of sparrows shrilled and chirped in the trees, excited by the mating of their neighbors. And a mockingbird established his territory in the one huge oak in the back yard by delivering his medley of songs vigorously day and night, and by swooping down to nip at stray cats who ventured too close to the yard.

The Sunday after Shad built the chicken house and enclosed it in a neat, four-foot-high picket fence, Elizabeth spoke with Emily Ingram outside the church after services, while Eric Ingram and Richard got into a discussion about the possibility of war with Spain. For, the previous month, in mid-February, an American battleship named the *Maine* had been blown up in Havana harbor, and while the proof of Spain's involvement in the disaster could not be established, most Americans agreed with the Assistant Secretary of the Navy, Theodore Roosevelt, that "The *Maine* was sunk by an act of dirty treachery on the part of the Spanish."

"Look at the men," Emily said to Elizabeth. "Underneath it all they're all warmongers. Every get-together we've been to lately that's all you hear. I don't understand all this nonsense, why they want war!"

Elizabeth answered, "In my opinion, they're like little boys playing soldiers. They remember the glory of the soldiers coming home after the Civil War, I think."

"They remember the glory, but not the horror. My father fought at Gettysburg and came home without his left arm. And the soldiers returning home here, Elizabeth, did not come home in glory."

"Nor did ours, only in a weary victory. My father was

sent home with a bullet lodged near his spine, and his brother did not come home at all."

"Oh, it's barbarianism," Emily said, fanning her face with her handkerchief. "Will they never learn? But who wants to talk about that. My Lucius sees your Shadrack at church, you know, and he says you planted a vegetable garden. Did you see Mr. Ziegler?"

Elizabeth was ready with all the answers, the questions, and any airs that might be required to accomplish her purposes. "Oh yes. And I have over two hundred bedding plants and shrubs, Emily. But although my family kept a garden for years, that was in Chicago. Frankly," she laughed, "I'm scared. I haven't the faintest idea where to plant what. You know, I've *no idea* what exposures are best for so many of the plants here on the island. But," she said cheerfully, "I'll just roll up my sleeves and—"

"My dear, Elizabeth! Two hundred plants?" Emily exclaimed delightedly. "What all did you buy?"

Elizabeth told her.

"Well, I agree with Mr. Ziegler about how to grow most things, but my advice is not to plant geraniums in the garden. In beds, their colors don't mix with other flowers. Put those in pots on the porch. Go see Mr. Boston and he can order you some urns and statuary too. Oh, and as for oleanders, you should . . ." Emily paused and placed her hand on Elizabeth's arm. "Listen, why don't you come to the house tomorrow and I'll *show* you. Didn't I mention once that you should come for lemonade in the gazebo? Yes, I think I did. There. Consider it an invitation. Tomorrow at two o'clock, if you haven't any other plans, dear, and I'll show you about the gardens and where things grow best here, considering light and shadow and prevailing winds. Do say yes, so that I can demonstrate how very knowledgeable I am about gardens."

"I'd be delighted, Emily, to take advantage of your expertise," Elizabeth returned smiling.

"Wonderful. And now, look at those ridiculous men gathered over there with your Richard and my Eric. An entire *mob* of them having the time of their lives talking. And all about silly, nuisance old things like war."

"The faculty is worried about the heavy infestation of insects, especially mosquitoes we'll have this summer because of the mild winter and wet spring," Richard said.

"Even worse than last September?" Elizabeth asked. "Why, even then one couldn't sit on one's porch without draping oneself like an Arab."

"As a matter of fact, they'll be worse. Isaac Cline was elected to write an article for the newspapers informing the people about the possibility of an epidemic of tropical diseases, and how to prevent them."

They were lying in bed after the lights were out, and she had asked him about the monthly faculty meeting he'd attended that day. He hadn't told her about what they were *most* worried about, though, because he didn't want to trouble her. They were anxious over the upcoming yearly session of the Board of Regents from the University at Austin scheduled to meet at the medical school the next Monday. There was always a bushel of rumors circulating among the faculty and students when

the board convened, especially when they met before the
bi-yearly session of the state legislature. The rumors
were always about such things as the possibility of the
professors' salaries being lowered, of lowering the
entrance requirements, of *raising* the entrance requirements, of moving the medical branch to another location,
and even of the dissolving of the school altogether. Funds
for running the school were scarce. Tax money alloted to
the university by the legislature had to be filtered
through the Board of Regents, and that august body
regarded the medical branch as a stepchild, and the state
constitution prohibited the use of tax money for running
expenses anyway. The professors' salaries were barely
comparable to those of other state schools, and no
surplus appropriations remained for funding a library, or
for new and better equipment for the medical branch.

This year, as in years past, the professors had dozens of
requests to present to the board, and they would do it
while shivering in their boots. Because the mood of the
board and the whim of the state legislature could dissolve
the school with the mere stroke of a pen. Will Kelly
would hopelessly request a skylight for the dissecting
room again, Rob Tate would ask for microscopes and
pathological equipment and funds for the library—for he
was the dean for the medical branch—and Jackson for an
increase in his yearly fifty-dollar appropriation for
surgical equipment. Richard would request more lab
equipment, and especially for more and better ventilation hoods.

Elizabeth would eventually hear the rumors and the
outcome of the board meeting scheduled for Monday,

and of the state legislative session scheduled in May, because she visited with several of the professors' wives, and there was no way one could keep a woman from hearing things anyway. But now was not the time to mention it. Their discussions in bed were reserved for pleasant things, such as her garden and the chickens they had purchased from Swenson, the dairyman—a dozen pullets, three setting hens, and a hen with thirty-two chicks— and of her visit at the Ingrams that afternoon. "How was Emily?"

"I was bursting to tell you all afternoon, Richard, but you stayed so late at the office there was no time. Their lot is a double lot, you know, and the entire grounds are nothing but lawns and gardens. We first had a chat in the gazebo in the rear gardens." She smiled into the darkness and told him *almost* everything, but not quite. Men had no business knowing everything women talked about or did. After all, ladies had to have some private moments. And he wouldn't understand half of it anyway.

She had worn one of the frocks made from a blend of linen and silk, woven at Harbour Mills last spring, an exquisite material dyed pale green. The frock was an afternoon dress fashioned for calling on friends at tea-time in spring. Her hat was small, made of straw, and decorated with a bouquet of small flowers dyed the same pale green as the dress.

Over a tall glass of lemonade, Emily had said, "That dress, Elizabeth, takes my breath. The fabric is so exquisite! Don't tell me it was woven in your father's own mills!"

"It was. In fact, Father displayed this fabric at the

1897 Exposition along with an excellent cambric . . ."
and thus she had discussed the excellent fabrics that
Harbour Mills produced, and how she had brought an
entire trunk full of fabrics with her to Galveston, and
how her father continued to send her any new or
especially lovely fabrics the mills produced. In the meantime, she casually mentioned how prosperous the mills
were, and dropped some prominent Chicago and eastern-
seaboard names while she was at it. Elizabeth had
mentally assessed the benefits of her background, and
during conversation in the Ingrams' gazebo, managed to
mention again the prestigious neighborhood in which the
Harbours lived, what kind of house, and how many servants. Naturally, this was done discreetly, inserted into
the conversation among Emily's elaborate vaporings
about theater personalities who had stayed at their house,
and parties, servant difficulties, costs of absolutely
everything, and trips she and Eric had made abroad.

Elizabeth picked up the conversation about trips
abroad as a maiden might pause and pick a wild flower
while skipping lightly across a meadow. "Ah, how
delightful London was," she said, "where Father and I
went shortly after Mother passed away. The ship we were
on was one of the best, though it seemed to me for the
price we were paying our state rooms could have been
larger. And there was absolutely nothing to do to occupy
ourselves. It seems to me something needs to be done to
improve things on passenger ships and to make crossing
the Atlantic a little more tolerable. Besides, the engines
kept me awake at night, they vibrated so."

"And they thud," Emily said, sipping her drink.

"Isn't there a new engine somebody is experimenting with in Europe that can make a ship travel thirty-five knots and which does not vibrate? I suppose Eric already knows all about that."

Emily tilted her head. "Not that I know of. But you know he depends on Damon to keep up with such things, though Eric's exasperatingly hesitant to try anything new."

"A pity. With things changing so fast, I'd think a company as large as Ingram and Sturgeon would have to keep up with the very latest innovations in shipping and transportation in order to *survive*." Elizabeth shrugged. "Oh well, that's for the men to worry about. I'm sure they're well-informed about the newest inventions and can handle things without *our* interference."

Emily's large, brown eyes were fixed upon her face, and Elizabeth knew she had brushed lightly against her most sensitive nerve, *the possibility of Ingram and Sturgeon losing money because they were backward, for heaven sake.* "I wonder," Emily began, "I wonder if even Damon knows about that new engine in Europe."

Elizabeth sighed and gazed about her at the Ingrams' gardens. "I certainly hope so," she said.

"Because with all the competition here, and competition growing in the Houston quarter, if Eric and Max aren't absolutely on top of *everything*. . . ."

Elizabeth smiled reassuringly. "Don't worry. You know you can depend on Damon. He has very sound judgment. But we mustn't mention any *new ideas* he might have to anybody except Eric and Richard, of course."

"Have you heard about any new ideas?"

"You know men. They never confide in us."

"Yes. I know. Well. I certainly won't tell anything I hear, not even to Matilda Sturgeon. I trust her, but I don't trust her daughter, Rosemary, further than I can throw my shoe. I don't see what Damon sees in that girl." Emily sighed too and looked up to study the climatis vine twining upon the trellis.

Now it was Elizabeth's turn to ask questions. "Oh?" she said softly. "Damon . . . courts . . . Rosemary Sturgeon?"

Emily smiled and said with a lilt, "Well, if you call taking her for drives in the country alone *courting*."

Elizabeth continued to observe Emily speechlessly while a heat rose from the pit of her stomach to bathe her chest and to show in a blush on her face. "Often?" she said.

"I don't think *too* often. Though I do wonder what he's been doing lately since he got back from Liverpool, and where he's been keeping himself evenings. Certainly not at your house *all* the time."

Tit for tat. Elizabeth discovered she wasn't the only wily woman around. "Well," she said, pausing to give thought to a suitable answer, "I know he's working on some kind of . . . project."

"That's what I had decided," Emily said. "You don't suppose. . . . What kind of engine did you say that was that they've just invented in Europe?"

"I'm not sure. But whatever happens, we women have to keep these men's minds off war and things, and onto bettering themselves and their businesses while they're still able. Don't you agree?''

Emily, suspecting that Elizabeth knew more about Damon's secret project than she was telling—but grateful for having been assured there *was* a secret project—replied, "Absolutely. We must present a united front if necessary. After all, Elizabeth, we women have a lot to gain if we do and a lot to lose if we don't." She smiled then as their eyes met in the most binding tie ladies can experience, a mutual conspiracy, however vague. "Tell me, dear, how did you come to know Dr. Morrison?"

Elizabeth told her.

"How romantic. But, of the two men, I'm surprised it wasn't Damon you decided to marry."

"Oh? Why?"

"Why . . . because . . . because. . . ."

"Because he's more like me than Richard?" Elizabeth smiled. "Perhaps, Emily, but you see, it was *Richard* who came to Chicago to ask for my hand."

Emily thought about that a moment, then set it aside saying, "Oh well, enough of this talk." And rising she added airly, "Come now, let's take a walk and I'll show you how my gardens grow. With silver bells and cockle-shells and . . ." Frowning she paused and asked, "Did you ever understand what the nursery rhyme meant by 'four little maids in a row'?"

Richard was saying, "And so it was decided that Isaac, because he's professor of climatology, which is the study of the relationship of climate to disease, should be the one to write an article for the newspapers. He says he'll urge people to install indoor plumbing, do away with cisterns and outdoor privies, install screens on windows and doors, fill in swampy areas, and do away with standing water of all kinds." When he received no reply, he suspected that Beth had been sleeping since her recitation of her afternoon at the Ingrams, and had probably heard nothing of his part of the conversation. So he turned over and was soon sleeping soundly himself.

Next day she had Shad out early to help with the planting. And they had been at it only an hour when the Ingram carriage came to a halt in the street, and Emily descended and came through the gate of the new, ironwork fence, saying, "I just *had* to drop by and see for myself how you were doing with your planting. And as an afterthought, I brought Lucius to help." Breathlessly she came to stand at the foot of the veranda steps, and with her hands on her hips she looked up at the house. "Land sakes, now. Isn't this the most charming cottage you've ever seen?"

Cottage? Elizabeth turned to look at the house, then back to Emily. "*I* think so," she said.

"It's that architect that did the Breckenridge house. Clayton. Nicholas Clayton did your house, didn't he? My, he's an artist, isn't he? But you see I came dressed in muslin, with gloves and trowel in hand, and I intend to help." She turned toward Lucius who had come inside the yard. "Go fetch the rest of the tools, Lucius."

"Emily, you're a perfect angel. And too good to be true."

212

"Well, now I don't know about that. Here now. Let's roll up our sleeves, so to speak, and get busy. At least let me advise you where to put your hydrangea and crepe myrtles and oleanders. And didn't you say something about palm trees?"

For the next three hours Elizabeth bowed to Emily Ingram's expertise, and the two of them instructed Shad and Lucius where to plant the shrubs and dig the beds. Emily had even brought cuttings from four of her "family" rose bushes which came "from England in 1780 with my great grandmother." They planted the rose cuttings in a curved bed in the back yard next to the Hoffmans' fence. "Turn a jar upside down over the slips for six weeks and they'll be rooted by then," she said.

After they had labored for three hours in the sun, Elizabeth directed Prim to make lemonade and asked, "Won't you come inside, Emily?"

"Oh, I'd love to see your house inside, dear, but heavens no. Not today, because I'd get dirt on your furniture. Let's sit on the veranda where it's cool."

So they sat in the wicker chairs with Emily removing her sun hat and fanning her face as she blissfully looked about her at the work they had accomplished; borders of shrubs and flower seedlings, a palm tree in front on the opposite side of the walk from the live oak, a beautifully shaped magnolia six feet high near the Hoffmans' fence, yews at the angles of the house, oleanders in corners and nooks, curved beds and hedgerows planted on the sides. Her gaze moved to the fancy fretwork on the veranda, the lovely bay windows, and finally to Elizabeth. "Oh, Elizabeth, coming here to your delightful place with

213

everything so new reminds me of when Eric and I were young and newly married. And it's always such fun to start a new yard."

"Any success I have with the gardens will be because of you, Emily."

"Nonsense. You showed a great deal of good judgment yourself and would have been successful without me. Which reminds me. Eric and I are having a garden party April the thirtieth. You and Dr. Morrison are invited. I'll be sending you a formal invitation. Absolutely everybody who is anybody in Galveston will be there. I have one garden party every spring, you know. We begin with dinner in the gardens and move in when it's dark. We always hire a band from New Orleans, and we have *so* much fun."

Elizabeth managed to contain her exuberance and said, "We'd love it." And was already calculating . . . Damon would be back from his trip up the coast, and Joe Bob would have finished work on the turbine engine. Hopefully, Damon would have presented Ingram with the project, and Ingram and Sturgeon could be stewing about it before presenting it to the board members, most of whom would certainly be at the Ingrams' party.

As if reading her mind, Emily said, "I've a notion that Damon's secret will be in the open by then, and if it has anything to do with the board of directors, Elizabeth, we certainly will have some stimulating to do." Fanning, Emily glanced at Elizabeth out of the corner of her eye.

Still fishing, Emily? Here's a nibble. "Not stimulating, dear. Softening. Spading up the ground so we can plant seeds for germination."

"Ah!" Emily smiled up at the ceiling of the veranda, giving that a moment or two of thought. "My dear friend, I think . . . I'm not sure yet . . . but I *think* we, you and I, are two considerably alike peas in a pod."

They laughed and sipped their drinks, then Emily said, "Incidentally, you mentioned not having a dressmaker in Galveston. My dressmaker can't take on any more clients, but I know a very good one who can. Her name is Dancey French and she lives over on Avenue M. She's very good, I've seen her work. I'm sure you'll like her. She's a friend of Damon's."

Elizabeth paused in sipping her drink, took the glass from her lips, and said, *"Another* one?"

And Shad and Lucius paused in their raking to look over at the ladies on the veranda, wondering at their laughter again.

Twelve

It was April second and a spring day of such brilliance when the pilot steered the *Mary Mae* through the Galveston channel that Damon, leaning on the rail of the bridge, had to squint even though he was wearing a billed cap. The channel was smooth and a deep indigo blue. The usual swarm of gulls which he had come to welcome as a sign that he was nearing land, besieged the ship with raucous cries and swoops and dives. And one bold bird landed on the rail nearby, eyeing him hopefully with bent beak and baleful eye, causing him to smile, because it reminded him of a lady he knew in Boston.

When the old steamer finally put into port, he disembarked at the pier with his baggage, hired a Negro boy on the wharf to carry it to the Washington Hotel where he kept a room, and made his way to Water Street where Joe Bob had his office over one of Ingram and Sturgeon's warehouses.

"Complete and ready to show," Joe Bob told him

moments later as he led the way down the stairs to the warehouse. "And more miraculously, the thing *works*. Parsons worked for *years* developing the turbine."

"Don't boast, Joe Bob. Parsons worked years developing the *principle*. I gave you the principle, all you had to do was build the engine."

In the privacy of the small warehouse which Joe Bob had kept locked, they set the coals in the small boiler afire, set a timer, pulled a lever, and the engine began slowly to hiss and clang, the drive shaft to turn the propeller. Damon watched the needle on the pressure gauge move slowly up to 200 psi's, the temperature gauge read 450 degrees Fahrenheit. In a full-size engine the psi should be around 800. This little engine was only a model, about a quarter the size the real engine would be, but the *principle* was there—the expansion of steam in a stationary turbine casing with the steam acting directly on the rotors and driving the shaft with the propeller.

Joe Bob shouted above the noise of the engine, "From the speed the full-size engine would drive the propeller, and considering the total resistance and displacement capabilities of the *Arundel*, I estimate two turbine units with twin propellers will drive her about twenty knots."

Damon threw down the rag he'd been wiping his hands on. "That can't be. Surely she'll do better than that."

"That's a good speed, Damon. If you want better you'll have to add another turbine or use another ship."

"Parson's *Turbina* got thirty-six knots."

"The *Arundel* won't. Not with her hull. The *Turbina* was specially built to demonstrate the turbine engines, long, low and lean as an arrow. But if the *Arundel* does twenty knots, she'll still be the fastest ship ol' I and S has."

Damon watched as Joe Bob shut the engine down, throwing a switch, pulling a lever, and releasing steam from the compression chambers. When the noise and clamor began to diminish, he said, "Are you good at saying prayers, Joe Bob?"

"Melissa thinks not."

"Well, one prayer from you is better than none," Damon said. "So start praying for me because I've got to give the cargo shipment report to Ingram in person, and after that . . . the labor pains should start."

"Good luck, then. I'll stay here. I've got some oiling to do on that crank shaft, it seems. But I'll be praying in the meantime, though I think the good Lord will wonder who the deuce it is down here who's asking favors all of a sudden."

"He'll probably also wonder, *Damon who?* But do it anyway. Whether it's poor quality or not, I need all the help I can get."

He gave the cargo inventory and the transactions reports to Ingram. To his dismay, Ingram was in an unusually foul mood. When the reports were done, Damon invited him to accompany him to the number four warehouse, saying that he had something important to show him. Ingram rose from his desk, still chewing on the cigar Damon had given him, and got his coat off the rack, saying, "I take it you finished your secret project then."

Astonished, Damon said, "Yes, but how did you—"

Ingram pulled on his coat. "Nobody can do anything

secret around this place, Damon, without somebody knowing it." As they paced down the corridor and the outside stairway, with Damon trailing behind, Ingram continued, "Emily's been on my back for a month. 'You're not keeping up with new inventions,' she says. 'Now you listen to Damon when he has new ideas. If you get behind, Eric W., you'll find Moran and Mayfield with all the business and we'll end up in a shotgun house on Winnie Avenue.'" Ingram shook his head. "If you weren't an honorable gentleman and Emily twice your age, I'd swear the two of you were in cahoots, and *illicit* cahoots at that." He stopped and glared at Damon. "What warehouse did you say?"

The turbine engine performed smoothly and perfectly, with Joe Bob first explaining the turbine principle, then Damon shouting the story of the Parson's engine and the trial run of his ship, the *Turbina*. Then Joe Bob gave all the facts and figures relative to a ship such as the *Arundel*, if fitted with two turbines, with her tonnage, cargo carrying capacity, what the engine's fuel consumption, propellor r.p.m.'s, and horsepower would be. He said he could guarantee a maximum speed of twenty knots on the open seas. He explained how the engines could be installed in the *Arundel* using parts of her existing engines, and using the old drive shaft tunnels. Then he expanded on the facts he'd already given, how the turbine used less fuel, had no vibration, and used less space because it was less complicated than the reciprocating engine, and how she would require less maintenance and sojourns in the shipyards for engine overhauls. "The turbine engine hums, while the old up-and-downer thuds," he said. And all the while, Damon recognized the glint in Ingram's eye, that of suppressed excitement, cautious speculation, and expectant hesitancy.

By the time Joe Bob shut down the engine, Ingram's expression was veiled in careful complacency as he chewed on his cigar and said, "I don't know, Damon. From the looks of it, the turbine probably *is* the marine engine of the future. But the expense of tearing down the *Arundel*'s existing engines and replacing them with a couple of turbines with separate drive shafts . . ." He shook his head. "It would be better to put the turbine into a new cargo vessel if we were going to try the thing out."

Damon was at once delighted at the prospect and dismayed about the delay which putting the turbine in a new ship would cause. He said, "But Eric, all we want now is to prove the turbine's capabilities. If it drives an old hulk like the *Arundel* at twenty knots, think what it can do for a new streamlined passenger ship, for instance. One with three or four turbines and quadruple screws."

Eric looked at his cigar and threw it aside. "Damned straw they sell nowadays, not fit to smoke and not fit to chew. That wasn't a Havana you just pushed off on me."

"Am I a magician?" Damon said, recognizing Ingram's change of subject as a delay tactic designed so that he could mull over the prospects of the new engine without having to give even the barest hint of a decision. "Am I supposed to push through a fleet of Spanish men-o'-war to buy Havana cigars? Not likely. I gave Cuba a wide berth as I said I would." Damon studied his own lit cigar and frowned in thought saying, "Pushed the *Arundel* at eighteen knots, Eric, last time out. And she came crippling in on one engine. She'll be dry-docked for six months and she's typical. What will that one overhaul alone cost you in trade?"

Ingram eyed him keenly. "I should have stuck with the clippers."

"Your fastest clipper did only twelve knots."

"Yes, and it spent very little time in dry dock."

"But her cargo capacity was only half that of your fastest paddlewheeler, which gave you only fourteen knots, incidentally, and only a third the cargo capacity of the *Arundel*. I gave you the figures on that and the difference in your margin of profit, which you've probably still got in your files."

"To the devil with files. I have those figures in my head."

And Damon knew he was probably right.

Steam engines had made Eric Ingram his second million after he and Max combined their two small shipping companies and built four paddlewheelers in 1880, even while they kept their fleet of square-riggers for coastal and Caribbean trade. Eric knew Damon had never steered him wrong yet, like Emily said. But money was tight at the moment. With Houston taking some of Galveston's trade and likely to take a lot more in the future, and with the expansion of intercontinental railroads, Galveston's future as a port did not glimmer as bright as it had in the past.

However, a fleet of steamers with the turbine engine, if it worked out and gave, say, twenty-six knots, could put the company ahead of Moran and Mayfield and the others in a year. Emily had said, "Don't be overcautious, Eric W. Overcautiousness did not characterize men like Bessemer, J.P. Morgan, Andrew Carnegie, and even Conrad Moran." The memory of her mentioning Conrad Moran did it.

Eric looked at Damon. "Suppose the board agrees to try the turbine, and it's successful in the *Arundel*," he said. "What do you suggest? Cast all caution to the winds, sell all our old steamers, and order . . . say . . . three or four cargo ships with the turbine engines to begin with?"

Damon was astonished at the enthusiasm such a suggestion represented, but he suppressed his exuberance, took the cigar out of his mouth and cleared his throat. "Well, I'll tell you, Eric. We ought not put all our eggs in one basket. We need to consider the future. There's another kind of engine developed by a man named Diesel, an internal combustion engine. It may prove to be something too, so maybe we should proceed slowly at first. Put the turbine in a couple of cargo ships and build a passenger liner with—"

"Bah! For I and S passenger liners haven't proved that profitable," Ingram said, holding out his hand to Damon palm up. "Cargo's where the money is, Damon, considering our port. At the port of Galveston the profit is in merchandise."

Damon had already reached inside his coat and withdrawn a cigar, which he now placed in Ingram's hand. "But passengers are the future, Eric, and can be the future of Galveston as well."

222

"Mmmmm." Ingram lit the cigar and turned to leave the warehouse as Damon threw Joe Bob a look of cautious triumph. First step taken. If Ingram didn't change his mind, the next step would be convincing Sturgeon and the other board members.

The two men paced out of the warehouse with Eric saying, "Joe Bob says it'll take nine months to a year or more to build two turbines?"

"Yes. Using our men and facilities."

"Mmm." At the bottom of the stairs that led up to his office, Ingram paused and looked at his cigar. "I thought you said you couldn't get Havanas anymore."

"Well, that was speaking as an honest seaman, Eric. But with a bit of illegal trading, I was able to purchase a couple of cartons of these from a Cuban blockade runner."

The two men regarded each other a moment, then Eric burst out laughing and clapped Damon on the back. "Ah, you blackguard. Let's go up and talk about ships." As they ascended the stairs, he added, "But of course, you know whatever you do, you must not say anything about this new engine to anybody, especially to the ladies, or the secret will be out. And that's the whole idea in proceeding with this swiftly . . . if we proceed with it at all . . . to get ahead of Moran and Mayfield and all the rest. Agreed?"

They paused outside Ingram's office door and Damon smiled tentatively, knowing that one lady already knew, through no fault of his own. "Agreed."

And they went in and talked about ships.

*   *   *

Shadrack killed the first two chickens early Saturday evening, and Prim dipped the headless birds in a washtub full of water and plucked them as she sat on the back steps humming. Small underfeathers drifted in the breeze across the yard and a scissortail flycatcher swooped down from the peak of the house, caught a feather in her beak, and flew to the little cupola on the carriage house where she was building a nest beneath the rooster-shaped weather vane.

In the carriage house, Richard was dressed in old clothes polishing the carriage while Shad groomed Blitz, and inside the house Elizabeth was ironing her frock for Sunday Church.

Next door Melissa had just decided to allow Cully to take his unfinished ship to the tub with him in order to mollify his disdain for having to take a bath, Joe Bob was lounging in the parlor immersed in the *London Monthly*, and Sissy was taking the rhubarb pies out of the oven which Melissa planned to take to the Morrisons for Sunday dinner.

Damon was downtown roaming the streets alone.

Since the discussion between Liz and himself about the great passenger liner she'd dreamt of, a passion had risen in him that began to keep him awake nights and intruded upon his every thought. It had swelled as he worked on the turbine with Joe Bob, and grown as he sailed up the east coast and back, and expanded until it had nearly pushed aside his enthusiasm for the turbine. Now all he was able to think about, it seemed, was the Big Ship, and even that was mixed up somehow with brief visions of shining red hair, piercing blue eyes, the soft curves and folds of a rustling blue dress, the lilt of a voice, a perceptive mind, the essence of a being who could never belong to him, not even in his dreams.

As he strolled along down Twenty-second Street, his thoughts, though disjointed, were of the Big Ship, the idea of it only a puzzle, the pieces of which were there in his mind scattered about but not yet fitted into the total picture.

Passenger liners had developed from the transoceanic paddlewheelers with their cramped passenger accommodations to the present day screw-driven liners with their expansive luxuries. Cunard's *Lucania,* for instance, one of the finest passenger ships afloat, could accommodate 1,800 passengers, and contained a dining room 160 feet long and ten feet high. She had large well-appointed berths with portholes for ventilation, and lavatories and water closets with running water in her first class staterooms, and a library with electric lamps, and a smoking room. She was a floating luxury hotel of great opulence to be sure. But what was it Liz had said about the Big Ship? She called it a floating *city. Not hundreds, but thousands of passengers. . . .*

The *Lucania*'s normal speed was about 22 knots. She had two three-cylinder triple expansion engines. Damon's Big Ship would have three, maybe four, turbine engines and give from 26 to 30 knots or more. . . .

He hadn't spoken a word about the Big Ship to Eric, nor would he until the turbine proved itself. In the meantime, there were a lot of questions he needed answers to, like how to build a ship with five to seven decks without making her top-heavy, how to arrange her hull for both cargo and passengers, how to shape it for maximum speed without sacrificing stability. That was the biggest problem.

He found himself suddenly on Strand and approaching a small crowd of people at the side of the street where he paused on the boardwalk and watched an organ grinder grind out a sour tune while his monkey picked up coins tossed to him from the dust. The creature was dressed in a red coat and a little cap which he tipped with every coin he retrieved, like the mechanical monkey he had become. He'd been so rigorously trained, he went about his task of gathering money for his master as mindlessly as any wound-up toy, his wizened, old-man's face a study in boredom. Damon did not toss him a coin because whatever the monkey retrieved did not belong to him. Damon suspected that at dinner the organ grinder would dine on beef steak and wine and the monkey would grub leftover vegetables from the master's dinner and count himself lucky to find a bit of gristle to eat. He went on, thinking that Strand Street was always a circus.

He turned on Tremont going south, paused in front of Jacobson's Jewelers where in the plate glass window an emerald necklace was displayed on a black velvet cloth, and he thought immediately of Liz. He turned away from the window abruptly. Two carriages were meeting and passing on the street. A dray beladen with bales of cotton rumbled by toward the warehouses near the wharves. And trudging off of Strand onto Tremont came Tony, the ice cream vendor.

Damon had to smile. How long had Tony been plying the streets of Galveston selling ice cream from his cart?

Probably forever. At least as long as he could remember. Year 'round the little Italian pushed the square white cart through the residential streets, the business district, and along the beach road, ringing his bell, and stopping to dip down into that mysterious cold box and hand a paper cone of chocolate, vanilla, or strawberry ice cream to customers young and old. Damon figured Tony had to be at least ninety. Rumor was he had amassed a million dollars over the years, living alone, God only knew where, and saving his coins.

Damon and Richard had several times been amused to see this ageless immigrant plodding down the street, with small boys too poor—or only momentarily penniless—taunting him from the safety of porches or from behind big trees, chanting, "Tony licks the spoo-oon. Tony licks the spoo-oon." And after a few moments of this monumental insult, Tony's acquired American self-control would give way to his Italian temper, which he would demonstrate forthwith by shaking his fist at the boys and shouting, "A-a-a-aya leetle basta! Ya fadda's no good, ya mudda's no good, ya leetle sonna beeches."

The taunting of Tony had become a tradition with Galveston's boys, and while Tony continued to ring the same bell, push the same cart with only an occasional new wheel over the years, the boys finally grew up, and like Damon, stopped the grinning, leather-faced little vendor on the street to purchase an ice cream—strawberry flavored—and try to get a glimpse inside the mysterious recesses of the cart.

Casey would waltz with the strawberry blonde, but there was no blond in her hair, only red. Damon went down the street unabashedly eating his ice cream, telling himself it was the Big Ship he kept thinking of.

He'd made up his mind during his stroll around town. He'd work out a basic design, and tell Joe Bob what the ship must contain, and they'd draw up a sketch and work it up and present it someday to Ingram and then carry it to the shipyard in Boston or Glasgow to have a professional marine architect draw up the plans from the basic sketch. But only if the turbine engine proved successful. For he believed a ship of the magnitude he was thinking of needed the most efficient and powerful engine in existence in order to succeed.

But he still hadn't figured out how one could design a ship to hold four turbines, six decks, and thousands of passengers and all the accommodations he wanted. If she's too high, she'll tend to list; too wide, she'll drag. *Liz, she's impossible. You've dreamt the impossible.* Still. . . .

After wandering about the streets a while longer, Damon at last went back to his room at the hotel and continued perusing and puzzling over the cross-section blueprint of the *Lucania* he had obtained in Glasgow.

And at the Morrison house Elizabeth hung her frock in the armoire in the bedroom and went downstairs to check with Prim about tomorrow's menu. Prim had finished plucking the chickens, and Shad was seeing to the brooding hens in the chicken house. Richard came into the house from the back door rolling down his sleeves, and went into the back parlor to read the *News*.

Next door Joe Bob and Melissa were sitting down at the table with a very scrubbed Cully, and Flop languidly scratched a flea lodged somewhere behind his right ear.

And except for the Jewish community, most of the rest of Galveston's citizens went about their business much the same way, preparing their bodies and their souls for another lazy Sunday.

Damon found the answer to his most puzzling problem after dinner Sunday afternoon, and since Joe Bob had gone to his office to study a problem he was having with the turbine's casing, Damon was able to carry the answer to him, an answer that had come from a most unexpected quarter.

In his office over warehouse number four, Joe Bob held Cully's model ship up between him and the window, saying, "You really are serious, Damon?"

"Look at her lines, Joe Bob. You yourself know Cully experiments with these things, and when he showed me the ship after dinner, I saw its advantages. Certainly the model is crude and primitive, but it's like the model of the turbine engine you built, the *principle* is there."

Joe Bob, still examining the ship, said, "I see a damn ugly model here that looks more like a Bowie knife than anything else."

"Knives cut. So do ships. Every cargo ship afloat is *round* compared to this. It's streamlined, designed to eliminate the least drag, to cut through the water *and* air."

Joe Bob lowered the model to his knee. "She'd hold half the cargo the *Arundel* does."

"You've missed her best feature. Her cargo capacity is in the *length*. Besides, to the devil with cargo. We're talking about a passenger liner."

"Oh yeah?" Joe Bob looked up with interest at last, and Damon began to confide to him his dream of the Big Ship, complete with all Liz's feminine trappings. And when he was done, Joe Bob was left stunned, as if he'd sustained a shock to his creative imagination. For ship design was his special love, and were it not for the fact that he had a family to support, he'd have studied naval architecture and taken it up as a profession.

Damon sat down in the chair beside his desk. "Let's say the turbine proves successful in the *Arundel* and let's suppose you help me design the Big Ship."

"Ingram and Sturgeon doesn't have that kind of money," Joe Bob said flatly. "In the worldwide shipping company pond, Ingram and Sturgeon Shipping Company is a small fish."

"We'll have to apply for a government grant."

Joe Bob nodded thoughtfully, sticking out his bottom lip. "That's possible. But what if Ingram still can't finance its part?"

"I'll . . . I'll have to go to another company with this."

Joe Bob smiled. "You're a loyal dude, aren't you."

"Only to God, my country, my brother, and myself. To anybody else it's strictly business."

Joe Bob laughed. "Well I'm wounded. I sure thought I'd be up there with God and your country."

"As my good friend, you are. And I'll naturally pay you for your time now, and if the idea ever sees fruition, you'll get a percentage of anything I earn from it. Will you do it?"

Joe Bob shrugged. "After all that, how can I refuse?

Though I think you're trying to ruin my marriage with all this extra work that'll keep me here nights. Have you taken a fancy to Melissa?"

Damon stood up. "You'd never know if I have."

Joe Bob laughed. "Oh yes, I forgot. You're loyal."

"I don't have to tell you to keep this thing a secret."

"Thanks for reminding me."

Damon went to the door saying, "Now I'll leave you to your drawing board, because I have a date with a lady."

"Another picnic?"

"Drive in the country."

"Uh huh. Well, thanks for the opportunity to work on your Big Ship, Damon. Because I think you're right. I think she's the passenger liner of the future. You might even remember me when you get rich and famous. Although I'm not sure I can please you with my meanial talent."

"Want me to send Cully over to help?"

Joe Bob picked up the ashtray on his desk and drew it back as if about to throw it at Damon. And he had gone out the door immensely pleased, and anxious to tell Richard about his plans. And Liz too.

Thirteen

Because he was a physician, John Richard was at ease in any crowd. Professionally he had attended rich and poor alike, and had even taught their sons. Damon suspected that his brother saw people as bodies, warm mechanical dolls rushing through life mindful only of the vivid present, giving no thought to the vague future and its inevitable end. The castes of society troubled him not one whit. One man was the same as another. Damon was sure that if John Richard had to decide which broken bone to set first, God's or the devil's, his unprejudiced mind would simply determine which bone was broken the worst and fix it before the other.

So John Richard was fitting into the crowd at the Ingrams' annual garden party as naturally as a comfortable chair. And Elizabeth, at ease in any crowd, was as accepted in the exclusive circle as a vase of fresh flowers.

Damon was supposed to be listening to Rosemary Sturgeon expound on the paintings of Renoir, as she had studied art for a year in Europe, and had done some things that were vaguely erotic. But he wasn't listening. Though physically standing near the gazebo in the Ingrams' backyard with a group of young gentlemen and ladies, mentally he was with Cully in his backyard Sunday. . . . *Me an' Jason tried her out in a pond, Cap'n. She whizzes through the water faster than any of my ships because she's skinny, an' she'll carry just as much cargo as the fat ones because she's long.* . . . And then he was with Joe Bob in his office above the warehouse when he had handed him Cully's model ship. . . . *I don't have to tell you, Joe Bob, to keep this thing a secret.* . . .

But now Emily Ingram was coming up to him again, still fanning nervously, saying, "Oh Damon. This old war has absolutely ruined my party."

It was the third time she had told him that and he assured her again that the war had not ruined the party, that the evening was young yet.

"But the men won't dance. They won't talk to the women. They won't do anything but talk in big groups and argue and I'm desperately afraid somebody will start a fight." And Emily went off again among her ferns and flowers, fanning and laying a hand on any other gentleman's arm who wasn't in the discussion about war, saying the same thing.

Poor Emily. Poor ladies. They were left to their own devices, standing around the yard in small groups, dressed in dazzling new pastel frocks with feather or silk fans and gorgeous hats which, once they went inside, they would remove to reveal extravagantly styled coiffures. They were left with nothing to discuss but each other's dresses, servant problems, and afternoon tea. Liz was among them but set apart from them. She was a jewel among jewels, dressed in a powder blue, breezy kind of material lavished in ecru lace, the lady and the dress meriting, if not contemplative admiration, at least a third glance. Damon smiled to himself when he caught a glimpse of her—Liz in her element. This is where she belonged.

The party was three hours old, and instead of the discussions about the war drying up, they were growing more heated. Because the younger set, which hadn't been in the groups of war-talkers before, eventually joined them and added the idealistic fervor of youth.

In the meantime, the band from New Orleans, which was installed on Ingram's garden terrace adjacent to the house, played on.

Damon, like the rest, was not about to be the only man left talking to the ladies, so he joined the group of men among whom John Richard had stood all afternoon, probably killing the grass under his feet because he hadn't moved an inch. The group, as far as Damon could tell, was no further into winning the war than they had been earlier when he had stood beside them and overheard their conversation.

Back in February, after the American ship *Maine* had blown up in Havana Harbor, the U.S. had appointed itself as intermediary and had sent word to Spain requesting three concessions, and since that time Spain had capitulated on every point except Cuban independence. McKinley had not wanted war but had begun to vacillate because of political pressures, and when Spain failed at first to agree to Cuban independence, he signed the declaration of war and Congress declared war on Spain on April twenty-fifth. That was five days ago. The news which had arrived only today was so new that the Galveston newspapers had not yet had time to print the story, but it was telegraphed to Galveston from other coastal cities and spread all over town by word of mouth. Commodore George Dewey had sailed from Hong Kong with a fleet of American warships toward the Philippines. So the talk of war was at a fever pitch on this, the thirtieth day of April.

For the most part, the crowd at Emily's party had not wanted to go to war with Spain, contrary to the general desire of the rest of the nation. The men here were bankers, or men with commercial interests, and war could not only complicate trade, but could tie up interests in foreign ports and cost them a great deal of money. In short, as Damon saw it, war was an inconvenience and a liability to them. But a younger faction, generally the college graduates from the universities in the east, were sympathetic with Assistant Secretary of the Navy, Theodore Roosevelt, who fired their idealistic enthusiasm for the liberation of Cuba, and it was this group who kept repeating with disgusting frequency, "Remember the *Maine!* To hell with Spain!" And it was this group with their young ideals and fearless ways of expressing them that heated up the tempers of the older generation of industrialists and merchants, and caused pressure to build up within each conversational group, reminding Damon a great deal of his turbine steam engine.

Abel Coffman who owned one of the largest cotton compresses in Galveston was saying, "No sooner had Secretary Long left for home than Roosevelt took over as secretary and sent an order to Dewey in Hong Kong to make ready in case of war. I'm a Republican, but I have to agree that Roosevelt's like a bullmoose."

"Well, bully for you, Mr. Coffman," young Michelson said. "Roosevelt did that on the advice of Henry Cabot Lodge, Mr. Coffman, whose politics you have applauded ever since I've known you."

Harry Borman, who was obviously holding more punch in his system than he was in his hand, raised his glass and said, "R'member the Spain. To hell with Maine."

He was ignored and the discussion, like the band, continued on.

No lady at Emily's gorgeous party liked what was going on. "Before you know it they'll all go traipsing off to Cuba to fight a silly ol' war that we've got no business getting into," one sweet young thing said in the group of ladies sitting in the gazebo.

"What do we care whether Cuba wins its independence or not? That's none of our business," said another.

Lord, thought Elizabeth, now *we've* started it. She fanned and looked across Emily's yard, abloom with oleanders and hydrangea, at the groups of men in sporty coats and trousers, some with hats, some not. The excellent band of ten men were dressed formally in black, split-tailed coats and playing Bach, Beethoven, and Tchaikovsky and nobody was paying them one whit of attention. And the men were all still, *still*, after three hours

236

and with dusk coming on, talking about the war.

Emily had gone into the house to oversee her servants' turning on the lights and would soon turn on the electrified Japanese lanterns strung in the trees and on the terrace. The Ingrams' house was a red brick and brown stone Gothic mansion with arched windows, colossal turrets and gables, and Elizabeth was dying to see the inside. Though she was enjoying herself and had not for one minute felt like an outsider, still, an element of fun was missing, and that element was strictly male in gender.

Finally the lights were on in the big house and there was a lull as the band moved indoors, followed by the ladies. Emily, frantic about the disaster of her party, fluttered among the gentlemen, shooing them inside, and the ladies smiled over their fans with, "Ah, at last," written plainly on their faces. But alas, the gentlemen only regrouped inside and started the whole campaign of fighting the war all over again.

The entire southeast wing of the Ingram house into which most of the party had moved was a ballroom with a polished parquet floor, a gorgeous white and gold coffered ceiling some fifteen feet high, and five long, wide windows facing south overlooking Broadway. These were draped in scarlet velvet and festooned in tassels of gold, but were open so that all travelers on Broadway that evening could see the brightly lit, gala event within Ingrams' house. That's what was so embarrassing.

Though the band, now elevated on a platform at one end of the room, continued their renderings of the masters, no one was dancing. The war had moved

PATRICIA RAE

indoors, the ladies were on their fifth version of their last trip abroad, and Elizabeth was furious.

Emily came to her at last and there were tears in her eyes when she said, "Oh Elizabeth. I'm ill. I think I'll go throw up any moment. It's dreadful. And I did so want to show you what a good time we have. I can't get Eric to budge. He won't listen to me. None of the men will listen to me. Oh, what are we going to do?"

We? Elizabeth thought, what *would* I do if this were happening at a party at my house? She looked at the band and said, "Emily, didn't you say the band could play any kind of music?"

Emily quavered, "That's what their credentials said. But what—"

"I have an idea. If you'll do your part, I'll do mine. Here's what I want you to do. . . ."

Three minutes later, she pulled probably the worst *faux pas* people had seen in years, but desperate situations called for desperate measures. She glided to a large group of men in which Richard and Damon were standing, and slipped her hand through the crook of Richard's arm and listened while Eric Ingram thundered redfaced, "Had McKinley the spine of a jellyfish, he'd have avoided this war. Spain had capitulated on the point of Cuban independence before he declared war. But he bent his will to the politicians, that's what he did. He was afraid moderation would ruin his popularity . . . and his chances for reelection in 1900."

"Now wait a minute, Eric," said a tall well-dressed gentleman whom Elizabeth had not yet met, "I was against war too, but you have to consider the pressures

238

the President came under, not just from political factions."

"Bah," Ingram said. "He gave up, Conrad. Fine President to have in power if we go to war."

Conrad, Elizabeth thought. He had to be Conrad Moran, Ingram's worst rival. Boldly, she took advantage of the pause for breath and said to Eric, "Mr. Moran is right. There were pressures from all sides on the President. Congress wanted war and so did the people. How could one man fight that?"

The gentlemen were stunned, and bent a rather comical gaze upon Dr. Morrison's attractive wife as she smiled charmingly at Conrad Moran and said, "And, Mr. Moran, you have to agree with Mr. Ingram too. Because without the support of the people and the interventionists in his own administration, he would risk losing the election of 1900. And let's face it, gentlemen," she said, sweeping the ring of stunned faces with a bright look, "that would mean a return of the free silver Democrats."

While the gentlemen stood suspended between amazement because she had spoken out on a gentleman's subject, and annoyance at her presumption to intrude, Elizabeth reflected that the discussions at Sunday dinner with the Swifts and Damon, and her own reading of the *Galveston News*, had reaped a reward at last. But lest she appear too unladylike to the men in the group, she tilted her head coquettishly and said, "And you big men are yearning to be soldiers. Now admit it. You recall seeing regiments of rebel soldiers in gray marching through the streets of home."

Somebody harumphed. It was bewhiskered Chadwick

Greenleaf—Greenleaf Merchandising—who wheezed, "My dear Mrs. Morrison. You have seen through all our blustering, I do believe. However, my dear, one point of your statement needs correction. We were *Confederates*, not rebels."

She raised her brows and said, "Oh? In Chicago we called you rebels. And you were, you know. You rebeled against the government of the United States, just as the Cuban revolutionists—whom you yourself call rebels—are rebelling against Spain."

The men laughed uproariously for the first time all evening.

Mr. Coffman hacked into his handkerchief and said, "We *were* rebels, Mrs. Morrison. But against government intervention in states' rights and—"

"Exactly," she said. "That and more. But that's over. The Civil War is done. And the Spanish War is out there across the Gulf, and there's a world of time to discuss it. *Later.*"

Suddenly, inexplicably, the band struck up John Philip Sousa's brand new, "Stars and Stripes Forever," excellently rendered even to the tootling obligato of the piccolo. Emily's guests at first were dumbstruck. Then they turned toward the band, and one by one the younger set began to clap in time with the march. After a few moments most of the older set had begun to clap too, and the old fogeys who didn't, eventually had to smile. Whatever patriotism, or war fever, or idealism still burned in the breasts of the guests were transferred to enthusiasm for Sousa's march. After one stanza the march was finished, and Harry Borman, who had forgotten what it

was everybody was supposed to remember, raised his fist
and shouted, "R'member the . . . R'member the . . .
R'member the Alamo!" The guests applauded laughing—
for who could argue with that?—and the band swung
easily into the old, dependable favorite, the "Blue
Danube Waltz."

It was then that Elizabeth turned to Richard and said
sweetly, and loud enough for the other gentlemen to
hear, "You, Richard, seem to have added as much to the
war as these other gentlemen, and you've also been as
inattentive to your wife as they have. Therefore, since
you've shunned your duty as a gentleman, I'll have to do
your duty for you." She curtsied beautifully and said,
"May I have this dance, dear, so that the *entire* evening
will not be wasted?"

Richard, falling into the harness like a milk-wagon nag,
smilingly encircled her in his arms, and off they glided
across the Ingrams' ballroom floor, he a little stiff, she as
graceful and vivacious as a blue heron. And Damon,
shamed like the others, but just as intrigued by the most
fascinating woman at the party, had to suppress his first
impulse, and seek out Rosemary Sturgeon instead.

In five minutes the passersby on Broadway could look
at the Ingrams' brick and stone castle and see, through
the open windows of the southeast wing, the ballroom
awhirl with pastel colors and gaiety enough to strike envy
in any middle-class breast.

Rosemary Sturgeon was as unlike her mother, Matilda,
as a mountain from the swamp. She was alive, a volcano
of a woman, beautifully serene on the surface, a seething
cauldron of emotions deep inside. Damon had the

opportunity on occasion to explore that seething cauldron, making it clear to the lady involved that the affair was only temporary in nature and that it was not to be mistaken for any involvement of a permanent nature nor was it to obligate him to her in any way socially. However, the lady tended to forget.

"Damon, Damon," she said as they danced on the crowded floor, "I don't understand your preoccupation tonight. Your charming sister-in-law is right. You must be like the others, sailing toward Cuba commanding a fleet of American men-o'-war."

"Liz said that?"

"And more. Yes, she is charming isn't she? Liz, you call her? You never gave *me* a nickname. Anyway, to me you men are like tomcats searching the neighborhood to invade someone else's territory with your talk of war." She smiled; her long, long lashes fluttered once. "Or is your mind on a feline in another port?"

He smiled down at her and did not reply.

"Ah. I know. You're wondering if Father and Eric and the other old coots on the board are going to approve your secret project."

His smile did not cease, but his face turned to wood.

"Don't be angry with me. Father let it slip at breakfast this morning that you were working on a secret project, but he didn't say what, except he mentioned steam. But don't worry. Even if I knew what it was I wouldn't tell a soul. As I've said before, you can trust me not to tell on you . . . about anything."

The "Blue Danube Waltz" was over, for which Damon would be forever grateful. Rosemary was seldom subtle

242

and the ears of most ladies nearby seldom deaf.

She was clearly piqued at his inattention and when he led her off the floor said, "I've promised the next dance to Conrad Moran. And I don't think a waltz with him could be as dull as the one I just suffered through with you." She turned to leave him, but paused and flung back at him, "Cat got your tongue?"

Damon looked over the crowd, found Liz's amber-red coiffure as easily as a beacon, went to her, took her from Richard without asking for the dance, gave a polite nod to Michelson who had come to take possession of her for the next dance, and whirled her into the crowd to the band's "Casey Would Waltz With a Strawberry Blonde."

"Damon. Rogue. I had just promised this dance to Wally Michelson."

"Young Michelson is a sap."

They danced a moment silently, a space of time in which he was aware of the movement of her waist under his hand and the damp, electric touch of her hand in his, a moment in which he relished the thought of Richard's wife as a woman, and not just an object of his deep affection.

It was she who broke the silence. "I'm surprised," she said. "My husband dances well. We had danced a little on the riverboat coming down the Mississippi from St. Louis, but somehow, how well he danced did not occur to me then."

Damon smiled. "Richard does everything well. Like picking you for a wife. Liz, you continually amaze me. I wonder if you're aware of how much you've endeared yourself to the ladies for breaking the ice tonight."

"Ice indeed. Heated discussions."

"I mean the ice that had frozen around the ladies' hearts. How they must have hated us. Rosemary was quite furious."

"Speaking of whom, she is dancing with Conrad Moran this minute and being very animated in conversation."

"Is she? That ass Sturgeon let it slip to her that I was working on a secret project."

"Suppose she tells Moran?"

"Rosemary?"

"Of course, Rosemary."

"She wouldn't betray me, Liz. She's kept many . . . confidences before."

"I'll bet she has. But only those which are beneficial to her . . . Shall we say, *socially?* And only when she is in an agreeable mood. Which tonight she is not."

He must have looked stunned, then worried, because she shook her head. "Oh Damon, how gullible you men are. I've spent fifteen minutes talking with her this evening and she spent the entire time telling me how you take her for drives and yachting and such, and how many secret lady friends you have. And she hinted she knew you were working on a secret project too, thinking she might find out from me what it was. And this minute she's talking to Moran and looking furtively this way."

"Furtively!"

"Don't look. I'll wager my entire wardrobe that she's telling him something like, 'I haven't the foggiest notion what the project is, but it has Father and Eric terribly excited, it's something to do with a steam engine, I think.' "

Damon stopped still as other dancers glided around them. "She can't."

"Oh yes she can. And she will. Hell hath no fury like a woman scorned, you know."

They started dancing again and Damon, knowing Liz was right, breathed, "God in heaven. She'd betray her father?"

"If it suited her."

"You're a suspicious woman, Liz."

"No. Only practical, Damon. And female."

The waltz ended much too soon and Damon led her from the floor, but couldn't take his eyes off her face because he read there the inevitable truth. Elizabeth knew the innerworkings of the female mind. He was horrified. If Moran got the barest hint of what he was up to, all would be lost. Conrad was shrewd, much more so than Eric, Max, or himself. He'd figure it out. He could set his vigorous mob of captains, agents, and marine engineers on a suspicion and turn it into a fact.

The grim phantom of Moran in his mind materialized into the real man, and Conrad touched Elizabeth's arm. "Damon," he said, "I assume you're ready to give Mrs. Morrison up for a moment?"

Damon inclined his head toward Conrad with a grim smile, seeing in his face the suppressed delight at what he'd just heard. And Liz bestowed on the enemy a bedazzling smile as he led her into the crowd of dancers, just as the band began the lilting "The Fountain In The Park."

Conrad Moran, delighted to have made the acquaintance of Dr. Morrison's lovely wife for the first time when she had blasted hell out of a stale discussion earlier, indulged his inquisitiveness about her in direct unveiled questions. "You're from Chicago, then, Mrs. Morrison?"

"Yes. Father is in textiles, Mr. Moran."

"Ah, yes," he said delightedly. "I'm acquainted a little with Chicago. Which mill?"

"Harbour Mills. I'm sure you've heard of them."

"Indeed, yes. Very progressive mills. Didn't your father once use Ingram and Sturgeon for shipping?"

"Yes."

"But found their rates too high, I'll wager."

"Well Father *is* a bit of a scrooge, I'm afraid."

"Scrooge? Let's see, that's from Dickens is it not, and refers to a man who was a miser. No, Mr. Harbour is not a scrooge. He is wise. Because he left Ingram. He should have come to me."

"I think he went to almost every shipping company in Galveston but yours, Mr. Moran. I think he must have gotten discouraged after speaking with the agents of two or three companies."

"My rates are high too, but not quite as exorbitant as some."

"I've heard that you aren't too solicitous toward the Galveston Wharf Company, Mr. Moran."

He said, "Shh. Don't let anyone hear you. The entire wharf company is represented here tonight and we don't want to reveal *too* many secrets."

"It's no secret."

They laughed again and Moran said, "Damon's been in port lately more than usual, I understand. Ah . . . have you seen enough of your new brother-in-law to become acquainted with him?"

"Oh quite. He takes Sunday dinner with us. But he is quite busy elsewhere."

"Elsewhere?"

"Yes." Conrad's gaze was fixed on her face, waiting for her to continue, and just when he had begun to despair that she would not, she tilted her head and said, "What's a sloop?"

"Sloop?"

"Yes. He's building him and Richard a sloop. And he's built this funny little engine, a scaled-down model of a steam engine to go on her, sort of an experiment."

Moran's face still had not changed, but some of the many lights in his expressive black eyes had gone out. "I doubt," he began musingly, "that a steam engine on a sloop would be very effective."

She smiled engagingly. "I don't know about that. All I know is that they keep talking about this little up-and-downer in relation to a sloop, whatever that is."

"A sloop can be a yacht . . . and if he's putting a steam engine on her, then. . . . If he's successful, I just might steal his idea and build racing yachts for profit."

"That would be terribly unfair, Mr. Moran, with Damon doing all the experimenting with it."

He laughed and said, "All is fair in love, war, and free enterprise, Mrs. Morrison."

The waltz ended and Conrad took her to where Damon stood slumped over a glass of punch beside Richard. Moran, smiling, inclined his head toward Richard saying, "I've just gotten acquainted with your very charming wife, Dr. Morrison. I hope you appreciate her value."

Then to Damon, "I'm afraid the secret of your project has been discovered, Damon."

Damon stared at Conrad, glanced at Richard, then his eyes flicked briefly to Elizabeth's serene face, and back to Conrad.

"I hope you realize, Damon, that even a scaled-down model of a steam engine for a sloop defeats your purpose. You'd have to reinforce her hull and that would add more weight."

Damon's expression remained blank.

"Don't be so secretive," Conrad said. "Anybody who builds a yacht and installs a steam engine in her has to be planning to enter the national cup races. No, don't look stunned. The ladies didn't betray you. I deduced it myself. So why be so secretive? Neither I nor Mayfield or the others have the time for such nonsense. Yacht racing is an indulgence which we can't afford at this critical time in the history of Galveston's port, and I'm surprised that Eric and Max are financing you, stingy as they are. I'm also surprised you're wasting *your* time on it too."

Damon smiled slowly. "Well, a seaman has to find some amusement to occupy his hours between trips, Conrad, and I can't think of anything more rewarding than . . ." he glanced at Liz, ". . . yacht racing. . . ."

Moran also glanced at Liz. "I can." Then to Richard, "Doctor, so you're a partner in this enterprise of Damon's. Do you think it will work?"

Richard swished the punch around in his glass and never batted an eye. "If you mean the little steam engine in a yacht, yes, I do. Naturally, the yacht will have sails too, just in case."

"Of course. But I warn you, there's such a thing as overdoing a good thing." Moran looked about him saying, "I need a glass of punch." He bowed to Elizabeth. "My dear Mrs. Morrison, I'm charmed. Damon, I wish you luck with your racing yacht. Dr. Morrison, I envy you a vivacious young wife. If you'll all excuse me, I need a dr—a glass of punch."

When Moran was gone both Richard and Damon looked at Elizabeth. She smiled and said, "You don't suppose when he finds out what you're really up to he'll be mad at me."

Damon laughed, feeling incredibly relieved, and replied, "My God, Liz. No. It's Moran who always says, 'All is fair in love, war, and free enterprise.'"

She took Richard's arm as she saw Emily Ingram approaching, and before that woman could embrace her, she gave a throaty laugh and said, "Well we've taken care of the war and the free enterprise, and now all that's left to be fair with is love."

Over Emily's shoulder as she hugged her gratefully, Elizabeth met Damon's gaze, brief, veiled, and oh so inscrutable.

Fourteen

Richard got to the school early, not soaked with perspiration for once. No more bicycle riding for him; those days were gone forever. The Board of Regents had met, and though they had not granted a single one of the professors' requests, they voted instead to raise their salaries. Though disappointed that they would all have to struggle for another year with inadequate and primitive equipment, Richard nonetheless had gone immediately to Houston by Houston-Henderson Railroad and purchased Beth a little Studebaker buggy and a beautiful bay mare. Now the larger buggy was his to use as he pleased. He had given the bicycle to Shad, and Elizabeth had the smaller buggy all to herself. And she needed it.

Beth was all caught up in her social clubs—the Jolly Sixteen and the Galveston Garden Club, which Emily had talked her into joining—and in paying and receiving social calls. She'd given a party the first of June and had invited all the doctors and their wives and a few other friends, and the thing had gone well because of Shad's entertaining and her own extravagant—and expensive preparations. They'd been invited to the Coffman's shrimp fleet launching party in May too, an event that delighted her more than her own, because only twenty couples of the aristocracy were invited, counting the Morrisons. That was what mattered, *counting the Morrisons.* And as a result of that, or her influence, or maybe because his practice had just begun to ripen like one of her pomegranates, or for some other reason he could not quite grasp, his private medical practice had begun to attract a few of the elite. Matilda Sturgeon seemed to have led the way. Then Chad Greenleaf came with his respiratory problems. Then all at once the fact that he had the only x-ray service in town seemed to lend some prestige to his practice in the eyes of Beth's friends.

At any rate, it did not take Beth long to see his need for a better office and she began to suggest that he move the office to a nicer location.

"We can't afford it right now, Beth," he had told her.

He should have known that wouldn't do. One day she left in the carriage, went to the real estate office on Twenty-second Street, and before the afternoon was done had gone to the bank and taken the savings from her trust fund dividends, and had paid a year's rent on a three-room flat above Eberhard's new drug store on Mechanic Street. He had been irritated because she had proceeded without him, more so because she had paid twelve-month's rent in advance out of her own savings. But eventually he got over the hurt and the blow to his pride, and since the thing was already done, hired help off the docks and moved all his office equipment to the more spacious flat.

The building was new, and the upstairs over the drug store had been designed for a live-in flat, consisting of three good-sized rooms painted ivory, with the baseboards, door frames, and mouldings in dark oak. He and Beth made the sitting room into a waiting room, the kitchen into a treatment room, the bedroom into an x-ray lab. She had the straight-back Morris chairs recovered in red leather, took the Civil War portable medicine chest which Damon had given him as a wedding gift, placed it in one corner of the waiting room, hung a painting of a ship over it which she had purchased from the art dealer on the Strand, and called it an "interest center." Then she added a large marble-topped center table to the middle of the room and stacked magazines and newspapers on top.

The rest of his equipment and his desk and chair she arranged in the kitchen, and arranged his medicines, instruments, and dressings in the cabinet, labeling everything, and organizing his entire treatment room until he couldn't find a damned thing. The x-ray room she graciously let him set up all by himself. A little at a time, she said, they'd add other fine touches to the office. What, he couldn't imagine.

He'd been in his office two weeks when Mrs. Jacobson wheeled Timothy into the office, creating quite a stir when the poor boy filled his pants and the seat of the wheelchair in front of five waiting patients.

He had just come from his office now after having prepared a slide for microscopic examination from a culture he'd grown from a sample of Timmy's feces. He hurried up the wide stairway of the medical hall to the second floor where Rob Tate had his three pathology labs, the best facilities in the entire school. In the beginning, Rob had two laboratories, one for normal pathology, the other for abnormal pathology. The third room had once been Richard's lab, but he had let Rob talk him into moving the chemistry lab to the basement, and in its place Rob had installed a lab for bacteriology.

With all that room, Rob still complained because of the architect's lack of practical knowledge of the requirements of a medical school, saying the labs were inadequate in arrangement and size, though he admitted the lighting was superb in all the rooms except Will Kelly's dissecting lab where it was needed the most. Luckily when he came to the medical school from Pennsylvania, Rob had brought with him his own collection of slides, both of pathological tissues and normal tissues, and a collection of tube cultures of some important bacteria, and a microtome.

Rob was like the rest of them, a charter faculty member who'd struggled from the beginning to keep the school going and indeed to improve it as quickly as possible. And, like the rest of them, had one goal in mind, to turn out the best damned doctors in the country.

Richard strode into the pathology lab and on through to the bacteriology lab where he found all two hundred and twenty-five pounds of the pathologist balanced on a stool and bent over an antiquated brass microscope. Rob looked up. "Oh hello, Richard. Sit down," he said.

Richard sat down and removed his derby and plopped it on Rob's table as the pathologist pivoted around to face him. "You have a question mark on your face."

"I've been x-raying since seven this morning and my whole body feels like a question mark. Have you much knowledge of *Salmonella typhosa?*"

"Typhoid bacilli? I certainly do."

Rob scratched under his beard as he always did when bacilli of any kind were mentioned, as if the very thought of it made him itch. He watched as Richard drew from his pocket the slide he'd prepared by taking a sample of Timothy Jacobson's feces, placing it in a culture medium, and isolating the bacilli from the feces by letting the bacilli grow in the medium, then smearing the growth and fixing it on the slide, then staining it with his own preparation. "You don't have a patient you suspect of having typhoid do you?" Rob asked.

Richard said, "Heavy rains all the month of June, and early heat. What we all feared. The patient has high temperature, diarrhea, abdominal pain, anorexia. Could be just dysentery, but I don't think so. See what you think."

Tate was not a man given to swearing, but the expression on his face as he took the slide from Richard showed what he was thinking and it wasn't Sunday School thoughts. He pivoted around to his microscope, removed the slide he'd been viewing when Richard came in, and inserted the one Richard had just given him. "I'd give my right arm for the new oil immersion lenses, Richard, and if my wife didn't need a new washing machine so badly—she still uses a scrub board—I'd buy a new microscope for the lab and fit it with the new lenses." He tilted the mirror to catch the light coming from the window, clicked the selected objective into place, applied his eye to the lens and began adjusting the instrument. "The slide I was viewing when you came in was *Necator americanus*, the ova of the hookworm, which, as you'll remember, I discovered," he said. "We've a continuous endemic plague of it all across the South, I've decided."

"You did that with this poor equipment and still didn't get any recognition?"

"Ha!" Rob shifted on his stool, still adjusting the microscope, his eye still peering through the lens. "What is it that you mix up down there in the basement that stinks to heaven every time the Board of Regents meets here, Richard?"

Richard leaned back in his chair. "I'm surprised you didn't recognize the odor. It's the same thing you learned to do as a freshman. I evaporate ammonia and hydrochloric acid which becomes hydrogen sulphide gas."

"And which almost drives us all from the building crying and coughing."

"Can you think of a better way to demonstrate to the board the need for better ventilation hoods in the chemistry lab?"

"It didn't work this year either did it?"

"No."

Rob sighed. "Richard, my friend, the slide which you prepared so ably with your new stain is an excellent example of *Salmonella typhi*."

"Blast!"

Rob raised his head and looked at him. "You'll have to isolate the patient immediately."

"He's an eight-year-old boy in a family of five children, he's dehydrated with high temperature, so I've sent him to the hospital and given strict isolation instructions. Also, his mother seems to be demonstrating symptoms, so I admitted her to the hospital and isolated her too. Because I believe, as you do, that typhoid can be transmitted from person to person somehow, as well as by contamination of food and water."

"I'd swear to that. Now come and see the slide yourself and learn the enemy well, for this stain of yours gives a clear picture. I'm experimenting with your other stains too, by the way."

Richard stood up, bent over the microscope, and applied his eye to the instrument's lens. "I wish you luck."

"Family of your typhoid patients poor?"

"No. Middle income. You know Jacobson's Jewelers. They have indoor plumbing at the house, but the neighbors on both sides have privies."

"Hmmm. Boy must have drank contaminated water at the neighbors."

"Impossible. He's an invalid. A degenerative muscle disease. Never leaves the house."

"Oh Lord, what a pity, Richard. Let's pray this is an isolated case and not the beginning of an epidemic."

Richard straightened and looked at the pathologist. "I already have," he said.

He went to the hospital and visited Timothy first. The diarrhea and abdominal pain had stopped, but his temperature was still fluctuating, and now he was chilling. Richard didn't like his color either. He was very troubled by the time he entered the women's ward, a ward very much like the men's, a huge room with beds lined up down two long walls, a window and mosquito bar at the head of each bed, a chair at its foot, a table in the center of the room serving as the nurses' desk. He took the chair and brought it to the side of Mrs. Jacobson's bed.

She was a stout, swarthy lady with shining black hair gathered neatly into a chignon at the back of her head. Her large, fearful brown eyes studied his expression as he told her that Timmy's diarrhea was better but that his temperature was still going up and down. He then began to explain that the typhoid bacillus could be ingested, by eating contaminated food or drinking contaminated milk or water. He paused, noting that she did not seem to understand, and it occurred to him that if she, a woman of average intelligence and education, could not understand such a thing as contamination and bacteria, how could the uneducated understand? In fact, how could anyone understand unless they were taught? The professors had made lofty assumptions, demanding that the people of Galveston remove their privies and drain their ponds, and all the while they weren't educating them as to *why* these things should be done. How *do* you explain that an invisible bacteria can be carried on the legs of a fly from a diseased cow to the platter of warm fish on the table? The doctors barely understood bacteria's relationship to disease themselves. How could they expect even the most educated men in Galveston to understand? It was no wonder his and Isaac Cline's articles were ignored by both the aloof city management and the puzzled citizenry.

He leaned toward her and asked, "Mrs. Jacobson, do you know what bacteria is?"

"No. I only know it is a disease you can't see except maybe with a microscope."

"That's almost correct. Now what I'm trying to do is establish where you and Timmy picked up this typhoid bacteria. I would like you to tell me first about your cistern."

"I understand," she said. "I will try, Dr. Morrison. The cistern is located on a platform behind the house. Our house is a two-story frame. The cistern is located under one of the angles of the roof where rain water washes down two slopes into a gutter and then pours into the cistern. Our cistern is screened because that's the city ordinance."

"And you do not use the cistern anymore for drinking water?"

"No."

"How about for washing?"

"No more. The water from that cistern never enters our house. We keep it only for emergencies. In case the pipe breaks that carries water from the wells across the bay, you know, like might happen during a bad hurricane."

"Your house is how old?"

"I'd say fifty years old, but we have new indoor plumbing put in five years ago, practically the first people in Galveston to have it."

Richard rubbed his chin in deep thought. "Your

neighbors have privies?"

The lady blushed and cast her eyes down. "Yes, on both sides and behind. You know how it is, doctor. Most of them have indoor plumbing, but they haven't removed their . . . outhouses. I guess they are like Mr. Jacobson, they don't really trust the city water supply or the invention of indoor water closets. And, like we keep our cistern, they keep their privies. Just in case."

Just in case. . . .

After a few more questions, Richard left Mrs. Jacobson, no more enlightened about the source of her and Timmy's typhoid than before. As far as he knew, there was no way Timothy could have come in contact with contaminated food or water. But there had to be a clue to this. The Jacobsons had four more children, and unless he could find the source. . . .

He decided to go to experienced, scholarly Dr. Matthew Cross, whose colleagues had forgiven him for insisting that their dengue fever epidemic last summer was really yellow fever, because in their most private thoughts, they suspected that he may have been right. Matt was a brilliant diagnostician, had done special studies on typhoid and tropical diseases, and was so well thought of by his contemporaries that he had been elected this year to the honorable position of vice-president of the American Medical Association.

Somberly, Matt looked up from the papers on his desk as Richard entered his office. "Richard," he said, "come in. Sit down."

Richard obeyed, plopped his derby on Matt's desk.

"I know what you came for," Matt said. "You've questions about your two typhoid cases eh?"

"You're quite perceptive."

"Not at all. Because if you hadn't come to me, I'd have come to you. The contaminated water problem in this town has been bothering me the same as it has you." Matt placed his arms on his big desk. "Well, what do you think?"

"The nurse at John Sealy said you have a case of typhoid too. What do *you* think?"

"First, I don't think my patient had contact with yours."

"Which means there may be more than one source of typhoid in town," Richard said. "Where? From what source did our patients contract typhoid?"

Frowning in thought, Matt opened the drawer of his desk and took out a box of cigars and held it open to Richard.

"No thank you, I only smoke the pipe."

"I know, but I had to be polite." He took out a cigar, shut the lid, and put the box back into his drawer saying, "Ever smoked one of those dinky cigarette things they've come up with, Richard?"

He nodded as he got his pipe out of one pocket, his tobacco pouch out of the other. "Jud Mason offered me one he had made once, saying he thought they were better on the respiratory system than cigars or pipes." Richard tapped tobacco into the bowl of his pipe and pulled the string to close the tobacco pouch with his teeth and stuffed it back into his coat pocket. Then he struck a match and held it to the tobacco in the pipe, puffed until the tobacco was lit, waved out his match, and tossed it into the trash basket beside Matt's desk. "The cigarette is too much trouble. All that pouring of tobacco into those little papers and rolling and licking to seal the tobacco in. By the time you've done with all that, you're out of the notion of smoking." He puffed languidly for a few seconds and said, "It's too much trouble. It'll never catch on."

They smoked in silence for a moment, then Matt said, "My patient got typhoid from cistern water, Richard. Washed her dishes in cistern water."

"Underground cistern?"

"Yes."

"Seepage."

"Undoubtedly."

"Is typhoid fomite-borne?"

"Who's to say? I think it is. I think it can be carried in dust through the air."

"Vector-borne?"

"Yes. Flies, mosquitoes, maybe even roaches and water bugs."

"Suppose out of a family of seven, only two contract typhoid. They have a cistern, but it's built up off the ground on a platform, is screened, and isn't used for household water. Dust isn't a problem; they live near the west end of town where standing water is the problem. The mother doesn't use the cistern water for drinking or cleaning. The boy is an invalid and never leaves the house. How did he contract typhoid?"

"The mother has typhoid?"

"Yes, but didn't begin to have symptoms until several days after the boy did. She's not the source."

261

"Hmmmm."

"It has to be something brought into the house which they ate or drank."

"Not necessarily. I think typhoid can be transmitted by a person who is carrying the disease, but doesn't show symptoms. Just a theory, you understand. But that person would have to handle the dishes or the food, because the typhoid bacillus has to be ingested."

Richard smoked and thought and said, "We could solve the typhoid problem here, Matt, with the minds we have, if only we had the money and the equipment to back us up."

"And the tropical fevers too, Richard. Pompous of us to say so, but true. However, look at Will Kelly. He's gone ahead and developed an embalming formula and process that's already becoming well-known and used in other medical schools all over the country, in spite of his lack of funds and equipment. The process may even end up being used by undertakers. And before long, embalming may become the rule instead of the exception. It may even be required because it kills disease in the—" He paused. "Richard?"

He raised his brows.

"How near the cemetery do your patients live?"

Richard puffed and thought. "Seepage?"

Cross nodded.

"They don't live close enough for that."

Cross looked disappointed. "Well, Rob Tate did some microscopic exams on the tissues of some of Will's embalmed cadavers and the tissues showed no disease. That's why Will can keep that dead house full of cadavers out behind the medical hall without it being a danger. Ever wonder what would happen if we had a hurricane that tore up Will's horror house?''

"You'd have a few ignorant people swimming the bay for the mainland, that's for certain.''

"And one professor of Principles and Practices of Medicine,'' Matt said, tapping the ashes off his cigar into the trash can. "Ghastly.''

Richard got out his watch, took note of the time, snapped the cover shut, and stuffed it back into his pocket. Then he stood up and knocked the tobacco out of his pipe into Matt's wastebasket. "I think I'll take a ride over to Avenue O to visit Mr. Jacobson and look around his place a bit.''

"Good luck, Richard. I wish I could have helped you more.''

"With all the studies you've done and papers you've written, I expected more help from you, Matt.''

"Be gone!'' Cross laughed. "At least I know dengue fever from yellow fever when I see it.''

"You haven't convinced me. I think you paid that Spaniard from the government last summer just to say you were right about the yellow fever.''

"On my salary? I can't even pay my grocer. If we go another two years again without a raise in pay, I'll have to get a tin cup and go 'round to you other professors and beg for handouts.''

"Let me know when you do,'' Richard said, "And I'll get my tin cup and go with you.''

It was risky taking Beth, but she wanted to go for a

drive, so she put on her hat and they took the buggy and the little bay trotter, driving under the tunnel of live oaks on Avenue I to Tremont, then south on Tremont, then west on Avenue O, while Beth chatted continually, barely taking a breath.

"Mildred Crabtree led a group of the Women's Temperance Union today and they went to some saloons on Strand and stood out in front singing hymns," she said.

"What was that supposed to do?"

Elizabeth shrugged. "Remind the patrons of the saloons about God, I suppose."

"What's God got to do with saloons?"

"Mildred thinks drinking is one of the most evil things one can do. And you know I really had to listen to a temperance sermon from her after our party in June. She found out we served champagne. I told her then that drinking was no sin as long as one doesn't drink to excess, until they're intoxicated."

"*Then* it's a sin?"

"Well, it's not exactly respectable, Richard."

"Next thing, Mildred Crabtree will be singing hymns in front of our house."

"Then I shall have Shad play the piano for her so she won't be off key," she laughed. "But seriously, we do have to be careful. Otherwise, we'll get a reputation in the neighborhood for being wine-bibbers."

"Bah. What we do in the confines of our own house is our own business."

"But it doesn't always stay in our house. Sometimes it goes down the street in a carriage singing in the rain."

"Does it?"

"Or comes up to bed wobbly on its feet."

"What happens in our bedroom is *also* our own affair."

"Richard!"

Smiling, he drew the carriage to a halt outside the Jacobson's house. The house was a typical two-story frame, painted white and built the usual five feet off the ground on a stone foundation, with huge hollyhocks blooming in the yard and honeysuckle growing on the fence. Every other house in the neighborhood was similar and reminded Elizabeth of the pictures she drew as a child—blue sky, white houses in a row, flowers, trees, white picket fences in front.

Mr. Jacobson was a short man with kindly eyes and dark beard, who let them in the house with the same ceremony with which he might have admitted the King and Queen of England, and introduced them to his four children; two little girls, six and ten, and two boys, four and twelve.

The Morrisons sat down in the immaculate parlor and Mr. Jacobson and Richard talked first of the weather, the shrimping this year, then of what Richard came for. He began to question Jacobson, kindly but steadily, and Elizabeth soon became uncomfortable listening to questions about privies, water closets, diarrhea, abdominal pain, sick neighbors. And growing restless, she looked around her, smiling at the two little girls peering shyly from around the door in the hallway, the smaller child Mary with two fingers in her mouth. Then at the boys, the older pretending to play with a toy pistol, the other under the parlor table watching her solemnly.

Elizabeth beckoned to the girls with her finger, and in a few moments they came to her shyly with their paper dolls.

"Mama bought the paper dolls in New Orleans," Rebecca, the older of the girls said. "But we played with them so much their clothes all tore up."

"So we gotta play wif dem wifout clothes," six-year-old Mary said soberly.

The smallest boy giggled and hid his face in the rag rug near her chair, while Eli, the older boy, blushed painfully.

"Their names are Lucy and Suzy," Rebecca said.

Elizabeth examined the well-worn cardboard dolls and said, "Do you have some paper and pencil?"

Mary nodded.

"If I may borrow some, I'll make Lucy and Suzy some new clothes."

Rebecca ran out of the room and came back shortly with tablet, pencil, colored pencils, and scissors, and Elizabeth moved her chair up to the parlor table and began to make the paper dolls a wardrobe.

Once, Mr. Jacobson offered her and Richard tea, but they refused, being afraid to take anything by mouth, and Richard continued his conversation with Jacobson while Elizabeth designed dresses, shoes, capes, and coats and the girls happily colored and cut them out.

By the time Richard and Mr. Jacobson went to the back yard, the boys were positively miserable with jealousy because of her attention to the girls. So she left the girls to their coloring and went with the boys through the long hallway to the back yard, where she had to exclaim over

Eli's collection of sea shells, examine a crotchety sand crab in a jar, and admire a smirking nanny-goat in a pen under a huge magnolia tree.

As she stood beside the pen where the goat had commenced to scratch her head on the fence post, she looked up to see Richard strolling about the yard with Mr. Jacobson, and she was suddenly struck by his fine appearance, handsome in his suit and bowler, looking up at the Jacobson's roof, at the cistern painted green, at the flourishing vegetable garden, at the neighbors' yard next door. And she handed the jar with its unhappy sand crab back to Eli and went over to join him, her heart inexplicably full of affection for him.

He was noting the distance from the neighbor's outdoor privies to Jacobson's cistern. No dirt street here, they were better paved than the Strand. No exposed dirt to speak of.

He looked at the cistern again, the privies, and determined that because the prevailing winds were amost always from the Gulf, the cistern was generally upwind from the privies. Maybe privies weren't the problem then. But what? A carrier, as Matt Cross had suggested? His eyes fell upon the children beside Elizabeth. . . . *Children beside Elizabeth.* . . .

"I almost lost the garden last spring, Doctor," Mr. Jacobson was saying. "Remember that week when it rained so heavy? Well, water stood in my yard and the yard next door for five days."

Richard brought his gaze from the children to Mr. Jacobson's face. "Water stood in . . . both yards?"

"Five days."

The neighbor's yard was higher than the Jacobson's; and more importantly, was crowned by a neatly painted privy. And undoubtedly underneath the privy was a cesspool, and fifty years of filth. Seepage. He looked at the neighbor's yard, then at Jacobson's. "The garden," he said.

Mr. Jacobson, a man of better-than-average intelligence, looked at his beloved cabbages, the turnip greens, the lacy carrot tops, the spinach, then at the privy in his neighbor's yard, and suddenly his face contorted in agony. He put his hand up to cover it. "Oh, Lord God," he breathed. "I'll plow up the garden, plow under the vegetables."

"Cooked vegetables wouldn't be a problem. And besides, we can't be sure the garden is the source of contamination."

"No. It is the source. I'll plow them all under."

Slowly, the three began to walk toward the house with Richard saying, "But if it's the vegetable garden, why were only your wife and Timmy infected?"

"Because. I see it now. The missus and Timmy are the only ones in our house who will eat carrots raw and the spinach raw and the cabbage raw. I can't eat raw vegetables because they give me stomach pain. The other little kids, they don't like the vegetables raw, but we try to make them eat some anyway." Mr. Jacobson shook his head in distress, his eyes filling with tears as he plodded to the house. "Every meal we say, 'Eat, Eli. Eat, Mary. Eat your carrots because they are good for you. Eat your slaw, Rebecca. Eat your spinach, Joseph. See how Timmy eats his spinach like a good boy?' Every day to the little kids, 'Eat your vegetables. Eat your vegetables.'" Something like a sob escaped Jacobson and he said, "We were only trying to keep them healthy, Dr. Morrison, like the books say. And all the time we were urging them to their death."

There was no more they could say to comfort the little jeweler, for he had retreated within himself in an agony of self-flagellation. And when Richard and Elizabeth left the house at last, he was still shaking his head as he shut the door, murmuring, "Eat your vegetables, eat your vegetables. . . ."

In the carriage going home, Richard put his arm around Elizabeth because they were both melancholy, and said, "Beth, typhoid's not very often fatal. Only about one in eight or ten die of it. Timmy Jacobson will be alright. So will his mother."

She smiled, but didn't reply. Well, he tried to shield her from all this, the unpleasantness of his profession, but he'd failed this time out of selfishness. Because he had wanted to be with her. Because he wanted her.

On a whim, he drove the carriage to the beach road and they watched the sun sinking low, riding the crest of the waves to the southwest, turning the beach momentarily to gold and her hair to fire. Richard said simply, "I love you, Beth."

All the way home she was silent, and once they were home, she dismissed Prim and Shad for the evening and turned to him, her back against the back door, her face flushed, her eyes glazed and very blue. And they stood looking at each other, in a moment so silent they could hear only their own breathing.

"Richard," she said softly. "I want a baby. Make me a child, Richard. Make me a baby."

He couldn't move for a moment, and then he took her into his arms and they went up the stairs together, and there he tried. Loving her, all of her, giving no thought to the inhibitions of society or the improbabilities of perversions, letting her own febrile passions guide his and not once or twice but several times all night and into the morning until they lay damp and drunk with spent passion, and a release that transported them both into a soft senseless slumber.

Fifteen

The telephone rang in the Morrison entry hall, rang incessantly until Richard stumbled stupefied down the stairs and mumbled into the receiver, "Dr. Morrison."

"Hello! Is this Dr. Morrison?" came a feminine voice over the line. "Hello! Hello!" There was so much crackling on the line that Richard could barely hear. The voice faded in and out, the line sputtered, and then the thing went dead altogether. He hung up the receiver mumbling to himself and started back up the stairs. The grandfather clock struck two.

When he was halfway up the stairs, the telephone rang again and he went back down and shouted into the receiver, "Dr. Morrison."

"Oh Doctor, thank God," came the voice again. "This is nurse Brumley at John Sealy. Doctor, Timothy Jacobson is vomiting black emesis and there's black stool in the bed."

Richard was fully awake now, but couldn't think what

271

to do. Perforated bowel was a complication of typhoid and would cause hemorrhage into the abdominal cavity which, if not immediately fatal, was almost always fatal within a few days. "I'll be there in fifteen minutes," he said.

He dressed quietly and was able to tiptoe from the room without waking Beth. In the kitchen he penned her a note telling where he was going. Then, pulling on his coat, he hurried to the carriage house where he found Shadrack lying in the hay in a corner asleep with a whiskey bottle in his hand.

Upon hearing Blitz whinny, Shad woke, and while Richard was taking the harness from the hook on the wall, he staggered to his feet. "Oh, Dr. Richard. I'm drunk and I admit it," he said mournfully. "I got a toothache an cain't stand no more pain."

He helped Richard hitch Blitz to the buggy saying the same thing over and over; and once, Richard paused and looked closely at him, seeing the swelled jaw, and the real pain in his eyes. "Why didn't you ask me for medicine, Shad?"

"Didn't start hurtin bad till you went to bed, Dr. Richard. Then I didn't had no heart to wake you. I swear, Dr. Richard, ain't touched non of the bottle since Miss Lizbeth laid down the law. Figured if I took one drop might take a passel o' others. Dr. Richard, this ol' black nigger been sober as a—"

Richard turned quickly to face Shad and said, "Shut your mouth. Mrs. Morrison would be angry to hear you talk like that." Then he said softly, "When she wakes, tell her to give you the bottle of pain elixir from the bathroom, and you take the amount it shows on the label. Only the amount it shows and no more. Get her to help you. Meantime, get sobered up before you take it or we'll have to carry you to the cemetery tomorrow. Do you hear?" He climbed into the buggy and took up the reins. And before he urged Blitz out of the carriage house and into the darkness added, "If I'm not back by breakfast, you take yourself over to Dr. Peterson and see if he can pull that tooth. Mrs. Morrison will give you the money."

"Yassuh, Dr. Richard," Shad said as Richard slapped the reins, and Blitz tore down the drive into the alley and off into the black streets, his hooves splatting reassuringly on the surface of the street which had been newly paved after the spring deluge back in June.

He had seen that Timmy was admitted to one of the hospital's private rooms instead of the children's ward behind the hospital, and tonight, he was glad he had; for when he arrived, unbuttoning his coat as he rushed into the room, the nurses were cleaning up the worst mess he had seen in years. Their superintendent had been awakened and had graciously come to supervise Timmy's care while awaiting his arrival.

One look at Timmy and the room, and Richard determined that the child, pale, crying, vomiting, was certainly hemorrhaging internally. He asked a few questions of the nurses—when the vomiting had begun, what Timmy's pulse rate was, his temperature. All the while knowing that only a drastic measure could save the boy—surgery.

But surgery was dangerous. Richard had done some surgery in his practice, but nothing of this magnitude.

And only one of the other doctors did surgery this dramatic, Bert Jackson. It did not take him long to make up his mind, for without surgery, Timmy was most certainly lost. With it, he had a slight chance. Richard had no choice.

He rushed out of the room and down the stairs to the foyer where a telephone was mounted on the wall near the nurses' reception desk, snatched up the receiver, cranked the bell, and waited until the operator said, "Number please."

"Hello! Central? Please ring 849, please." He waited, ignoring the nurses who came rushing out of some of the patients' rooms to see who was shouting in the hospital in the middle of the night; and in the meantime, the line went dead. He cranked the thing again and waited. "Central? Now listen carefully, Miss. This . . . is . . . an . . . *emergency,* so do not let this line go dead. Now please call—Now, Miss, be calm and listen to me. Please ring 849. Yes, thank you." He waited, looked down at his shoes.

Bert Jackson's voice came on the line. "Hello, Dr. Jackson here."

"Bert? Richard Morrison. Sorry to wake you."

"Quite alright, Richard. What's the matter?"

"I've an emergency here at John Sealy. Typhoid patient with perforated bowel."

"I say, Richard. Is it the little boy?"

"Yes."

"Oh God. Hemorrhaging is he?"

"Yes. Blood in the emesis and feces. I don't think he can make it through surgery, Bert, but we've got to try."

Richard touched the tips of his fingers to his head. "I'll call his father. . . ." Hello! Hello! Bert?"

"Yes, Richard, old boy. No need to shout, we've a good line. I'm just thinking. If he dies we could be blamed and not the perforated bowel, I assure you."

"Do we have a choice?"

"No. Just wanted to remind you. It's the risk we take as surgeons, you know. But listen, now Richard, I want you to assist me, to give the anesthetic. Will you?"

"Of course. Of course."

"Good boy. I'll be there shortly. Meanwhile prepare the patient for surgery."

"Consider it done."

As Richard dressed in the surgical garb which consisted of a white smock and trousers, he kept telling himself again and again that Timothy might live, thanks to modern surgery. The discovery and use of anesthetics only twenty years or so ago had made the miracles wrought by surgery possible, and thanks to donations and funding by local city philanthropists, John Sealy Hospital was fairly well-equipped with the latest instruments and equipment. Richard thanked God for that. He also thanked God for Bert.

Dr. Bertram Jackson was only thirty-five that year but already well-respected by his colleagues at the medical school. Born, raised, and educated in England, Jackson probably had the best education of any of the professors at the school, because he had obtained both a bachelor of medicine and a bachelor of surgery, and had gained his teaching experience at Manchester Hospital as a resident surgeon. He was a strict disciplinarian when teaching students in the operating room at the medical hall, and tolerated no inattentiveness or lethargy. Students must be on their toes every second.

After Richard had dressed, he decided to wear one of the cotton surgical masks in order to prevent his inhaling the ether and because he was unaccountably uneasy being so close to an open surgical wound without wearing one. Usually no one wore a mask in surgery but the surgeon, so in order to prevent Jackson's thinking he wanted to steal a bit of this thunder, he explained his preference to Bert before he went in to give the ether to Timmy. Jackson nodded saying, "Very well, Richard, so long as you speak up loudly through the thing so that I can hear what you have to say."

While Richard put Timothy to sleep by fitting the cotton-filled ether cone over his face and dropping drops of liquid ether into the funnel of the cone, Dr. Jackson was carefully washing his hands at the sink in the room, then dipping them in a solution of phenol, and drying them on a sterile towel. Two nurses and the nursing superintendent, dressed in clean white uniforms, had been assigned to assist, to pass instruments to Bert and run any necessary errands.

Bert came to the table, hands folded almost reverently, gave a hand signal because talking was kept at a minimum during surgery, and a nurse handed him the proper instrument. He carefully made an incision through skin and fasia just below Timmy's umbilicus, and as the wound filled with blood, sponged the area with sea sponges, and sutured the bleeders as deftly as Beth stitched her needlework.

Richard noticed that the amphitheater which surrounded the surgical room was filling with medical and
nursing students rousted out of their beds for the
purpose of seeing a difficult emergency surgery, though
it was just after four in the morning.

The surgery room was surrounded on three sides with
rows of theater seats, the floor was tile instead of wood,
and the tables of instruments were wrought iron, painted
white. The electric lights here came from fixtures
hanging from the tall ceiling.

It bothered Richard that some of the people in the
gallery were coughing and that one nurse kept sneezing.
*If bacilli can be airborne on a speck of dust, why can't they be
airborne on droplets of water through coughing or sneezing?*
He writhed a little inside the starched smock.

Jackson had entered the abdominal cavity now which
Richard could see was filled with fecal matter, and he
peered at him over his mask. "Don't like the looks of it,
Dr. Morrison."

"Nor do I."

"What say?"

"Nor do I."

Jackson sponged some of the matter carefully,
unavoidably getting some of it on his bare hands. Then he
took from the nurse the needle and kitgut—or "catgut,"
as everybody called it—and began to suture the perfora-
tion in the bowel. Carefully, painstakingly Jackson
sutured. Then he sponged a little more. At last he began
to close the wound, and Richard removed the ether cone
from Timothy's face.

Outside the amphitheater, as the little patient was

being taken to his room, Jackson pulled off his mask and regarded Richard gravely. He shook his head, "I say, Richard, that was a nasty hole and the abdominal cavity was filled with stinking material. I don't give the boy much of a chance."

Richard didn't either and went to his office on Mechanic, hung his THE DOCTOR WILL NOT BE IN TODAY sign on the door, and went back to the hospital to join Mr. Jacobson at Timmy's bedside.

The boy woke at noon, but could not respond when his father spoke his name. A little after two o'clock, Timothy Jacobson died quietly in his sleep.

Richard went home after that and found Shad had gotten his tooth pulled, and though still red-eyed and lethargic from his ordeal, told Richard he was in "fine fettle, considerin'" and that Miz Lizbeth had gone visiting.

Feeling desolate and out of sorts, Richard went to his library and sat in his horn chair for several minutes, staring out the window across the room. Then he got up, went to his desk, took a sheet of paper out of the drawer, dipped his pen in the inkwell, and began writing.

Ten minutes later, Prim stuck her head in the door and said, "Dr. Richard, you best be eatin' you a bit of somethin' lest you faint and fall on the flo. Let Prim bring you a nice piece o' cheese and a slice o' light bread."

"No, thank you, Prim."

"Miss Lizbeth will be mad if you don't eat nothin' all day. How 'bout me bringin' you a piece o' hot apple pie?"

"I'll just wait 'til dinner, Prim."

"Then how 'bout a cup o' nice hot tea? Dr. Richard,

you got to put somethin' in your stomach for it to eat, or that stomach will end up eatin' you."

Richard looked up, pen poised above the paper on which he had been writing. "Alright," he said. He picked up the paper to read what he'd written:

A little boy died today. He was eight years old and a victim of a degenerative muscle disease that had left him an invalid since the age of three. But this little boy did not die of the muscle disease. He died of typhoid. To our knowledge, his muscle disease could not have been prevented, but his contracting typhoid could. He was a victim of the apathy of Galveston's citizens.

Richard looked up as Prim brought the cup of tea, then his gaze drifted out the window beyond the veranda to the young magnolia in the yard, to the vine on the fence. For what purpose was he writing this, as a purge for his own miserable feelings? At first he'd thought he was writing it to be published in the Galveston newspapers. But what did Galveston care about a little boy who had died of typhoid? What had that to do with anybody else?

Richard wadded the paper up and tossed it into his waste basket. Like Isaac Cline had said, *The island seems to cast a spell of euphoria upon its people; the climate is an opiate that renders them insensible to the dangers of sea, sickness and satan.*

Isaac was a voice crying in the wilderness, reminding the people that the city was vulnerable to the ravages of the sea. The ministers of Galveston and even Mildred

PATRICIA RAE

Crabtree kept reminding them of satan. Then who was
left to remind them of the reality of sickness in their fair
isle? The physicians.

He took up his pen again, dipped it into the inkwell on
his desk, and began the story of Timothy Jacobson all
over again.

July fourth, the German band played in Central Park
for the city's annual Fourth of July picnic. Strangers
came up to Richard and Elizabeth to compliment him on
his story about the little boy which had been published in
the *Galveston News*. Others were overheard to say that of
course a doctor with a good salary could have an indoor
water closet, but what about those who couldn't afford
it? Should they be practically accused of murder? After
dark that day the citizens of Galveston left the park in
droves and went to the beach area where Mr. Dealey had
set up a fireworks display, and after an hour of lemonade,
popcorn, and fireworks, those who cared to dance went to
the dance held in the beach pavillion.

The favorite talk of the day was that on June 30th,
General Shafter's troops had begun their advance on
Santiago, and on July first (or second, nobody knew for
certain) former Secretary of the Navy, Theodore Roosevelt, who had resigned his position on the cabinet and
had been appointed lieutenant colonel over a ragtag volunteer cavalry called the Rough Riders, advanced
against, and helped to drive out, the Spanish from Cuba's
San Juan Hill. The mood in Galveston that Fourth of July
was patriotic . . . and cautious. The immense confidence
which the American people had displayed in their ability

to drive the Spanish from Cuba had mellowed. For it had become apparent already that though the United States had a better navy than the Spanish, her army was ill-prepared, ill-equipped, and just plain ill. Word was that more Americans were dying in the Philippines from tropical diseases than from battle wounds.

Then, as July grew hotter, so did the war. On July 17th, General José Toral surrendered Santiago; on July 25th, America's General Miles and his troops occupied Puerto Rico. Then early in the morning of July 23rd, Richard woke to see the south window of their bedroom aglow, and when he looked out, saw the entire sky alight. In the distance he could hear the clanging of fire engines, and he woke Beth to tell her he was leaving the house to see what was on fire. Thoughts of the tragic forty-block fire in 1885 caused him anxiety as he dressed to go out. He met Joe Bob outside the house and they left together. When they returned at seven in the morning, Melissa and Elizabeth were having tea in the kitchen. Richard told them that Nicholas Clayton's beach hotel had burned to the ground.

On August 12, Spain signed a preliminary peace treaty, and the war was over.

There were mixed emotions in Galveston at the ending of the war. Some thought that the war had been too short; others felt there should have been no war to begin with and were glad the whole silly fracas was over. One of the favorite stories that circulated in Galveston about the war was about a Civil War veteran, who had fought on the side of the Confederacy, "Fighting Joe" Wheeler, who, during the confusion and mayhem of one of the battles in Cuba, had shouted, "We've got the damn Yankees on the run!"

"That just shows you what I've said all along," Elizabeth said over her needlework one day when Richard told the story to her. "The Rebels continue to call northerners Yankees because they're still fighting the Civil War."

In mid-October, the Jolly Sixteen elected to sponsor an outing for the senior students whose previous three years' grades fell within the top ten category, to celebrate the beginning of their final year at the medical school. The students were allowed to bring one friend each, and as it turned out, only six brought their favorite girls. When the old city physician Dr. Larry Brice heard about the outing, he offered the Brice pleasure yacht, the *Charlamagne*, provided the Jolly Sixteen could produce a yachtsman knowledgeable enough about sailing craft to negotiate the bay in safety, to carry the party to the western end of the island where it was decided the clambake should take place. The ladies in the auxiliary looked immediately at Elizabeth, who possessed, in the form of her brother-in-law, the perfect candidate for captain of the *Charlemagne*.

So on the night when Damon blustered into the Morrison's back parlor carrying an enormous roll of preliminary sketches which he and Joe Bob had worked up of his Big Ship—which now seemed to occupy his every thought—Elizabeth took advantage of his expansive mood and asked him to sail the *Charlemagne* for the outing. When he was assured that both Richard and Elizabeth were going, he agreed to do it. The other brave

persons who volunteered to be chaperones were Cora
Mae Cline and her husband, Isaac.

But on the morning of the outing, the telephone rang
early in the Morrison household and Richard came into
the bedroom where Elizabeth was pinning on her hat to
say that Mrs. Thornhill, alas, was in labor.

"Oh Richard!" she exclaimed, stamping her feet in
dismay. "Mrs. Thornhill just *had* a baby not too long
ago."

"That was nine months ago, Beth. But don't be upset.
You can go to the clambake without me. You already
know some of the students, and you'll be with Cora Mae
and she's one of your favorite people. She'll keep you
company."

"But everybody will have a beau or a husband but
me."

He smiled and put on his hat, watching her throw a
little girl's temper tantrum, jerking the scarf of her hat
tight under her chin in dismay, and said, "Beth, Damon
can substitute for me."

She froze and turned slowly and looked at him, but he
was already going toward the door saying, "I'll have Shad
drive you to the pier." And then he was gone.

Sixteen

As the *Charlemagne*, with her billowing white sails, her mermaid figurehead, her handsome captain at the helm, and her eager students—practiced if not proficient at hoisting and furling sail—plied across the bay and back down the island, poor Cora Mae remained bent over the starboard rail retching in green and purple agony, wanting nothing to do with Elizabeth or her husband Isaac, or the students or life itself. It never occurred to Elizabeth to get seasick, so she enjoyed the companionship of the students and the six girls who accompanied them. She also became acquainted with Isaac Cline, a genial middle-aged fellow with brown mustaches, twinkling eye, and a perpetual pipe in his hand.

Dr. Cline had just returned from Mexico, having been sent there during the war by the chief of the United States Weather Service. President McKinley had been more afraid of West Indian hurricanes than of the Spanish Navy and needed the best weather forecaster possible in the area. He also needed a diplomat and Isaac turned out to be both. Since the Yucatan Peninsula was only 150 miles from Cuba, it was considered a strategic place for establishing a weather station, and Cline was chosen to persuade the President of Mexico to allow the U.S. to set up weather stations on the peninsula and along the Mexican coast. He was successful, and five stations had been set up. When the brief war was over, Cline was allowed to come home.

Most of the voyage, Elizabeth's attention was divided between listening to Isaac talk, of handing poor Cora Mae a damp handkerchief for her head (Oh, go away, Elizabeth—thank you for the handkerchief—and let me die in peace) and of being caught up in the antics of the students and their sweethearts.

Marvin Haversham, who she knew as the nephew of Galveston's own Dr. Holcomb, did not have a girl, but he brought with him a hand organ which he played well and on which he accompanied the students as they sang some of the merrier popular songs. The main one which they kept repeating was, "Throw Him Down McCloskey":

> "Throw him down, McCloskey, was the battle cry,
> Throw him down, McCloskey, you can lick him if
> you try. . . ."

Or there were times when he played something all to himself while the others gave their attention to spinning yarns, telling anecdotes, taking turns at the helm, and getting by with whispering to their girls, or winking at somebody else's when they thought their chaperones weren't looking.

Elizabeth did not consider herself much older than they and so was often as much in the fray as the students, surrounded by them during the entire voyage. They referred to her as "Old Beaker's Wife," or "As-a-Matter-Of-Fact's Lady." It was at this time that she first heard of the two nicknames which the students had given Richard.

She also enjoyed watching Damon at the helm, easy-going, squinting across the bay, the wind rumpling his dark hair, his open-necked, white shirt tight against his broad chest, occasionally throwing back his head to laugh at the monkeyshines of the young men. Something inside her ached for . . . something of him. Something she could not, would not consciously confront. Once during the morning when she came to lean against the mast near where he stood at the helm, and, catching her hat when a gust of wind threatened to blow it off, she said, "I notice you're not sailing out of the bay."

"And you'll also notice I'm staying well in sight of shore," he said.

"Why? I thought we might sail out into the Gulf."

"I'll not do that for several reasons, but the main one is that I'm responsible for nineteen people aboard this yacht, and this time of year is especially a bad time for squalls. I'm not going to risk getting caught at sea with a bunch of landlubbers."

"But some of the students seem to handle sail well."

"In calm waters. But I don't know what they can do in a storm."

"You really distrust the sea, don't you?"

286

"I hate the sea," he said intensely. Then smiled and looked over at her. "Treacherous as a woman." Watching her hold on to her wide-brimmed hat which was flapping in the breeze like a sail, he said, "Liz, why don't you take that thing off?"

"I can't. I'd burn."

"Pray tell me what's wrong with looking more like an Indian than a lily?"

"I'd freckle too."

"What's wrong with that? There's no way a few freckles can ruin your— Some of the prettiest girls I know have a few freckles."

"And I'll bet you know plenty of girls, Damon."

"Enough." He smiled amusedly at her, their gaze met, held, he looked away. "Mrs. Cline feeling any better?"

"No, poor thing. Perhaps we should land this thing and end her misery."

"Let's do that then. I'm hungry as a bear." He called, "Rolf!"

"Aye, aye, Captain," answered the student who considered himself first mate.

"Take the helm. I need a cigar. Keep her steady as she goes."

"Aye aye, sir."

The yacht stood a mile or so off the island, paralleling it, going west-southwest. Elizabeth staggered a little going back to the stern until Damon took her arm and steadied her until they came to the circle of students. Cora Mae was sitting against the side of the ship, her color less yellow than it had been, and after Elizabeth dampened the handkerchief again with water from the

287

keg and gave it to her, she joined the students who were still listening to Dr. Cline's stories. Damon had just joined them and was holding a match to his cigar, having turned his back to the wind until the thing caught, then sat down beside Isaac.

". . . so I said to the president of Mexico, 'Señor Presidente, to have weather stations along the Mexican coast shall benefit the United States because we can forecast rainstorms and hurricanes and telegraph the information to Washington so that our fleets can avoid the bad weather. Mexico can only benefit from any advantage the U.S. has over Spain.'" Isaac shrugged, "So—"

"So you got your weather stations," a student said.

"I did." Isaac pointed his pipe stem at the student. "There are more ships destroyed by hurricanes in the West Indies than by any other enemy."

The girls were hugging themselves at the thought of storms at sea, which, of course, made sailing all the more thrilling.

Dr. Cline pointed at Damon. "Captain Morrison has seen many a storm, I'll wager. Eh, Captain?"

Damon nodded. "Aye," he said taking the cue along with the limelight. "I've been to Boston, Great Britain, around Cape Horn, through the Suez even, but never have I seen such weather as the West Indian storms."

"Oh tell us about it!" the girls demanded at once, their young faces upturned, reflecting a hopeless infatuation with their dashing captain.

Damon with a serious face began to spin yarns the like of which Elizabeth had never heard. Having read *Two*

Years Before The Mast, she noticed that Damon's tales were so similar, if she hadn't known better, she'd swear he took his own stories right out of the book. Yet, he elaborated more about whales, schools of dolphins, the California coast, his experiences at encountering pirate ships in the open sea, and of a skirmish or two at sea with privateers.

The students listened in awe at the captain's relaxed, easygoing yarning and stole arms around the girls. Damon paused once in order to shout an order to Rolf. The student called back, "Aye, aye, sir."

"But have you ever been in a hurricane?" asked one of the girls, named Sue.

"Several."

"What happened?" asked Sue's friend, Janet.

And Damon lit another cigar and began a new yarn. As the yarn unfolded Elizabeth became aware that he was embellishing it a little, and she looked around the circle of students who were hanging onto his every word; the girls, at least, believing all of it; then she looked at Isaac who met her amused look and winked. Cora was even smiling by then, wanly, over in her corner, undecided whether to continue to be sick or enjoy the voyage.

At last Damon finished his tale and took the helm again. The students, fascinated by the hurricane story, were not yet ready to drop the subject, but Damon began to let some of them take the helm and soon they were caught up in that.

"I didn't know it took such arm muscles," one student said.

"Oh, Captain," sighed one of the girls, "I'll bet you

have *lots* of arm muscles."

What Damon replied to that Elizabeth would have relished knowing, but the students were singing again and the sails were flapping like sheets hanging on the line on a windy day, and she could not hear his reply.

A half hour of sailing across the bay brought them midway down the island and it was time to move in to shore.

The city of Galveston was built on the eastern end of the cigar-shaped island. The west end was populated mostly with a few small farms and dairies, leaving a wide swath of sandy beaches on the coast side, and on the bay side, little inlets, coves, swamps, and a few vacation houses built up on pilings driven deep into the sand.

Damon called orders to "all hands," and watched their struggles as a few made a mess of things, while others, more adept, corrected them. "Look alive, men! Lay aloft and furl the top sails! Clew down the royal yards! Haul down the flying jib! Steady at the helm! Stea-ea-dy."

The *Charlemagne* dropped anchor in Lafitte's Cove and the students lowered the boats into the water and helped the squealing girls with their flapping hats and long skirts into the boats. Rolf, who was a loner, preferred to "read a good book" in the company of a jug of rum and stayed aboard to do anchor watch.

When the bottom of the boats scraped the shore in two or three feet of water, their young men carried them the eight or ten feet to shore. Isaac carried Cora Mae, and there was nothing left for Damon to do but to carry Elizabeth. Somehow, his carrying her struck her as funny and she began to giggle as he waded ashore with her, her arms clinging around his neck.

"Now Liz," he said. "I've never carried a lady like this in my life and I could really consider this romantic if you weren't married to my brother and weren't laughing at me to boot."

"I'm sorry, Damon," she laughed, "but you looked so grim. I guess I'm just getting soft in the head."

He might have replied that her head wasn't the only place on her that was soft, but he didn't. But his thoughts must have showed on his face, for she blushed when he set her down upon the dry land ever so gently. She thanked him, straightened her hat, and went to Cora Mae where she sat on a large log, some of the color having returned to her cheeks. They watched the girls wading from where their beaus had set them down in two or three inches of water. Dutifully, Elizabeth called, "Careful, girls," because they were tending to lift their skirts too high where one could see the lace edges of their drawers—which was probably why the students had set them down in the water instead of on dry land. Her duty done, Elizabeth enjoyed watching the students struggling to pull the huge boats up on the shore while Damon, no longer ship's captain for awhile, laughed at their efforts. Then he and Dr. Cline came to the log where Cora Mae sat and Elizabeth stood, and they all watched the silly youths wading in the shallow water of the cove hunting clams, the girls squealing and pretending to be afraid of the clams and other things they brought up out of the water for them to see.

The whole lot of them had grown younger during the voyage. College cares had fallen away, the results of each young lady's years of cultivating the art of sophistication had vanished. "Better to be young while you can," Isaac said as they stood watching.

When enough clams were gathered, and more, the youths dug pits while the girls gathered kindling, and the fires were lit, embers raked, clams were put on screen wire over the coals in the pit, and Elizabeth and Cora Mae tucked potatoes into the embers. After the girls spread the quilts and tablecloths under the ancient cedar trees, Elizabeth and Cora Mae brought out the other side-dishes, fresh vegetables and fruit, loaves of light bread, cheese, and little cakes. Damon and Isaac set up the kegs of beer and crockery coolers of lemonade. Soon the clam shells had opened and everybody gathered 'round for the feed.

The talk at mealtime was about Jean Lafitte, Galveston's very own pirate. His settlement called Campeche had been established on the east end of the island where the city now was, his house called the Maison Rouge, the remains of which one could still see. What was so fascinating was that just east and south of the very spot where they were now picnicking, the pirate and his men had fought the battle of Three Trees against the Karankawa Indians.

Marvin Haversham, who was the bard among the students because he was the only Galveston resident among them, and was the authority, told the story. "It seems that a hunting party went out from Lafitte's settlement, and among the game they found was a young Indian squaw, which they kidnapped and took back to camp with them. That kind of act wasn't particularly popular with the Karankawas, so they painted themselves up and came down upon the camp, drove all the hunters away except for two, which they killed, and took back to their village with them, and ate."

The girls, being Galveston citizens, had heard the story before, but were extra scared this time because conditions required it, and they oooohed and ahed and some even hid their faces in their hands. The very thought of cannibalistic Indians having once been near the place where they now sat, almost offset the ambivalent thrill of somebody their age being carried off by pirates.

Elizabeth had heard the story before, the day she and Richard picnicked at the grove, but she was inclined to shudder at the thought of the Indians too. And of the pirates.

Damon added his say to the story. "Some say Lafitte buried his treasure near here, and people come digging around and all they've been able to find so far are skeletons."

The girls shuddered and murmured nonsensical things.

Yes, Galveston island had had its share of horrible things; pirates, cannibals, fires, hurricanes. . . .

Sue asked, "Dr. Cline, has Galveston ever had a really bad, bad hurricane in all its history?"

"Indeed she has," Dr. Cline said. "Back in 1867 they tell me."

The students scooted forward, the circle drawing tighter so that no one would miss a single word of Isaac's tale.

"Galveston has been visited by several hurricanes in

her past, but probably the worst in history came in 1867, October third.'' Dr. Cline took out his pipe, the youths who smoked did the same with their pipes and cigars, and all waited expectantly while the doctor filled his pipe and began. ''I believe it was a Wednesday night. The winds had been from the east all day. By Thursday morning the rain started. All day it rained and the wind blew from the east harder and harder. Small trees began to fall and debris blew from buildings. The water in the streets no longer drained and grew deeper and deeper. Folks say you could look out over the city and see water covering the entire island. People waded in water knee deep to find shelter on higher ground, which you know is not really very high, the highest being right around Broadway, a little over eight feet above sea level. The floors of the buildings on the Strand were two to four feet under water. This lasted all day until about three o'clock in the afternoon. At last the rain stopped, but the wind continued into the night. There was a lot of wreckage uptown, debris in the streets, ships torn from their moorings at the wharves.''

Dr. Cline puffed silently a moment while the youths waited. ''Then there was the hurricane of 1886 that was bad, but the town of Indianola over on the mainland took the brunt of it, 100 mile-per-hour winds which left over a hundred-fifty people dead, and so demoralized the town that the people moved away and Indianola died of natural causes, you might say.''

''Ooooo! Can that happen here?'' asked one of the girls.

Elizabeth had noticed a student named Jannock, a

handsome, sullen youth who wore a Stetson hat and boots, and who was, as far as she could tell, the best yachtsman aboard the *Charlemagne* that day. He now spoke up, "It can happen and probably will."

Dr. Cline took the pipe out of his mouth and squinted out across the bay. "Well, I think the island is vulnerable. But it's seen many hurricanes and we've survived fire which devastated forty blocks of the city, so it seems to me that Galveston would die hard."

Jannock said, "Then do you have any idea, Doctor, why the idiotic town of Galveston never built a sea wall?"

There was a stunned silence for a moment, then the attractive Sue Yates exclaimed, "Marshal Jannock! Calling Galveston idiotic is not only ungentlemanly, it's not fair!"

Jannock shrugged. "The city government is stupid, Miss Yates. Galveston lies low in the sea. And does anybody know why it doesn't make an attempt to protect its seaport interests?"

The ladies were all Galvestonians and protested all at once, and something was said in the confusion about Houston, though Elizabeth didn't quite hear what. One of the girls stood up and threw down a clam shell. "My father happens to be on the city council, Mr. Jannock. And I demand that you take back what you said about the city government!"

"I don't retract the truth."

The girl quickly proceeded to remove her shoe and strode toward the youth, wielding it over her head. Jannock held his arms over his head saying, "Hey Sig, get your girl off me, will you?"

The other students were enjoying the scene, half agreeing with Jannock, though they wouldn't say so. All of them except Marvin Haversham were from other cities, either in the state or out of it, and Galveston citizens had been as unreceptive to them as they were to other outsiders. Like the citizens in many other towns in America at the time, Galvestonians weren't any more impressed with institutions of higher learning than they were with insane asylums. This was a situation that Elizabeth had become aware of, but did not understand.

When the clamor died down and Jannock had taken another chew off his plug of tobacco—for he chewed instead of smoked—Isaac said, "The sea wall. Ah yes. I believe it was after the hurricane of 1886, the one that devastated Indianola, that the people of Galveston began to clamor for a sea wall. The city management agreed that the city needed a sea wall. A plan was even drawn up for the building of a dike all the way around the island except on the bay side. The city management considered it, but by then several months had passed, and the hurricane that destroyed Indianola was all but forgotten. Consequently, the plan for the sea wall was dropped."

"Blame that on the city government," Janet said to Jannock.

Jannock paused in his chewing and squinted at the delicate girl and said, "Idiotic."

At that Marvin Haversham threw down his cheroot and stood up. "I've listened to enough of your mouth, Jannock. Either you shut it up or get ready to back it up with your fists."

"Hey, hey!" Isaac said, getting to his feet.

Elizabeth got to her feet also, saying, "You girls hush too. We're here for fun, not fighting. Come! All of you. And have dessert. The ladies' auxiliary has baked some delicious sweets. To the dessert quilt with you!"

They rose and went to the quilt covered with oil cloth on which the ladies had spread cakes and cookies and candies. Elizabeth and Cora Mae passed out the chosen desserts and the students were like children again, wanting some of all of it. But the gloom of the recent disagreement still hovered over them all, while Jannock and Haversham stood apart eating their dessert glumly.

They might have dropped their disagreement if Janet had not gathered up her skirts and swished them around and around Jannock's feet, taunting as only a pretty girl can, tilting her chin up. And enjoying his sullen but rapt attention, she said, "If Galveston's so stupid, Marshal Jannock, why does everybody in the country call her the Queen City of the Gulf?"

Jannock's eyes did not miss her feminine form, moving with impertinent freshness beneath her yellow frock, or that the color of her smirking lips was red.

"In Houston," he said, still hunched over his piece of cake, "we call her the Old Lady by the Sea."

Sue called to him from her place beside Cora Mae, "At least we don't hang people and shoot them in the streets."

"No, you just slit their throats quietly down at the wharves."

Elizabeth went to Janet, took her gently by the arm and said, "Girls, hush. All of you. No more of this!"

But Marvin Haversham had had enough. Red-faced he said, "If Houston has that kind of attitude about Galveston why doesn't it build its own medical college, Jannock, instead of sending its people to Galveston to get their M.D.'s?"

"We're working on that," Jannock said, "among other things."

"Do you mean that dinky channel up Buffalo Bayou?"

"Deep enough and getting deeper, Haversham."

"That's stupid, Jannock. Houston will never be the seaport Galveston is."

"You can be sure of that, Haversham."

Isaac Cline came between them, but Marvin Haversham, with fists clenched and smiling grimly said, "I think it's time to invite you to the field behind the trees, Jannock."

"If you want a fight, we'll do it here." And Jannock cast his piece of cake aside.

Then both students, with fists doubled up, began to circle each other with Isaac saying, "Alright now, men . . ."

But before he could intercede, Jannock said, "The city you're all so ready to fight for, Haversham, is a sump hole, a cess pit, and you're all too blind to see it."

"Yeah? Well, I'll tell you, Jannock, if God were to give the world an enema, He'd start with Houston, going right up Buffalo Bayou."

"Haversham!" Isaac grabbed the front of Marvin's shirt and twisted it up under his chin, saying, "Apologize to the ladies, Mister."

Marvin by then was pale and trembling with fury; his

298

opponent was flushed but calm. The ladies whom he was urged to apologize to were all laughing and clapping their hands, except for Elizabeth and Cora Mae.

"I said apologize to the ladies, Haversham," Isaac said furiously.

Marvin turned to the cluster of girls. "I apologize." Then to Elizabeth and Cora Mae, "I apologize, Mrs. Morrison, Mrs. Cline."

"Now go your way, Haversham," Isaac said. Then to Jannock, "No more of this talk out of you either, Jannock, or you'll hear from the faculty about this matter."

The two students turned and went in opposite directions along the shore of the bay, but not until they had glared at each other one last time.

It was then that a girl near the bay cried, "A shark! A shark!" giving the rest of the young people an excuse to break away from their discomfort, and they all ran toward the sandy shore. There was no shark, of course, only a dead sea trout, but the distraction served to relieve the tension nevertheless. Now that the crisis was over, Cora Mae told Elizabeth, "I'll never volunteer to be a chaperone again."

During the fray, Damon had remained aloof, standing with one foot propped on a log, smoking thoughtfully. When Elizabeth came to stand before him, hands on her hips with a questioning look, he said to her, "They were both right, you know."

"Well, a lot of help you were!"

"Not any of my business."

Exasperated she said, "Well, I thought you were supposed to be a substitute for Richard."

He looked at her long, searchingly, softly, causing her to become suddenly very warm; and though his eyes and his expression revealed nothing, he said, "I'll never be a substitute for Richard, Liz."

The sun was low over the island when the *Charlemagne*, with sails billowing white in the blue dusk of sky and water, glided through the channel on her way back to port. The students and their girls had sung all the way accompanied by Marvin's hand organ. Jannock did not participate, nor did he intrude, but leaned on the rail on the starboard bow and watched the island gliding by.

Isaac Cline took the helm once while Damon leaned on the nearby mast and smoked, and Cora Mae, half-seasick, half not, seemed to enjoy the students' singing. Elizabeth stood near the starboard rail watching the city growing closer, a tapestry in blue and white, a tiny town woven against a background of indigo. Her town. Her island. Her people. She was as much a part of it now as the bay or the beach or the fragrant inland gardens. She was woven into the tapestry of Galveston with silk threads and loving care. And yet, there was still this feeling of a thing left undone, a vacant place, a thread left unstitched.

I'll never be a substitute for Richard, Liz. Damon's words kept going over and over in her mind, his eyes guarded, not revealing the full meaning of what he was saying. *I'll never be a substitute for Richard, Liz,* had begun to cause her inexplicable pain; for she had no way of knowing how wrong those words could be.

Part Two

Seventeen

Richard hadn't admitted a patient to the hospital since Mrs. Jacobson was discharged last June. But old Mr. Hyde, a retired seaman who had lived alone for over twenty years, had suddenly become bedridden at home with a "stoppage in the bilge, pain abaft, and a general weakness of the entire hull, Dr. Morris." So Richard had hospitalized the old fellow in order to perform some laboratory tests on his blood and feces, but Mr. Hyde had become so enamored of the gentle, loving care and attention of the nurses, and of the best provisions he'd partaken of in years, that he had all but refused to leave the hospital when Richard pronounced him fit, having purged him of a bad case of hookworm.

The "old men's ward," as it was called by the entire staff at John Sealy, was one of the most depressing places in the entire hospital, old fellows lying in their beds, few with families left to visit, all their friends having "passed on," and most of them with no disease or malady of any kind that the doctors could detect, very patiently waiting to die.

Their care was what was bothering the little nurse in charge of the first floor, spunky Miss Hanes who had developed from a green, scared little novice to a proficient nurse whom some of the medical students would have liked to court, had it not been forbidden for students to fraternize with the nurses.

As Richard was looking over the nurses' reports of Mr. Hyde's condition for the day, Miss Hanes approached him quietly and said, "Dr. Morrison, please excuse me for interrupting, but may I ask your advice about something?"

Richard turned to her. "Certainly."

"I love this ward, Doctor, in fact I chose this ward over the entire hospital in which to work. I feel like I have twelve old grandfathers to look out for, but our duties here are becoming more than three nurses can do. We need more nurses on this ward on all shifts. We have approached the superintendent with the problem, and also the administrator and both say that unless the doctors recommend more help here, they see no need to change things."

Richard studied the nurse a moment knowing she was right.

"The old fellows are constantly complaining," she said. "They're so helpless that we have to do absolutely everything for them, bathe and feed them, change their clothing, give medications, which of course is our duty; but we just can't give them the attention they require if we don't get more help."

Richard smiled and said, "Miss Hanes, have you gotten the impression yet that these patients are not quite as helpless as they seem?"

She bridled at once, blushing as she always did when he spoke to her. "No indeed!" she said.

"Well, I wonder if maybe they are just lonely for attention."

Plucky Miss Hanes ruffled her feathers like an indignant young hen and said, "Dr. Morrison! I couldn't agree with you less!" Then after a moment's reflection said, "Well, anyway, that's beside the point. I'm wondering if . . . well, if you. . . ."

Richard handed her Mr. Hyde's chart and said, "I'll mention the problem at the faculty meeting next week, Miss Hanes, and see if I can get the other doctors to agree to request more nurses on this ward."

"Oh, thank you, Dr. Morrison," she said. "I knew I could count on you."

It occurred to Richard briefly that Miss Hanes could approach any of the other doctors with the problem and he wondered why she had picked him, who seldom used the hospital facilities. . . .

In the old men's ward, Richard approached his patient's bed and said, "How are you today, Mr. Hyde?"

"What say?"

Richard leaned close to Mr. Hyde and shouted, "The nurses say you had a bad night, Mr. Hyde."

"Eh?"

Richard took the old man's ear horn which was propped up beside his bed, and handed it to him. Mr. Hyde blinked at it a moment, then took it and stuck the small part in his left ear. "What say?"

"The nurses say you had a bad night."

"Had a fight? I sure as hell did, Dr. Morris. See that old man over there?" He pointed to his roommate in the next bed. "That old barnacle snores like a battleship. T'ain't no sense in such a thing so's I tol' him to batten his hatch or I'd keel haul him down one side of his bunk and up the other. He tol' me to shut my mouth!"

"You had no trouble hearing that?"

"What say?"

Richard gave it up, and since the "old barnacle" in the next bed was eyeing them both maliciously, he decided to say good day to Mr. Hyde and let well enough alone.

"Well, try to sleep now, Mr. Hyde," he said, "and maybe you'll have a better night tonight."

"Quiet?" said Mr. Hyde as Richard turned to leave. "No t'ain't quiet atall, Dr. Morris. Never heard so much snorin', singin' out orders, and yarnin' in my life. A feller can't get his rest in this place with all that fracas goin' on noways. . . ."

Richard left the ward, went out the door of the hospital to his horse and buggy, gave the stablehand a coin, and turned Blitz west on Strand street. He had given two lectures that morning, one that afternoon, and knew that by now the corridor outside his office would be standing full of patients. Not only that, but he had scheduled six of Dr. Holcomb's patients for x-rays that afternoon, which he'd have to work his own patients around somehow. If it didn't already cost him a considerable amount to run the x-ray machine and the equipment for it, he'd hire someone to help, and teach him how to use it. What he really ought to do was charge the doctors for the service, but they'd only charge their patients for it and that wouldn't be very popular with anybody.

He had scheduled the x-rays as soon as he could. That morning six longshoremen had been injured in an accident on pier 19 when a rope connected to a boom, which was lifting a load of cargo from the hold of a ship, had broken and sent several hundred pounds of cargo careening down upon the men on the pier. Dr. Holcomb, the longshoremen's company doctor, had requested x-rays as soon as possible. That was three hours ago and Richard was feeling rushed and pressed for time, and the thing that was bothering him the most was that he couldn't see how he could possibly take Beth to the opera tonight.

He stayed late at the office often, was called from parties to attend patients frequently, weekends he prepared his lectures. Beth seldom complained, because she was busy in her own right, though he often had to prevail upon Damon to take her home after a party.

But the opera. . . . This was opening night and she had had a new ball gown made for the occasion, they had already purchased their tickets, his formal evening attire had been cleaned and pressed.

He shook the reins to make Blitz go faster. But he needed to pause to get priorities straight in his mind. What was more important, Beth going to the opera? Or preparing x-rays for six injured men? There it was, the solution. Beth would have to either stay home, or find someone to go with her.

Damon.

He'd ask Damon to take her to the opera. He'd arrived in port the day before from one of his long voyages to Liverpool. Yes, he would do that, though Damon was caught up in what Joe Bob called "working the bugs out of the turbine engine," a project that once begun had met with more difficulties and had experienced more setbacks than even pessimistic Ingram had expected. Demonstrating the principle of the turbine engine had been one thing, building the thing from scratch was another. Then there had been the matter of securing a license to build the turbine from the patentee in Great Britain, and the agreement by I & S to pay the required royalties.

When Richard arrived at his office, eight people were waiting outside his door, grim with impatience and none too friendly because he was almost an hour late. He unlocked his door, bade them enter the waiting room, and made haste to his treatment room, shut the door, and went directly to the telephone on the wall.

He found Damon where he thought he'd find him, at the shipyards. And when he asked him to take Beth to the opera that evening, he was none too eager, but agreed to do it.

Expecting to feel relieved that Beth's evening would not be ruined, Richard discovered that his inability to take her himself bothered him a great deal all afternoon as he saw his patients, administered treatments and medications, then admitted the six accident victims, and with Dr. Holcomb's help, made twenty-two pictures altogether.

He didn't know what was wrong with himself. All he knew was patients kept coming in, the longshoremen probably had over thirty fractures if they were all totaled together, and he had at least eight hours more of work to do before he could go home.

But he kept reasoning with himself that Beth *was* going to the opera. Why then was he so miserable about it?

The old lady in the seat next to Elizabeth leaned toward her and said behind her fan, "This reminds me of Baroque opera, dear. Don't you think so?"

To quiet her, Elizabeth smiled and nodded, although she wasn't at all acquainted with Baroque opera and wasn't sure Baroque had ever been performed in Chicago or indeed in any other city in the United States. But if it had, surely it would have been performed in Galveston, for some of the greatest opera stars had performed here in the Grand Opera House.

She fanned and listened to the aria, enjoying the performance on the stage, the bright costumes, the innovative scenery, and Damon by her side. Which surely must account for how very warm she was, for it was January, after all. And how tight her corset seemed to be!

The old lady leaned toward her again and whispered loudly, "I've just decided who you are, dear. You're Elizabeth Morrison. I thought I recognized Captain Morrison. Myrna Coffman pointed you out to me at the Fourth of July picnic. I never go to parties, so I seldom meet many new people any more. I'm Mary Louise Shraeder."

Elizabeth glanced around her to see if the lady was disturbing anyone. Surely she must be. Shraeder— Shraeder Freight and Shipping—of course.

"How do you do," Elizabeth whispered, but thought, *Dear Lord, make her hush;* for whispering at the opera during an aria was considered much more improper than whispering in church during a sermon.

"Where is your Dr. Morrison, dear?" Mary Louise Shraeder asked.

"Busy at the office," whispered Elizabeth. As the old lady pursed her lips and nodded knowingly, Elizabeth could have bitten her tongue, because the excuse sounded . . . so *suspicious.*

Someone behind them leaned forward at last and said, "Will you ladies please be quiet?"

She glanced at Damon, who was enjoying the incident more than he was enjoying the opera. Mrs. Shraeder tightened her mouth, blinking rapidly, and bent her attention once more to the stage.

She was aware, so aware of Damon sitting stiffly at her side. In fact, he had been rigid since he arrived in the carriage to escort her to the opera, arriving dressed handsomely in his evening clothes, almost grim with determination, unhappy to be substituting for Richard, uncomfortably accompanying her among the lavishly attired elite in the lobby. When he wasn't mistaken for Richard, he was being asked where in the world Dr. Morrison was. *Busy at the office,* he would reply briefly. He had not met her gaze since the yachting party back in October, seemed aloof and ill at ease. She felt beautiful tonight. Her new green satin was the most stylish dress at the event, her hair was up in curls, and her mother's emerald brooch was at a strategic place upon her bosom where the scooped neck of her bodice almost—but not quite—

revealed the cleft there, which Damon seemed determined not to notice.

At the intermission they had risen but did not find it necessary to promenade in search of acquaintances; for the acquaintances came by to greet them where they stood, to ask after Dr. Morrison, to express their regret about the six injured longshoremen. "And isn't Galveston lucky to have the only x-ray doctor in the state?" Elizabeth had enjoyed telling them that Richard, in that capacity, was called a roentologist, because she loved to roll the word off her tongue, and it sounded so important. "Yes, aren't we lucky to have the first roentologist in the entire state of Texas?"

But then, Galveston always prided itself in being first with everything; here the first Catholic Church in Texas was dedicated, the first telegraph operated, Galveston had the first gas lights, the first hospital, the first electric lights, the first nursing school south of St. Louis, the first medical school west of the Mississippi, and yes, Richard was one of the first faculty members at the school. . . .

Galveston was here tonight, as represented by old Mrs. Shraeder, and there in Abel and Myrna Coffman; and there, front row center, Eric and Emily Ingram, Matilda and Maxwell Sturgeon, and behind them, Conrad Moran, across the aisle, Dr. and Mrs. Judson Mason, Mr. and Mrs. Nicholas Clayton; in a gallery, Dr. and Mrs. Will Kelly, and behind them, Mr. and Mrs. Ed Ketchum, and in the back of the balcony even Tony, the little ice cream vendor. . . .

The orchestra was building to a crescendo, cymbals crashed, the tenor's voice vibrated within the hall. The

311

orchestra thundered the finale, the scarlet curtain fell, the applause thundered through the hall.

"Bravo! Bravo!" called male voices within the audience. "Bravo! Bravo!" Galveston audiences were famous for appreciating cultural entertainment. "So agreeable to perform for," entertainers had said of them. "Bravo! Bravo!" Applause roared through the hall. The lead soprano and tenor came from offstage to take their bows, once, twice, three times.

Elizabeth dropped her fan and Damon ceased applauding, bent down to pick it up, and handed it to her. Their eyes met for one dizzy moment and perspiration broke out in beads upon her forehead.

Bravo! Bravo! These were her people, her town. They were all here, all of them at once. She stopped applauding to fan herself.

The audience rose, still thundering their applause, and she and Damon rose also. Bravo! Bravo! Here, the entire aristocracy. Here, nearly every physician, every businessman, every merchant, in their finery, in their best, here eager for the best of everything, together in this red brick Grand Opera House. All of them, Galveston in this theater all at once. Here, tonight.

But what if there was a fire. . . .

Suddenly a coldness came over her, a cold perspiration broke out over her entire body and she imagined a vivid scene, a fire sweeping over them all, the building falling. But the fire was suddenly a flood, a thunderous, roaring torrent of rushing dark waters and buildings flying apart, and debris. . . . The debris. . . .

"Liz!"

He caught her as she swooned, and when the mists cleared from her vision, Mrs. Shraeder was waving her smelling salts under her nose. "It's the vapors, Captain Morrison. You should take her out of the hall, it's ghastly warm in here."

"Yes, yes. She'll be fine. Excuse me. Excuse me," Damon's voice said, and she could feel his grip around her waist, his fingers digging painfully into her arm. "Excuse us, please. Yes, she'll be fine." And they were moving down the row and up the aisle. "No, thank you, she'll be. . . ."

Was the roaring, then, in her own head and not in the house?

The cool January breezes touched her face, his arm was around her and they were outside. Yes, and Shadrack who had brought them was there waiting at the curb in the buggy.

"Lord, Cap'n. What's the matter with Miz Lizbeth?"

Damon got her into the buggy saying, "Get us home, Shad, before she faints again."

The buggy began to move, swaying, swaying, *swaying too much.*

Seeing that she was pale and wavering in the seat, Damon put his arm around her and made her rest her head against his chest. "God, Liz. What's wrong with you?" He asked, his lips against her forehead.

"I'm not sure," she said softly, "but I think I'm going to. . . ."

"No, God. Please don't faint again. Three more blocks to go. See? We're passing the Breckenridge house. Lord, Shad, can't you make this thing go faster?"

"But I think I'm going to. . . ."

At last the carriage swayed to a halt and Damon jumped from the buggy and took her into his arms, carried her through the gate, up the walk, up the steps, shouting, "Prim! Prim!" And then when Prim opened the front door, he carried her through into the entry. "Get her smelling salts or something, Prim, she's sick."

Prim bent and took a look at Elizabeth and said, "Lord, Cap'n Damon. She's got the natal sickness."

"The what?"

"You just stay with her while I run for Miss Lissa. An meantime I best be sendin' Shad for a basin!"

Damon carried her to the parlor where he lay her down upon the sofa. He knelt beside it, holding her hand. "Liz, you scared me. You were so pale, so sick-looking. Are you in pain?"

She shook her head no.

"Are you sick to your stomach?"

She nodded.

"Feeling faint?"

She nodded. "And I think I'm going to—"

Shad brought the basin just in time. She sat up so suddenly that it caused Damon to fall backwards, sitting down hard upon the floor. There he remained, watching her retch into the basin again and again. Befuddled, he realized that though he had given medication to sick men before aboard ship, and he was a physician's son and a physician's brother, he had never, never seen a sick woman before. God. It was ludicrous!

Melissa came bustling through the front door, into the parlor, and took command as if she knew exactly what

314

was wrong with Liz and what to do about it. "You, Damon, please go to the library if you care to stay, but just leave us alone awhile," she commanded. "You too, Shad. Go. Both of you. Shoo! Shoo! This is women's business. Prim, fetch a damp cloth and a cup of hot tea." Then she knelt by poor Liz and began to smooth back her hair as she retched.

So, bewildered and worried, Damon left the room and wandered into the library to await further instructions. In a few moments, Melissa came to the library and asked him if he could please help get Elizabeth up the stairs. He sprang to his feet and with a face grave with anxiety crept into the parlor while Mel and Prim struggled to get Elizabeth to her feet.

But her knees gave way and Damon went to her, picked her up and stood holding her in his arms while her skirts swept the center table. "Where are we going with her?"

"Up to her room."

Suddenly, Damon couldn't remember exactly where their room was, for he'd seldom been upstairs, but he carried her up thinking she was light as a feather, and as he went was absurdly aware of the contours of her body against him and of the soft places, and of her fragrant coiffure tickling his throat. Suddenly, her body began to shake and when he looked fearfully down at her, he saw that she was giggling. All the way up the stairs she giggled, and he thought, By God, now is she getting delirious?

He carried her inside the master bedroom and lay her down upon the bed. His duty done, Melissa shooed him out and told him to telephone Richard.

Well, he could certainly do that! He wondered why he hadn't thought of it before now. He flew down the stairs to the entry hall where he rang central and asked the operator to give him 493, the number for Richard's office. The telephone rang and rang. No one answered. He hung up the receiver and stood slumped over in the hallway wondering what to do. Then, in a sudden burst of fury, he plunged out the front door, leaped into the carriage, and sped off down the street.

Several horrible things kept going through his mind as he urged the horse on faster into the night. Among his misgivings was the disconcerting thought that Richard might not actually be staying at the office all these nights. Was he being unfaithful to Liz? No, he told himself, not Richard. *Anybody* but Richard. Still. . . .

But he found the lights on in the flat over the drugstore, and rushed into the building, up the stairs, and burst into Richard's office where he found him placidly hanging up an x-ray print to dry.

"Why the hell didn't you answer your telephone, John Richard?"

He looked across the examining table at him and said calmly, "Because it didn't ring."

Damon was so relieved that all he could think to say now was, "Liz is sick!"

Richard studied him. "What do you mean?"

"Sick! Sick! She fainted at the opera. Then threw up in a basin at home!"

His brother continued to study his face, then looked over at his desk and said contemplatively, "Hmmmm."

"Look, John Richard. I don't give a damn what you've

316

got to do here, you belong home with Liz. *Right now!*"

Richard smiled calmly. "Yes, I rather think you're right."

While he watched, Richard moved slowly, deliberately cleaning up his mess, in no hurry, puffing on his pipe, and every now and then pausing to ask a question. "Did she have abdominal pain?"

"No!"

Richard hung up the last print and said, "Was she nauseated before she fainted?"

"How the devil would I know?"

He puttered a little more until Damon was livid with fury. When Richard picked up an x-ray plate to put it away, Damon snatched it from him, slammed it down on the table and said, "It's time you left, John Richard, and to hell with all your bloody equipment!"

"I've never seen you quite this upset, Damon."

"You want to know why, John Richard? Because you've been neglecting Liz. You went up there to Chicago and fetched her down here, put her in a gilded cage, and then proceeded to neglect her. All this medical equipment, that damned machine of yours, you should hire somebody to run that thing."

Richard went to the coat rack and took down his top coat, saying, "Perhaps you're right."

"She could be mourning herself into an illness over being left alone every damn night of the week."

"Oh, I doubt that's the case," Richard said, pulling on his coat. "Quite the opposite, probably."

Damon didn't like his brother's offhand manner. Didn't like it at all. "Damn it, John Richard, am I going to have to drag you out of here by the collar? *Hurry up!*"

Richard paused and raised his brows as he put on his hat. "Mind if I get my bag?"

Damon glared as Richard got his black bag off the desk, sauntered past him to the door, carefully locked the door behind them, and went down the stairs and out into the night.

They went back to the house in separate buggies with Damon arriving first. Not waiting for his brother, he went inside and found Melissa coming down the stairs acting every bit as casual as Richard had. Prim came down behind her and when she saw Damon, ducked her head giggling and went off to the other part of the house, leaving Damon standing in the entry wondering if he was going mad.

"How is she?" he asked Melissa.

"Better. Is Richard home?"

"He's very carefully putting away his precious buggy."

"That's good."

"Well, can I go up and see Liz?"

Melissa's gray eyes smiled at him a moment and she said, "I suppose it's alright since Richard will be up shortly."

It was casting propriety to the winds, but to hell with propriety. At the bedroom door he knocked tentatively, and she called to him to come in.

When he went in, she was propped up in the bed with several fat pillows, dressed in a white nightgown with lace at her throat and wrists, and with a quilt pulled up to her waist. She had let her hair down and it waved in

318

luxurious folds upon her shoulders and down past, the longest hair he'd ever seen. He had never seen her hair like that before, and was paralyzed at the sight of her.

"Damon. Come on in and please don't look so tragic." And raising her brows added in a lilting voice, "Come on. I won't bite you."

He went in slowly, stunned at how young she looked, how like a girl, how pale and how beautiful.

"Do sit down, Damon," she said. "You don't look at all well."

He sat down in a rocking chair near the window and said, "Liz are you alright?"

"I'm fine now. Though I'm terribly embarrassed. I know I must have caused you a great deal of—"

"Don't be embarrassed," he said. "And please never give it another thought. I just wonder. . . . Did I do anything to . . . to cause this?"

"You? No," she laughed softly, the laugh catching in her throat. "No, not *you*."

Richard rapped on the door frame. "May I come in?"

Damon sprang to his feet almost guiltily and Richard came to the bed, kissed his wife saying softly, "What is this, Beth?"

Damon turned away, turned his back on the both of them. While Richard plied her with soft questions, a fury rose in Damon again, a fury he could not explain, and after a moment of listening to his brother's gentle murmurings, Damon, beset with guilt, anger, and hurt, plunged out the door, and as he descended the stairs, heard the door of the bedroom close softly behind him. Melissa was in the parlor drinking tea, so he went to the library where he could be alone. To think.

In his nervousness, he cast his glance over the books on the shelves, all the while thinking, typhoid? Wrong time of year. Malaria? Yellow fever? Also the wrong time of the year. One of those mysterious female troubles? Could be a monthly visitation. No, women don't usually throw up with that. Or do they?

Many titles on the books were familiar. But there were medical books here too. He took one out and opened it blindly. There was a lithograph that showed a man sitting in a chair with a tube coming out of his abdomen and a woman holding the other end of the tube pouring something into it from a pitcher. He slammed the book shut and stuffed it back on the shelf, went to the only sane chair in the room, took out a cigar and lit it, smoking morosely until Richard came into the room and carefully placed the black bag on a shelf.

"Prim's made a crock of hot buttered rum, Damon, and I've asked her to bring us a mug to celebrate." Richard, smiling, went to his horn chair and sat down.

"Celebrate?"

"Yes. Congratulations, Damon. You're going to be an uncle."

Damon stared. "Uncle?" Then it all came together at once. Lord, what a fool. Slowly he covered his eyes with his hand and after a little began to laugh softly, laughed until Prim brought the generous mug full of rum.

"It's all part of the process," Richard explained when Prim had left. "The nausea, fainting. The baby will be due about . . . let me see . . . August."

Still laughing, Damon said, "August is a damned

hot month."

"For a man wise to the ways of the world, Damon, I have to say you were splendidly ignorant concerning this matter."

"John Richard, I've been around few females in that particular condition." He looked at his brother, that temperate ass who seldom drank, sipping the rum like a sailor. He toasted him with his mug, "I congratulate you, brother."

After a sip or two, Richard proposed his own toast, "To fatherhood. May it live forever."

"Without fatherhood, there would be no forever."

After they had drained their first mugful, Richard rang for another.

Minutes later, Damon said, "I overheard Melissa say something about Aunt Martha. It seems to me that every-woman's got an Aunt Martha and nobody's particularly happy about her visits. Every Aunt Martha in the world seems to be a bitch, John Richard. And it just occurred to me. There's a connection."

Richard nodded soberly, "A definite connection."

"Which is another puzzlement. I never dreamed you were fertile."

Richard frowned. "Women are fertile, men are virile."

Damon shrugged. "All the same. It takes . . . one of each."

Richard nodded philosophically and swallowed his rum.

"But it's sad, John Richard, sad because Liz was so beautiful. She had on a green dress with a low . . . and her . . . and what was even more beautiful about Liz was her hair, up there in her room, her hair goes down to her . . ."

"Damon, you still get indiscreet when you've had a bit too much to drink, so I'll invite you to abstain from talking about my wife. Don't even *think* about my wife."

Sometime in the blur of the next few moments, Richard must have pulled the bell pull, for Prim appeared at the door saying, "Another one, Dr. Richard?"

Richard said no and told her to send Shad in. Once she was gone, Damon pointed at him and said, "Hey, remember the time we stole that jug of corn liquor from old man Koppel's barn?" And they reminisced about how they had soaked the biscuits from their mother's kitchen in the liquor and fed them to the chickens, how the chickens staggered about and ended up stretched out on their sides upon the ground, alive, but definitely intoxicated, mouths open, tongues sticking out . . . and when Shad came to the door, the brothers were paralyzed with laughter, Damon bent over, Richard stretched out almost prostrate in the horn chair. So Shad began to giggle too, standing in the doorway giggling, "Hee, hee, hee, hee," and finally bending over to slap his knee, not knowing what he was laughing about, but whatever it was, it was hilarious.

Richard and Shad recovered at the same time, abruptly, and Richard scooted upright in his chair and looked over at Shad.

"Yessir, Dr. Richard?"

"I believe Captain Morrison could use some . . . help getting up the stairs. He will be staying with us tonight. Put him in the guest bedroom, please."

Shad grinned at Damon. "Yessir, Dr. Richard."

Still laughing, Damon let Shad steer him to the door. "Congratulations, Shad," he said as they began to ascend the stairs. "You're going to be an Uncle Shad."

"Yessir, Cap'n Damon."

"Shad, some women are fertile and men are virile."

"Yessir, Cap'n Damon."

"And when they . . . come together, that makes them virtile. Now, my brother, he's a virile man. He knows how it's done and as a result, I'm going to become an uncle."

"Here's your room, Cap'n Damon. Jus' guide your feet that way. . . . That's it. . . . Now here's this nice soft bed Miz Lizbeth keeps all clean and nice."

Damon fell upon the bed with a groan and a sigh and rolled over on his back. "It takes two," he said. "And when one is beautiful, you get results."

"Yessir. Now if you'll hold up your feet, I'll be gettin' your boots off, Cap'n Damon."

"But before the baby comes, Shad, you understand, the lady has to be sick. So-oo sick. Even if she's beautiful."

"That's a misery, Cap'n."

"Why?"

"'Cause Eve done et de apple in de garden of Eden, Cap'n, dat's why."

"So did . . . What was his name? Adam? What happens to Adam?"

"He done got to wuk by de sweat o' his brow all de days o' his life, Cap'n. Now I jus pull off yo trousers so you be—"

"No! Oh no! You leave my trousers alone, Shad. In this house, I keep my trousers on at all times."

"Aye, aye, Cap'n."

"If it's a boy, we'll name him . . . we'll name him John Richard Junior."

"Yessir, Cap'n, Damon. Now I'll tell you good night."

"Boy should always be named after his father. An' if it's a girl, we'll name her after her mother, Elizabeth Lucinda. Did you know Mrs. Morrison's middle name is Lucinda?"

"Yessir, Cap'n. Goodnight, Cap'n."

Downstairs, Richard had remained seated in his chair until Shad reappeared. "Anything else, Dr. Richard?"

"That's all, Shad. Thank you. You and Prim are excused."

"Jus' want to extend my congratulations, Dr. Richard."

"Thank you, Shad. As you go out, please take Captain Morrison's carriage to the shed and take care of the horse."

"Yessir. Good night, Dr. Richard."

When Richard heard the back door close, he got up out of the chair. None too steady on his feet. None too steady at all. He stepped carefully out of the library to the stairway. But he found that the first step was impossible to negotiate, for once he raised one foot off the floor, he tended to lose his balance. He tried again and again, and finally turned, went to the back parlor, and curled up on the newly upholstered empire sofa where he fell asleep, deeply, pleasantly, serenely asleep.

Eighteen

Although Dr. Isaac Cline had recorded the lowest temperature ever recorded in the city in February, and the bay had frozen solid for several days, spring came early that year, and Elizabeth's garden came alive and flourished. The flowers that had wintered over burst into bloom in late March, the annuals having seeded the previous fall, pushed up through the fertile soil and were blooming by May, creating a riotous border of blooms to complement the debut of the oleanders.

Also by the first of May, Shad's three brooding hens had hatched three "batches" of chicks, and he went about boasting to his friends that he had "forty chickens in the pen, and a pig in the poke." For Prim was pregnant with her first child.

Mildred Crabtree came across the street in April and when she saw Elizabeth's swelling belly said, "Every woman in Galveston seems to be in a family way. It's a sign of war or a catastrophe, mark my words."

Prim began to bathe her own loins daily in dish water, for the old negro said that would lessen the pain of child birth, and she drank the bitter juice made from milkweed once a day to encourage the production of breast milk, and she avoided looking at the moon lest the child growing within her be born with a harelip.

In early May, Mildred came across the street again and told Elizabeth that the baby would surely be a boy because she was carrying it low, and not to eat strawberries this year, lest the child be born with a disfiguring birthmark. Richard said that was utter nonsense, and that Mildred Crabtree expounded more superstitious nonsense than Prim did.

One day, Elizabeth was out weeding her front garden and Cully was out in the street throwing a ball to Flop. When he saw her, he sauntered over, bouncing the ball for Flop to catch.

"Throw the ball on the lawn, Cully, not toward the garden," she admonished him. "How are you today?"

He came to stand beside her and said, "Miss Lizbeth. Why are you getting fat?"

She smiled and said, "Prim says I swallowed a watermelon seed, Cully."

"Don't tell the things other people do, Lizbeth. I'm in first grade and I know better."

She put her hand on his shoulder and together they went to the veranda steps, a thing they had gotten into the habit of doing, Cully always exploding with questions, and finding Elizabeth the only grown-up wise enough to answer the truth. She took his grimy hand and placed it on the swell of her abdomen where the baby was moving, writhing under his hand. Cully's face was thoughtful at first, then his eyes took on a new light and he smiled up at her.

"What do you suppose it is?" Elizabeth asked.

Cully took his hand away politely, unabashedly. "It has to be a baby," he said. "When Julie Wineburger's ma had her baby, she wasn't fat any more. So I don't believe the story about the stork. I decided babies grow inside their mothers. Now I know."

Cully threw the ball down the walk and Flop brought it back, laying it at his feet. This had become a constant game with Flop. Cully, or whoever was available, would throw the ball, Flop would chase it and bring it back, and this would go on and on until the ball-thrower would become weary. But Flop never tired of it, though his master grew tired and the ball grew wetter.

"What I wonder is, how the baby gets inside." Cully threw her an embarrassed look and added, "But don't 'splain that, Lizbeth, 'cause I'm not old enough yet."

She had to laugh and hugged him briefly, a thing that pleased and embarrassed him at the same time.

Damon had come back after a three-month voyage in April and when he saw Elizabeth, though she had discreetly attempted to disguise her belly which was growing so huge so fast, he said, "You've taken on more cargo than your hold was meant to carry, Liz. Next thing, you'll be shipping sea." And they had smiled, sharing a special rapport they shared with no one else on earth.

Ding-dinga-ding. Ding-dinga-ding. A familiar bell sounded now and Elizabeth looked down the street as Cully rose. "It's Tony, it's Tony!" he exclaimed.

Suddenly, she was consumed with a desire for chocolate ice cream and she hurried inside the house to her sewing box, took some coins out of it which she kept there for this purpose, and she and Cully went out to the street to wait for the little vendor on the walk under the oaks.

Ding-dinga-ding. Down the street he came, and from across the street in the shelter of the Crabtree veranda Jason called, "Tony licks the spoo-oon," and giggling, disappeared into the shrubs.

Elizabeth and Cully agreed that Jason was being rude.

Ding-dinga-ding. Life was sweet and good. It always had been for Elizabeth, but now she was wonderfully pregnant and this was spring, the flowers were blooming, the birds singing, and life was better than ever.

"Tony licks the spoo-oon," giggled the shaking shrubs across the street.

Elizabeth put her hands on her hips. "One more time and I'm going over there and scold Jason for that," she told Cully.

"Sometimes I don't like him," Cully said.

She had heard Tony's response to the neighborhood boys' chiding before, it was always the same; *Aya leetle basta. Ya fadda's no good. Ya mudda's no good. Ya leetle sonna beeches.* It was as if he was responding according to what was expected of him. Mildred Crabtree had expressed her dislike for the little vendor for that reason.

Ding-dinga-ding.

"Tony licks the spoo-oon," sang Jason again, and Tony raised his fist and said, "Aya—," and seeing Elizabeth at that moment, lowered his fist. "Ah, good morning Miz

Morrison. A good day. A good day to Mr. Swift too."

"Good morning, Tony. We would like two double chocolates," she said.

"Ah si. Very good," he said as he flipped open the lid on the cart, and taking the fabled spoon, dipped two dips of ice cream into the paper cone and handed it to Cully. Then he dipped three dips and handed it to Elizabeth. "Two for you, Miz Morrison, and one for leetle bambino, eh?" he said and charged her for only four dips.

Back on the veranda Elizabeth daydreamed and consumed her ice cream and Cully let his melt over his hand, letting it drip to the step where Flop happily washed the step clean with his eager pink tongue.

Elizabeth floated these last days of her pregnancy in a serene world; her parties had lost their glamour, but she enjoyed receiving her friends and acquaintances at home. The Ingrams came over for whist occasionally, the Sturgeons came to take them for drives, Emily came often for tea, and one of the Jolly Sixteen was there every day. Life was sweet.

As soon as her doctor, Lawrence Smart, who chaired the Obstetrics and Gynecology department at the medical school, said that the "dangerous" months were over, she and Richard fixed up the third bedroom, moving out all the trunks and purchasing a wicker cradle and a rocking crib. The room had been painted a pale green, so Elizabeth and Melissa sewed white organza curtains for the long windows, and then they sewed baby clothes, knitted little sweaters and caps and bought yards of gauze with which to make diapers. Now that her time was close, she began to long for the baby, to visit the nursery just to look at the little wicker basket and touch tiny dresses lying in the chest.

It was a good time to have a baby, she decided, with life being so sweet. Neighborhood children were playing in the street with the newest fad, roller skates; there was news that the horseless carriage was growing popular in the north; and President McKinley and William Jennings Bryan were already campaigning for the next year's elections.

She mused and smiled to herself for a while before she noticed that Cully wasn't eating his ice cream. "Cully?"

He looked up at her and let his eyes go back to his ice cream. "Lizbeth, may I give my ice cream to Flop?"

"Aren't you hungry?"

"I don't feel very good."

She looked at him closer. Indeed, his eyes did look dull, the usual precocious intensity was not there. She felt his forehead which was hot to the touch. "Yes, go give the ice cream to Flop in the street, then bring the cone back so we won't mess up the pretty street. Alright?"

He nodded and went out to the street and Elizabeth went into the house to telephone Melissa. Telephoning was easier than going over these days. Later Melissa called back. "Cully does have a temperature," she said, "I've put him to bed and he fell right to sleep. When Richard comes home, will you have him come over, please?"

Richard came home at five, and when Elizabeth told him about Cully, he went next door carrying his black bag. By the time she had crocheted two squares for the baby's afghan, he came back and went directly into the library to put up the bag. She called to him, "Richard?"

He stuck his head into the parlor.

"Well?" she said. "Is it measles?"

He smiled. "I hope it's measles," he said and started up the stairs.

"Hope it's measles!" she exclaimed. "John Richard Morrison!" He was halfway up the stairs on the landing when she came into the entry. "What do you mean you hope it's measles?"

He said, "A boy will get measles sometime in his life and it's best to get them now." He turned back and hurried the rest of the way up the stairs. She heard the bathroom door shut behind him and water running in the lavatory. Somehow, she had the feeling that he wasn't telling her everything.

At dinner he warned her not to go near Cully and he had asked Melissa not to come over; for if Cully had measles, she should not be around him at all, nor should Prim.

Next day Cully's temperature was high and rose gradually all day. By evening he was vomiting, Melissa told her over the telephone. He was complaining of headache and ached so much all over that he could not rest. Elizabeth was worried now and the minute Richard came home from the office, sent him over to check Cully. He came back somber.

"Is it measles?" she asked.

"Can't tell yet," he said and hurried up the stairs to the bathroom, shut the door, and she could hear water running in the lavatory again.

Next morning Melissa called. "Beth, Richard was here early this morning and when I told him Cully had diarrhea, he just sort of went pale." Melissa paused, and though she was attempting to keep her voice calm, there was a note of hysteria in it she couldn't conceal. "Beth? Why would he want to take a sample of Cully's stool with him?"

Elizabeth's hand went to her throat. "Oh, Mel. I don't know."

After she hung up the telephone, she went to Richard's library. From the shelf that held his medical texts, she took down a book titled, *Symptoms*. Inside was an index for disease symptoms. Her finger went down the index. *Abdominal pain, Anorexia*. Next she looked up the symptoms, *Elevated temperature*, then *Diarrhea*. In this manner she traced all of Cully's symptoms and discovered that many illnesses had the same symptoms except for maybe one or two differences. Measles showed a rash on the fifteenth to eighteenth day. And diarrhea wasn't a symptom in measles except in the very young. And under *Diagnosis*, a stool culture wasn't required. She kept reading and tracing and at last found that typhoid had all the symptoms. But a stool culture wasn't mentioned there either. She sighed a sigh of relief, until she realized that the book could have been written before anything was known of bacteria in stool. She checked the date the book was published and discovered that it was indeed an old one, published in 1886. After that, she went into the front parlor and sat a long time upon the sofa. When Richard came home early, she said, "It's typhoid, isn't it?"

He took her by the shoulders and said, "Beth, I took a sample of Cully's stool. The culture hasn't had time to grow yet, but . . . Rob Tate did find typhoid bacilli in the stool."

"Oh God no, Richard."

"Listen to me, Beth," he said shaking her gently. "Typhoid is only occasionally fatal and Cully is strong." He straightened then went to the piano and leaned on its top, looking out the bay windows, musing aloud. "I wish Cully could stay home. Near me. I could look out after him better here than I could if he was at the hospital. On the other hand, if there's an immediate emergency as there was with . . ."

"Timothy Jacobson?"

"Yes. Then, he could die before I was able to get him to the hospital. I'm going to have to weigh one factor against the other in deciding where to let Cully recuperate, at home or at the hospital."

The same moment she realized that Richard was deeply disturbed, the infant kicked suddenly. She rose and went to him and smoothed back his hair. "Richard," she said softly. "Why not tell Melissa and Joe Bob the alternatives and let *them* decide."

His furrowed brow smoothed out and a smile grew upon his lips. He took her hand and held it, saying, "Yes. Yes, that's the right way, isn't it? That's the wise thing to do. You're right, Beth, as usual."

The Swifts felt safer with Cully at home, because there was nothing to be done at the hospital for Cully that couldn't be done at home. And as Richard explained, the only advantage to having him in the hospital was to be there in case emergency surgery was necessary.

Cully's fever rose steadily, and on the eighth day, the characteristic rash of typhoid broke out on his chest and abdomen. Fluctuations in his temperature occurred after that, as the fever began to subside. During one time when his fever was low and it seemed Cully was better, Richard plied him with questions trying to discover where he could have contracted the disease. Finally, it became clear. Cully and Jason Crabtree had gone to sail his ships in a shallow pond very near the medical school and Cully admitted they had drunk some of the water.

The first thing Richard did was to go across the street and inform Mildred and Frank Crabtree, then he checked Jason who did have a slight temperature and was put to bed. Then he called the mayor of Galveston and informed him about the pond.

The next day, just when it seemed Cully was getting better, his temperature rose sharply, his eyes became glassy and he became so lethargic he could barely speak. But when he did speak, he whimpered that he couldn't turn his head, "'cause my neck is stiff." Hearing that, Richard paled, and Elizabeth, marooned at home, could detect a quiet panic in him as he telephoned Rob Tate.

Tate checked Cully and agreed with Richard's tentative diagnosis. "It's one of the complications that can set in when one has typhoid, as you know, Richard. Thank God he's at home where he can be watched continually. Because it does look like encephalitis."

Encephalitis? "Sleeping sickness," Richard explained to the Swifts and to Elizabeth.

Elizabeth had her fill of staying home awaiting tidbits

of news about Cully, so after she heard that Rob had agreed with Richard about the new diagnosis, she gathered up her skirts and went next door.

Melissa was wan, her large eyes dark and sunken with fatigue. Joe Bob was pale and worried, but he, at least, would go to bed. Melissa would not.

Elizabeth cajoled and pleaded with her to go to bed to rest. "I'll sit with him, Mel, please go to bed."

Melissa wouldn't leave the room, but because of Elizabeth's presence, she was able to doze in her chair. Daylight faded, night came and Richard could not make Elizabeth go home, nor would she rest in another room at the Swifts, not as long as Cully's fever raged and he remained unconscious, not as long as Melissa stayed up like she was.

The men came and went like day and night and Melissa and Elizabeth took turns dozing in their chairs, propped with pillows, with Sissy bringing food in and Flop coming and going, but mostly dozing on the rag rug by Cully's bed.

Richard came to her once and said, "Beth, please let me take you home."

"I'm fine, Richard."

"You're tired. You're endangering the baby, Beth."

"I'm fine and so's the baby."

Melissa also tried to persuade her to go home.

"No, I'm fine, Mel. Truly I am."

Twenty-eight hours after Elizabeth first came to stay, Damon arrived home from a voyage, and when he appeared in the doorway of Cully's room, Elizabeth went to him and they embraced briefly as was their custom, and when Damon came into the room to see Cully, the look that became etched upon his face in that moment endeared him to her for the rest of her life.

Moments later when Melissa told him how long they had been sitting up with Cully, Damon turned to Elizabeth and said, "Go home, Liz."

"No. I'm fine, Damon."

"Melissa, you go to bed."

"I'll be alright, Damon."

Damon sat down in a rocking chair and later Richard came in, checked Cully, said there was no change. Joe Bob joined them after a while, and the five of them sat silently watching, waiting, listening to him breathe . . . the death watch?

What a quiet, warm night for it, thought Elizabeth. A kerosene lamp dimly burned upon the chest in the corner, the lace curtains blew softly at the windows. Damon sat in the rocking chair in a corner, Melissa in a rocking chair at the foot of Cully's bed, Joe Bob sat on the window seat, Richard in the straight chair beside the bed, and Elizabeth propped with pillows in the padded rocker. The rasp of a cicada could be heard from outdoors somewhere, and the song of the mockingbird in the Morrisons' oak tree next door.

Once Damon looked over at Elizabeth. "Liz, go home."

"I'm fine," she said rocking, feeling perspiration beading upon her upper lip.

"John Richard, if you don't take her home, I will," Damon said.

"I won't go," she told him.

"Then I'll carry you," Damon said.

336

"I don't think you're able anymore," she said.

"I can try."

But no one left and no one spoke again until they noticed that Cully's breathing grew deeper, deeper, quieter, so gradually that for a time no one was sure it was happening. Then they looked from one to the other and saw in each other's faces that it was true. Richard rose and bent over Cully, touching him, lifting the lids of his eyes, feeling his thin little wrist, and then he turned toward them, the lids of his own eyes heavy with fatigue. "He's better," he said to Melissa. Then to Joe Bob, "By heaven, I think he's been spared."

There was quiet, cautious rejoicing. Joe Bob took Melissa from the room at last. Damon volunteered to stay the rest of the night, for the others were spent with fatigue.

Nearly three days, Elizabeth had spent in Cully's room, leaving only to use the bathroom, dozing in the rocking chair, taking her meals from a lap tray, keeping Melissa company, keeping her talking about other things besides her fear of Cully's death, placing cool cloths on Cully's feverish brow, helping clean his bed and change the diapers they had begun to place between his thighs. And it wasn't until Richard took her home and Prim, herself heavy with child, helped her undress and step into the tub of tepid water, that she let her mind recognize the weariness her body felt, had felt from the beginning of her watch, and the light but steady ache in her abdomen.

Richard put her to bed and drew the draperies even though it was still dark outside, for it was after 3:00 A.M.,

337

and climbed into bed beside her.

"We helped him live, didn't we Richard?"

"Yes, Beth. I think we did."

"I love our friends. We're so alike, the five of us."

"Yes, we're lucky."

"We're rich, that's what we are. Cully drew strength from us, drew health to fight the disease with until we conquered it."

He was silent a moment, then said, "Yes. Perhaps you're right. Now go to sleep, Beth, you're exhausted."

"The five of us. I think we can conquer anything, don't you?"

He rolled over to face her and rested his arm across her breasts. "And you are our inspiration, Beth."

"Am I?" She smiled into the darkness. "I'm glad. I like that, Richard. Yes. I'll sleep now. With Damon there with Cully, I know he'll get well now. He loves Damon so."

"Yes. Yes. I think he will," Richard said and withdrew his arm from her, rolled to his back and listened while her breathing began to come in a deep, slow rhythm as she slept.

Nineteen

When Elizabeth woke late that morning Richard was already gone. She thought of Cully, wondering if he was still improving, and sat up quickly only to double over with a sudden, stabbing pain in her abdomen. She clenched her teeth, the room spun. "Prim!" she called as she moved to the side of the bed. "Prim!" Suddenly she felt a wetness beneath her, her hand went to her gown, and when she brought it up, saw that it was damp with blood.

Her world was suddenly engulfed in pain so excruciating she could neither cry out anymore nor move. "Prim," she whispered. "Oh Lord, Prim." Perspiration began to bead on her face and by the time Prim found her, her gown was soaked in blood, perspiration, and tears.

She was only dimly aware of Prim crying out, making her lie down, of Prim screaming, "Shad! Miss Lissa! Oh Lord help!" and running from the room. "Shad! Oh God, Miss Lissa!"

She was aware of faintness, of becoming detached from herself as if she were vaguely observing someone else in such awful pain lying there, her abdomen knotted up in a hurt that never let up, and her breath being pushed from her until she grasped the mosquito netting and tore it down from the bar.

Two things entered her mind in the interval of time it took for Prim to bring Melissa; that the pain was not normal birth pangs, and that the baby was not due for two months.

Melissa's face appeared above her in the haze, twisted in horror. Mel's hands came to her face and applied a soothing, cool cloth, murmuring something Elizabeth couldn't understand. She fainted for a time and awoke with someone prodding her body, and Richard's face appeared over her. She was panting with exertion and from the pain, the steady pain, and there was another pain now, a climbing pain, climbing, climbing, to unbearable heights and then going down, down, down, and then up again and down, a different pain, a pain that came and went; but the constant pain remained. Two pains. She did not know one could experience two pains at the same time. But she did not cry out at first, but panted and fought the sheets, the hands that came near her face. She saw Dr. Smart's bearded face above her, her doctor's face, and tried to speak but had no strength.

Then, "Rich—ard!" she cried. "Rich—ard!"

The house was on fire, it was the theater again and everybody was being drowned in hot liquid, and only Damon could save her. "Damon?" she whispered. "Damon, Damon, Damon. . . ."

". . . abruptio placenta. . . ."

". . . something for pain?" she heard Damon say. "My God, Dr. Smart, can't you give her. . . ."

She reached toward his voice.

". . . can't because of the baby," Richard's voice said.

Dr. Smart said, "Never mind the baby, Richard. It's too late for the. . . ."

She gritted her teeth and bore down against the pain.

"Get out, Richard. Mrs. Swift can help me now better than you. Go on out with your brother." Then Dr. Smart said, "Elizabeth? I'm going to give you something for the pain. Try to keep still a little while longer. Elizabeth?" His kind face came near her and she blinked back the heat pressing upon her face. "Elizabeth, do you hear me?"

She nodded.

"Bear down for me, dear, the next time the pain comes."

"Pain's all the time," she panted.

"I know. But when the big pain . . . there. Here it comes. Now bear down, bear—"

She bore down again with all her might, teeth clenched. And then again. She rested, and then the pain was followed by another.

"Bear down, Elizabeth."

She bore down and gave up, panting. "Tired," she gasped.

"I know, but you must help me. Bear down, Elizabeth. That's right, keep it up."

She climbed up a very tall mountain, a very tall, craggy mountain with many tall, jagged peaks that hurt, and then she slid down on the smooth other side only to have to climb again, up . . . up . . . so difficult to go up . . . and so easy to go down. And over and over she climbed the mountain, coaxed by Dr. Smart. But then she slid into a sea of warm water, a smooth sea, in a ship that hurt only a little, and into a dark place from which she did not want to emerge.

The rain was all she heard at first, a steady rain. The quiet broken only by the rain on the roof. Then she heard the telephone jangle downstairs.

There was very little pain now.

It was evening. A dim light was on in the room, her tiffany lamp on the dresser.

Someone was holding her hand. As she turned her head to see who it was, Richard looked up.

"Richard. Oh, Richard . . . where's Damon?"

His face registered a stinging blow, but only briefly. He looked across the room and she turned her head to see Damon approach her bed. "Liz?"

She touched Richard's face and smoothed the worry lines from his forehead. "Where's Melissa?"

"She just left, Beth. She's been here all day," Richard said.

"Cully?"

"Awake and ate some grits this afternoon," Damon said smiling.

She smiled too. "Is it night?"

"Yes."

She looked at Richard. "How long have I been asleep?"

"About twelve hours," he said.

She reached for Damon's hand and held each of their hands in hers and said weakly, "Look at you. Both of you so grave. This isn't the end of the world, you know."

The brothers glanced across the bed at each other and Damon sat down in the chair beside the bed while she said, "Damon you're always gone, but you manage to be here during every crisis."

"Don't talk, Liz. Just rest."

"Yes." She nodded. "I'm tired." She shut her eyes for a moment, still gripping both their hands. Then she opened her eyes again. "Please see that Prim gets her rest, Richard," she said. "And both of you go to bed. You look so awful."

Richard touched his lips to her hand. "Are you hurting, Beth?"

"A little."

"I'll give you something."

"I'd be grateful."

It was five days before she could bring herself to ask whether the baby had been a girl or a boy. Painfully, Richard told her it was a boy and that there had been a graveside service for the infant with only he, Damon, the Swifts, Shad, Prim, and the rector attending.

"When I'm able, I'd like to go and put flowers on his grave, Richard," she said. "What is on the stone?"

Richard, sitting beside her bed, ducked his head, then raised it to face her. "Just 'Infant Morrison' and the date, 'May 22nd. 1899.'"

Later she asked what had caused the miscarriage and

he explained that it was called abruptio placenta, the tearing of the afterbirth from the lining of the uterus; he had no idea why it had happened.

Convalescence was slow because she had lost so much blood, but tall, dignified, bewhiskered Dr. Smart came daily and there was always someone in her room during the day, Melissa, Mildred Crabtree, one of the doctor's wives, Emily, Matilda, other lady acquaintances. In the evenings the gentlemen came calling too, the doctors, and others to pay brief calls.

Elizabeth was grieved at having lost the baby and she wept frequently at first, especially during the first weeks when she was so physically weak. But life beyond her bedroom door beckoned her, life that was sweet and full of promise and things that were new and friends that were yet to be discovered. And Dr. Smart had said there was no reason why she should not have another pregnancy. So she graduated from the bed upstairs to the sofa in the back parlor after two weeks, and by late June was up on her feet again and going about the house doing small chores.

That Jason Crabtree had not contracted typhoid was a wonder. Mildred said it was by the grace of God. Melissa asked her why God's grace had not included Cully, and Mildred, for once, had no answer.

But Cully was well now, though pale; his youthful mental and physical energy returning enough that he was tutored in June to make up for a month's school lost.

When the due date of Elizabeth's baby arrived, the grief was lessened a great deal by the launching of the *Arundel* with her twin turbine engines and twin screws, two years and two weeks from the date work had begun on them; and Damon was in command with Joe Bob in the engine room.

Richard drove Beth and Melissa down to the wharf in the buggy and they watched as the *Arundel* slipped quietly out of the shipyard, through the channel, between the jetties, and out to sea. It was a wonder that though six men had worked on the turbine engines for two years, no word of it had leaked out to the other shipping companies, which was a credit to Ingram and Sturgeon's influence, and a show of high regard for Damon. Therefore, whatever success the turbine engines might have was not yet heralded by the press.

It was only a test run for Damon's new engine, and if it was successful, his plans were to use the engine in the Big Ship, a dream only Damon and Elizabeth shared.

The *Arundel* was gone a week, and then she slipped into port as quietly as she had left. However, Damon had telegraphed ahead to Ingram the news: NO TURBINE BREAKDOWNS. TWENTY-EIGHT KNOTS.

The telegrapher relayed the message to Ingram, and as Damon had hoped, spread the news around the railyards adjacent to the wharves as smoothly as if he were spreading warm butter on a slice of toast. So that when Damon disembarked on the pier, he was met by a welcoming committee from the Wharf Company, and a delegation from each of the Galveston-based shipping companies, his brother, his brother's wife, and his friends.

Among the small enthusiastic crowd on the pier that afternoon was Conrad Moran, surprisingly as excited at the success of a new type of steam engine as Ingram.

During the congratulatory orgy that occupied Damon as he disembarked from the *Arundel*, Conrad approached the Morrison's carriage where Richard and Elizabeth sat, and doffed his square crowned hat to Elizabeth. "Well, Mrs. Morrison," he began, glancing at the *Arundel*, "she's indeed successful as a steamer after all, but I don't believe she's much of a racing yacht. She's fast, but her size would disqualify her for the national cup races."

When she laughed, he joined her, then shook hands with Richard saying, "Dr. Morrison, I'll be forever wary of your very charming wife. And so should you. For every gentleman in Galveston would be honored to have her clinging to his arm as she is to yours."

Richard said, "It's not Elizabeth I'd be wary of, Conrad, but of gentlemen with your good tastes, but questionable manners."

He bowed, "I deserved that. You see, I'm terribly jealous of Damon Morrison for many reasons. Excuse me." Conrad nodded to Elizabeth and then walked away to meet the hero of the event who was coming toward them smiling.

But Damon did not reach them before Conrad came to stand before him. Face to face they stood, two strikingly handsome men, both tall, both impeccably shrewd. They stared at one another for a moment before Conrad offered his hand, which Damon took, and while Richard was talking with Max Sturgeon, Elizabeth overheard a strange exchange between Damon and Conrad Moran.

"Shakespeare said, 'An honest tale speeds best being plainly told.' You kept your secret well, Damon, from us all, until your purposes were served and then you telegraphed it to the world. Well done. I congratulate you doubly."

"Another quote from the bard, Conrad. 'There is no virtue like necessity.'"

"How long will you continue to pan for fool's gold?"

"Until the river runs dry."

"Then you can take your pick and shovel to the hills, Damon, or you can join my camp where the vein is already discovered and needing only a partner in the enterprise."

"The vein you speak of is shallow, Conrad."

"I'm afraid that's true and I have been considering other camps. I've lately discovered there's other gold in them thar hills, as they say."

"Have you?"

"You know I have. You've been watching Moran and Company the same as I've been watching you. You and I are of a kind, Damon. We're alike. You see, I've already experimented with the turbine principle. And I, like you, didn't let the experiment be known lest I fail and appear a fool. Well, I failed, but no one knew it. Fools who seek to remain undiscovered must suffer alone." Conrad paused. "But now, I bow to your success. I've a new mine to explore and your little experiment has given me more hope for success."

"Rome wasn't built in a day, Conrad."

Conrad smiled, glanced at Elizabeth and told him. "True. But if I had a . . . confidante like your brother's very charming wife to look after my interests, as she has yours, my secret would be safe in the meantime, would it not?"

"Liz . . . Mrs. Morrison is simply loyal to her family."

"Yes. But not simply. Shrewdly. And that intrigues me. Normally, the womb keeps the female brain a useless trifle."

There was silence for a moment and Damon's voice said, "One more step in the direction which your conversation is taking, Conrad, and I'll be obliged to paint the entire pier with the blood from your nose, using your mustache as a brush."

"Then I withdraw from the contest, Damon. I meant no insult, only to express admiration. Here comes your able Mr. Swift, who I'm sure, pardon the pun, had a hand in making the engine a success. So, until we meet again, Damon."

Elizabeth glanced toward them in time to see Damon only incline his head toward Conrad, then he came on to the Morrison's carriage where she held out her hand to him. "Congratulations."

"Thank you. You're looking fit, Liz."

"Damon," said Richard. "I have to shake your hand." And he did, just as Cully's shrill cry cut through the afternoon air. "Cap'n, Cap'n," he cried, running from his parents, and came to stand beside Damon so that the captain could muss his hair. "Cap'n, can I go aboard the *Arundel?*"

Damon rumpled his hair saying, "Not now, Cully, because the longshoremen are starting to unload her cargo and it's not safe." But when Cully ducked his head in disappointment, Damon said, "But how would you like to go aboard a real square-rigger?"

"Oh boy!"

And off they trooped together, leaving the rest of them behind; Richard and Elizabeth to take the Swifts home in their buggy, the bigwigs of the wharf company to seek more information about the turbine from Ingram and Sturgeon, and Conrad Moran to stand with gold-headed cane in hand to envy Damon his success, and Ingram and Sturgeon their most excellent captain.

Twenty

The first week in August, Prim had a baby girl up in the carriage house before Elizabeth was able to call for help. Prim had two pains, and by the time Shad ran for Elizabeth and Elizabeth put down her knitting and ran up the stairs of the carriage house, the baby girl was there on the bed between Prim's knees. The birth caused Elizabeth no consternation—for she instinctively knew what to do—but the baby itself did. Because, though the child had Negro features, it was white, or almost so. However, when Melissa came to help and saw the child, she told Elizabeth that Negro babies were born like that, appearing almost white, and that they darkened during the first few hours after birth. Richard came from the office, spent an hour taking care of the afterbirth, and three hours from the time Prim had her first pain, she was sitting up nursing the tiny child at her breast, with Shad grinning and shaking his head in constant wonder.

By September, Elizabeth and Richard were back in the

swing of parties and picnics and gala events. The Morrison house became once again alive every few weeks with a gala affair of some sort, which often included their aristocratic friends who came to enjoy the Morrison hospitality in their most charming cottage, with their excellent trained manservant who, rumor went, came from some prestigious New Orleans estate. No one seemed to know the New Orleans family's name, nor from what teacher the manservant had learned to play the piano with such excellence.

Elizabeth, ever the gracious and charming hostess, kept her social stratospheres apart. If the classes should mix, it had to be at public events. Outwardly, the fact she still grieved for her child did not show, nor were her friends aware of a burning within her, a burning that seemed to have its beginning in her womb from which it spread to engulf her heart and her loins, and finally that vulnerable place in her mind called reason.

For she loved Damon, and where once she recognized the fact with reticence, she now admitted to herself that she desired him passionately. Her daydreams became romantic and fanciful, her dreams in sleep, passionate and exhausting, and she would often wake in the night and move close to her husband, moving and sighing until he woke to her hand upon his chest or his neck or in his hair, and he would make love to her while she pretended . . . pretended. . . .

But knowing all the while the thing was wrong and loving Richard all the more for his innocence. If he noticed a change in her, he must have attributed it to a reaction from the loss of their child, which indeed in part it was.

Physical strength returned to her quickly and by the time the annual Halloween masquerade ball rolled around, Elizabeth was as fit as ever.

Abel and Myrna Coffman were of German descent, spoke German fluently—and therefore were qualified by ancestry and the solid fact that they were shareholders and members of the exclusive Garten Verein—to rent the garden club's octagonal pavillion for the ball. The Coffman circle of friends included the entire aristocracy along with another circle of less monied but nevertheless prominent citizens, most of whom were of German descent, making their annual ball more like Ezekiel's wheel within a wheel. The Coffmans had rented the pavillion every October 31st—except for Sundays—since 1892, and the ball had become as much a tradition to the Coffmanites as the city's own annual Fourth of July picnic.

The Morrisons received Myrna and Abel's engraved invitation a month before the ball, and Elizabeth could not help but gather her skirts, hurry to the telephone, and call Richard.

"What, Beth? What?" Richard shouted over the line.

"Richard, hush. Don't shout. The invitation says . . . here, let me read it: 'Please come dressed in the costume which expresses the character you most want to be.'"

"Alright, Beth, but suppose I like who I already am?"

"Oh Richard!"

Of course the request was a tongue-in-cheek thing and Elizabeth had her Queen Victoria costume made, an outlandish purple brocade satin and taffeta ball gown, embellished with fake pearls and jewels and lace and with a hoop under her skirt that took both Prim and Melissa to get her into. She also wore a dark, brown wig to hide her hair, and a black satin mask covered with purple sequins to match her dress.

Richard went as Benjamin Franklin, excellently attired with a bald pate—except for a fringe of shoe-polish brown hair around the edge of the bald spot—small round eyeglasses perched over his brown mask, a brown suit with tails, ruffled-jaboted shirt, calfskin shoes with large silver buckles, and carrying a kite in his hand. Elizabeth never saw Joe Bob laugh so hard as when he saw him, and Cully jumped up and down on the porch clapping his hands. Flop sat on the veranda beside Cully tilting his head this way and that trying to understand why such familiar scents came from such strange persons.

They took Richard's carriage and arrived at the Garten Verein, which consisted of several attractive buildings—bowling alley, club house, pavillion—surrounded by geometric gardens and garishly lit with gaslights and lanterns. As they walked from their carriage through the garden paths to the pavillion, they laughed seeing the others arriving, and the laughter lasted all evening.

The pavillion, which most people likened in appearance to a carousel, but which reminded Elizabeth more of a giant gazebo, was another Nicholas Clayton masterpiece, and every Galveston citizen knew its history. It was said that Clayton conceived the plan for the pavillion and the grounds one evening, and spent the entire night at the drawing board. The long, wide windows all around were already alight, and dancing had begun with the German band playing a waltz.

Guests were masked and costumed and the greatest fun was guessing who was who. Little Bo Peep greeted them and brought them to Samson; so Elizabeth concluded Bo Peep was Myrna and Samson was Abel—there was no mistaking Myrna's chirping voice or Abel's frequent "harumph!"

The group to which Little Bo Peep took them was in the process of discussing the recent campaign speech by William Jennings Bryan, who it seemed had foreseen that the gold and silver issue was of fading interest to the American people and had begun new tactics. While the men talked, Elizabeth's eyes played over the riotous guests, telling herself it was not a sin to look for Damon; no, she was not being unfaithful to Richard in the least. There. She was sure the pirate was Damon, no mistaking the walk, the way he held his head.

"Most honorable queen," said a voice at her side. "May I have this dance?"

She turned, her huge, billowing skirts sweeping the gentleman's boots, and beheld a mustached fellow in tights, cape and sword, bowing low, a plumed hat pressed to his chest, the black eyes beyond the black mask those of a villain. The voice, however, was that of Conrad Moran. He swept her and her voluminous skirts onto the dance floor.

"So you must be, let me guess, Sir Walter Raleigh," she said.

"At your service, milady."

354

"If you are who I think you are," she said, "I rather expected you to come to the ball as Julius Caesar."

"I considered it, but decided the forum was too full of Brutuses. Sometimes I can't tell a Brutus from an Antony."

She laughed.

"I think I know the laugh," he said. "Which makes my decision easier. May I have the last dance of the evening?"

Suddenly on her guard, Elizabeth said, "Why?"

He only smiled and whirled her away from the pirate and a milkmaid dancing close by. The German band played a combination of classical and popular waltzes, the lights burned brightly, and Elizabeth's heart was lighter and gayer than it had been in many months. After the first dance, Sir Walter Raleigh took her to the punch table and got her a glass of punch, and while she sipped her drink, Cleopatra came up to them dressed in a filmy pajamalike thing that one could almost see her legs through, her breasts indecently encased in sequined cups sewn over chiffon. Elizabeth decided she must be Rosemary Sturgeon.

Little Bo Peep and Martha Washington—surely Emily—came to talk over the hilarious costumes. "Wouldn't you know Nicholas Clayton would come as a priest?" Martha Washington said. "Look at Ed Ketchum. Where do you suppose he had that costume of a blood-hound made?"

Elizabeth said, "I'm quite sure the gentleman dancing with the Dutch girl is supposed to be George the Third, and is surely the mayor."

"Look," Martha Washington said, "Noah is Chad Greenleaf."

Bo Peep said, "Are you sure?"

"Of course I'm sure."

"Well, then you shouldn't tell. It will spoil the party," said Sir Walter Raleigh. He turned halfway around and joined the pirate, the bloodhound, George Washington, Benjamin Franklin, and Napoleon Bonaparte, who stood in a circle with drinks in hand discussing, of course, the upcoming national elections.

Elizabeth heard Napoleon say, "Roosevelt will be nominated for Vice President, watch and see. America is ready for a hero and he's made himself a hero."

"What do you mean he made himself a hero? He *is* a hero, charging up that hill in Cuba, risking his life with a bunch of cowboys and college graduates, no trained men behind him at all," George Washington said.

"Heroes are fools. The two are synonymous," the pirate said, and Elizabeth thought, Yes, he's Damon, for certain.

"But that's what makes heroes," said Sir Walter Raleigh. "Risk."

"I know what you're referring to," said Napoleon. "To Mr. Lafitte's new idea. And indeed it is absurd to think Galveston businessmen would go along with it."

"To build an empire on an unperfected steam engine is indeed a risk," said George Washington.

"Well, our company's policy in regards to the turbine engine is Wait and See," said Napoleon.

"Which is the attitude of most of the Galveston shipping companies and why they will always be small ducks in a large pond, gentlemen," said Sir Walter Raleigh. "They operate on certainties rather than exploring possibilities."

Little Bo Peep rolled her eyes under her pink mask and took Napoleon's arm. "Come, you awful stuffy bunch," she said. "We're letting a perfectly good band go to waste. Dance with me, Napoleon."

Elizabeth smiled at the pirate and said, "Jean Lafitte, I presume?"

The pirate bowed low. "May I have this dance, Rosemary?"

Before she could reply, and knowing he was only pretending to think she was Rosemary, for what reasons she couldn't discern, she let him whisk her onto the dance floor. At first she was disappointed that he pretended such a thing. But on the other hand, Felicia would not behave as Elizabeth Morrison would, so she relaxed in his arms, feeling free to do a bit of flirting. "Do your hunters still carry off Indian maidens, Mr. Lafitte?"

She felt him stiffen ever so slightly, then gradually, gradually he too relaxed. "Only when they're hunting," he said.

"Do *you* ever go hunting?"

"Occasionally."

"And the maidens?"

He shrugged smiling. "I'm seldom sure. However, they're *not* Indians."

Blushing under her sequined mask, Queen Victoria said, "Sir Walter Raleigh asked me for the last dance, Mr. Lafitte. What does it mean?"

"That Sir Walter is a scoundrel."

"Why?"

"You should know why, Rosemary, you've been to every Halloween masquerade ball for the past five years."

"Oh yes. I forgot."

"How could you," he said. "I'm hurt."

"Hurt?"

"That you should forget what the last dance of the ball means. Because the last two of them we danced together."

"Did we?" Jealousy consumed her.

He laughed, clearly enjoying the ruse and whirled her around the floor, his hand on her waist light but simmering there like a hot coal. Being this near to him was intoxicating on one hand, and curiously absurd on the other. She wanted at once to laugh at him and for him to hold her closer.

Finally the dance ended and for the rest of the evening, she danced with almost every gentleman at the ball, even with Benjamin Franklin.

"Are you still feeling alright? You've been on your feet a long time," Benjamin Franklin asked as they danced.

"I feel fine. And I'm having a marvelous time."

"That's all that counts," Franklin said philosophically.

When at last the band began to play, "After the Ball," suddenly Sir Walter Raleigh was at her side, sweeping his plumed hat to his abdomen. "My dance, milady," he said, bowing low so that his sword poked out behind him.

But the pirate appeared like a ghost out of nowhere saying, "Pardon me, but I believe the queen has given *me* the privilege," he said.

"You?" said Sir Walter, his hand going to the hilt of his sword. "I rather thought I'd have a tussle with Benjamin Franklin rather than you. But I should have known."

"This is Franklin's first masquerade ball, Sir Walter. He probably doesn't know any better," the pirate said.

"And you didn't inform him, Mr. Lafitte? That's curious."

"Not at all. Just cautious."

"At any rate, this dance is mine."

"Enjoy it then, Sir Walter, while I dance with the queen."

Chuckling, she let the pirate guide her across the floor; he was exuberant, sweeping her around, her hoop skirt brushing everybody in its way until she laughed aloud. It was wonderful fun having two handsome swains vie for her attention, especially for this mysterious last dance, but more fun because she was in his arms and all the fantasies and dreams of her days and nights came together in the reality of his touch, his arm around her, his hand holding hers, perspiring into hers, his breath bathing her face in its sweet warmth, his smile upon her. Lights whirled above, the band played. And then it was over, the band stopped playing, the lights went out, and the guests oooed and ahed as if the thing was unexpected.

But Elizabeth had guessed correctly; when the lights went out, tradition dictated that the gentlemen kiss the

ladies with whom they were dancing. So proper
gentlemen kissed their friends' wives on the forehead.
Swains stole the first kiss from their sweethearts, and
forbidden loves were only following tradition if they
kissed. Others hesitated on the brink of indecision. His
lips touched her forehead, but there was no indecision in
Elizabeth. She raised her face to meet his lips, felt his
breath hot and quick upon her face. Indecision, a
moment's hesitation, a stiffening of his entire body. But
Damon's honor held.

The lights came on, and the guests removed their
masks. There was high fun and ridiculous hilarity all
around them, but Elizabeth and Damon removed their
masks slowly, and there was no fun in discovering what
they already knew.

Damon looked down at her, his face reflecting a
bewilderment which went as deep as his soul, and
without another word, he turned from her like Joseph
from Potiphar's wife. And fled.

"I see Damon rescued you from Moran," Richard said
going home in the buggy.

"Yes, I suppose he did," she said with a cheerfulness
she did not feel.

"Moran can be a swain sometimes when it comes to
women."

"Can he?"

"They say so."

"Who did you dance with last?"

"When I saw you were taken, I asked Rosemary Sturgeon."

"Oh?" She looked at him. "Disgusting costume she was wearing."

"Was it?"

"You know it was." They rode in silence a moment before she said, "Well?"

"Well what?"

"Did you kiss her?"

"Of course."

"Of course. On the cheek?"

"On the forehead, of course."

They were silent the rest of the way home with Elizabeth becoming angrier and angrier. Because Richard *did* know about the tradition of the last dance, and because he *didn't* ask how Damon had kissed her. Or even *if*.

Twenty-One

Damon had a problem; how to explain to a tightfisted, nearsighted pessimist such as Eric Ingram, a vision as unprecedented and incredible as a 30,000 ton, stream-lined, turbine-driven transoceanic passenger liner. The task would have been insurmountable if it hadn't been for his important connections. Indeed, it took a great deal of preparation and diplomacy to prepare such an infertile mind as Ingram's for the planting of the most fantastic idea of the century, Damon's Big Ship. Actually what it took was a bit of spading and a great deal of manure. It took giving his sister-in-law the cue so that she could begin the manure-spreading, preparing the soil, she called it, first with Emily Ingram; that's what it took. Damon had no idea what Liz said to Emily or how Emily conveyed it to Eric. The only thing he knew was, Ingram wasn't unduly surprised or negative when he unrolled Joe Bob's excellent sketches of the Big Ship.

Ingram simply gazed silently as Damon turned over

page after page of the sketches showing the outside of the steamer, the longitudinal cross-sections of the deck plans, sketches for the engine room, bridge, the cargo hold, the staterooms, the dining rooms, the library, the smoking room, game rooms, clinic, and sketches of architectural details.

Damon had begun by saying, "I had an idea for a new passenger liner, Eric, I want you to see. Joe Bob and I worked it up." And he had been talking and explaining for over an hour until he was talked out and emotionally exhausted.

"You're a dreamer, Damon," Eric said once during his monologue. "Of course you know this kind of thing is absolutely impossible for a company the size of Ingram and Sturgeon. She's incredible, unprecedented. . . . Streamlined, isn't she?"

"For speed and maximum cargo-carrying capacity."

"Mainly human cargo."

"Yes."

"Four smokestacks, eh?"

"Yes."

"Beautiful! My God. . . . Funny. Emily tells me lately that she wants to go abroad in a really enormous passenger liner for the pure luxury of it, simply for the cruise and never mind the destination. And I told her she would get bored and she said not if the ship has a circulating library and so on and so on, and I had the unmitigated short-sightedness to tell her there were plenty of ships like that on other lines and she said not in the proportions *she* was talking about. I should have known you were going to come up with this idea. This is strictly a

Cunard or a North German Lloyd ship. Big stuff, Damon."

Damon sat down in the chair before Ingram's big, carved mahogany desk. "Suppose we apply for a government grant?"

"Still too much, if this estimated cost is correct."

Of course Damon knew that. And probably the only line in the world that could afford the Big Ship was Cunard or the German lines. Certainly no American line that he knew of. Still, there was an outside chance that if Ingram and Sturgeon bought the idea there was a way that I and S could become one of the greatest lines in the industry. With I and S having liners like the Big Ship built, and being based in Galveston to boot, it could help turn Galveston, with its vacation resort potential, into one of the most important seaports and resort towns in the world. The city was a natural for a tourist resort, like Hawaii, and with a luxury liner of the size and magnitude of the *Lucinda*—which is what he was calling the Big Ship now—surely the businessmen of Galveston would benefit tremendously, and would be willing to invest in her. It seemed to Damon that lately the trend in economics was for businesses to merge, to consolidate, to form enormous corporations. And shipping was big business and getting bigger. With the Philippines now in the possession of the U.S., they were a perfect naval base for penetrating the vast markets of the Orient. A more available market for trade. Of course, Ingram and Sturgeon Shipping Company couldn't raise the capital to finance the *Lucinda*, but they could invite the visionary Moran and maybe even Mayfield and Shraeder too, to consolidate and become one enormous corporation. But that was a wild dream, like shooting for the moon, and he wouldn't mention consolidation to Ingram just yet. Better to let I and S work the ground by itself, if it could, for a government subsidy and the support of Galveston businessmen. Then if that failed, there would always be consolidation.

Yes, he was shooting for the moon, but like Liz had said last year when Joe Bob complained that Damon was never content, "Joe Bob, contented people never invent anything, discover anything, or improve anything."

Eric, looking morose, flipped through the sketches again saying, "I've always dreamed of doing something like this. Max seen this?"

"No."

"Suppose I show Max and get his reaction, Damon. Then present this to the board, just to tease them a little. And suppose the board favors approaching the Coffman, Greenleaf, Crowley, Crandall, Henderson crowd for financial backing? You'd have to take this to a naval architect, get specific plans drawn up, and we'd have to apply to the U.S. government for a grant."

"Of course."

"This thing's very interesting. Wish we could swing it. . . . But would the ship pay for herself, or make us all bankrupt?"

"It's a chance we'd have to take. But have Galveston businessmen ever invested in anything that failed?"

"Good point," Ingram said flipping through the sketches. "Quadruple screw, turbine-driven?"

"Yes."

"Unprecedented in passenger liners."

"It's a new development, as you well know."

"I like these damn smokestacks. . . . Take four or five years to build this thing. If . . . just suppose we decide to take this to the naval architect in New York or Glasgow . . . just to get a more specific estimate of the cost . . . how would I contact you when you're off to San Francisco for four months?"

"Telegraph me in San Francisco at the El Padre Hotel. But don't string me along with this, Eric, unless you're really interested in developing it."

Ingram sighed. "Sometimes I get confused who's the boss around here, me or you?"

"Anytime that happens take a look at your bank account, your shares of stock and compare them with mine. Then you'll know."

It was December when he presented the plan to Eric, and shortly afterward, after the first of the year, he sailed down the coast, around the Horn, and up the West Coast with a cargo of household items, mostly furnishings, reminding himself of a damned peddler like those who used to go from farm to farm in a wagon selling pots and pans and paper fans. He'd rather have been sailing to Glasgow or New York with a commission to build the *Lucinda*. Because there was risk in letting Ingram dilly-dally with the idea, as if I and S could possibly dig up enough financial backing to build a ship as enormous as the *Lucinda*, risk of the idea leaking out.

During the entire voyage to the West Coast and back, Damon felt ill at east because his idea was out in the open. Hopefully at this point, when the other lines heard about it, they would become enthusiastic enough to want to be a part of it. "Our policy is wait and see," Braxton May-field had said at the Halloween ball. So far, none of the other lines had even built a turbine engine. Incredible how slow American shipping enterprise was to change. But that had been the pattern from the beginning, America lagging behind in naval technology. She was just now toying with horseless carriages, while Europe had been driving them about for years.

People who are content never invent anything, discover anything, improve anything. Or desire their brother's wife. Liz at her needlework. Liz in her garden party frock. The soft places when he carried her ashore in Lafitte's Cove and up the stairs when she had fainted. Liz, her anguish and pain when she lost the baby. In her ball gown on Halloween and how close he had come to. . . . No. Get your mind off your brother's wife and onto something else, anything else. Like getting round the Horn in January and up the West Coast and dealing with the agents in San Francisco bay.

When he arrived in San Francisco, there was no message waiting for him at the El Padre Hotel. Just as he expected.

But it meant the board had not turned down the idea, and he was glad, glad because Galveston would benefit if it was accepted. When it had become apparent to him and Joe Bob that the liner was bigger and more important than any ship afloat, that his own company would not be able to handle it, his idea had expanded to include a beautiful island paradise on Galveston island, develop-ment of the entire thirty miles of beach on the coast side, the entire island a resort paradise for surf bathers, deep sea fishing, yachting, resort homes on the west end of the island, extensive planting of palms and oleanders over the entire island, not just in the city itself. Galveston, developed all along the bay side for shipping. Galveston businessmen could only profit, and to profit they'd have to invest, and their first investment would be to attract passenger trade, and the beginning of that was the *Lucinda*. Let Moran handle the cargo, let Ingram handle the passenger trade, Mayfield the immigrant traffic—or *consolidate*. The wharfage company could lower the wharfage rates and make up the capital in tourist trade and passenger services. Entirely plausible, profitable, and sane.

In high spirits Damon put the *Arundel* into the port of Galveston in early May. Talk at the wharf—conveyed to him before he ever left the ship—was that a faction in China called the Boxers had rebeled against foreigners and foreign-held property in China, and many foreigners had been killed. Armed intervention seemed inevitable, an ironic twist since there had been such a to-do after the war about annexing the Philippines as a base for commercial trade with the Orient. Damon hoped the whole damned mess wouldn't end up in war again. He smiled as he threw the last of his shirts into his bag preparing to disembark, realizing he was beginning to think more like Ingram and the rest of them. Like them, he favored free trade. He favored Hay's Open Door policy. His dream depended on it.

Still intoxicated with his possible dream, he disembarked from the *Arundel*. And at the end of the gangplank at the wharf, stood Liz.

She said nothing, only smilingly came to him, and he took her into his arms as naturally as if she had been his own wife. But the usual brief embrace at meeting her after a long voyage, the sisterly hug, the brotherly brevity, wafted off somewhere on the gentle seabreeze, and he pulled her against him and kissed her lips warmly and lingeringly before it even occurred to him it was wrong. He drew away from her, shocked. "Liz—"

"Hush," she said, putting a finger to his lips. "Damon, I didn't intend for that to happen."

"Nor did I."

"Then we won't talk about it."

"Shouldn't we?"

"I came only to tell you first the good news. Joe Bob says Ingram and Sturgeon are feeling out the Galveston businessmen about financing your . . . idea. The board members are skeptical about it, but they have an entire whisper campaign going on among the wharf company and the businessmen about your ocean liner."

He smiled. "And the bad news?"

"Richard has been ill. No, don't be alarmed. It wasn't serious, but he did miss his last three weeks' lectures at the college. It's something strange; we don't understand what it is. First, these burns appeared on his hands which he thinks had something to do with the x-ray machine; then he became weak and pale, absolutely lost all his energy, began to throw up frequently. Rob Tate said he was anemic. But after three weeks at home, he's much better."

He took her arm and together they walked to her carriage. "If he's been unable to work, how are his finances, Liz?"

"Well, the Board of Regents didn't give a raise to the professors this year, and they didn't grant any of their requests, but we're financially alright."

"Do you need money?"

"No. We're fine."

"Promise?"

"I promise."

"Is Richard still at home?"

"Yes, but Rob Tate says he'll be able to return to his office by the first week in June. That's three weeks from now, so I imagine Richard will return next week instead. You know him, has to be busy every minute."

"Yes, I know. I love my brother, Liz."

They had reached her little Studebaker buggy with its spirited mare and he helped her up into it and held the bit as she wrapped the reins around her dainty wrists. Smiling down at him she said, "So do I, Damon."

And he stood wondering that he had actually just kissed those lips and still the world kept revolving, the sea gulls never paused in their squawling and circling, nor the longshoremen in their loading and unloading on the docks. The only change he could detect was in the shine of her eyes and the high color of her cheek and the heavy pressure in his own chest which he did not want to identify.

"I'm glad you're home," she said.

"So am I."

She shook the reins and he released the little mare, the carriage jerked forward, and he watched as it sped away down the street to the south. John Richard, he thought, the pressure in his chest revealing itself at last, what am I doing to you, brother? Worse, what am I doing to the three of us?

Elizabeth could tell that Mildred Crabtree had come to her on a serious mission. There was no mistaking the determined set of her chin, the tightness of her mouth as she sat erect and fanless in the Morrison front parlor. Mildred never fanned when she had something religious or serious to discuss. Elizabeth was afraid someone had seen Damon kiss her at the wharf last Tuesday and had conveyed that delicious tidbit to Mildred. She sat waiting for the blow, but when it came, it wasn't what she expected.

"Elizabeth, please understand I mean no harm," Mildred began, "only to warn, because I consider you one of my very best friends and because I think so highly of you. I have it from a very reliable source that you and some of your friends were actually seen bathing in the surf last week."

Elizabeth was so stunned—and so relieved—that all she could do was burst out laughing. "Mildred! Is that all?"

"All? It's enough. Brother Bill says that sea bathing in such costumes is a prelude to habitual lasciviousness."

Elizabeth laughed again. "Mildred, not one more inch of skin is exposed in my bathing suit than in this dress I'm wearing now."

"Skin no," said Mildred tightly, "but form yes. I've seen those suits, Elizabeth, and they do reveal form. I'm

371

only telling you this, please understand, because I don't want you to be the target of any gossip."

After last summer's confinement, Elizabeth had been *so* happy to be in such fine health with a new summer arriving, that she had accepted an invitation from Betty Milford and Ruby Yates, friends in her garden club, to go bathing in the surf. Galveston beach was a sunny crescent of yellow-white sand, a long, clean beach that sloped gently to the water's edge and more gently still out to sea. Horse-drawn bathhouses could be rented where bathers could change from street dress to swim suits and step out into the shallow surf without being duly exposed to the view of people on the beach road, and to prevent getting sand on their stockings and shoes. The day she took Cully and joined Betty and Ruby at the beach, it was lined with the bathhouses and the Gulf water washed around dozens of bathers—mostly women and children— and early tourists lay on the beach under umbrellas enjoying refreshments from the concessions along the road.

Elizabeth had gone to Hardy's Ready-to-Wear on Tremont and purchased a beautiful suit and brought it home, unwrapped it hurriedly and held it up for Richard to see.

"Look, Richard, isn't it beautiful?" she said, holding the suit up in front of her.

Richard was still at home convalescing from his bout with the mysterious illness, and looked up from his paper, took the pipe out of his mouth, and said, "What is it, a sailor suit for Cully?"

"No! It's a bathing suit for me!"

"Kind of small isn't it?"

"Oh, Richard. It's the very latest thing. Hardy's just got it in from New Orleans." She held the thing up again for him to see.

Actually it was rather strange looking. Though the navy skirt would come well below her knees, she would have to wear dark cotton stockings to cover her legs—or maybe striped ones, she wasn't sure yet—and canvas shoes. The top was daring, but not any more so than her party frocks, with its V neck in front. The sailor collar was embroidered in back with red birds and under the front of the collar a red scarf was tied.

Richard smiled and said, "Beth, I'm only teasing you. Put the thing on and go to the beach. You've been inside too much the past year. And anyway, I'm of the same opinion as Damon; you should get some sun, look more like an Indian than a lily."

They had immense fun bathing in the warm surf, laughing, splashing, and when she came home afraid of freckles and saw the burns on her arms and cheeks, feared the worst. But, no freckles appeared, only a high color to match her exceedingly high spirits.

She smiled at Mildred now and said, "I'm not worried. We did nothing wrong. There'll be no talk about my bathing in the surf."

"Oh, but there already is."

Elizabeth returned lightly, "Who and what?"

"Now don't be angry with me," Mildred said touching her bosom. "I'm only telling you this to prevent further gossip. It wouldn't be so bad if you were single, though that's bad enough. But being a married woman . . . well, people will tend to think you're trying to attract attention of the most salacious kind."

"Salacious! Mildred, I was only taking Cully for a swim and with two very respected ladies!"

Mildred looked truly distressed, saying, "Oh, now I've made you angry, haven't I? And I meant only to help." She reached for the handkerchief she had tucked inside her sleeve and began to fan with it. "It's just that Brother Bill has been preaching about Galveston's loose morals, so many ladies of the night, so much no-telling-what going on behind the drawn shades of people's houses. He says it's high time Galveston and the rest of the world took notice of the signs of the times. Wars and rumors of wars, loose morals, too much thought about . . . well . . . things in the bedroom, even between husband and wife."

"Oh Lord. There's been wars and rumors of wars since the beginning of time, Mildred. And even things going on in the bedroom between husband and wife."

Mildred was fanning faster. "And the medical school . . . Elizabeth, did you know that Dr. Kelly and his students actually cut up naked human bodies, forgetting decency and that the body is the temple of the soul?"

"The soul has long departed those bodies, Mildred."

"And while I'm at it, please don't be mad at me, but some of the ladies in the missionary union of our church object to Dr. Morrison's machine."

By now Elizabeth was furious and fought the urge to lose her temper entirely. "Whatever for?"

"Well, it seems to them, that if the machine could see

through the skin to the bone, what about its ability to see through a lady's or gentleman's . . . *garments?*"

"Stop it!" Elizabeth stood suddenly. "Stop it! I've heard enough of this!" Tears flooded her eyes as she clasped her hands tightly to keep from striking her neighbor. "Your Brother Bill, Mildred . . . what he needs is a *woman.*"

"Elizabeth!"

"Yes, even one of those ladies of the night who would let him into her bed at night. That sanctimonious milquetoast wife of his you brought over here for me to meet, does *she?* Poor frustrated man! And as for Dr. Kelly, he is a decent man seeking cures for diseases and maladies that afflict human beings. And Richard, that decent, sweet, self-sacrificing gentleman, ruining his health with that machine so that people's bones can be mended correctly to prevent deformities . . . how dare anybody talk about him. Have you seen his hands?" Weeping freely now she said, "Scar tissue all over that will never heal. Never!"

Mildred had risen from her chair and pressed her handkerchief to her bosom and reached out toward Elizabeth with the other, wailing, "Oh dear Lord. I've hurt you. Oh dear, Elizabeth, I've hurt you."

"Yes. Yes you have. But let me tell you, Mildred, I'm *glad* Galveston has beaches and ladies of the night. And I'll tell you something that will truly shock you." She caught her breath and said, "Those hands of Richard's, I want them to *touch* me, to make love to me. I not only let him touch me out of duty, but I *encourage* it. Go tell that to your friends. *Tell* them!"

"Oh my Lord," breathed Mildred faintly, her eyes

swimming in the vagueness of an imminent swoon.

"Yes, I encourage it," Elizabeth whispered passionately. "And now, please excuse me, because I think I'm going to be sick."

Mildred followed Elizabeth into the entry and watched as she flew up the stairs, then weeping and moaning to herself, bustled out the screen door, scurrying for home.

But Elizabeth did not become sick. She ran into the nursery instead where she sat down in the little oak rocker, and rocking, wept in fury for awhile. Then, thinking back on what she had said to Mildred Crabtree, the entire thing became funny, and she laughed thinking, Poor Mildred.

Still rocking, the tears drying on her cheeks, she said to herself, "I shall bathe in the sea again, and I shall continue to enjoy Richard's love, I shall continue to dream of Damon and yearn for his visits. I shall bask in parties and visit with my friends. I will enjoy life and living, and I will continue to love Galveston in all her beauty and with all her faults, and continue to thank God for my good life. And life shall continue to be good and sweet. And someday soon I hope to become enormously pregnant again! Yes, pregnant again I shall be! Somehow."

Twenty-Two

It took a lot of parties; Emily's garden party in May, the Sturgeons' shrimp fleet ball in the Octogon beach house, the Coffmans' ice cream social at the Garten Verein, Elizabeth's old-fashioned singalong in June, the watermelon feast on the beach, the Fourth of July city picnic, the Trinity Episcopal Church social July 20th, and the fish fry in central park in August, to prepare the soil of Galveston's master minds and city fathers for the planting of the idea of Damon's *Lucinda* by Eric Ingram and Max Sturgeon and some of the other cautious, vacillating board members.

Every businessman knew that the city was in financial trouble due to political gerrymandering and financial jugglery, its budget consistently exceeding its income, although its citizens were some of the richest per capita in the world. And so the time was ripe for planting. Over champagne and Havana cigars and Galveston's own homemade cheroots, men toyed playfully and almost

embarrassedly with the idea of a great luxury passenger
liner, the first of its kind to sail the seas, and maybe a
sister ship just like her, of resort hotels, of the extension
of the beach down the entire length of the island, of
island avenues planted with tall palms, and streets lined
with oleanders, of yachts for hire, of deep sea fishing, of
tourists flocking to the island in droves, of buildings
rising tall downtown, of many shops and boutiques, of
wharves stretched down the length of the island on the
bay side, of giant cargo ships in port and plying the
channel. And Galveston could then thumb her aristocratic nose at swamp-infested Houston and strut down
the annals of history a big sister to New Orleans, a com-
petitor of New York City, and respected by her European
cousins.

But Elizabeth said, "Why can't we just build the liner
and remain the port we are. Why *must* we turn our island
into a resort?"

On the subject Damon and Elizabeth often argued for
hours. And once she had stood up from her chair in the
back parlor, threw down her embroidery, gathered up her
skirts, and with chin up and mouth tight, swept past the
Morrison brothers, out of the room and up the stairs with
Damon following and shouting after her, "I'm sorry, Liz.
I lost my temper. I apologize. Galveston *isn't* becoming a
sick old lady, and you *aren't* just being backward. I apologize, I say!"

So the summer of 1900 was one vibrating ambivalently
with destiny. The seigniorial families, the bankers, the
financiers, real estate brokers, shipping magnates, merchants, and the Galveston-based government officials

smoked Havanas and cheroots and pipes in their libraries, drank mint Julips in their gazebos, and discussed the future of Galveston.

Meanwhile, an outbreak that summer of what was thought to be malaria had occurred in the American garrison at Havana, and a commission consisting of Drs. Walter Reed and James Carroll were sent to investigate. The epidemic turned out to be yellow fever. In July, as an experiment, a man named Lazare allowed himself to be bitten by a mosquito suspected of being infested with yellow fever and Lazare did indeed contract yellow fever and die. The experiment strongly supported the theory that a certain type of mosquito did cause yellow fever. The tropical world awaited the final results of the investigation.

The thing was on Richard's mind as he climbed the stairs of the medical hall. With the yellow fever season almost over, he and his colleagues could heave a sigh of relief that there had been no epidemic that year. Perhaps once it became established that mosquitoes did cause yellow fever, the cities like Galveston would do something about their sanitation and standing water, and a way could be found to eradicate yellow fever. The means used to eradicate yellow fever pests could eradicate malaria, dengue and perhaps even typhoid as well.

Richard, glad to be plodding the wide corridors of the building again, had felt his strength return with Beth's tender ministrations. His office practice was again flourishing, and he was wearing rubber gloves now to prevent further burns from the rays of the x-ray machine which somehow seemed to be associated with his recent illness.

The new term was scheduled to begin October 15th, and he had just set up his lab equipment in preparation for the term and wanted to see what Will Kelly was up to.

He found him sitting at his desk in the dissecting lab carefully penning the words, LIVER, on a label stuck to a jar. Kelly looked up when Richard entered and said shrilly, "Come in Richard. Look at you. Fit and in fine fettle, as you Texans say. I see you set up the chemistry lab already for another year."

"I thought you were on vacation," Richard said, taking the chair near Kelly's desk as Will's dog rose up from under his desk and came to him to be petted.

"I leave at three o'clock today. Weather warnings and all. I checked with Isaac this morning about the tropical disturbance in the West Indies heading for Florida and he seems a little concerned. Seas are choppy between here and New Orleans and he advised me to take the train out instead of a steamer. He ran up the storm warning flags this morning." Will set his pickled liver on the desk and leaned back in his chair. "I hear you bought some new lab equipment."

"Well, I couldn't start a new term without new equipment, so I borrowed a little money and ordered some new burners and such," Richard said as he scratched the dog's head.

"Rob Tate bought a new microscope and a dozen rabbits. Thinks he's going to do some studies on typhoid. Thinks if one can vaccinate for rabies, why can't one vaccinate for typhoid? He made a pen for the rabbits out on the gallery above the main entrance. His lab opens out onto it."

"How about you? If you're off to Florida for a couple of weeks you must be ready for the new term too."

"I am. I need to get out of here for a while. Look at me. Pale and sickly looking because there's no light in here and this is where I spend most of my time." Kelly pinned Richard with one of his ice-blue gazes and said, "I've complained for nine years about needing a skylight in this lab, Richard, to no avail. I've finally come to the conclusion that for the lab to have a skylight, it would take an act of God."

Later Richard looked in on Rob Tate on the second floor.

"Ah, Richard. Welcome," Rob said when he entered the pathology lab. As Richard wandered over to peer out at Rob's pen full of rabbits, Rob said, "Come see this magnificent microscope. I can fit it with oil immersion lenses." Rob was seated at his desk which was stacked with papers. "Pardon the mess, Richard, but I've been going over hospital records from January to June, sent them off to the bindery so we can incorporate them into the medical school library for case studies. Here, now take a look at this microscope. See what you think."

When Richard had looked at the slide of Rob's pet *Necator americanus*, he nodded smiling. "Wish you had an entire lab of these microscopes, Rob?"

"Yes. But of course that would take a miracle," Rob sighed.

"About your rabbits, you anatomy and pathology professors are making a zoo out of the medical hall."

"Ah, sounds like a true chemist. What I'm doing is experimenting with a typhoid vaccination using the

381

rabbits. Will's dog is here because he's leaving on vacation and is boarding the dog for me to look after. Intends to lock him up in his office, papers on the floor, you know, for him to do his business on. And then I'm supposed to let him out to run once a day." Rob straightened in his chair and said, "We've come a long way, the school has, though, Richard. In spite of everything. Shoulder to shoulder we've fought a good fight and UTMB has survived. More. It's grown in enrollment and in reputation. And in nine years we've managed to turn out quality physicians able to make the highest grades on the state examinations." He tilted his head and squinted out his window. "You know, I've got this feeling lately, Richard, that our struggles here at the school are about over. It seems to me that with the coming of the new century, we are on the brink of something. . . ." He looked at Richard, ". . . something enormous."

Richard went back to his office and tended to his patients; then later, going home, noticed the sky—blue, with only wispy clouds. Will Kelly should be well on his way across the mainland headed for Florida. Hopefully the tropical disturbance would be played out over land by the time Will and his family reached the state.

As he drove Blitz into the drive from the alley, he noticed Beth's neat flower borders were still blooming profusely even for September; Shad's vegetable garden was still producing more than Beth and Prim could can. Joe Bob was weeding the garden in his yard and paused to shout a hello, and the curtain at the Hoffman's window on the other side was pulled to as he dismounted the carriage. Strange people. He and Beth had lived here for

382

three years and had seldom seen or spoken to their next-door neighbors to the east. Beth had tried to befriend them, but they wanted nothing of their neighbors and preferred to be left alone.

Shad took over the horse and buggy saying, "The buggy needs a shine, Dr. Richard. The salt spray's been heavy today, what with the seas churnin' like they is."

"I advise you to shine it today, then Shad," he said looking up at Beth's palm trees now eave-high and bending with a stiff breeze from the north. "We might need to shut the storm shutters later, maybe by tomorrow morning, but I doubt it."

Beth met him at the door as he went inside, and he kissed her soundly.

"How does the school look to you dear?" she said returning to her salad-making.

"Much better than the weather," he replied. "Storm flags are up on the Levy building. I guess Isaac Cline earned his keep today. It looks like we may have a little rain from the tropical disturbance in the Gulf, maybe by tomorrow." Richard pulled a couple of Elmira's numerous, beribboned twigs and the toddler giggled and hid her face in Prim's skirts.

Elizabeth said, "Did you see Rob?"

"I saw Rob and Will both. Rob has rabbits in the lab he's doing experiments on, and Will has a dog in his. What's Prim got in the pot?"

"Don't you dare lift that lid, John Richard," Elizabeth said. "That's jambalaya and you'll let out all the steam and ruin the rice. Go read the morning paper. I saved it for you, since you left before Shad could bring it in. Go

383

on! Shoo! Out with you!"

He caught her roughly around the waist and planted another kiss on her lips when Prim wasn't looking, then released her and went to the parlor where his paper was laid out on the center table. Settling in his rocker, he fixed his pipe and shook out the newspaper.

Allied forces had occupied Peking. The Boxer Rebellion was soon to be over, it seemed. Further down he read where William Jennings Bryan had made a speech in Virginia. The *News* had printed the Galveston census at last. The population was 37,789. He thumbed through the paper until he reached page eight where the U.S. Weather Bureau in Washington, D.C. reported the tropical storm now over Southern Florida. The storm was moving northward with winds up to forty-eight miles an hour. The article went on to say the center of the storm would probably continue to move northward; that would make it hit the mid-Atlantic coast and miss the Gulf altogether. Which seemed rather far away to make the seas near Galveston so choppy today.

He thought of Damon out there in the Atlantic, somewhere in the West Indies, and hoped he'd missed the storm. That concerned him some, but he reasoned that his brother was a superb ship's captain and he had been through storms before in less seaworthy ships than the *Arundel*. And the Weather Bureau report was twenty-four to thirty-six hours old by now anyway and the storm should be inland and Damon should be out of it. Besides, according to the *News*, the storm was only a tropical disturbance, nothing more. Certainly nothing for Galveston to worry about, thank God. Nothing at all.

Twenty-Three

Second mate Michael Stephens had fought the helm for four hours now as the *Arundel* pitched and yawed about in rough seas churned by gale-velocity winds upwards of sixty miles per hour. The mountainous swells rose, crested, tumbled down, roaring white with spin drift; visibility was almost zero.

"Barometer reading, Mr. Cunningham," said Damon to his first mate.

"Twenty-eight point six five, sir."

"Mr. Cunningham, I do believe the storm is veering to the west, which should put it heading for the Louisiana coast."

According to the weather station in Havana, the storm was expected to pass from Cuba to Key West, Florida, and on inland from there. But a hurricane was as unpredictable as a woman and they had been steaming on the periphery of it since the third watch.

"If I read the signs correctly, sir," began Mr. Cunningham, "the storm is veering west and we are either sailing into it or it's gaining in intensity, sir."

"It's the latter. Note the direction of the wind and the swells, Mr. Cunningham. It's veering west and we're steering west-northwest."

"Then the thing's gaining strength and headed for New Orleans, if my calculations are correct, sir."

"Your calculations are correct in my opinion, Mr. Cunningham, and we may find that city a shambles when we put into port there. So since the ship is faster than the storm, we'll remain steady as she goes and take our time, bear away from it. Have the engine room cut the forward engine."

"Aye aye, sir."

The sea had not diminished its churning nor the wind its intensity as the *Arundel* put into the port of New Orleans. By that time, it had become obvious to Damon and his crew that the hurricane had veered on a course almost due west, leaving in its wake a stream of wrecked vessels along eastern Florida and the Mississippi and Louisiana coasts. When he disembarked from the ship, he literally ran through a pounding rain and gale winds to the dispatch office near the wharves.

"It's a big 'un, alright, Cap'n," the telegrapher shouted above the roar and whine of wind. "Did considerable damage in Key West and we haven't had no reports since she blew through here, but she's headed toward the Texas-Mexico border, far as we can tell. Texas had better look out!"

"Can you get a dispatch out to Galveston?"

"As I understand it, Cap'n, a weather bulletin has

already gone out; looks like Galveston will only get the edge of the storm, though. Anyways, the lines blowed down here early this morning and I can't send and I can't receive."

Damon, with rain dripping off the hood of his slicker and the end of his nose, looked out the dispatch office window toward the west. If New Orleans had been a port located immediately on the ocean, he could not have seen the heavy seas for the downpour. But he would not have seen the sea anyway, only that fair island in his mind's eye, the Queen City of the Gulf, naked, and so vulnerable to the ravages of the storm.

The storm would cause a bit of wind and rain after all, Richard decided as he stepped into his trousers. It was six A.M., September the 8th. He had four x-ray plates to look at before Barry Holcomb came for them on his way to his own office. As Richard shrugged into his suspenders, he looked out the window and saw that the sky was pink in the dawn light; pink and white resembling a graveled surface. When he'd gone to bed near midnight, stars were shining and he had thought then that the storm would miss Galveston altogether. Now it looked like Galveston might have a bit of wind and rain later on.

Downstairs little Elmira was whimpering in her high chair when Richard came into the kitchen. "Morning, Prim. What's the matter with Elmira?"

"Oh she has the colic, Dr. Richard, and the bowel runs too."

"Don't give her any more milk, Prim. Try weak tea."

"Weak tea? Lord, Dr. Richard, you say weak tea?"

"Weak tea."

"Then weak tea she gets. How much sugar?"

"None."

"None? Lord, that child won't drink weak tea with no sugar."

"Try and see." By then Richard had picked up the *News*, dutifully bought by Shad earlier that morning from Commodore Cooley, the old peg-legged seaman who sold the *News* on the corner of Strand and Tremont from morning till night calling, "Dabey Naw. Dabey Naw." Nobody knew for sure if the fellow had really been a commodore or not; it was just a title somebody had given him once that stuck. Richard shook out the folds in the paper and sat down at the table.

The first thing that caught his eye was a storm warning. According to the article, the storm which had headed due north struck the Florida coast then veered west, and yesterday afternoon was located between New Orleans and Galveston still headed due west. Richard figured that would make it hit Texas in the vicinity of the Texas-Mexico border. The article confirmed his deduction by stating that though the weather bureau had no late advisories as to the storm's movement, it was believed the "tropical disturbance" had changed its course or spent its violence before reaching Texas. Richard turned the page and scanned it for any article concerning the investigation in Cuba by Drs. Walter Reed and James Carrol on yellow fever, a thing most interesting, especially now that they were establishing that yellow fever was indeed caused by a specie of mosquito, and Havana, Cuba had begun extravagant programs of sanitation and drainage systems because of it.

"The child likes the tea," giggled Prim. "Look, Dr. Richard."

Richard peered over the pages of the newspaper at Elmira sitting in her high chair briskly nursing a bottle of amber-colored tea with a nipple on it that was more like the color of Beth's breast than Prim's. When the child saw Richard peeping over the paper at her, she let go of the nipple, grinned, showing four gleaming white baby teeth, and emitted her first word, the inevitable, "Boo!"

After a breakfast of ham and eggs and biscuits, Richard got his coat and hat and went out to the carriage house where Shad had already hitched Blitz to the buggy. "Morn', Dr. Richard."

"Morning, Shad. Brisk wind."

"Yes sir. The horse is jumpy," Shad said. "Reckon some critter or other came into the yard last night. Ain't never seen ol' Blitz actin' like that. An' Little Bit done kicked till she put a hole in the stall."

"There's a storm in the Gulf. Maybe that's what's got them upset," Richard said climbing into the carriage. As he took the reins he was remembering the days when he and Damon were boys and how their father's cattle had become spooked before a storm, sometimes even before a cloud appeared. "Somethin' in the wind, I reckon," their father would always say. Richard looked down at Shad and said, "Tell Mrs. Morrison that I said she shouldn't go bathing in the Gulf today like she'd planned, will you? The sea's probably still rough because of the wind."

"Sure will, Dr. Richard. But Miss Lizbeth, she don' listen to me." Shad ducked his head and shook it, giggling. "But I'll tell her. I seen the bay this mornin' and it's bilin'. Ain't never seen the bay bile like that before."

Richard looked up at the sky. Millions of birds were winging across the island high up, winging against the north wind from the south, headed, it seemed, for the mainland. A drop of rain fell on Richard's cheek. He clicked his tongue, and Blitz sprang forward at a trot.

When Elizabeth came down to breakfast at seven, a light rain was falling outside, and the wind was driving it into the glass-enclosed service porch. She chucked Elmira under the chin and said to Prim, "Looks like my plans are ruined for the day."

Prim poured beaten eggs from a bowl into the cast-iron skillet on the stove. "Dr. Richard told Shad to tell you not to go bathin' at the beach, Miss Lizbeth, for the sea is choppy today. I done talk to Sissy and she say the waves is high and makin' a *terrible* noise."

"Sissy always exaggerates."

"Look out yonder at the wind, an' you'll see," Prim said. "Say, that child Elmira done say 'Boo' to Dr. Richard this mornin'."

"I told you she was a precocious child." Elizabeth, smiling, went to the porch and could hardly see out. The wind, oddly from the north, was driving the rain against the window. But she could see her palm trees bending in the wind and Shad closing the storm shutters on the carriage house windows.

The telephone rang in the entry and presently Prim called her to it. It was Emily.

"Lord, Elizabeth. Max rang Matilda to tell her not to go

390

down to the beach. The breakers are tremendous and there's a foot or so of seawater in some people's yards down near the beach."

Elizabeth talked to Emily only a minute because there was so much noise on the line, and the party line kept breaking in and hanging up. She went back to the kitchen to eat breakfast. The more she thought about the breakers on the beach, the more excited she became. How beautiful they must be, the sea raging in one of its many moods. Her rival, the sea, and yet she loved it. Damon said once, "I hate the sea . . . it's treacherous . . . you'll see, Miss Harbour . . . somehow I know you will."

She sprang up from her chair and went upstairs to her room, found her oilskin slicker in an old trunk and ran down the stairs pulling it on. In the entry she pulled up the hood to cover her hair and put on her gloves. When she came into the kitchen, Elmira shrieked at the sight of her, and Prim looked up from the dish water and exclaimed, "Lord, Miss Lizbeth! What are you up to?"

"I'm going to go see if Melissa and Cully would like to see the breakers on the beach."

"Now Miss Lizbeth, Dr. Richard say—"

But Elizabeth slammed out the back door and ran over to the Swifts where she found Melissa sitting at the kitchen table nursing a cup of tea and "under the weather" because Aunt Martha had come to visit that morning. But Cully was excited to see the breakers, and Sissy helped him into his rain gear and he and Elizabeth went to the carriage house to have Shad harness Little Bit to the buggy.

Shad protested, but Elizabeth cut him short. "Dr.

Richard said for me not to go sea bathing. Well, I'm not. I'm only going to look," she told him.

Still, Shad moped over to the wall, took the harness from the peg and said, "That mare, she's skittish, Miss Lizbeth. Don't reckon you ought to go at all."

"I can handle Little Bit. She's always skittish."

Shad threw the hitch muttering, "But today she's skittisher, and so was Blitz." He hitched the little mare to the buggy and Elizabeth and Cully climbed into the seat.

"Please, Miss Lizbeth, there's a storm acomin' an I jus' don't feel right lettin' you go like this," Shad whined.

"Then you can drive us, Shad."

"I will, 'cause if I don't, you'd go anyways," he said, and climbed onto the seat beside Cully. "Giddap, Little Bit."

The beach and the beach road were crowded with sight-seers exactly like Elizabeth and Cully. The streetcars were filled with people getting off at the beach to watch the breakers, the awesome heave of the angry sea. Because of the crowds along the midway where the myriad concession stands were lined up, Elizabeth had Shad drive off the road and onto a high place where they could get a better view of the sea. Little Bit was clearly disturbed and kept stamping her hooves and tossing her head and swinging her white face around to look at Shad with baleful eye.

Business at the concessions was going on as usual, or better. Tony, the ice cream vendor, was plodding down the sodden beach road dressed in a slicker, pushing his cart and ringing his hand bell which was barely audible above the thunder and roar and crash of the breakers.

Cully would laugh and clap his hands at the daring bathers on the beach when a particularly giant wave would bear down upon them, causing them to run screaming up the beach in delight. But after a while, gradually, one by one the bathers drifted away from the water as the swells grew slowly larger and dashed at the Pagoda bathhouse stretched out over the Gulf.

It was awesome, and Elizabeth delighted in seeing it, the sea in a fury driven by an unseen force from the southeast against a north gale; dark-gray seas, heaving in mountainous, foaming swells and crests, merging into an equally angry, leaden sky, the drenching cold rain obliterating the horizon.

All bathers were ashore now, the little bathhouses were pulled ashore eventually and lined up in rows behind the concessions. Cully pointed suddenly. From the south a giant roller was coming in, dark, foam-crested, and crashed onto shore carrying with it two of the little bathhouses, flinging them into the concessions on the midway.

"Oh Lord," Elizabeth gasped, feeling her first wave of alarm.

Another roller—*crash*—carrying the other bathhouses with it, dashing them to splinters into the concessions. Another wave—*crash!*—sending foam as high as the telephone wires, carrying with it debris almost all the way to the beach road. Water was lapping now at the very walls of the Pagoda and the other giant bathhouses which stretched out over the beach and over the surf. CRASH. Two concessions went down, splintered into wrecks.

CRASH! Others flew into a million pieces, and now the owners were vacating them, carrying goods with them, dragging machinery onto the beach road. Sightseers huddled along the road laughed and shouted good-natured taunts at the concessionaires. The fierce wind drove rain under the carriage top, drumming against Elizabeth's and Cully's rain gear. CRASH! More concessions flew into oblivion and the waves washed sand and debris onto the street car tracks.

The telephone and electric lines strung above the beach road upon crosslike poles were sending up an eerie singing now, and there was no sound to be heard from anything but the wires and the sea.

Little Bit tossed her head and made a move forward. "Ho, now," Shad said, and turned his dripping face to Elizabeth. "Miss Lizbeth, I reckon we ought to go now."

Not while the breakers are so thrilling, she thought. "In a minute, Shad," she said and examined Cully's slicker to see if he was staying as dry as possible. He was squinting out to sea with a grimace against the awesome sight.

Presently they saw a hansom approaching down the beach road and Elizabeth recognized Isaac Cline's spotted horse. The hansom was pausing occasionally, the driver shouting to the crowd now standing in drenched huddles along the road, and then moving on. When he drew near, Elizabeth waved to him and he pulled the hansom up beside the buggy. "Mrs. Morrison!" he shouted above the roar of the sea. "Go home! The worst is yet to come!" And without further ado, he went on further up the road and she could still hear him shouting, "Get to higher ground. The worst is yet to come!"

Cully stood up in the carriage, watching the giant breakers, the sea swelling, encroaching now over the beach road, and he sat down shuddering, his teeth chattering. Then he turned frowning to Elizabeth. "I think I'd like to go home now."

Elizabeth put her arm around the boy, nodded to Shad, who gratefully gave the little mare her head, and the buggy turned about in the muddy street and sped homeward.

The storm warning flags atop the Levy Building where the weather bureau was located were shredded by the time Richard left his office at noon. The rain was being driven hard by terrible winds that had shifted from north to northeast. Water was running in the streets now. He could see the churning water of the bay already swamping the wharves. The electric wires along Mechanic were sending up an eerie singing like souls mourning in hell, and he experienced his first alarm.

Blitz bore the animal terror of wind, rain, and flying debris with infinite patience, splashing through the water for home. Richard had decided to go home for lunch and check things out there. Shad should have closed the storm shutters and secured the doors of the carriage house. A load of hay should be put down for the horses, because it might not be possible to get to the carriage house tonight. Apparently, the hurricane was closer than anyone had expected.

When he arrived at home, drenched to the skin, Shad took over the horse and buggy, shouting above the howl of the wind and the thunder of rain that he had secured all storm shutters and doors and put hay down for the horses.

The light was on in the kitchen when Richard went in. The smell of coffee and salt pork cooking with black-eye peas wafted to him as he stood on the porch shedding his coat and hat.

Elizabeth came to him saying, "Look at you. Your suit is ruined. When it dries it won't even be big enough to fit Cully. And the odor is awful."

"Wool smells that way when it's wet," he said, "It's not me, I swear."

She laughed. "I tried to ring you but all the lines are jammed. I wanted you to come home. Melissa and Joe Bob are here."

He went with her to the table in the kitchen where Joe Bob and Melissa sat with a cup of coffee in front of them, and Cully ran to him shrilling, "Dr. Richard, me and Lizbeth went and saw the waves." Then he proceeded to tell what they'd seen down at the beach, his face reflecting a mixture of fear and exhilaration.

When he was through, Richard said to Elizabeth, "Was that very prudent, Beth? Little Bit could have run away with the buggy."

"Oh hush. Shad drove us."

Prim set a cup of steaming coffee in front of him as Joe Bob said, "I went by the weather bureau office, Richard, and there was havoc there, people coming in asking the Clines about the weather. The telephone was ringing incessantly. All Isaac Cline and his brother could do was tell us to get to higher ground. Seems he doesn't like the way the Gulf is moving in *against* the north wind. Usually a north wind drives the sea out. But something's driving it in against the wind."

Prim moaned, "Oh Lord, it's a hurricane!" But her consternation about the storm was short-lived when she saw Flop heading for the dining room carpet with his ball. "Cully you mind and keep that ol' wet mop off the dining room carpet, you hear?"

Richard set his cup down. "Isaac seems to think the storm's approaching?"

"Seems that way."

"Well, we've had hurricanes before, I hope everybody knows what to do."

Shad came in the back door just then, slapping his hat against his leg saying, "Hooo eeee! That rain is comin' down like it was poured out'n a boot. The flower gardens are beat down, Miss Lizbeth, and I had to shut the chickens in the chicken house. They was standin' out in the rain and drowndin'. Stood aroun' with their heads up in the air to let the water run off their backs. Only thing wrong with that was, the water was runnin' into their beaks. Ain't nothin' dumber than a chicken!"

"Sounds like the people down by the beach," Cully said. "An me and Lizabeth are chickens too." The little boy went off on a tangent going around and around the table saying, "Bock, bock, bock," and flapping his arms while Melissa corrected him. "Cully? Behave! Cully!"

"Did Cline say how long he expected this storm to last?" Richard asked.

Joe Bob shook his head. "No, but he was clearly worried."

"Frightened and frustrated," Elizabeth said as she reached for Cully and hugged him to her. "He was going all up and down the beach road telling people to get to higher ground, that the worst was yet to come. He was almost in a frenzy."

Richard didn't comment. He was thinking the weather looked bad enough that there would be people hurt from flying debris and probably some would become ill from exposure.

She had persuaded Joe Bob and Melissa to stay for lunch. During the meal the talk was of the storm and what each of them had seen, and Prim and Shad strained to listen from their table on the service porch.

Halfway through the meal, the telephone jangled and Richard said, "Somebody has gotten through," and got up to answer it.

The crackling on the line was worse than usual, but the voice on the other end said, "Hello, Richard? Rob Tate. If you feel you can leave your house for the afternoon, I think we need you at the hospital. There's some injuries coming in, flying debris. And there's only a few of us doctors left that haven't gone on vacation. Do you mind?"

Richard hesitated only a moment before he replied, "Not at all, Rob. I'll be there shortly."

He went back to the dining room and asked Joe Bob if he was going to be home the rest of the evening and Joe Bob said he was. Richard asked him to keep an eye on things—meaning Elizabeth and his house and servants.

Elizabeth said, "Oh Richard, do you have to get out in this awful weather?"

He truly wished that he didn't but . . . "I'll be alright," he said, "and Joe Bob will tend to things here."

"Oh, I'll be so worried."

"Don't be. Just stay inside," he said, "And no more daring rides to the beach."

Elizabeth looked at the west window in the kitchen where the rain was washing down, obliterating the view of the Swift's house next door. And shuddered.

Twenty-Four

It was almost 2:00 P.M. by the time Richard reached the hospital. Slate blown off the roofs of houses had begun to sail through the air, striking the sides of buildings and the trunks of trees like missiles. Water was flowing down the streets as if they were canals. Trees were bending double. His second alarm of the day came when he saw the row of cottonwood trees on the side of the hospital lying over with their roots torn from the ground, reaching up in a tangle like gnarled hands clutching at the sky. Behind the hospital he left the carriage and the frightened Blitz with the stable hand, and went inside.

Within, the hospital creaked and groaned and shook with the gusts of wind. Light fixtures swung eerily. Rob Tate met him on the first floor ward. "I anticipated injuries, Richard, but most of the people coming in have only minor cuts and abrasions and are mostly just seeking shelter. They're afraid their houses won't stand

400

up to this wind, and some from the south end say the Gulf's up in their yards two feet or more."

For the next hour, refugees from the storm continued to stream in through John Sealy Hospital's front door; the Negro hospital had been evacuated and its patients brought to John Sealy and taken to the second floor. Rob told Richard once during the afternoon that he was glad the corridors were wide, that more people could be put on cots and bedded down there. He and Richard and Bert Jackson sutured flesh wounds and applied antiseptics to small cuts and abrasions. Nothing of a serious nature had come in yet, though the refugees from the storm told of rising water and increasing winds.

About 2:30, Rob came to Richard, who was washing his hands in the first floor treatment room. "Intern Zachery Scott over at St. Mary's Infirmary came by and said he tried to buy a railway ticket out of the city at noon but the trains have quit running. The railroad agent said there was water over the tracks across the bay. Have you tried to telephone lately?"

Richard said no.

"I have, and the lines are dead."

Richard turned to face Rob. They stared at each other, both experiencing the same uneasy feeling, knowing that the island was now cut off from the rest of the world.

Drenched refugees from the storm were now pouring into the hospital bringing with them soaked bedding, canvas bags of food, and tales of water rising from the Gulf and bay sides. One male orderly with a pockmarked and sallow face kept coming to the doctors bearing tales of woe from the refugees. The Gulf and the bay had met at last, the entire island was covered with water, there was wreckage of outhouses, sheds, fences, and barns. Slate was blowing off roofs, whizzing through the rain-drenched air like bullets. Telephone lines were down, and outside the hospital the water had risen and was now knee-deep.

Rob came to Richard around 3:00 and said, "Richard, I'm worried about my family. I've no idea how my cottage is withstanding the wind, and my wife and children are alone."

Richard was leaning against the table on the second floor ward listening to the nurses try to quiet terrified women patients, worrying about Beth and his own house. he said, "Go home, Rob. There's four doctors here, and a dozen interns. Nurse Hanes just told me the nurses have all moved from their building across the street because it's coming apart, and they are all on duty. I think your duty now is with your family."

"I agree," Rob said. "I've been doing nothing the last hour but directing traffic. I advise you to go home too, Richard. The cuts and bruises we've had can be treated by interns who need the practice and who are bachelors with no families to worry about. Bert's gone home and so has Weatherly. We can always come back later. This storm can't get any worse."

"I think I'll go in a little while. Meantime, don't you think we'd better move everybody up to the second floor?"

Rob looked toward the shuttered window. They both felt the building quake. Kerosene lanterns now lit dim corridors and wards, and nurses by the dozens were hurrying to and fro. The whole place, curiously, smelled like rotten eggs. "Yes. Ten minutes ago that unappetizing orderly who keeps giving all the gruesome details of the storm said the water is rising steadily." Rob took out his watch and thumbed it open. "Three o'clock. Too bad. I had decided to take a week's vacation starting tomorrow. I was going to ask you to feed Will's dog and my rabbits. Looks like I might not get to leave with the water over the railway bridge." He looked at Richard. "But surely by morning the water will have receded. Want me to stay and help get all the old patients to the second floor?"

Richard shook his head. "No. There's plenty of nurses and interns. Go to your family, Rob, but be careful. I understand the wind's gotten quite brisk."

Richard tarried, suturing and treating wounds, feeling guilty about leaving and feeling guilty about staying. Rob Tate had been gone about thirty minutes when the storm tide caused the water outside the hospital to rise two feet in five seconds, probably indicating that the wind had shifted toward the south.

He came down from the second floor ward when he heard about the sudden rising of the water and saw Barry Holcomb below. He was shouting orders to the nurses, trying to appear calm, but betraying his excitement by his confused commands. "Get the patients up to the second floor. Those that can't walk will just have to go up by themselves. Dr. Brice, organize the orderlies to carry the bed patients. You, nurse, look sharp!"

Nurse Hanes hurried to Richard as he came down the stairs, her huge, brown eyes on his face. "Dr. Morrison, what will we do with the old men's ward?"

He said, "We'll capture every orderly and intern we can find to carry them up. Meantime, let's get them ready to move."

When they entered the old men's ward, every one of the helpless old fellows—the lame, the arthritic, the toothless, the deaf, the almost-blind—were sitting up in bed, wide-eyed, their faces a collage of fear as they watched the doctor and the nurse entering their ward.

"Alright, gentlemen," Richard began calmly, "water's risen a bit outside so we have decided it would be prudent to move you fellows to the second floor. Now we'll start first with bed A and proceed—"

The old men all at once peeled off their covers, swung out of bed, pushed and shoved each other going out the door into the corridor; and when Richard and Nurse Hanes went out behind them, aghast, they saw the eighteen patients from the old men's ward pushing their way up the stairs to the second floor with such agility, they left many young orderlies and nurses behind. Richard estimated soberly that the old men's ward had been vacated in fifteen seconds.

The Morrison house, built on a foundation of red sandstone, stood two or three feet higher off the ground and was newer than any of the other houses in the neighborhood, and was therefore considered stronger. Neighbors began their trek through roaring wind and torrential rains to the Morrison's house shortly after two o'clock. They arrived drenched, shuddering with fear and excitement. Shad built a fire in the back parlor stove, and Prim and Sissy made tea by the gallons. Elizabeth,

Melissa, and Mildred Crabtree served. The back parlor eventually filled with anxious neighbors. On the stairs their children huddled clutching toys and dolls, while Cully entertained them with tales of watching the waves on the beach that morning, embellishing the story a little at first, and a great deal later on. The tales began to include whales and dolphins being thrown from the sea upon the concession stands, and sharks swimming up the beach road. And eventually there was even an octopus chasing people on the beach. But his tales were no more incredible than those told by the grown-ups later on.

The roar of the wind outside was steady now and the house groaned and quaked. So far as Elizabeth knew, not a slate had blown off their roof. Her garden, though, was totally destroyed. Water was at least a foot deep in the yard, and Shad had brought the chickens into the carriage house with Little Bit. At four o'clock Melissa counted twenty-two people in the house including children.

Dark came early. There was no electricity. Kerosene lamps were lit just after four o'clock and still neighbors came. Three who rang the Morrison's doorbell after four o'clock when the water had risen three feet in only a few seconds, were the Hoffman's from next door and their German maid. Humbly, they asked for shelter, and Elizabeth welcomed them into the house. Shad had to force the door shut behind them, an indication that the wind was swinging to the south. Elizabeth invited the Hoffmans and their maid to join the other neighbors now filling the front parlor.

In the kitchen, Sissy, Prim, and Melissa were already

preparing huge kettles of stew, pans of corn bread, and pots of tea and coffee; for dinner time was approaching and it appeared that the storm would be going on yet a little while longer. Joe Bob had suggested calmly that the people be offered dinner soon because it looked as if they might eventually have to vacate the first floor. Shad and his friend, Eddie Grimes, had carried baskets full of canned goods up from the basement where water was now three feet deep, and from the vegetables that Shad had grown and Prim and Elizabeth had canned during the past summer, the ladies were preparing delicious stews. The fare was laid out on the Morrisons' dining table. Neighbors, consisting of the poor from down the street to the east, and the immigrants to the north, and Negro servants, the young and the old, the ragged and the rich, filed by and filled their cups and their plates, while the storm raged, the wind velocity increased, and water continued to rise without.

The poor who otherwise would never have had occasion to step through the Morrisons' doorway, received tea in china trade cups poured from Grandmother Hansley's silver teapot in the elegant dining room, and dipped stew from iron kettles into Elizabeth's best crockery and china plates. And the Hoffmans and their maid sat among their neighbors whom they had seldom spoken to before.

Only on the periphery of Elizabeth's consciousness was she aware of tales told by the refugees from the storm, of floating outhouses, uprooted trees, downed telephone poles, flying debris, houses inundated down near the beach, wreckage floating down streets which at first had resembled rivers and now could not be defined from the yards, nor the boundaries of the island from the sea. She hoped the chicken house would not wash away, or the fence, or her palm trees. She could not see out the shuttered windows.

By five o'clock, water lapped at the front steps and Joe Bob suggested that Shad bring as many of chickens inside as he could. And he said softly, "I'll help you unlock the stall door and let Little Bit have her freedom. Because if the water gets much higher, she won't have a chance to survive in there."

At 5:30 the wind roared, the rain thundered against the roof, debris was flying through the air and pelting the house. There were two coops of hens on the service porch and Little Bit, who had swam to the back door and demanded entrance, stamped her hooves beside the coops. It was dark. Elizabeth wept inside for Richard, afraid to think about where he could be, of the hospital so near the bay. And, as water began to seep under the front door, she thought—but wasn't quite sure—that she heard above the roar and howl of the storm, the dismal tolling somewhere of a bell.

All he could think about was getting home. Water was waist deep here near the hospital and he thought wildly that it must be nearly that deep at home. It was almost dark, an eerie dark. A heavy veil of writhing black clouds obliterated the setting sun and lowered like a shroud over the city. The wind was fierce, howling, stripping shingles and limbs and siding and other rubble from invisible objects and flinging them through the air. It drove lumber and other debris through the swirling waters, an incredible amount of wreckage sweeping past, or inflicting his body with stinging blows. Arms raised, he waded west and had fought the rush of water and debris for ten minutes, shocked at the amount of lumber washing past, wondering where it all came from, before he realized that the enormous mountains looming dark and sweeping past were . . . *roofs*. Roofs off houses. The missiles whizzing through the air were mostly slate and it occurred to him they could be lethal. Planks and lumber and rubbish swirled past.

Once he stepped in a hole, went under the water, came up, and instinctively grabbed a plank washing past. He thought he heard cries above the roar and howl of wind but was not sure. Lightning lit up the place frequently but he could not be sure where he was, did not recognize anything. Surely, if he went south, away from the bay, the water would be more shallow. . . .

A man washed against him suddenly, thudded against his side, naked, staring. Instinctively Richard grabbed him. But the thing was dead, a cold white corpse, sleek and grimacing in death—*yes, death*—and with a gasp of horror he let it go, and stood for a moment paralyzed with panic, until he heard cries in the distance. He turned slowly in the water to see where they came from.

A roof bobbed menacingly toward him . . . there was a man on the peak of the roof crying out . . . Richard plunged ahead to help—*you spend your life learning to help*—but the roof disintegrated before his eyes and the man was swept screaming past into darkness. Too late.

What is happening . . . ?

Other cries came to him from out in the night, screaming for help—or was it the wind? The sea, the salty sea water dragged off his coat, and suddenly he realized for the first time that he was going to drown. Yes, like the corpse that had washed past him with a grimace of pain on its startled face, like the cadaver that had dragged at his trousers with dead fingers clutching, a sexless, macabre *thing*. It was as if he were wading in the Gulf; there was no earth, and all was dark. And the frenzied wind drove stinging rain against his face, and buildings and trees were stark and white in the flashes of white lightning, and wreckage swept and swirled about him. A plank knocked the breath from him, but he grabbed it and held to it. His feet could still touch the ground occasionally and he struggled forward for home.

A tree, an entire tree swept toward him, its branches reaching, reaching like the gnarled fingers of a demon coming toward him, and in a quiet terror, he watched it swirl suddenly away from him. But he saw sitting upon the tree a boy, a boy quietly riding the tree surging past. A small roof swirled past, and upon the roof hunkered a dog with head down, riding the raft first north then south and then out of sight. North? South? How could he be sure?

Folly. He knew he was lost. He had been whirled and dunked by the washing sea and now did not know his directions for certain. He should have stayed at the hospital as Nurse Hanes had urged him to do. *Oh, Dr. Morrison, please. Stay. You'll be drowned and I'm terrified . . . stay . . . with me . . . don't you see? . . . can't you tell that I. . . .* He should have started home earlier, but now it was too late—too late to turn back. He would still be there if she had not urged him to stay. He left in a hurry, fleeing what she had almost said.

Another roof bore down upon him, a mountain coming fast, and he was unable to prevent its striking him, for in the water and against the wind, he moved slowly as in a dream. A corner of the roof struck his head, and for a moment he could not see. Then in a flash of lightning, he caught a glimpse of two people on the roof clinging. He reached for it but his hands slipped and the water washed over him while he floundered, floundered until he came up to the surface again just in time to see the others on the roof slip quietly into the black swirling water and debris.

Now there was nothing to do but swim home. It was not for him to ride the currents or be carried by the will of the tides, but to go home—if there was a home—and he swam first against the current, then with it, the current a fickle thing. Only instinct told him he was still going south. But his head ached from the blow and he was not much of a swimmer. His lungs ached with his exertion; ached, and the cold penetrated to his bones until at last there was nothing to do but grab the square piece of planking which thudded against his side and hold on. The lettering on the plank read, CORGIE'S RUM. For a time he gasped with exhaustion, clinging, bending his head down to keep the rain out of his face.

Then he heard a "Halloo," which seemed human. He listened and heard it again. Suddenly a boat surged into view, a boat and three men. A boat barely larger than a bathtub.

"Halloo," Richard called, surprised at the weakness of

his voice, and the boat swung sideways and two of the men hauled him over the side, tugging, grunting, until he was aboard.

"Carrying all we can to safety, govnor," cried the older man as he took up the oars again. "So we'll be going to Broadway where houses are still standing."

"To Avenue I," Richard gasped. "Avenue I if you can." Then, absurdly, he pointed to nowhere. "Out there! Help those out there!"

"Would take a ship the size of the Cutty Sark, govnor. I'm getting all I can find. Been at it since three o'clock."

Richard passed his hand over his face. "There's roofs. Where are they coming from, for God's sake?" he shouted.

"Mostly the south and east and west, govnor. The whole south and east side's washed away."

"God help us all, sir," cried the other man at the oars. "The island's under eight feet of water south of here."

The two rowed and the little boat inched south against the impossible gale, two men risking their lives to save others. The third man in the boat with Richard was another victim of the storm. As Richard looked at him closely in the flashes of lightning, he realized that the man was in a severe state of shock.

South the boat went, battered with debris, in the water and out, with Richard attempting to make the man in shock speak, trying to relieve his fear, but it was no use. He was like a dead man still alive.

Now above the roar of storm there came a eerie sound, an eerie and unnatural sound. Corpses were out there, but these voices were alive. In the strange phosphorous glow of the angry sky, Richard recognized the Rosenburg school and as the boat tossed past, the eerie sounds became singing, singing of hymns.

"The place is full of Negroes," cried the older oarsman. "Reckon they figure on singing their way through the pearly gates, govnor. I figure—"

Suddenly the man in shock began to scream in terror, screaming until Richard saw that he was about to stand up and capsize the boat, and he grabbed his arms and held him down, struggling, and then began to shake him, to shake him back to his senses, but to no avail. He raised his hand to slap him, hoping to silence him, and if that failed to knock him senseless with his fist before he caused them all to drown. He slapped him once and raised his hand again, and . . . there was nothing to slap, nothing but the bloody stump of a neck. The oarsmen cried out oaths and Richard, horror-stricken, released the body slowly, staring at the man slumping over in the boat without a head. No head at all.

"My God, it's the slate," cried the older oarsman. "It's like knives being thrown."

The storm was a monster, a shadowless entity raging and grinning with glee and howling with fury, an executioner, ripping the clothes off its victims, decapitating, drowning, crushing, shredding, tearing—

"You better throw him overboard, govnor, so that—"

They were engulfed abruptly. There was a tearing sound, a screeching sound like nails being pried from planks, and Richard found himself floundering in the water again, and there was no boat, no men, no oars.

But his feet touched earth, the water was more

shallow. His tears mixed with rain and sea water as he pushed on first against the current then with it, knowing at any second a piece of slate could decapitate him, or slice off his arms, or a tree could—or a plank—

A horse swam by, a horse surging forward, swept aside, and out of sight. He thought of Blitz in the stable behind the hospital. There was no stable behind the hospital anymore, the orderly had said, grinning.

Clinging to a plank, leaning into the gale and driving rain, moving south, Richard's mind grew calm. How many dead? Mortality rate twelve. Maybe thirteen. Cause of death? Decapitation, drowning, crushing injuries. . . . His head throbbed. *Beth.*

There were corpses sweeping past, dead white in the phosphorous light, all naked from the surge and pull of water and wind.

Though the roar of the storm was deafening, somewhere, somewhere he heard a bell. A bell tolled frantically. St. Mary's? No, Sacred Heart. And the Sacred Heart Cathedral was near home. The bell clamored, the storm gleefully tolling the bell for the corpses washing out to sea. But the bell led him homeward as he clung to the plank, half-walking, half-swimming until he came to Avenue I. Here the shapes that loomed on either side in the darkness were trees, stripped, but still standing, houses damaged but not gone, battered by debris, the shattered and splintered remnants of residences. There, the Hoffman's house was washed crooked on its foundation. And home. The house stood. Yes, and there was a light in the window of their bedroom. . . .

He made his way slowly to the door, having to swim the

last eight or ten feet to the veranda where he waded chest deep to the door. Shad had boarded up Elizabeth's precious oval, etched-glass window, shielding it from the storm. He beat on the door and shouted. Beat and shouted. Locked out of his own house with the water creeping ever upwards, lapping against the back of his neck.

Then the door opened and Shad's arms pulled him inside. Shad's beautiful face mirroring his terror and gratitude at the same time. Richard waded panting through the entry in waist-deep water, waded to the stairs and up to Beth where she pressed her face against his torn, wet vest and he held her warm, dry body against him for a long moment.

"Oh Richard," she said, pulling away from him. "We stayed downstairs as long as we were able," she began. "We moved as much of the furniture up to the attic as we could and a few of your books. There's almost thirty people here. Oh, Richard, did you know our garden is lost?"

He blinked at her, and then together they started up the stairs where he met Joe Bob coming down to meet him. The two men stared at each other, Joe Bob's face asking a silent question, Richard's giving the answer.

Shad threw a quilt over his shoulders and Richard went on up to the landing where the stairs turned and where several Negro men, women, and children huddled together. He looked up, strangers peered from the upper hallway over the banister, the banister Elizabeth had leaned on the day she first saw her beautiful new home.

He made his way up the stairs, passing among strangers to the second floor hallway, where weary, frightened people huddled together on the floor or stood leaning against the walls. Elizabeth said nothing more to him for a while, sensing in his muteness a horror he could not yet begin to comprehend. A little child asked for a drink of water somewhere in the crowd.

In their bedroom where he went to find a dry shirt and a pair of shoes—he had lost his shoes hours ago—he counted six children sleeping on their bed. The guest bedroom was full of people, familiar and unfamiliar. In the nursery sat Melissa and Cully, Flop, Mildred and Frank Crabtree, Jason, and the Hoffmans from next door. Strangely no one asked him about the outside, they did not have to. It must have shown on his face.

As he sat down in the hallway, he learned that in the attic with the grandfather clock, his horn chair, and some of their furniture, stood Little Bit who had climbed the stairs of her own accord when the people were hesitant to do so, and four of Shad's hens.

Few spoke. What was there to say when death was at the door pounding to be let in, with water still rising higher and higher, creeping up the stairs steadily inch by inch, and with the wind taking the house and shaking it in its fury, shaking it as Richard had shaken the man without a head. And over all, away, barely audible through the roar of the storm, the frantic clamor of the bell in Sacred Heart Cathedral.

As he sat in the hallway with Elizabeth, she dabbed at the bleeding wound on his forehead where blood oozed and didn't stop. He finally took the handkerchief from her and held it there, having discovered that blood and seawater tasted the same, it was all the same. From sea water life must have emerged. To the sea it

415

would return. . . .

The house shuddered, the several lanterns' lights flickered, the howling maelstrom without lashed at the house and drove the sea against it, the sea and debris, lumber, and medieval horrors.

Neighbors who must have earlier spoken of wreckage and death and rescues now waited in silence, waited for the house to cave in, to disintegrate as they had seen others do. Every moment could be their last; they only hoped, as Richard and Elizabeth did, that it would happen quickly and be over. Be over. . . . How easily one accepts death when the time comes, Richard mused passionlessly.

He held Beth in his arms for many hours, huddled in the hallway of the upstairs, and every time a piece of furniture scraped and thudded against the ceiling of the downstairs rooms, Beth flinched. All was quiet now, except once in a while a neighborhood youth named Mark called up from the landing to those on the second floor, "Water's halfway up to the landing." And again, "Water's just risen a good four feet in less than a minute!" From the six Negro families huddled together on the landing came an eerie hymn, repetitious, sliding, moaning, rising and falling, resembling the howl of the wind.

The rest of the people who awaited death, waited in silence.

After awhile—it must have been ten o'clock or eleven or even midnight—he thought he noticed an abatement of the wind, but he wasn't sure. Finally, he was almost sure of it. Out of habit, he took out his watch, realizing in that instant that it was a miracle it had not washed from his pocket. It had stopped at 5:35. He hugged Elizabeth once, then rose. The eyes of every person in the hallway looked up and followed him as he walked to the stairs where he saw Joe Bob standing on the landing, thumbs in the waist of his trousers, looking down the stairs. He went down to the landing to join him.

Below, he could see Elizabeth's tea pot floating on the surface of the debris-filled water and thudding against the second step below the landing. He saw their furniture floating, little islands in the sea.

"I think it's dropping," Joe Bob said. "Inch by inch, I think the water's receding."

The rain still thundered on the roof, the wind still raged and howled, but . . . there was an abatement. Yes, Richard was sure of it.

Flop was housebroken and he'd held his control long enough. When Richard joined Joe Bob on the landing, he had eagerly followed. He was a good dog, not given to such abominations as had been committed by the mare in the attic; so, hoping things were in order downstairs and that someone would let him out the door, he eagerly looked up at Joe Bob first and then Richard. He was twice as excited when Cully joined them.

Cully looked down at the water filling the entire space of the stairwell below the landing—a boy poised on the brink of destiny—looked up, and seeing the first bright hope on his father's face since the storm had begun, said, "Papa, are we going to live now?"

It was at that precise moment that Flop spotted something bobbing on the surface of the water. He tilted his head. Yes, it was the ball, and without warning, he dove into the water swimming after it. A nerve-shattered

Cully shrieked, "Flop! Flop!" and Joe Bob grabbed his arm just as the boy slipped on the slime-coated steps at the water's edge and plunged head first into the water.

Joe Bob cursed and waded down into the water where Cully floundered, and he reached out and touched his head. But at that moment, the gale released its hold on the sea, and with one mighty sweep, the waters covering the island rushed back to the sea. Back, back, the storm tide rushed, carrying with it more death and destruction than before. Shutters on the south sides of houses ripped free, and furniture crashed through south windows. Residences that had withstood the constant battering of wind, rain, and debris, went down, and with the violent receding of the storm tide, Cully was flung out of Joe Bob's reach and crashed with his dog out the boarded-up window of the Morrison's front door.

Negroes on the landing screamed in terror and Joe Bob and Richard flung themselves down, down into the entry, down into the debris and slime and out onto the slime-coated porch, screaming, "Cull-ll-y!" and the storm flung the screams back into their faces, the wind still violent and unyielding. And somehow Melissa knew, and set up a scream that went on and on as Joe Bob and Richard stood on the littered veranda. Water still swirled upon the veranda steps, flinging debris against the banister. Out there was darkness, death, and destruction, but Joe Bob went out. Richard started to follow, but a light encircled him, and he turned to see Shad standing on the veranda holding a hurricane lantern.

Richard shouted above the roar of wind, "Get back, Shad. Let me have the lantern, I'm going—"

"No sir," Shad cried. "All respects, sir, but I'm goin'

out. I'm goin' to light the way and hunt for poor lil ol' Cully." He sobbed and cried, "Now Miss Lissa, she needs help, Dr. Richard, and *you is elected.*" And with that, Shad waded down the steps into the receding waters.

Richard turned, undecided, and saw Mr. Hoffman from next door coming down the steps. "I must help," was all he said, and followed Shad out into the raging storm and down into waist-deep waters.

It took a long time to quiet Melissa, to settle her down in Elizabeth's arms, to keep her from going downstairs and out. Elizabeth held her, Mildred Crabtree held her hand, Richard held Elizabeth. The terror-stricken neighbors had quieted down again and began, after awhile, to get as comfortable as possible, dozing in each other's arms. Richard held Elizabeth, her head resting on his chest, and finally some time in the night, the steady rising and falling of her breath told him she was sleeping. He listened for Shad's voice, or Cully's or even the barking of a little dog, but heard nothing but the house creaking on its foundation, the wind howling, the roar of the sea, the frantic clamor of the bell in the Sacred Heart Cathedral, now tolling for Cully.

His senses had become dulled, his muscles ached from exertion and shock, but he listened until he heard the howl of the storm as it abated to a low moan and the sound of the sea grew fainter . . . and fainter . . . and farther away. The rain still thundered on the roof and was now leaking through the attic floor, to drop to the carpeted second floor hall.

With eyelids half shut, hovering between sleeping and

waking, and holding his wife to him, Richard heard the death angel slowly pass over them. The rain slackened, the wind abated so gradually no one else noticed. The bell had ceased its clamoring, and tolled now slower and slower . . . the sound of the rain lessened more and more . . . the bell tolled slowly. And then there was only a trickling sound of water running off the roof into the gutters and out into the yard. And the bell rang once . . . twice . . . and fell silent just at dawn.

He sat unmoving for a time. The round, stained-glass window above the landing took on a glow. Little Bit stamped her hooves above them in the attic, but there was no sound outside the house, only an eerie silence. No birds heralded the dawn, no rooster crowed, no cow lowed. Richard drew away from Elizabeth and she blinked awake, looking around her for Melissa, who was asleep beside her. He stood up, noticing that everybody else was still asleep in their exhaustion.

He made his way to the landing and the Negroes stirred as he passed by. Then carefully he descended the flotsam-coated stairs and went into the entry, unaware that Elizabeth was following him.

Outside, the sky was cloudless. And in the light of dawn Galveston whispered *havoc*. He stared aghast at the wreckage; most of the houses on their street still stood, but everywhere there was death, carnage, and destruction, and down the street were mountains of debris that was once Galveston. Only then did the impact of the disaster impress itself on his brain, and Elizabeth heard him breathe softly, "Oh my God. . . ."

Twenty-Five

There was no sound. There was no wind. There was no garden, no palm trees. Beyond the twisted fence every house left standing was defaced. Verandas were gone, houses tilted on their foundations, roofs were caved in, fences had vanished. And beyond, as far as the eye could see, destruction—mountains of wreckage, mounds of debris, piles of lumber scattered like straw.

Elizabeth creeped onto the veranda and could not believe what she was seeing, could not believe the silence, or the odor, or the aura of havoc that enveloped the atmosphere in a spectral vacuum. Every vestige of her garden was gone. Only the big oak still stood in the front yard; only a few of the largest oaks along Avenue I still stood, split and broken. And debris was everywhere.

Richard spun around to face her, his face anguished. "Go inside," he commanded her.

It was then that her eyes fell upon a dead man lying in the yard near the veranda.

"Beth, I said *go inside!*"

She stared; the dead man was naked and bloodless, lying face up, his eyes reflecting a nameless terror seen in the night.

Richard took her by the arm, but she shook off his grip. A dead cow lay in the street among unidentifiable debris, its legs stretched stiffly; and in the oak in the front yard, a ragged sofa was wedged, and a naked little girl was hanging face down between the branches, her hair streaming down and tangled among the limbs. A scream came from a distance. A wailing started close by. Someone shouted down the street. A child began crying somewhere. Galveston was waking to the horror, the devastation.

Elizabeth's hand went to her mouth and a strange sound escaped her.

Richard ushered her inside against her will, both of them slipping and sliding on the slime left on everything by the Gulf. He was not gentle with her; there was not time for it. He commanded, "See if there's any canned goods left to feed the people. Get busy, Beth, it's the only way."

She stood frozen in the entry, her arms spread out, her mouth open, as immovable as the dead man against the veranda or the child in the tree. . . . The furniture was soaked and broken and covered with a brown silt and green slime . . . in the library Richard's desk stood up on end, his books scattered everywhere on the floor and soaked and buried in silt . . . silt a foot thick on her floors, her beautiful carpets, and the walls were black with muck clear up to the ceiling. . . .

"Beth!"

. . . The beautiful plaster moulding broken away in places and filth-encrusted. Her piano half-in, half-out the bay window, carried almost all the way out through the windows to the porch when the water had rushed out of the houses, when Cully—

"Listen to me, Beth," Richard said, taking her by the arms. "Prim's coming down now. Both of you get busy. Find food, if possible. Something with juice. There'll be no water. Do you hear me?"

. . . Her tapestry was gone. Grandmother's silver service was scattered in the front parlor. . . .

Richard turned to Prim, Prim large-eyed and terrified, carrying her drowsy child in her arms, coming down the stairs to the entry. "Prim! Find canned food for these people. There'll be no—"

Prim set up a careening howl that started other people crying out as they filed down the stairs behind her, a high-pitched wailing that rose in crescendo. Little children who did not know, ran out onto the veranda with Richard grabbing them, pulling them back inside, saying to the stricken parents, "Don't let them go out. There's . . . *horror* out there." He took hold of Mrs. Wineburger's arm. "Please, there's—" But she went on. He turned to the youth who had reported to them every inch of rising water the night before. "Mark?"

Like dead people, inhabitants of Hades, they filed down the stairs into the entry; like zombies, survivors of the valley of the shadow of death, they came down, faces white with apprehension, but drawn by a force stronger than fear; they must know, they must see.

And Melissa was among them, Melissa, who overnight

had turned old and drawn, moved as if hypnotized down past Richard. "Melissa!" And shaking off his grasp she went to stand on the slime-coated veranda.

. . . Her medallion-backed sofa green with slime, her pictures washed away, her beautiful little china statues scattered and broken. . . .

And finally even Richard gave up and went with the others, out onto the veranda, out to view the unbelievable destruction that was Galveston.

Shadrack was coming up the veranda steps at that moment, saw Melissa on the veranda, shook his head; and Melissa and Sissy quietly moved like ghosts down the steps, picked their way among incredible debris, going home.

Shad came to stand before Richard, soaked and coated with grime and said, "Warn't no use, Dr. Richard. There's death and destruction at every step. You cain't stir the dead with a stick, an' we ain't . . ." He broke off sobbing a moment and then continued, "We ain't never goin' t' see Cully no more."

Richard turned away and leaned his head against the veranda post. "Joe Bob?"

"He be along in a minute. But he ain't half in his head, Dr. Richard. Says he's goin' home and be alone for a while with Miss Lissa. Then he 'tends to go huntin' again. But 'tain't no use, no use atall."

After a long silence, Richard said softly, "Mr. Hoffman?"

"He done gone home. Gone home tired and hurtin' in his joints. He say Cully never climbed the fence an stole his strawberries like the other neighborhood kids has

424

done." Shad began to gaze around him distractedly again, the whites of his eyes flashing as he said, "There's dead folks everywhere, dead and dyin'."

Richard plunged into the house unable to bear any more of the morbidity that permeated the air, that battered every one of his senses, the devastation, the death, the cries out there; and for a moment his mind teetered on the brink between sanity and insanity.

But Beth was sitting on the stairs.

Richard and Shad brought the sofa down from the upstairs and he led her to it and sat her down, and then brought down the hens and Little Bit.

Outside, the carriage house still stood, but there was no chicken house, no pen, no palm trees, only the big oak with slime hanging from it like Spanish Moss. Beth's carriage still sat in the carriage house and Richard thought vaguely, unless it's oiled and cleaned, the salt water will rust it. The upholstery was covered with slime, and there was no hay.

Four shutters were torn off the south side of the house, one window was blown in on the first floor. There were many slate shingles gone from the roof, the veranda sagged at one corner where the post was broken, and the house was pockmarked on all sides by flying debris. Slime coated the siding all the way around as high as the second story windows. So much work to do.

When they went back into the house, Prim had found some canned peaches and they had breakfast on peaches; everybody but Elizabeth, who sat on the sofa in the back parlor, hands folded in her lap, still, pale, and unmoving. Except she shuddered occasionally and her teeth chattered, Richard noticed.

He went upstairs and got a quilt and the pain medication from the bathroom, took it down and draped the quilt over her shoulders and made her take the medication. When she was sufficiently sedated, he carried her up the stairs and put her on the bed, went down, gave Prim instructions about how much medication to give her, and gave Shad instructions about cleaning up. He turned then to his duty, a duty he was bound to by the nature of his profession, and began the trek toward John Sealy Hospital.

There's death an' destruction at every step. Every step. Every step that Richard took was carefully chosen as he wandered vaguely down Avenue I going east. In his own neighborhood there was devastation that defied imagination—gardens, trees, fences gone, verandas ripped off or sagging for lack of support, roofs partially or completely gone. The level where the seas had risen was clearly visible upon the once white-painted frame residences, a black-green slime from the ground to about the level of the second story. Debris had battered every residence like his own, leaving the siding pockmarked. Shutters were ripped off, windows broken. Lumber enough to build an entire city lay tossed in heaps in the yards and streets. And in places the yards had washed so that there was no defining the line between the street and the yard.

The farther east he went, the worse the destruction, and suddenly before him—before him now was a vast wasteland, mountains of lumber, heaped and packed and strewn where once blocks of small frame houses had

stood. *My God, I can see all the way to the Gulf!* My God,
my God. . . .

And there were bodies, corpses naked in the sun, man
and animal, snakes and birds, and the sun beat down with
a peculiar intensity not usual for that time of year. And
there were no mosquitoes, no insects, no live birds.

The first five human corpses he came upon, sprawled
upon the heaps of lumber or lying face down in the street,
he examined briefly to see if they might possibly be alive.
But after a while, the sight became so common that he
simply shook his head and passed on, grieving, passed on,
picking his way north along the same route he had swam
and struggled over the night before.

There were live people out too, searching among the
ruins calling out, "Mary?" or "Zack! Zack Wakefield?"
An old couple was poking with a stick among the ruins,
the old lady clutching a jar of vegetables, poking,
poking. . . .

Chilled to the bone in spite of the heat, Richard saw the
red medical-school building long before he reached it; its
walls were standing then . . . and John Sealy Hospital
was intact too, but there was a wall of debris heaped
twenty feet high, which must have shielded them from
the surge of sea on the bay side and the Gulf side too. But
the medical hall. . . .

As he picked his way forward among the debris, he
could see in the early morning light that the dome of the
medical school building was gone, the pointed dome over
the middle of the roof, and the cupola, and every spire
and turret gone, as if a giant hand had plucked off every
point and protrusion. As he neared it, the rubbish around

427

it seemed to bar his entrance, but he climbed over broken lumber and uprooted trees, sheets of twisted tin, slipping on stinking sea slime. He picked his way through and over broken furniture and household goods, soggy brush, dead animals, and slipped twice, tearing his coat and ripping open the back of his hand, and finally was able to step through the giant archway under the front entrance. The basement was knee-deep in water and full of floating lumber, but Richard made his way to the lab on the east side. Lab?

His chemical tables were shattered and tossed in a tangled heap, beakers and test tubes and bottles were broken and flung everywhere and floating in green water amidst stinking flotsam. The gas and water pipes were twisted, broken, and flung into the heaps of broken lumber and debris. And the corpse of a woman, which Richard suspected was one of Will's cadavers, floated face down among the litter, her long, dark hair moving restlessly upon the surface of the water.

He stood for a long moment feeling more hopelessness than he'd felt even the night before, depressed, weighed down by despair. Then, unable to progress any further in the basement because of the wreckage barring his way, climbed the wide stairway holding to the rail to keep from slipping on the stairs, up to the first floor. There was damage here, broken windows, water standing, still dripping from upper floors, but not the mess there was in the basement.

Up the stairs he went to the second floor where he found the pathology labs in a wet disarray, but not destroyed. He went to the entrance of the gallery where the rabbits were kept and saw that there was no pen and no rabbits there. He thought of Will's dog and had just turned from the gallery determined to check on the animal, when he saw a rabbit hop out from behind an overturned waste basket, pause, eye him with its placid rabbit's eye, then hop on.

Out in the corridor, he came upon Will's dog, excitedly chasing first one rabbit then the other, so caught up in the chase he paid no attention to Richard.

He made his way then to the dissecting lab on the third floor where there was even worse destruction than in the basement. Part of the dome had crashed down into the lab. Will's tables were broken and most of the shelves which had held his carefully collected specimens were destroyed. Broken jars and organs lay scattered in a miasmic fog of formalin diluted with rain water. A nine-year collection of specimens destroyed! Richard looked up then and beheld . . . *blue sky*. And the lab was as bright and sun-filled as any yard.

It was almost eight o'clock when he reached the hospital. It had fared well, but the Negro hospital had been destroyed, the nurses' dormitory destroyed. St. Mary's Infirmary two blocks away had been damaged, but not beyond repair.

Rob Tate had already arrived. The wards and corridors were filled with victims of the storm; the interns were hollow-eyed with exhaustion. The nurses had managed the refugees through the night, working in shifts, but sometime just before dawn the injured had begun to stream in.

Though the hospital was virtually undamaged, there

were no lights, no water, and little food, and the hospital's ambulance service was already bringing in more patients. Among the seven doctors from the medical school and the six city physicians—who decided to split up with half of them going to St. Mary's to help—there was no exchange of tales, nor did any of them relate their personal horrors. They set to work grimly, all of them in their own state of shock, and began, as men all over Galveston, to repair the damage done by the storm.

They treated victims of shock from the cold, and bleeding wounds, and abrasions and fractures, knowing that soon, surely the severely injured would be arriving. As morning wore on, the orderlies who were sent out in the ambulance coaches came in with tales of horror, and the doctors slowly began to realize the magnitude of the disaster.

They learned that the entire east, south, and west sides of the city had been destroyed. Only a U-shaped portion of the city, roughly between Forty-fifth and Eighth Streets and as far south as Avenue P, had escaped total destruction. *Total.* The area of town within the U was severely damaged, but the structures outside the U no longer existed.

Isaac Cline. The doctors did not say so, but each saw it in the others' eyes. Isaac was the only doctor who lived outside the U-shaped area, close to the beach. Isaac was the only physician in town who had not come to John Sealy that morning and no one had seen him at St. Mary's.

The doctors heard that huge cargo ships had been torn from their moorings and flung adrift, that the wharves and the warehouses were damaged. There had been four, five, and six feet of water in the downtown district. City hall was a shambles, area schools were all damaged, some beyond repair. The school Richard had passed the night before in which he heard the Negroes singing was badly damaged. The orphanage near the beach was destroyed and most of its inhabitants swept away. No one knew much about the damage west of the town, except that Swenson's Dairy farm had been erased from existence, and that Mr. Ziegler's Botannical Nursery—called "Ziegler's Folly" because he had dared erect a hothouse constructed entirely of glass—had vanished, and Mr. Ziegler with it. Babies had been born at St. Mary's Infirmary during the storm and many victims cast adrift into the black waters of the night were pulled to safety by the nuns at St. Mary's. Intern Zachery Scott had become a hero during the night. Rumor—which he denied—was that he had carried two hundred patients from a frame building to the infirmary.

The orderly who had irritated Rob Tate and Richard the day before with his tales of woe, was full of worse today. The dead were everywhere, on land, in and under the wreckage. Hundreds floated in the bay, hundreds more were washing ashore upon the beach by the calmed water of the Gulf, and the cemeteries were a nightmare.

Once near noon, Rob and Richard stood grimly listening to the orderly tell that he had stood at Ninth Street and from his vantage point had counted thirty-eight bodies, and that was not counting animals. Rob and Richard looked at each other, then looked out the window at the bright sunlight. It was eighty-five degrees.

As the day wore on and John Sealy filled up with storm victims, there was more grim news. There was no gas in the city, no electricity, no water, no telegraph, no telephone, and the railroad bridges to the mainland had been swept away. Ironically, only those who had persisted owning cisterns had water, and that was surely contaminated. Galveston was devastated, and the doctors began to wonder how much destruction there was; how many lives lost.

Word came at noon that the mayor and several of Galveston's businessmen had met downtown to decide what must be done, and had deputized someone to carry a message to Houston by yacht to be sent to the Governor of Texas and President McKinley, that Galveston had sustained a great deal of destruction and loss of life.

By three o'clock word came to the exhausted physicians that a Committee of Public Safety had been formed, with Police Chief Ed Ketchum and an Ohioan named Fayling appointed as operational deputies. "But what are the operational deputies for?" asked the sallow-faced orderly.

"What for?" thundered Dr. Matthew Cross incredulously. "To stop the looting, that's what they're for!"

Rob Tate, who was carrying a tray of instruments across the treatment room, said, "And to start clean-up proceedings, I hope to God."

When word got around that two Yankees were in charge of patrolling the island, three of the older doctors didn't like that a bit and said so.

Later the doctors heard that the first thing Ed Ketchum had done was to close down the saloons, and since the Ohioan, Fayling, had previous experience in dealing with rioters, he and Ketchum had begun to recruit volunteers to form a militia.

By then, it became apparent that the number of injured people were indeed overwhelming, but very few had sustained injuries serious enough to require hospitalization. There were lacerations, contusions, abrasions, fractures, but where were the seriously injured? Young Dr. Haversham put the question into words. "Why aren't we getting in any critically injured patients?" he asked the three doctors who were gathered around the crockery cooler of boiled cistern water that had just been brought in by a deputy of the militia.

Rob Tate lowered the dipper from his lips and said, "Dr. Haversham, the critically injured *drowned.*"

Richard, who was wiping grime off the front of his shirt with a handkerchief, paused and raised his head to look at Rob. Yes, those who were unable to swim or hold on to floating objects, just . . . simply . . . *drowned;* for in the black frame of mind that had stayed with him all day, he had kept remembering his ordeal of the night before.

At five o'clock, he trudged for home, so weary he could barely place one foot in front of the other. He had been awake for thirty-five hours. The doctors had agreed they must work in shifts from then on, that those who hadn't slept for twenty-four hours should go home first and come back at dawn. The devastation he'd seen that morning was all around him; bodies still lay on piles of lumber, bloating, bloating in the heat. But he was so tired, had seen so much, that he thought nothing,

nothing could disturb him anymore.

Until he saw the drays.

Trundling among the mountains of wreckage down paths barely cleared of debris, came the mule-drawn drays, not carrying bales of cotton, or barrels of wheat, or groceries from the market, or lumber from the mill, but bodies stacked three and four deep, fifteen to twenty human bodies piled on top of each other, limbs hanging stiff out the sides. Richard halted and watched in morbid fascination as a dray stopped and the two men on the seat got down, lifted a body from the wreckage, lay it on top of the others, and climbed back onto the seat. Then the dray moved on. He'd heard at the hospital about the warehouses down at the wharves which had been turned into morgues. . . .

Nearby an old lady sat in a rocking chair on top of a pile of lumber, rocking, rocking. . . . A mother carrying a child was lifting a plank up from a heap of rubbish calling, "Mack?" Men were rummaging through piles of lumber while drays awaited close by.

By the time Richard got home, he was sick. Prim met him at the door.

"Dr. Richard, Miss Lizbeth wouldn't let me give her no more medicine. She come down and sit on the sofa, just sit and stare an' don't say nothin' to nobody. I helped her up to bed just an hour ago."

"Alright, Prim."

He went up the stairs and into the bathroom, forgetting there was no water to flush with, and threw up the beans and cornbread the nurses had prepared for the doctors at noon. But Prim had set a pail of dirty sea water beside the water closer and he poured it down and flushed it out. To go where?

It was not yet dark, but Elizabeth was in the bed in her night clothes, awake. He said nothing as he peeled out of his clothes down to his underwear and crawled into bed beside her.

"Don't bother to draw the net. There's no mosquitoes left," she said lifelessly.

"Did Prim have to help you up to bed, Beth?"

"Yes."

"Are you feeling better?"

"No."

"I'm sorry."

"It can't be helped, John Richard. Nothing can help us. You see, we are lost."

"No, Beth."

"Yes, we are lost. Cully's lost. Melissa is insane, and I'm dying inside, Richard."

"No."

"The old red rooster was drowned in the loft of the carriage house."

"Try not to think about it."

"Our baby is washed up out of the cemetery, Richard. Mildred—"

"Hush, Beth."

"Mildred Crabtree says there are coffins floating in the bay."

"Oh God, Beth, be quiet."

"There's corpses all over the beach bloating in the sun." Her voice was hoarse and dead. "And Damon is drowned at sea."

"No he's not."

"Yes. That would be the last thing we'll find out. The crowning blow."

"Damon is safe."

"There'll be no food in the house soon and none on the island."

"There's a committee working on that, Beth."

"Papa will think I'm dead—"

"We'll telegraph him as soon as possible."

". . . and he'll be right. I'll be dead by then, Richard."

"No. I won't let you die, Beth."

"You can bury me on the beach with—"

He slapped her face before he knew what he was doing, a stinging blow she did not seem to feel, then enfolded her in his arms. She wept upon his chest, until darkness came and the rumble of the laden drays in the street fell silent.

Twenty-Six

He left early in the morning, before dawn. Outside, the rescue efforts had apparently gone on all night by lanternlight, because there were people still buried alive beneath the wreckage. As he made his way down the street going east, he couldn't tell in the predawn glow that any time had passed, that any progress had been made in cleaning up since he'd passed this way yesterday. He had heard yesterday that bodies were being carried to the warehouses on the wharves where attempts were being made to identify them by means of jewelry, clothing, or characteristic marks—corpses lying side by side under canvas sheets. Somebody was going to a lot of trouble, Richard concluded, and were to be commended, but the smell was—

"Halt!"

He froze.

"Stay where you are, mister."

He turned slowly around and saw emerging from

behind a head-high mound of wreckage the form of a man with a rifle slung over his arm. He approached Richard cautiously, and then his taut body relaxed. "Dr. Morrison. I thought I had me a looter."

He recognized Ed Ketchum and relaxed too. "Ed. You're out early."

"Never went to bed. It's like this, Doctor, I've got a job to do just like you, and every bit as gruesome."

"I know, Ed. I've heard."

"You probably haven't heard the half of it though." Ed pushed his hat to the back of his head and mopped his face with a handkerchief. "We've had Negroes, Mexicans, whites, living ghouls out stealing already. The committee formed a sort of quasi-military organization and the mayor put the city under what you might call martial law. Would you have ever thought it? We had to. We're even gathering up all the guns we can find in the city to give to the militia. We're deputizing responsible citizens to head up work crews and see that there's no more looting. Had to do it, Dr. Morrison." Ed lit up a cigar, puffed twice and took it out of his mouth and looked at it. "Now we even hate to smoke because all this lumber's drying out and when it does, one spark and—*poof*—the rest of Galveston goes up in smoke."

Richard looked out over the vast wasteland of rubbish.

"Not only that," Ed went on, "there's ghouls, people stealing jewelry off corpses. I've had my gut full of that and don't intend to put up with any more of it. I've got orders, and so have the men, to shoot to kill anybody we catch looting. Don't have the time or the patience to put

438

them in jail or any of that. City hall's a shambles anyway."

"Has there been any progress cleaning up?"

"That's a problem. Yesterday we had volunteers. You can appreciate the fact that we've got to get the dead cleared out of here before. . . . And nobody wants the job, of course. Now, I predict we'll have to start forcing men to do it at gunpoint, if you can imagine that." Ketchum took off his hat, put it back on, and looked up at the sky. "Cloudless. Another hot day. Yeah, it'll be another hot one." Looking at Richard somberly he said, "Doctor, the more we hunt, the more we find. I guess the death count will be near a thousand before all is said and done."

Richard passed his hand over his face.

"Well, I've jawed at you long enough," Ed said. "I'd better let you be getting on to your duty. They've been hauling people to the hospital all night."

"I'll see you around, Ed."

"Yeah, Doctor. I guess you will."

Prim brought her a slice of toast and hot tea, but she couldn't eat, couldn't drink, though her throat was dry and parched.

"Miss Lizbeth, now Shad hunted down the tea and the bread, and traded canned vegetables for it, and this is your breakfast. You got to eat. Keep up your strength," Prim urged.

She tried, and slowly, slowly ate the toast. The tea felt good going down and after a while she put on a dress, smoothed her hair a little in front, and went downstairs and sat down upon the sofa. The house smelled of decaying slime and mold and mildew. She did not know when Richard left. Did not care. Did not care about anything, not him or the house or the servants. There was no joy, no joy at all. And she had a fear, a fear of something she could not define, nameless and threatening and foreboding, a gloom swallowing her up, a menacing cloud ready to consume. It stunned her, walled her off from everything outside herself, and she was so tired. So very tired.

On the periphery of her vision she knew Shad was shoveling, shoveling sand from the floor into buckets and hauling the buckets off. He'd worked yesterday hauling sand out, and her front parlor floor was now visible so that she was able to see that her beautiful carpet was ruined. Did Prim really tell her yesterday that Shad found the tapestry under the silt covering the entry floor?

Even Shad walked slowly, moved slowly, walled off in his own misery. But he worked, keeping busy, hauling sand and shoveling. And in the kitchen Prim was boiling water and washing, washing. *You have to get busy, Beth. It's the only way.* When had Richard said that?

There was confusion in the kitchen now and a scream. But what was one more scream? The city was full of screams and so was the night. They'd taken the dead man out of the yard, the child down from the tree, Prim had said; and the dead cow from the street, Mildred Crabtree had told her sometime, but then Shad had found snakes floating in the basement. What was one more scream?

Sissy was suddenly before her shrieking, "Miss Lizbeth. Miss Lizbeth. You got to come please help Miss Lissa!"

And Prim was shouting, "You get out, Sissy, an' leave her alone. She got troubles of her own!"

But Sissy kept screaming, "Miss Lissa's goin' out to fin' Cully, an she's all by herself!"

"I say get out'n here, Sissy," Prim shouted. "You can see for yourself she ain't in no shape!"

But Sissy continued, "Miss Lissa don't do nothin' but sit in Cully's room and rock. Don't eat, don't sleep, don' talk, just sit and rock. And Mr. Joe Bob has had to go help clean up. Now she say she's tired of waitin' and she's goin' out to fin' Cully!"

There was a tussle between Prim and Sissy, and angry words, and Shad broke it up, restraining Prim, with Sissy on her knees now so that Elizabeth could see her face. "Miss Lissa *needs* you. She won't listen to me. Please, Miss Lizbeth, make her come back!"

Elizabeth said softly, "Melissa."

And Prim set up a fuss and a howl and the tussle began again, but Elizabeth rose slowly and said, "I'll go, Prim. I haven't any other choice."

"No. Miss Lizbeth. No! I been out there an' I seen! I ain't lettin' you. Dr. Richard will kill me if I let you go! You got no business out there."

Shad, still half out of his mind from shock and grief, said, "Prim, hush now. Miss Lizbeth gotta do what she gotta do, and there's no way out of it."

Shad was right, of course. There was no way out of it.

She went out into it, out where dead people floated in ponds of stagnant water and snakes hung from trees, and an injured cat lay kicking in its death throes upon a hill of devastation. She picked her way through muck and sludge to the street and saw Melissa already half a block up the street, up the littered flotsam, debris-covered street, picking her way along, and she showed no surprise when Elizabeth came to her. The sweet face that Elizabeth loved was gone, and Melissa had grown old and drawn. The lively gray eyes, gone, and there were only sunken orbs with no life in them. She took her cold hands. "Come back home with me, Mel."

Melissa shook her head. "I can't. I've waited long enough. I have to know. Is Cully alive or dead? I have to know. I have to know whether to hope or to grieve."

"Mel, there's too many—too much—"

"If he's under the rubbish cold—"

Elizabeth knew. Yes, a mother would have to know. Shuddering with fear, she joined her and they held to each other, making their way west on Avenue I.

Where does one begin to look for a little boy in all this? Wreckage was everywhere. As they passed down Avenue I and came to Fifteenth Street, they turned going south. On Broadway, houses were damaged to be sure, some beyond repair, roofs caved in, porches gone. And farther on, wreckage and lumber, slime, silt, sodden clothing, trunks, pots and pans, pools of fetid water, dead animals. And before them, beyond Broadway, wreckage; a mountain range of it heaped twenty feet high, a dam made of shattered houses from the south part of town, a wall of debris which probably saved Broadway and

Avenue I and houses further north from being swept away when the storm tide receded with a rush to the sea. Cully must be there. It made sense to them both.

Two blocks beyond Broadway, they came to the dam of wreckage and as Elizabeth and Melissa approached, clinging to each other out of fear of the unknown, they saw two mule-drawn drays standing by. Elizabeth gasped. On the dray nearest to them were bodies, nude or only partially clothed, a pile of human bodies flung upon one another like so much trash, and the insulting stench of rotting flesh—which had touched only the edges of their consciousness until now—assailed their senses. Melissa, who was proceeding about the business of finding Cully in an orderly manner, neither gasped nor drew back, but raised her apron to her face to quell the odor as if she did it every day, and went ahead where several men were clearing debris, hunting, and where two corpses lay on the ground having just been pulled from the wreckage. Elizabeth hung back, suspended between horror and fascination, and a groaning in her soul that all but paralyzed her.

"Ma'am, what are you doing?"

Melissa looked up at the man on a horse, a uniformed man who was carrying a rifle slung over his arm.

"I'm looking for my little boy," she said, and dropped her apron and raised both her hands toward him. "Have you seen a little boy with black hair wearing blue trousers and white shirt?"

"Respectfully, ma'am, no. And I advise you to go back home, ma'am, for there's no way of finding your boy here. And this is no place for a woman." The man's eyes were blue, his face kind, but his expression was grim.

Melissa turned just as Elizabeth did and saw the bodies being flung into the dray, and one of the workers, oblivious of the two women close by, was saying "They ain't as easy to handle today. Yesterday they were stiff. Today they're bloated and squashy." And with a heave, they tossed a woman's body on top of the pile.

The other man said, "By tomorrow we'll have to use shovels. God damn, Bill. I'm not going to do this tomorrow. I'll swim the bay to get out of here if I hafta."

"Well, for today soak your handkerchief in alcohol, Alex, it helps a little for a while."

The man on the horse said, "Lady, please go home. There's too many. You'd never find your boy."

The men were still shouting, tossing bodies onto the dray. "Yesterday I was careful with these. Today there ain't time to be gentle; for they've ceased to be human and are now carrion."

"It's either us or them," said the other.

The man on the horse had dismounted and stood holding the reins. "You see how it is, ma'am," he said to Melissa. "Besides, it's apt to get dangerous. We've orders to shoot to kill looters and we've killed a few already this morning. There's some unholy things going on and you got no business traipsin' around. Now, I'll have to ask you kindly to move on, please ma'am; for the pile of wreckage where your friend is standing is full of corpses we think, and we've got orders to get them out."

"Oh, but my little boy—"

"Move on, ma'am. Now, that's an order."

Elizabeth went to her and they moved away. Melissa's

eyes darted everywhere as they picked their way west along the edge of the dam of wreckage. They saw among the mounds of broken lumber household items and toys, cook stoves, broken furniture, a sewing machine, a rag rug, a doll carriage. Elizabeth stooped to lift a sodden paperdoll—Suzy?—from the mud, and once Melissa fell on her knees and picked at a piece of sodden blue cloth on the ground, thinking it could be Cully's trousers. It became apparent to Elizabeth that Melissa had no concept, did not want to recognize, the extent of the death and destruction, nor in fact did she. And now she was ill, almost gagging with the stench—*and it was Suzy*—and the continuous assault of horror upon her senses, making her light-headed and almost faint.

Suddenly another man on a horse came up behind them and drew the reins and dismounted. Elizabeth saw that it was Ed Ketchum. "Oh Ed," she breathed, glad to see someone she knew. "Ed, Ed!"

"Mrs. Morrison! My Lord, ma'am! Mrs. Swift! Do Dr. Morrison and Joe Bob know you ladies are out here?"

"No, but Melissa's Cully—"

"I know, Mrs. Morrison. Joe Bob is heading up one of the clean-up crews and is helping us impress men into work groups. The men have to help clean up the dead or they won't receive any provisions at the ward head-quarters. I don't imagine most of us could eat anyway, though." He said to Melissa, "Now Mrs. Swift, your husband is in as good a position to find your little boy as anybody. What you gotta understand is, there's a thousand bodies in this wreckage, and we've been working on finding them for twenty-four hours straight.

445

Most of the volunteers have been working that long without sleep. Joe Bob and several others have enforced our decision that every able-bodied man in Galveston has got to hunt the dead and haul them to the warehouses." When he saw that Melissa was beyond reasoning with, he looked at Elizabeth. "Mrs. Morrison, it's dangerous for you to be going around like this. We've shot several looters robbing the dead and desecrating them every way they can be desecrated. We've armed the Galveston militia to patrol, because we've already had ghouls coming in from the mainland bent on looting. There's even maniacs photographing the nude corpses. Pardon me, Mrs. Morrison, but I can't be delicate. You have seen the uniformed men? Our militia and what's left of our artillery men at Fort Crockett are rounding up every rifle and handgun in town and every horse we can find, and still we're short. I wouldn't be surprised if the governor didn't put this town under *real* martial law before all is said and done. Anyway, we can't guarantee your safety out here at all."

Elizabeth gathered her wits about her enough to ask, "Ed, if you were looking for one of your children, where would you look?"

Ketchum's face underwent a series of expressions that included horror, pain, relief, horror again. "Mrs. Morrison, if Mrs. Swift is bent on looking for her boy and I can't persuade her otherwise, the only reasonable way is to go to the warehouses. We've turned them into temporary morgues. But I don't recommend it at all."

The two women exchanged glances.

"I don't recommend it because . . . well, because it

isn't pleasant. But the deputies there have tried to keep a record of every corpse and any identifying clothing or jewelry. But that was yesterday. Today, it's a different story. My advice is to go straight home. *Now.*"

Melissa said, "Do you know if Joe Bob looked in the warehouses?"

"No ma'am, I don't. But I don't think he's had time. Now my advice is go home. Please, Mrs. Morrison, you're a responsible woman. Take Mrs. Swift home. It's not safe."

Elizabeth thanked Ed and the two moved on, with Elizabeth saying, "Mel, you can see it's hopeless."

"I have to go to the warehouses, Beth. If Cully's there waiting, and I didn't come for him. . . ."

Yes, a mother would have to try.

It was a ten-block trek through incredible carnage to the wharves through the edge of the business district. From a distance, Elizabeth saw the building where Richard's office was, still standing and only slightly damaged. The water line marked the brick building showing how far the seas had risen, not quite to the second floor where his office was. But the rubble around it and the other buildings was incredible.

There were men everywhere going through wreckage, men on horses and on foot. Elizabeth and Melissa were stopped four times by patrols, and always Melissa's pitiful reply was the same, "I'm going to the warehouses to look for my little boy."

The temporary morgues were clearly identified by the coming and going of drays; and Melissa was almost as excited now as the time she had met Cully at the depot

447

after he had come home from visiting his grandparents. Elizabeth was hesitant and moved slowly, not wanting to do or see any of this, but like Shad said, there was no way out of it. She kept thinking that surely after so many horrors a callus grows on one's soul and one more horror doesn't shock any more.

But she was wrong.

They went into the large warehouse where the day before, bodies had been brought by dray and placed carefully in neat rows on the concrete floor, catalogued and covered. An overpowering odor of decaying flesh pressed against them as they entered the warehouse. Flies swarmed everywhere, and the air here was heavy and hot from the sun beating down upon the tin roof. They were not the only ones looking for a loved one. There were mothers and fathers looking for children, an old man searching for his wife, a youth looking for his parents, a young girl looking for a friend; forty or fifty people searching, filing down the rows of covered forms upon the floor, lifting canvases, dropping them, and moving on.

They went first to the makeshift desk and asked a man with a badge if he'd catalogued a little boy with a white shirt and blue trousers. The man, his shirt soaked with sweat, shooed the flies away from his face, and turned the pages of a ledger, ran his finger down four or five pages, shook his head and told Melissa. "Ma'am, all I have here is approximate ages. You understand that most of these people here . . . are not clothed. However, my advice to you, if you want to persist in this, is look for the corpses under the canvases that seem to be your boy's size. I can't tell you any more. I'm sorry."

Melissa turned away and raised her apron to cover her nose and mouth. Elizabeth bent down and tore the hem from her petticoat, covered her nose with it, and began to follow her down the rows.

How many dead faces of children does one have to see before one is numb? Never. Never in a thousand years. Elizabeth gave up after three, and went to the door of the warehouse and sat down on a crate, holding the torn cloth to her face, gagging and shooing huge blue-bottle flies from her face. She began fanning her face feverishly because of the heat, and finally weeping, rocking back and forth weeping silently because of her misery, because she knew they would never find Cully, because of Melissa's stoic grief, and Richard's placid face gone horrible to see, that calm face etched with weariness, his dear, swollen, passionless eyes. And because of Galveston.

Oh, Galveston, she wept, what did we do to deserve this thing worse than the destruction of war or plague, to cause your beauty to be wiped off the face of the earth, to massacre your good people with such mutilating violence? Through seas of tears and an eon of time she looked toward the wharves, and beyond to the bay laden with debris and flotsam and wrecked boats and ships wrenched from their moorings. *Damon, please come to me.*

Through her tears she became aware of men working, working at the drays and trudging past her into the warehouse, their faces hidden behind handkerchiefs, unidentifiable, coming into the warehouse. Drays were being driven inside too. Canvases were being lifted, and flung aside, and the dead were being tossed back into the drays.

What are they doing?

She rose and backed away, away until her body was pressed against the door of the warehouse.

They're taking the bodies out on drays.

And the drays with their stinking burdens were trundling down to the wharves, to the piers where barges and flat boats were moored. And they were unloading the bodies onto the barges, tying pieces of broken concrete to the bodies. . . .

The man with the badge came to stand in the wide door of the warehouse where a soldier stood. Elizabeth heard, "The doctors at John Sealy Hospital met with the commission this morning and said we've got to get the dead out of Galveston or there'll be pestilence, a plague that'll wipe out the rest of the city. They say rotting flesh breeds the worst kind of—"

She must protect Melissa from this. Elizabeth went to her, Melissa still moving between the rows, lifting canvases, dropping them, moving on. "Mel, let's go home. It's hopeless. Please, Mel, *right now.*" She expected an argument, but Melissa straightened and looked at her, and nodded in agreement. Elizabeth was able to get her out of the warehouse and away, away before she saw what was happening on the wharves, and on through the littered streets to home, to Avenue I with its broken, brooding oaks hanging with flotsam like Spanish Moss, and its twisted fences and broken verandas, its littered, strewn yards and debris-filled streets. Its inhabitants were out milling about in the wreckage like sleepwalkers.

Melissa went into her own house, calm, weary, and Elizabeth went to hers. Prim stood in the entry, watching her without speaking as she climbed the stairs and went into the bathroom where she took off all her clothing and poured the boiled water into the basin and washed her body and her long hair. Then she went nude into the bedroom with her damp hair wrapped in linen and crawled between the cool sheets.

She lay for a time listening to Shad scraping the shovel on the floor below, and Prim's broom making a swish-swish-swish sound on the veranda. Had she really gone with Melissa through the wreckage and down to the warehouses looking for Cully? Or had that been another horrible nightmare? She wasn't sure. She began shuddering, trembling so violently the bed shook, the bedsprings making sounds like the drays in the streets, and she moaned with pains more agonizing than those she had felt when she lost the baby, the baby washed up—

Outside the sun still shone bright, and the air was getting warmer, and so very still.

Early that morning the doctors at John Sealy Hospital had met and agreed that something had to be done about the hundreds of bodies that lay bloating under the wreckage and lying on the beach and floating in the bay. The usual mosquitoes that inhabited the island were strangely absent, and so were the buzzards. Even the sea gulls had not returned after the storm. But carrion flies were thick and hungry, and were everywhere. The doctors were keenly aware that putrified flesh was the ideal breeding place for the worst pestilences known to man, and that flies were the ideal carriers. It was apparent, that second morning after the storm, that over a thousand people had lost their lives, along with countless household pets and livestock. The situation was critical and becoming more so with every hour the sun beat down upon the island with such relentless heat.

At seven o'clock in the morning, Drs. Cross and Tate left the hospital and went to the building on Tremont to meet with the Committee of Public Safety. The logical thing, the doctors said, was to burn the wreckage where it was, corpses and all, instead of wasting time dragging out the dead bodies and risking the spread of disease by hauling them through town to the warehouses.

"But if a wind gets up, the burning could spread and burn down what's left of the town," said a committee member.

"Besides, we're still finding live people beneath the wreckage," said another.

It was then that one of the members suggested loading the bodies onto scows and carrying them out to sea. Dr. Cross protested that they'd just wash back up on shore. Another committee member said they could be weighed down with concrete. The idea was voted on and passed.

Rob and Matt came back to the hospital still seething with fury because of the decision, and at noon word came to the hospital that the first load of corpses from the warehouses had been carried out to sea.

Meanwhile, Richard and the other doctors had not had time for tea, coffee, lunch, or even a pause for a smoke. The injured came in droves. It was apparent that John Sealy Hospital and the city's physicians were unable to handle the volumes. St. Mary's Infirmary was so severely damaged that it would be another day or two before it could admit any patients. Outside help was mandatory.

Richard glanced once at the list of cases brought to John Sealy; all minor, but all requiring medical and surgical attention. There were abrasions, abscesses, bruises, contusions, lacerations, dog bites, snake bites, puncture wounds, fractures, dislocations, crushed limbs, internal injuries, sprains, cellulitis. There was rheumatism, a case diagnosed as malaria, colitis, myositis, lumbago, vertigo, hernia, diarrhea, hysteria, and cramps. While he stood running his eyes over the list which was kept near the front door on the first floor, Nurse Hanes became very busy, and though he tried to ask her a question or two, she didn't hear, and refused to meet his gaze.

Then the word got around that Dr. Isaac Cline had been admitted to the hospital. Though Isaac had been a victim of the storm, he had gone to the weather bureau station yesterday to record his observations of the storm; but today, he had succumbed to injuries that he had sustained in his struggle for survival during the hurricane. Richard visited him in the men's ward and learned that although Isaac's house had been swept away in the flood, the only member of his family still missing was his wife, Cora Mae.

With Isaac's depressing news burning into the doctors' consciousness, the tales of looting, rape, the shooting of looters who were caught desecrating the bodies of the dead, were even more horrible than they would have been otherwise, and kept battering their nerves like the debris had battered their residences during the storm. They seriously began to wonder if the nightmare would ever end.

The sallow-faced orderly—whom the doctors had all come to dislike, who somehow had appointed himself their informer since they were confined within the hospital walls—kept coming to them describing in detail the shooting of looters in the streets, how the militia found a man chewing off a lady's finger to get to a ring on her swollen hand, of sprawling bodies on wreckage, how the corpses went "splat" today when tossed upon each other.

Late in the afternoon Richard was in the treatment room with Rob Tate, cleaning up after they had sutured some particularly bloody wounds. Both of them were glum and pale with exhaustion when the orderly came in with more tales, and kept going on and on with them. "But the awfullest yet," the orderly said, "is they shot a looter desecrating a dead woman. I mean he was . . . you know . . . can you imagine doing that to a—"

Rob turned and his fist shot out and caught the orderly full in the face, knocking him to the floor, and he would have pummeled him further if Richard had not caught his arm and held him. Then Richard told the orderly, "Get out of here. Keep your mouth shut about what you see. If I hear of your coming here carrying any more tales like that, I'll knock you down myself."

The orderly, still on the floor, scooted backwards out the door of the treatment room until he reached the hall, then scrambled to his feet and disappeared.

Rob sat down on the stool, bent his head down to his knees, and tried to keep from crying.

*   *   *

The situation in Galveston seemed hopeless, yet somebody was going about the business of survival in an orderly manner. The doctors learned that all edible provisions in Galveston had been sequestered and distributed to the various wards of the city. From each ward headquarter—usually the residence of the ward chairman—a citizen could receive provisions according to the number of persons in his family. If the gentleman in the family did not help in the clean-up proceedings, he did not receive rations. It had to be that way, the doctors agreed, if the people were to survive.

Richard worked till midnight, all of them did, knowing that unless they got help from somewhere soon, every doctor in Galveston would break down. And there was little food, barely any drinking water to keep them going.

Because of the late hour and the dangers that lurked in the night, the John Sealy ambulances carried the doctors home. Blitz and the Morrison carriage which Richard had left in the stable behind the hospital the day of the storm, had been swept away. Only two ambulances had survived the storm and none of the horses. The horses now drawing the ambulances had been donated. Richard was determined that tomorrow before he left for the hospital again, he would instruct Shad as to how and where to go to secure food for the house. He was also considering sending Beth away, getting her off the island before— Send her to her father until things were improved. Yes, that was the sensible thing to do.

At home, Prim had left a candle burning on the newel post of the stairs, and Richard took it and went to the bathroom. There he washed himself in the boiled water left beside the lavatory, then crawled naked into the bed beside his wife. When he touched her, he discovered that she too was naked, damp with perspiration, and drowsy with weariness or sedation, he wasn't sure which.

"You didn't open a window did you, Richard?"

"No."

"I've been in bed since one o'clock this afternoon."

"Have you."

"Emily's Lucius came to check on me for Emily. He says Emily stayed in bed all day yesterday in hysterics and kept calling my name until Lucius had to come check to see if we were . . . alive."

"Mmmm."

"Melissa and I went out today looking for Cully. We'll not go out again, I promise. It's bad isn't it, Richard? The situation on the island, I mean. Some people are leaving the island. But I won't. Not for anything in the world. Even though things are getting worse. Aren't they?"

He snored softly in answer.

Twenty-Seven

Two days after the *Arundel* steamed out of the port of New Orleans, her new turbine engines humming steadily, she approached the Galveston ship channel from the south, south-east, and as Damon stood in the pilot house, first mate Cunningham said, "Storm clouds off starboard bow, Captain."

Damon squinted at the horizon where the city of Galveston should be rising white above the rolling sea, every muscle tense with apprehension; for since they had left the port of New Orleans, they had seen an incredible amount of debris in the sea, left, no doubt, by the hurricane which had plowed west growing in intensity as it went. *So much debris so far out,* he kept thinking. He raised his glass to his eye.

"Captain, the clouds seem to be hovering low over Galveston bay," Cunningham said.

Damon lowered his glass and handed it to the first mate. "It's not clouds, Mr. Cunningham. It's smoke."

"Smoke?" The first mate took the glass and lifted it to his eye.

"School of dolphins dead ahead, sir," called second mate Stephens from the helm.

Damon squinted ahead. Flashing white . . . something . . . bobbed on the surface of the water among broken lumber.

"My God!" exclaimed the first mate, peering through the glass. "My God, Captain! It's bodies! Human bodies!"

Damon took the glass from him and lifted it to his eye. "Mother of God," he breathed.

By the time the *Arundel* steamed slowly between the jetties between Bolivar point and the eastern tip of the island, it was apparent that Galveston had suffered incredible damage. An icy hand clamped over Damon; his crewmen gaped in fear and horror at the floating debris, the bobbing human and animal bodies in the channel. And stared in terror at the pall of black smoke which hung over the city in the still, hot, afternoon air. Small craft had been dashed to pieces in the channel, large vessels set adrift—litter which Damon had to pilot through himself. The wharves were damaged, and the warehouses along the piers were crushed.

At the Ingram and Sturgeon's broken pier they anchored the steamer. No longshoremen appeared to moor her. His own crew lowered a boat and carried the bowline to the pier and secured her. Damon, clutching his bag, moved down the gangplank slowly, grim with apprehension, his eyes narrowed, taking in such a scene of ravagement he could not believe it.

The smell—God in heaven, the smell—

Armed and uniformed militiamen stood on the wharves and surrounded the crewmen as they stepped onto the pier. A man in army uniform with rifle in hand stepped in front of Damon. "Your name, sir," he said.

Shocked, Damon answered, "Morrison. Captain Damon Morrison of the Ingram and Sturgeon Shipping Company. What—"

"You're not a relief ship then, Captain?"

"Relief?"

"What's your cargo?"

By now Damon was irritated. "The usual. Lumber, brick, iron oar—What is this? Who are you and what's going on?"

The officer, a young man no more than twenty, said, "Holocaust, I think, Captain. You don't know, do you?"

"We're two days out of New Orleans."

"I see. Then you probably aren't aware that a hurricane hit here Saturday, wiped out the entire south, east and west parts of town. You wouldn't believe it, sir. I'm with the artillery division at Fort Crockett. We were wiped out, many of our men swept out to sea. The city has organized the police force, the army, and a militia of citizens to patrol the island and direct the work crews. It's like a war here, Captain. You'd think after three days things would be getting better on the island." He shook his head. "It ain't. It's getting worse."

"Avenue I. What about Avenue I?" Damon said, breaking out in a sweat.

"Got a wife there?"

"Yes. No. A brother."

The crewmen and the eight passengers from the

Arundel had gathered around them now listening, and the soldier, clearly enjoying being the bearer of the news, continued; "Well, nobody was spared, you understand," he said. "Everybody had damage. We figure now there's over two thousand dead. Lying all over the island. The governor put Galveston under martial law, and we've got troops coming in tonight or tomorrow, they say. State militia. You see, every man on the island is being forced into work crews to go through the wreckage and dig out the dead. Carried barges full of corpses out and dumped them in the sea yesterday. Had to get rid of 'em because of the heat and the possibility of disease, you know. Think that worked?" The soldier shook his head. "It didn't. This morning they came floating back in. Littered the beach like so many hundreds of dead fish. And the ones we're still finding in the wreckage, we're having to shovel into the wagons today. God, they're disintegrating with rot, Captain. They're falling apart."

Crewman Donaldson turned abruptly, fell on one knee, and vomited off the edge of the pier. A moaning went up from one of the passengers. Damon's own stomach was churning, the faces of the crew and passengers reflected various stages of white, blue, and yellow disbelief.

"This island usually has carrion birds. Wouldn't you know there's not a damned vulture to be seen? Only the human vultures coming in from the mainland. That's why my men are guarding the wharves."

"The smoke—" began Mr. Cunningham.

The soldier jerked his thumb toward the brownish black cloud hanging low over the city. "Five of the doctors over at John Sealy Hospital met with the Commission of Public Safety early this morning and demanded we get rid of the dead. Didn't like the idea of dumping them in the Gulf in the first place. They recommended we burn them."

A sailor fell with a thump on the pier, but no one paid him any attention and the soldier continued, "We started out digging trenches along the beach to burn the washed-up corpses in. Think that was the way?" He shook his head. "Too slow. About an hour ago at noon, we had to start piling bodies and wreckage together and setting the whole mess on fire."

There was an awful taste in Damon's mouth now, as the crew one by one turned away to retch into the water along the pier.

"You men," called the soldier undaunted, "I'd advise you not to pick up anything. We're shooting looters. Better if you joined in the cleaning up too, if you want to eat. Saloons are all closed anyway. If you care for a drink, the work crews on burning detail are the ones they're passing liquor out to, keeps them going, you know." Then to Damon he said, "Best you be finding your brother, if you can, Captain. I'll tell you what, sir. After yesterday, I won't be eating any fish or seafood around here for a long time."

The soldier stood aside and Damon moved on in a daze. Militiamen in a variety of uniforms, Fort Crockett soldiers, men in plain clothes with badges, armed, stood aside to let him pass.

There was wreckage everywhere, like the carnage of war. Brick buildings caved in along the wharves, roofs gone, broken lumber and debris everywhere. Dead animals bloating in the streets. Telephone poles were down. He covered his nose and mouth with his handkerchief, for the smell that permeated the town was of rotting and burning flesh. He staggered toward Strand, drunk with horror, sick with fear. There were men everywhere going through wreckage. He was stopped repeatedly by patrols and learned to say simply, "Captain Morrison, just put into port." And was allowed to pass on. *Captain Morrison just put into port. Away when Richard needed me. Away when I could have helped Liz.* His mind kept avoiding the question, though not straying far from it, darting at it, and flying away before he could ask himself if Richard and Liz were alive. His friend's faces went through his mind; Eric, Max, Emily, Matilda, Rosemary, Dancy French. And once he came to the Strand, Tony the little ice cream vendor, and Commodore Cooley, the peg-legged newspaper peddler—*Dabey Naw*—Joe Bob, Cully, Melissa, Ed Ketchum, Reverend Kahn. . . .

He made no attempt to seek Wakefield, the agent for the company. It didn't matter. He only hurried through the streets heading for Avenue I as the sun beat down, the smell of rotting flesh grew worse, the smoke hung dark over the city. *Halt. State your business, mister. Captain Morrison, just put into port.* Damon stepped on a human arm sticking out from under an overturned cook stove and the sound of it made him begin to run, run toward Avenue I, groaning audibly, with a crushing pain in his chest that did not let up until he stopped in the shade of the broken oaks on Avenue I and leaned against an iron fence and retched repeatedly in the street.

*   *   *

Elizabeth had retched all morning, since the burning had begun on the beach. Shad had shut all the windows in the house and the shutters too, and boarded up the window which was broken and the one in the front door. Lanterns were burning in every room in the house for light and to help staunch the odor, and still the stench of burning flesh permeated the house. Prim and Shad had done their vomiting earlier and then had resumed the business of living.

The floors downstairs had been scraped and swept and Shad said that when they were dry, he'd replace the warped boards and varnish the floors. But the fallen plaster moulding would have to replaced by a plaster craftsman, the walls repapered, the entire house repainted inside and out. Most of the furniture could be reglued and polished. The rest would have to be refinished and reupholstered whenever Billingsley and Sons were able to reopen their shop on the Strand.

Shad had been working on the furnace in the basement all morning until the militia came for him and made him go out on a burning detail. That made Prim have to go to the neighborhood ward headquarters for their allotment of food, having to take Elmira with her because Elizabeth was still so sick, and Prim wanted the comfort of her child with her anyway.

And now, consumed with that nameless fear which had paralyzed her for three days, sick and alone in the dimly lit house, she wanted to scream, to start screaming until help came. Help from fear and nausea and the continued horrors of the outside that would never cease to grow worse and worse and worse. She'd felt better that morning early as she began to help Prim scrub the cook stove—until the burning started, until Mildred Crabtree came over with news about what the smell and the smoke was, and that the corpses had washed up on the beach.

She'd felt better working, so with that in mind, she made herself rise from her place beside the water closet, and wash her face, wash out her mouth with glycerin, smooth back her hair; then she went downstairs thinking how strange it was that she felt so weak. The trek outdoors the day before with Melissa had drained the remainder of her strength. But she must come back to life, must get busy again, must stop behaving like the sickly, weak-minded kind of woman she detested. Everybody else she knew was having trouble coping with the terrible ordeals too, but Mildred Crabtree, who had wept for half a day after the storm, was now up scrubbing her house. Lucius said that Emily, who had screaming hysterics for hours, was now giving shelter in her big house to six homeless families. Matilda had fainted half a dozen times and been abed with headaches and was now up helping to feed several families. Elizabeth had been too sick to invite strangers into her house, had not cared.

Going through the dining room, she saw that Prim had left the back door open, which was strange, and she made her way into the kitchen telling herself she would have to remind Prim and Shad to keep the doors closed at all times.

"Now lookee here."

She stopped just inside the door of the kitchen and caught her breath; for beside the cabinet stood a man she had never seen before, a shabby and unshaven man with a battered hat and stained clothing. He smiled. "Now ain't this dandy?"

Irrationally, she demanded, "How did you get in here?"

"Aw, lady, I just walked in," he replied, indicating the back door with his hand. "Just like you fancy folks to leave your door unlocked with all those bad fellas out there scroungin' around."

Feeling her heart begin to thud with fear, she said, "Please leave this house! You've no business in here."

"Don't I?" He laughed showing yellow teeth. "Sometimes, lady, it takes a little bit of messin' up from a storm or somethin' fer a man to better hisself. Lookee at your house, lady. Ain't that a shame?" he said gazing around him. "Messed up all your purty wallpaper." He looked at her again. "I done been in the front parlor," he said gently. "All them fancy china dolls broke up and that purty sofa all soaked and smelly now. And them drapes all dirty and them carpets out on yore warsh line. Near makes a feller like me want to weep. Septin' I know you probly can buy more. *Cain't ya?*"

She stepped slowly along the kitchen table, hoping to circle around it and run across the kitchen for the back door. "I asked you to get out of here before I call my servants."

"Aw there's no need to do that. I only came in lookin' fer food. You got any food, lady? Or a gun? I need a gun, you see, because a feller cain't go around out there unarmed lest some varmit or other tries to rob him."

"There's no food or guns in here."

465

"They ain't? Shucks. An here I came all the way from up around Houston. You folks here in Galveston think you got all the bad luck from the storm, but you didn't, lady. They's destruction and dead people for miles inland too. Say," he said brightening, "I'll bet you got a little money. So's a fella could buy hisself some supper."

She had begun to tremble and clutched her apron so that he couldn't see her trembling hands. "No, no. I don't. The flood washed it all away."

"Aw. Now ain't that a pity? No gun, no food, no money." The man gazed around him and Elizabeth took another step toward the door. "An' in a fine house like this too," he said facing her again. "You know what I grew up in? A shack, lady. A tarpaper shack. My Ma had to go a hundred yards a day to a spring for water, and me an' my brother— Now I wouldn't recommend your dartin' out that door, lady," he said reaching into his trouser pocket. "For you see I have this here knife and I didn't come here to palaver with no fine lady and have her call the neighbors on me."

This is why she was afraid, why she hated Richard for leaving her with only Prim and Shad. She just hadn't been able to put a name to it, hadn't known why she felt so alone. She had to try hard to keep from screaming, in rage more than fear, to try to keep calm and not excite the man, and meanwhile seek a reasonable escape when he wasn't watching her.

"Now you ain't got no gun, no food, and no money, but you got a purty face. An hair like new copper. An' I'll bet your skin is as smoo-ooth as silk." He spread his arms, the one hand still clutching the knife. "Now what do you reckon I ort to do about that, lady?"

Somebody darkened the door of the service porch, another man's form; not Richard, not Shad. She could not see who, only a form against the glare of the sunlight, pausing, watching. *Another one? Oh, God how many are there?* Another second and she would scream, scream until at least Melissa would hear; but no, then they would get Melissa too. . . . The floor creaked under a foot, but the man with the knife did not hear. His breath was coming in quick, excited pants, his eyes were intense upon her face, and then he grinned and said something foul.

Suddenly his head snapped back as the side of Damon's hand slammed into his neck. The knife flew across the room. Damon grabbed him by the collar and turned him around and hit him again and again, pounding his face until blood flew, spattered the stove, the floor. Then he took him by the collar out the door, and she could hear him dragging him around the side of the house. She slipped into a chair, trembling, and put her head on her arms. "I think I could have made it out the door . . . I think I could . . . oh, Lord, I think I could . . ." she kept saying.

"Liz."

She raised her head and said, "I thought you would never come back."

"Did he harm you in any way?"

"Not yet."

He stood over her now and asked, "Richard?"

"At the hospital working. Always working."

"Joe Bob and Melissa and Cully?"

467

"Cully," she quavered rising, and reaching her hand toward him she whispered, "Cully. . . ."

His face twisted as if she had slapped him. "Oh Lord. . . ." He took her into his arms gently. And after a moment he said into her hair, "Liz, my God, you must have been through hell."

"I'm still in hell, Damon," she said against his chest. "And now so are you."

He held her close for a moment, then at arm's length so that he could see her face. "That ghoul, I nearly killed him. Had to drag him to the militiaman on the corner. Liz, I'm almost mad."

"Such horrors as are out there, Damon, does strange things to people."

He took her face in his hands, his eyes looking into hers. "I want to kiss you again, Liz. I think I'm crazy. I'm insane with relief that you're alive." His eyes traveled from her face to the ceiling as if looking into the rooms above, then back down to her face. He put one hand on her shoulder and ran his thumb over her lips, his eyes intense, his mouth grim. "I need to kiss you. And more. And more, Liz."

She could feel the blood surging through his body causing a slight shuddering of his beloved frame. She shut her eyes for a moment, opened them, and said, "You blame yourself, only, for wanting me?"

"Only."

"Fool," she said taking his hand in hers. "You're either blind or a liar, Damon."

"Help me, Liz."

"No," she said pressing his hand to her breast. "Because, you see, I love you."

"As your husband's brother," he said faintly.

"No. As Damon, just Damon."

The sound of Prim's voice as she spoke to Elmira outside the house drove the necessary wedge between them. The pain left his face as he released her, and he looked down at his hand. As Prim came into the back door, through the service porch to the kitchen, Damon, still staring down at his hand said, "I think . . . I think I've broken my hand."

He had. She wrapped it in strips of torn sheeting following his directions; and when Richard came home shortly, he unwrapped it, examined it, and said, "I'll have to splint it. You've fractured the fourth and fifth metacarpals, Damon."

"Well do it gently. It hurts like the devil."

They were standing in the library with Elizabeth looking on, her hands wrapped in her apron. Richard took the strips of gauze which she handed to him from his black bag and began to wrap them around a small piece of wood, making a tight roll with which he could splint the broken hand. "Next time, use your fist," he said, "not the side of your hand."

"You're really particular, John Richard. Is there any *particular* way I should hold my mouth next time I rescue your wife?"

Richard looked at Elizabeth now sitting erect in the desk chair, color in her cheeks and light in her eyes for the first time in three days. He shook his head. "No," he said. "No, I guess not."

He took Damon's hand and put the roll into it, and took the strips of gauze, pressed the tiny fractured bones on Damon's hand with his thumb. His chest felt constricted; yet he reasoned, *why* SHOULDN'T *she be glad Damon's home? I'm glad Damon's home, and because of it the world* DOES *seem brighter, in spite of the funeral pyres burning on the beach, and the corpses washing up on the shore and the threat of plague hanging like a pall over the city.*

"Whacked him good?" he asked.

"Knocked the breath out of him. Almost killed him," Damon replied flinching.

"He was marvelous," Beth said. "And just in time."

"Just like in the plays. Ouch, John Richard."

"Then I have to thank you, Damon, for rescuing my particular damsel in distress."

"You're ever so welcome."

"Except next time, bloody him in the yard. You made too much of a mess of things in the kitchen," Richard said, smiling for the first time in three days.

It was an hour or more after Richard had splinted his hand before Damon could ask what happened to Cully. That was the way he was. Richard told him briefly what happened, and Damon showed no grief, just sat immobile for a time. Then he asked about Eric and Max and other friends. It was at this time that Elizabeth learned some things she hadn't known about the storm.

Trinity Church had been damaged, the entire south wall had vanished, leaving the interior exposed to the elements. Prim and Shad's church, the Mount of Olives Baptist, was totally destroyed. Various churches throughout the city were in ruins; none had escaped damage. Sacred Heart Cathedral was a shambles—the only portion of it left standing was the west tower in which a bell had been tolled by the wind during the hurricane.

Also Mr. Ziegler, the German nurseryman who had sold Elizabeth her palm trees, shrubs, and bedding plants for the last three years, had vanished. His entire nursery stock and hothouse gone without a trace. Swenson's Dairy west of town was wiped out too, not a cow or a barn stood where the dairy had once been. Old familiar town characters were missing. Peglegged Commodore Cooley was found in the wreckage on Tremont naked and dead, though his pegleg remained still attached to its stump.

"What about Tony?" Damon asked, his uninjured hand now rubbing his knee over and over again, the only indication that he was disturbed.

Richard told the story he had heard at John Sealy: A family marooned on a roof during the height of the storm saw Tony clinging to his ice cream cart, bobbing on the surface of fifteen-foot deep water near the beach. The cart floated like a cork, they said. Their six-year-old boy slid off the roof shortly afterwards and Tony was able to swim to him, grab him, and while debris battered the little vendor, he managed to get the boy into his cart. The cart was swept away from the roof with the boy in it, and Tony went under the water never to be seen again. The family on the roof were swept out to sea, they think, and back again, but the roof held together and they survived. They found the boy the next day at St. Mary's Infirmary where they went for shelter. The ice cream cart had swirled around the infirmary's second floor windows and some nuns had plucked the boy out of the cart and pulled him through a window to safety. "There's all sorts of stories of heroism, miraculous rescues, and reunions you wouldn't believe," Richard said.

Elizabeth had hurt so much so deeply the last few days that the loss of Tony and Commodore Cooley and poor Mr. Ziegler barely touched her. Talk of the storm went on at the table in the kitchen where Prim placed before them dried beef and canned corn and peas in plates she had scalded and scrubbed.

"Dr. Tate saw Nicholas Clayton yesterday morning at the medical school," Richard said. "He tried to speak with him, but he said Clayton was in a daze, stood looking at the building for a long time, tears in his eyes, and when Rob asked him inside, he shook his head and said, 'I've seen too much already.'"

At this Elizabeth pushed her plate away. "Excuse me," she said and stood up.

The brothers, who had barely taken notice of her all evening, looked up at her surprised, and Richard said, "Beth?"

"I can't listen to any more of this, Richard."

"Please sit down and I'll try not to say any more about it," he told her, then said to Damon, "She hasn't seen how it is out there yet, and won't if I can help it."

Elizabeth sat back down. "Oh haven't I?"

While the brothers listened, she related the story of her and Melissa's trip through the streets looking for Cully, of the drays and the workers, of the warehouse with its rows of bodies under canvas. And of her watching the men load the bodies on a scow. It became evident to them that she had seen worse than either of them, and when she was through telling it, Richard's face was grim and pale, and Damon's was intense with horror, anger, and resentment.

"I didn't know," Richard said softly.

"No," she said. "No, you didn't. You didn't ask. You're too busy at the hospital. You came home late and left early. You did not inquire about our protection. You have not seen Melissa or Joe Bob. All you can think of is that hospital and your medical school." She rose again and said softly, "Damn your hospital *and* your medical school, John Richard." With that, she excused herself politely and bustled out of the kitchen. While the brothers looked at each other, they heard her going up the stairs.

While Richard's face took on a flush not common to him, Damon said, "Well, you know of the danger now, don't you?"

When Richard didn't answer, Damon said, "Look, John Richard. Nobody could have imagined what dangers would come out of the destruction. It's beyond comprehension. I guess people thought it was over when the storm was, but it looks to me as if it has just begun. I have a revolver in my bag, the one Father gave me years ago. I'll leave it here, law or no law. Because you're going back to the hospital tonight aren't you?"

"I have the night shift," Richard said morosely.

"Prim and Shad should stay in the house then with Liz."

Richard looked up from his plate. "You're not staying?"

"With you gone and me alone in the house with Liz? Hell no!"

Richard saw his alarm and smiled. "It *would* cause talk, wouldn't it."

Damon stood up, studied his brother grimly, then said, "With every able-bodied man needed, I can't stay. I'll

473

volunteer for the night shift clean-up. But here's some advice. Go see the mayor—you've done it before—and see that Shad is allowed to stay here with the women. He can watch Joe Bob's house too. We can't leave the women alone without protection."

Richard rose and took out his watch which he kept forgetting had stopped at 5:35 on Saturday evening, September 8, 1900, and said, "I'll try to see Ed Ketchum and get him to write a pass for Shad and permission for him to stay here. I'll leave now and see if he's still at the meeting hall."

As it turned out, Richard didn't have to find Ketchum; for just as he and Damon were preparing to go out the door, Ed, having received word that Damon was in town, rang the rusting doorbell beside the Morrisons' boarded-up door, and the three men went to the parlor, lit up cigars and pipe, and began a conversation that lasted an hour. Ed said, "We need everybody that can sail a ship, Damon. We're the fifth largest seaport in the United States but we haven't got three seamen in town left to sail the yachts we need. People are fleeing the island in droves, afraid of hurricanes, afraid of pestilence, unable to endure the sights and smells of destruction, I guess. Many have lost everything they owned. Now we've got supplies and doctors and nurses from the interior waiting on the mainland, needing transportation over. We've got supply trains on the way from Chicago, San Francisco, New York, and God knows where all. Had the first shipment of supplies come from Houston last night along with the state militia, and we had no way to ferry them over to the island."

Ketchum, enjoying a moment's break from his gruesome task, nonetheless couldn't get it off his mind, and lit up another cigar and continued, "You'll have easy detail, Captain. Like Dr. Morrison. At least it's easy on the stomach, maybe. The workers are the ones. They've reached the limit of human endurance and the deputies have had to threaten them at gun point today to make them keep up the work. We even had a couple of riots, men unable to stand anymore, but you'd be surprised what you can stand when you're staring into the barrel of a Winchester. We're trying everything to help. I'm passing out bourbon and smelly cigars and rags soaked in alcohol to the workers, to keep them steady on the job and to help kill the odor a bit." Ketchum looked at Richard. "There's more doctors and nurses and medical supplies coming by rail, as I said. The country doesn't comprehend what it's like, but they're shocked, and America is rallying to help us. And believe it or not, nobody is rallying more than Houston."

Richard obtained written permission from Ed to let Shad remain at home in exchange for Ed's good-natured demand that he not let the ladies Morrison and Swift go "galavantin'" off again unescorted.

Later Richard and Damon left the house together to go their separate ways. Richard had left Elizabeth, Prim, and Shad with instructions concerning their safety, and Damon had left the gun.

As the men parted on the street below, Elizabeth could see them clearly from the upstairs window in the glow of the fires that lit up the night.

Twenty-Eight

Sometime during the night, water from the city's receiving tanks was restored to parts of the city, and the Morrisons' neighborhood was one of the lucky ones. The next morning, Prim went down to find sandy water running into the kitchen sink, and Elizabeth awoke to the sound of the water closet in the bathroom flushing of its own volition.

On Monday, Dr. Tate had sent a message via boat to the mainland to be telegraphed to the Board of Regents in Austin, stating that the medical school building was severely damaged and could not possibly be opened for the next academic session. On Wednesday, September 12, the professors of the medical school received a terse telegraphed reply from the president of the board;

THE UNIVERSITY OF TEXAS
STOPS FOR NO STORM.

The doctors were relieved to hear that St. Mary's Infirmary would soon be fit to take in more patients, and the city board of health had formed an auxiliary committee which was divided into district committees for the purpose of establishing hospital facilities in the various wards, and emergency hospitals were being set up in buildings and tents throughout the city.

On Tuesday evening a number of volunteer Houston physicians had arrived in Galveston along with medical supplies and the state militia, and came to John Sealy Hospital on Wednesday morning to meet with the doctors there. Among the doctors who went out to the wagons to help carry in medical supplies that morning was one of the medical school's own graduates, young Dr. Marvin Haversham. Richard was fortunate enough to see him rush out to help another of the school's graduates— who was now a practicing Houston physician—carry in a heavy trunk of supplies. He witnessed the exchange of looks between Dr. Marvin Haversham and Dr. Marshal Jannock, a pause in time and space of only a moment in which much was said and not a word spoken.

News came to the hospital that day that the *Galveston News* had published its first official paper since the storm, and Dr. Cross read from the issue that the mayor had received a telegram from President McKinley expressing sorrow that Texas had been visited by such a calamity and had instructed the Secretary of War to render all assistance possible. Then and only then were the doctors reminded that the presidential elections of 1900 would soon be upon them.

Meanwhile, funeral pyres continued to be formed of

the splintered wreckage, human and animal bodies were piled on top of each other, kerosene was sloshed over all, and the entire putrified mess set afire. Pyres burned over the south part of the island, all along the now-ragged beach. At first efforts were made to discover if anyone remained alive under the wreckage before it was set afire, but the 85-degree weather persisted, the sun beat down, the flies swarmed, and the workers' patience grew shorter. And there were still hundreds of bodies still buried in the wreckage. Now it was thought that from 2,000 to 3,000—or more—were dead in Galveston.

Richard worked at the hospital from Tuesday evening until midnight Wednesday, and on Wednesday Elizabeth and Prim scrubbed the pots and pans and crockery and china, the stove, the walls, the floors. As if possessed, Elizabeth worked, scrubbing on hands and knees, hair streaming down from the "toddle" on top of her head, scrubbed until her back ached and her hands bled. Then she and Prim went to the Swifts, and with Sissy, scrubbed their house. After an hour or so, Melissa came down to help, moving slowly, but *moving* nevertheless.

Richard came home at midnight too weary to speak, slept till nine the next morning, ate breakfast, and trudged back to the hospital.

On Thursday, Elizabeth began to watch for sails moving out in the bay. There were only a few. Somewhere there would be Damon. *I need to kiss you. And more. And more, Liz. . . .* His words were branded in her memory, and her very flesh desired him. Her passion, which she had tried to quell with scrubbing and cleaning and staying busy, still burned out of all reason, and was

478

mixed up somehow with the intense fear she had of being alone. All care for Richard had vanished, all caution gone with the fickle winds of reason. Besides, Richard hadn't touched her in over a week, maybe two weeks. She half-way wondered if tragedy couldn't make someone even as insensitive as he impotent. She felt no guilt for wanting Damon.

From the guestroom window on the north, she watched the triangular masts moving in the bay and began to pace the room before the window in a mounting frenzy.

Finally in the afternoon, she could endure no more of it, and forgetting her hat and gloves, flew down the stairs and out to the carriage house. "Hitch Little Bit. I'm going for a drive," she said breathlessly to Shad who was mending a shutter on a carriage house window.

He said, "No, please, Miss Lizbeth. Dr. Richard wouldn't want you to go out. I done let you once, but I'se duty-bound not to again."

"You have no choice, Shadrack. I told you to hitch Little Bit to the buggy. Now do it!"

Shad looked stunned first, then ducked his head and did as he was told, but he kept shaking his head over and over, and when she climbed into the buggy, she thought she saw tears in his eyes.

But never mind. She drove away and guided the little mare through the paths barely cleared through the wreckage. The mare was more skittish than usual and kept tossing her head and shying away from the piles of wreckage; for *who knows what lies beneath?*

At the wharves most of the activity seemed to be near

the I and S pier and she drove the buggy to it, where cargo was being unloaded from a small sailing vessel. She got down, tethered Little Bit, and went among the sweating longshoremen and stevedores asking, "Do you know when Captain Morrison will be putting into port?" over and over until at last one of them said, "He's on the *Lucy Ann,* ma'am, and you're lucky, because that's her dropping anchor yonder alongside the *Arundel.*"

She waited in a fever, waited until her nerves were strained to the breaking point, waited until she saw him coming from amongst the longshoremen and the stacks of supplies on the pier.

She ran to him, and with fear in his eyes he embraced her briefly, then held her at arm's length, questioning only with his eyes. He smelled of sweat and smoke and there was a two-day growth of beard on his face. "Please, Damon. Can you come home a while? We're afraid," she said desperately. "The fires are everywhere now, and there's men with guns, and strangers are still roaming—"

"Liz." His eyes were intense, his mouth set in a straight line.

"Please say you will. Please, Damon. The water is on at the house. You can take a bath. Shad was able to buy groceries today for the first time, so there's food. You can rest in the guest—"

"Liz, listen to me," he demanded as he peeled her arms from around his neck.

Because there was no desire for her in his eyes, and because she saw his resistance, his restraint, she became instantly panicky. "You're going to say no, aren't you? Yes, I can see it." Fear consumed her, tears sprang to her eyes and as he held her wrists she cried hoarsely, "Damon, please help me. I'm going mad. The smell, the strangers, not knowing—"

"Liz, listen—"

Suddenly she did go mad and tore her hands from his grip, stepping backward, and in a breathless rage cried, "You have no feeling. No heart. You and Richard. Men. All you can think of is—"

"Liz, listen."

"I hate you, Damon. I hate you," she cried. "You and your brother. Hate! Hate! Hate!"

He was suddenly shaking her, shaking her violently, shaking her until her teeth chattered, and the longshoremen on the pier, who had paused enjoying the scene, were not able to hear him say, "God dammit, Liz. We've found Cully."

She blinked. Through her tears of rage his face was horrible, horrible to see.

He released her and said, "Or what is left of him."

Shame is what she felt first. Shame. Her trembling hand went to cover her mouth.

He fought for words, stumbling in his mind among the ruins of his shattered memories and the horrors he'd seen. "In the bay," he whispered. "I saw him on the scow that was picking up the bodies caught in the pilings where the railroad bridge used to be." After a moment he said, "Go to Melissa. Don't tell her yet, only go to her. I'll find Joe Bob and fetch Richard, and then we'll come to tell her. Meanwhile, Liz, you go to her." He shook her again, more gently this time. "You be there, Liz. Do you hear me? *Be there.*"

Then he turned and went along the pier toward the Ingram warehouse, and left her trembling alone on the pier.

Melissa asked if she wanted tea and Elizabeth said she did, and they sat mostly silent in the Swifts' parlor. While they tried to make conversation, Elizabeth kept listening for the carriage, and at last it came. Melissa looked out the window, pulling back her lace curtains. "It's Joe Bob. And Damon and Richard. What a surprise!" As Elizabeth shut her eyes and tried to steady her hands, Melissa said, "Now what do you suppose . . ."

At the door she flung her arms around Joe Bob saying, "You must be famished, dear. All of you. I'll have Sissy fix you some dinner." She uttered a strained little laugh. "I have only bread and bacon, but we'll do our best with it, won't we Beth?" Nervously she said, "Sit down for now, and I'll have Sissy fetch you some tea while we wait for dinner. *Sissy?*"

The five of them sat in the Swifts' parlor, the men grim, avoiding Melissa's eyes as she forced a nervous chatter, totally uncharacteristic of her. "Well, I suppose the work is going on as usual? Richard, you look exhausted. Damon, you need a shave. And you, Joe Bob, just look at *you!*"

Elizabeth hadn't seen Melissa so animated and talkative since the storm and thought, *she must know,* but was holding on to the last straw of hope before the finality of it.

"Sissy is getting the kitchen in order again," Melissa went on. "Did you know Shad did all the cleaning up of

482

the sand in the house? I'd never have gotten it—"

Joe Bob interrupted saying, "Melissa."

She paused, her face frozen, her hand still in the air. Joe Bob couldn't go on. Neither could anybody else. It was Melissa herself who finally voiced the impossible. "It's Cully, isn't it?" she asked softly.

No one could answer.

"Yes." She nodded. "It's Cully. He's dead, isn't he?"

Joe Bob nodded gravely.

Melissa looked at Damon. "Are you sure?" she whispered.

He nodded.

"How? How can you be sure?"

Damon moistened his lips, and with palms up managed only, "His clothes . . . Melissa, I saw him. It was Cully."

The pressure in the room, if it could have been ignited, would have blown them all to heaven. Melissa sat straight and stiff, her moist gaze went to the window. She said nothing, her hands clutched tightly in her lap.

Joe Bob said, "Melissa, we've . . . already . . . he won't have to be . . ."

She looked at him. "Cremated?"

"No. We buried him, Mel. The three of us. Just now."

She turned a fierce, moist gaze back to the window. A thin line of perspiration had formed on her upper lip, and her cold hand reached out for Elizabeth's and gripped it painfully. "Cully . . . Cully hasn't died in vain, you know," she said to no one in particular. "Something good will come out of this, just you wait and see." She stood up and said to them furiously, "Cully didn't die in vain. You'll see."

Joe Bob went to her then, and as the tears came at last, they went together up the stairs, two of the five who could conquer anything.

Richard gave Elizabeth a bottle of tablets to give to Melissa to help her rest. "Two every three hours, Beth. It's all any of us can do now. She'll sleep, but stay with her. Can you do that?"

She took the bottle and nodded. "I have no choice."

Richard said, "Joe Bob will have to go back to work shortly and so do I."

Elizabeth looked to Damon, their eyes met in their mutual agony. "And I have a ship to sail," he said.

Twenty-Nine

For a week Richard continued to work day and night at the hospital. Damon sailed back and forth across the bay carrying refugees to the mainland, and supplies and relief workers to the island. The cleaning up of debris and bodies continued, the funeral pyres burned day and night, and the city remained under martial law.

Two and three pieces at a time, Shad carried the Morrisons' furniture to Billingsley and Sons in a rented farm wagon to be restored, and he and Prim continued cleaning the house while Elizabeth scrubbed down the walls and peeled loose plaster, and beat out her carpets on the wash line. Shad repaired the broken post on the veranda and raked the debris out of the yards and rebuilt his chicken pen from lumber piled in the street.

As Galveston began to realize that at least 5,000 of its citizens had been killed during the hurricane, hope began to rise with the streaming in of supplies from the interior. Tents were set up for the 10,000 homeless, donations for provisions poured in from individual philanthropists and from organizations, and even from school children from all over the country. On the thirteenth, the telegraph was in operation and Richard sent a message to Elizabeth's father:

HOUSE DAMAGED. NOT DESTROYED. BETH WELL.

The banks opened on the fourteenth, and during that week, the first mule car ran between Market and Twenty-first Street, to Broadway, and out to Fortieth Street.

A week after the storm, on the morning of September sixteenth, Elizabeth was sitting at the dining room table gluing the arm on one of her precious porcelain statuettes, a little china lady in hoop skirt dancing, when the scream of Sissy next door brought her to her feet. She and Prim ran out the back door, and there in the Swifts' back yard lay Flop.

He was bedraggeled and dirty, his long hair matted, his body scrawny and shivering. Where he had been, and what rigors he had endured, nobody would ever know. Melissa was standing on the back porch, looking at him, and then turned and went inside the house. Elizabeth, assuming Mel was going to wake Joe Bob who was asleep upstairs having worked the night shift, bent down and stroked the little dog and he submitted to her tender attention, moaning softly and pleasurably at her strokes.

"Get out of the way, Beth."

Elizabeth turned toward the house where Melissa

grimly stood on the porch with Joe Bob's rifle in her hands.

"No, Mel," Elizabeth whispered. "Oh, don't, Mel."

"Get out of the way," Melissa said, her voice trembling.

Elizabeth, having been awash in a sea of shame as real as the Gulf itself because of her cowardice since the storm, was on the verge of backing away in fright. For she realized that in Melissa's distracted frame of mind, she could easily pull the trigger of the rifle without a qualm, no matter who was at the other end of it.

"No, Mel."

"Get out of the way," Melissa said again as she cocked the rifle and raised it and took a wavering aim, weeping audibly.

Flop did not seem concerned. He sat with head down, eyes blinking rapidly as if awaiting the blow he must surely deserve, while Elizabeth remained on one knee beside him.

Melissa sobbed, the barrel of the rifle wavered, and Elizabeth pleaded, "Please, Melissa. It wasn't Flop's fault. He loved Cully. Please."

Melissa wept aloud, took aim again, the barrel wavered and pointed at the famished little shank of hair and bone on the ground. She aimed, and held, and wept, and Elizabeth turned away and clamped her hand over her mouth while Prim and Shad hovered together in the yard and Sissy went screaming into the house for Joe Bob.

But the shot did not come. Melissa lowered the rifle, and weeping aloud, dropped it and fell to her knees. Flop went to her apologetically and she wept into his fur.

But it was Elizabeth who took him home and fed him warm milk and a small portion of canned broth. He slept on the service porch that night and followed her around next day in the house. He never went back to the Swifts. It was as if he had decided he should not grieve his master's parents by depending on their succor. So he attached himself to the Morrison household where he would remain for the rest of his long life.

That same morning members of the Board of Regents, and the president of the University of Texas visited Galveston, toured the medical school, and left the city in a state of shock as profound as any the doctors had treated yet.

Next day was Sunday, and in the afternoon, Mildred Crabtree came over and waited fanning rapidly until Prim had set the tea tray on the center table in the front parlor and had left the room before she announced, "Mr. Crabtree and I have decided to leave Galveston."

"Oh, Mildred," Elizabeth said, pausing with the tea half-poured.

"Of course you know our hardware store was badly damaged and thieves have taken so much of the stock, and a dead cat was found in Frank's office up over the store. Pew. We'll never get the odor out. And we didn't have any storm insurance." She laughed shortly, and continued, "Of course you've heard nobody in Galveston has any storm insurance except for the bagging mill and the cottonseed-oil mill. We just thought; well, we've had storms before and there wasn't that much damage. I blame that ol' Commodore Maury who was supposed to be such an expert on storms. He certainly must be turning over in his grave, wherever it is, telling everyone that Galveston wasn't in the usual storm path. You think this is the last storm like this? No indeed. Thank you, dear. Your teapot has a dent in it now, doesn't it? The Lord has seen the iniquity of us all. We've decided to move the business to Houston like everybody else. Do you know Conrad Moran of Moran Shipping Company? Of course you do, you're in the clique. Rumor is he's moving his company to Houston, although you understand that's just rumor."

When Mildred took a sip of her tea, Elizabeth opened her mouth to express surprise, but she wasn't fast enough.

"But I have some good news," Mildred said, setting down her cup. "That German nurseryman who sold you your shrubs and things . . . what was his name? You know, with the gimpy leg? Ziegler. Yes, Ziegler. I could never understand why he used all that glass on that hothouse knowing this island was subject to hurricanes even though he says he devised a storm-proof protection system using gunny sacks and braces. . . . Anyway, just wait till you hear! This morning Frank and his work crew were clearing debris over in Sherman Square, and what do you suppose they found? Old man Ziegler under the wreckage. Alive. After seven days, mind you. Can you imagine his being swept this far away, and Cully being swept to the south and ending up in the bay on the north? Strange. Well, anyway, they didn't know who Mr. Ziegler was at first until they got him to the hospital and some of the doctors there recognized him. They treated him,

Frank says, and fed him and they say he's going to be alright."

Elizabeth laughed and clasped her hands together. "Oh thank God. There really are miracles!"

Mildred's face suddenly paled as she pointed a finger past Elizabeth. "Oh good heavens!"

It was only Flop coming into the parlor to check out the visitor.

"Yes," Elizabeth said smiling. "Another miracle. He came home yesterday."

Mildred sighed. "The dog comes home but his master is dead. Hello, doggy, you poor thing. It's enough to make you wonder. But then one mustn't question the ways of the Lord. Is Captain Morrison staying with you?"

Elizabeth flushed and shook her head.

"That poor man. Such a shock to come in and find his town desolate. Was he distraught?"

"Shocked. Not distraught."

Mildred watched her face carefully, fanning, sniffed and looked away. "Certainly is a devoted man," she said, "to his family."

Coloring, Elizabeth said, "More tea?"

"No, I must go," Mildred said rising and looking out the bay windows. "I'm packing, you know. Paid four thousand dollars for the house and we're putting it on the market for four hundred and hope and pray we get that. People are fleeing Galveston in droves and I shouldn't think there'd be—Oh, here comes Dr. Morrison home in the middle of the day. He walks home doesn't he? A carriage can hardly pass in this debris. Your curtains are going to have to be replaced, aren't they dear? Well, I'll run on and be seeing you later. If you run short of food, send Prim over because we have plenty. Those lace panels still need cleaning, don't they? Hello, Dr. Morrison."

Richard nodded coming into the entry.

"You look weary. Did you have a good day?" Mildred asked.

"Smashing," he replied.

Mildred laughed. "Well, bye bye, Elizabeth. You too, Dr. Morrison."

Richard shut the door behind her as she bustled out. "What kind of maxims has she delivered today?"

"The Crabtrees are moving to Houston."

He sat down in his horsehair rocker. "Isn't everybody?"

"No they're not. *We're* not."

He smiled at her, glad to see that her usual pluckiness had returned. "I brought home the *News*. Want to see it?"

"No, I've just had the news," she said. "Tea?"

He scratched Flop's head saying, "Believe I do," and tossed the newspaper onto the center table while she rang for Prim. "*News* says there's a new horseless carriage they're experimenting with. A steamer. Runs on steam instead of gasoline."

"You need that like you need another patient, Richard."

"I've got good news. Your nurseryman, Ziegler—"

"I heard. How is he?"

"Another day of rest and good food and we'll be able to release him. You know that Bert Jackson specializes in corrective surgery of the bones and joints? Well, I believe he's talked the old boy into having corrective surgery done on his hip. Did you hear about Clara Barton?"

"No."

"Came into Texas City this afternoon. They'll ferry her and her hordes and supplies over some time tonight or tomorrow."

Prim set a clean cup on the tray, and while Elizabeth poured she said, "Terrific! Clara Barton knows how to organize and distribute food and supplies. All of it so much needed. Ten thousand homeless, Richard. That's awful."

"What's needed at this moment, though, is something to help the workers. We're getting workers in now at the hospital so sick they can't stop vomiting, and with diarrhea, their nerves shattered. They say it's the smell more than anything. I keep telling them camphor. Take a lump or two of camphor and somehow tie it under your nose. More effective than alcohol and not as damaging to the lungs. Doesn't burn the eyes."

"Camphor?" said Elizabeth handing him his cup of tea. "Where could one get that much camphor?"

"Supplies coming in. The hospital's full of it."

Her mind wandered a moment as he said, "Have a good day, Beth?"

She brought her gaze back to his face and smiled. "Smashing," she said.

She was the one who conceived the idea of making little bags out of gauze, placing three lumps of camphor inside, drawing the attached strings and fastening them around the head so that the bag would rest on the lips and block out the incredible stench of decay and burning flesh. In the little Studebaker buggy, she took her idea to each of the members of the Jolly Sixteen—only now the medical auxiliary was the haggard fifteen. Cora Mae had been missing but her body had been found under the very wreckage that Isaac and their children floated to safety on. The auxiliary, sick of doing nothing to help in the relief work, were enthused and eager about the idea. They met at the Morrisons' on the twentieth, cut and sewed and made little bags of camphor which they packed up and sent to Ed Ketchum who passed them out to the workers, and which proved, within a single day the most effective "odor stifler" they'd used yet.

Not only did the medical auxiliary make life-saving camphor bags, but once Clara Barton had set up her relief stations, Elizabeth helped rally the auxiliary and many of her other friends to help at the relief stations. Melissa, Emily, Matilda, Rosemary, Helen Greenleaf, Myrna, and a host of the other prim and privileged put on aprons, tied scarves around their hair, and started first at the Santa Fe depot to sort out clothing and supplies, to mend, roll bandages, and dispense camphor bags.

Clara Barton, a thin, angular lady with a severe countenance and dressed always in black, commanded each post, going from one work area to the other, surveying the work, making demands and giving advice and instructions. She was a lady of such powerful character that even headstrong Elizabeth almost quailed in her presence.

But not quite. Her friends would always remember her standing before the venerable Red Cross President and saying, "No, Miss Barton. Camphor bags in sheeting will not work. It must be gauze. Three thicknesses, no more and no less."

The Red Cross President looked Elizabeth up and down as a not-very-proper gentleman might do, smiled and said, "Very well. Three thicknesses of gauze it shall be!"

The mounting possibility of pestilence in the city continued to alarm the doctors in town more than the amount of injuries. The city physicians were more inclined to believe that the free use of disinfectants and the bracing salt air would dispel any outbreak of pestilence. The medical school physicians believed in the disinfectants and were not so sure about the salt air, and were delighted when word came that three carloads of disinfectants, mostly lime, charcoal, oil, and carbolic acid, had arrived by barge from the mainland, and that many more were expected. The disinfectants would be spread all over the city and in the inlets and coves of the bay.

On the twenty-fourth, the faculty of the medical school, still swamped with patients at John Sealy and St. Mary's Infirmary, received word that the Board of Regents of the school had met in Austin and had ordered the medical committee to proceed at once with having the medical hall repaired and the equipment replaced. The Board had immediately appropriated five thousand dollars for the purpose, and had decreed that the next session would begin November fifteenth, only one month late.

The professors were stunned at the Board's sudden generosity, and dignified Dr. Bertram Jackson did a little dance in the first-floor corridor at John Sealy Hospital.

Meanwhile Ingram and Sturgeon Shipping Company had abandoned all considerations of Damon's luxury liner, and Damon, sitting in Ingram's now-dilapidated office on Water Street, was both furious and relieved; furious because of the rejection, relieved—he didn't know why.

"We tried to sell the idea of the liner along with Galveston as a major seaport and resort island to the businessmen of the city, as you well know; though all of us had qualms about it at the time. Well, the good Lord made our decision for us," Ingram said as he sat behind his peeling desk.

"The good Lord?" Damon said incredulously. *God is everything,* Cully had said. *Even the bad things? Even those.*

"We got thumbs down, Damon, for obvious reasons. The board decided such an enterprise is unfeasible, over-indulgent, besides being foolhardy to begin with, and the liner could in no way repay the cost of its financing, and now it's just simply impossible."

"Their conclusion is a lie."

"And you are a visionary, Damon. You've got to realize the stockholders of the company are made up mostly of Galveston businessmen who have all suffered severe financial loss because of the storm. Only two of them had storm insurance. Many of us have lost as much as two-thirds of our investments. That's what made Galveston so rich, Damon. Her businessmen made their fortunes in Galveston, then turned right around and *invested* it in Galveston." Ingram shrugged. "That's what happens when you put all your eggs in one basket."

"Will you flounder then in your losses for another eight, ten, twenty years while Houston keeps sucking dry the teats of our commercial trade?"

Ingram raised his brows. "You *are* angry, aren't you? For your information, the stockholders of the Galveston Wharf Company met yesterday and proposed to borrow $400,000 for four years to repair and restore the wharves. A New York firm is ready to loan us the money. At six percent interest. Does that sound like building an extravagant passenger liner or making Galveston the seaport you dreamed of? For that matter, do you think any of us really *want* the island—all of it—to become a tropical paradise teeming with tourists from all over the country, coming here to litter our beaches and crowd the channel with their fishing yachts, and philander with their mistresses? Not if we can help it. I was momentarily dazzled by the brilliance of your idea. I've been dazzled in years past by the same idea. But now all I want is the peace and quiet of the island again. I want the militia the hell out of here, the wreckage cleaned up, the beach graded and smoothed, the streets paved, the piers repaired, the buildings restored, some kind of protective dike around the island, my wife's gardens and the trees and the oleanders replanted. And I want the horrible memory of this disaster erased from my mind, just as I intend to see that every vestige of destruction from the storm is erased from this island."

Damon sat a moment in the quiet, watching Eric's face, red with his pent-up anger at what he had earlier called "the good Lord," turn to its natural color again as he picked at the peeling varnish on his desk top. Damon said, "I have suffered too."

Ingram ducked his head, raised it, said, "We all have. Everyone of us. Take your plans to Moran. He's moving his western branch to Houston. But he can't afford that liner either, Damon. Take it to Cunard's branch in New York."

Damon took the roll of sketches off Ingram's desk. "I wanted the liner to benefit Galveston. We're a natural seaport carved out by God, improved by the government, but misused and exploited by the Wharf Company. We're the seaport for the entire southwest, even the midwest. My God, Eric. You call me a visionary? I call my ideas common sense. And good business." He rolled the plans for the *Lucinda* tightly. "Alright. Keep Galveston like it is, like it was before the hurricane, and Houston will slowly absorb your commerce. It'll grow and Galveston will wither on the commercial vine."

Eric leaned back in his chair, took out a Galveston-made Virginia cheroot, and lit it saying, "No, not wither. We'll not allow that. But neither will we become another New York City, or for that matter another Caribbean-like tourist resort." He puffed now, half-angry, half-mollified. "Take your plans to Moran, Damon. His ambitions equal yours. Who knows, maybe the two of you will put that liner of yours together and change the entire concept of transoceanic passenger travel."

Damon did go to Moran that same day, and laid his plans on the table which Moran was using for a desk. Conrad had a cigar clamped between his teeth and said around it, "Sit down, Damon. They turned you down at I and S, didn't they?"

Damon did not like Conrad particularly, probably because he represented the worst in himself, and there was no point in pretending he did. This was business, so he did not sit down, he simply opened the plans out on Conrad's table, set a bookend on one end, an ashtray on the other.

Moran bent over the sketches—the side view of the *Lucinda* was first—and after a moment he took the cigar out of his mouth and laid it in the ashtray. He turned to the second page, the longitudinal cross-section of the interior, and studied it a full three minutes. He turned the seven other pages, perused them, and at last looked up. "What the devil, Damon? I thought you were trying to build another floating palace. This thing is a floating *city*."

"Complete with boutiques, barber shops, hair dressers, library, clinic—"

"Same thing that's on the seas now but much bigger, larger in scope, fancier, and powered by four turbine engines. With quadruple screws, no less. My . . . Lord. . . ."

"If I had the capital, we could take this thing to a naval architect and then to one of the giant corporations. I'm not guaranteeing somebody else hasn't beat me to it, you understand. Maybe Cunard or one of the other big lines already have it on the drawing board. But I don't think so."

"So you want me to finance the hiring of a professional designer, the architectural planning, the model testing, and the building of a turbine engine for demonstration purposes if necessary. Am I correct?"

"You know you are. I know your ambitions are to build up your eastern branch and you'd be smart to merge with one of the giant corporations, with yourself as an indispensable member, and this baby can invoke your engraved invitation."

Conrad grinned. "Ah. So well put. However, I'll need to think about it before I decide. Tell you what, I'll just take these to an engineer to see if the quadruple screw idea—"

Damon reached for the plans. Moran clamped his hand back onto the page. "On the other hand, we've no time to lose, have we?"

"No. And you mentioned something to me once about a full partnership. You said for me to sell my stock in Ingram and Sturgeon and invest it in Moran and Company, and that no matter what it amounted to, you'd hang the rest and make me a full partner in the company."

"I said that and meant it. And I'll tell you why. Regardless of your superior attitude toward me and your so-very-apparent scorn of my company, I need you. You see, I've got the money, the ambition, and the business sense, but I haven't got a creative cell in my brain, nor an inventive one in my entire body. I'm the fabled ship without a rudder, a liner without a helm, and that's fatal. I want you to be the rudder." He shrugged comically and said, "Not very poetic, but apt. I'm not content to remain a small company sending out half a dozen cargo ships and a dinky so-called passenger liner or two. No, I want to make a mark in the history of shipping. You're my pen." He shrugged again and grinned. "Still not very poetic, but apt. Besides, I need somebody I trust to manage the eastern branch and you're disgustingly trustworthy."

"Then you'll finance me?"

Conrad shrugged, spread his arms. "You're my partner. And incidentally, I've been sweating it out that I and S would manage to come up with the backing for this and I wouldn't have a chance at it. But alas, fate has interceded in my behalf. *Our* behalf." He rose and offered Damon his hand and Damon took it, though it galled him to do so.

However, he took pleasure in saying, "I'll transfer my shares in I and S to Moran, Morrison and Company tomorrow. But I'll have to tell you this, the storm almost wiped me out along with I and S."

But Conrad was unperturbed and sat back down and took out the box of Havanas from a trunk beside his table. "Well, the stock I really wanted anyway are those cells in your brain. Your capital which I require is just an act of good faith. Sorry you're almost wiped out." He handed the opened box to Damon. "But what is it Eric Ingram has got in the habit of saying lately? Oh yeah, 'That's what happens when you put all your eggs in one basket.'"

Thirty

Deliberately, he picked the evening before he was due to sail to break the news to Elizabeth and Richard. He invited himself to dinner and, knowing that celebrations occasioned the only drinking sessions he and his brother ever had together, he brought his own bottles of good cheer secreted away in his travel bag, which was full of fresh linen, just in case it was necessary to spend the night in the guest room.

They started with wine at dinner, which turned out to be a more sumptuous fare than he had partaken of since his arrival back in Galveston four weeks earlier. It was Yankee food; New England boiled dinner, Elizabeth called it, fresh light bread, and apple pie. He gorged and complimented and let his brain absorb as much of Elizabeth as he could during the meal, to pack away in the storage trunk of his brain. For time was short.

She was almost gay. The color had returned to her cheeks, the awful white pallor of her lips was gone.

"Dinner lately is always a surprise," she said from her end of the dining table. "When the grocery stores finally displayed their canned goods for sale, the labels were all soaked off. We just bought up boxes of them, and every time we open a can it's a surprise. Luckily everything we opened this evening we could use in the boiled dinner, and the fresh beef, Damon, is a luxury. I hope you're enjoying it."

"Indeed I am," he assured her. And to Richard, "Your fear of typhoid and malaria didn't develop did it?"

"No," he said. "But it still could for a number of reasons. Overcrowding is one reason. Families crowded in the same houses together, the filth and lack of sanitation, high temperatures, huge increases in flies, and the water supply. Most people used cistern water the first few days after the storm. Didn't have any choice. A plague we haven't had, but mild epidemics, yes."

"Then your office practice is booming?"

"Yes, and I've got four ladies who're pregnant, a thing I've come to dread."

"More bread, Damon?"

"Yes, please."

"This is to be kept among the three of us," Richard went on. "None of us doctors want to cause any more panic than we already have, but there have been several cases of malaria—at least we think it's malaria."

"Because of the return of the mosquitoes?"

"I don't know. We haven't half the mosquitoes we had before the storm. Because of the smoke. Anyway we've had cases of gastro-intestinal catarrh and dysentary. And we've even had a few mild cases of typhoid. All of this more than the average number of cases. But not plague and no serious epidemic yet. Thanks to the disinfectants spread all over the city."

"Then you feel you're free from any more catastrophies?" Damon said to him.

Richard studied Damon's face. "You keep asking questions that lead me to believe you're checking to see if all is well with me. You keep saying *your* instead of *our*. Are you moving or something?"

Damon nodded and drank the rest of his wine, glimpsing Elizabeth's face, seeing her shock. "I'm no longer employed with Ingram and Sturgeon. I asked Eric to keep it a secret. I've joined Conrad Moran and am going to manage his eastern division in New York."

Elizabeth's face was bright red and she stared at him silently. Then, "How can you just leave Galveston like that?"

"It's only for two years, Liz."

"Two years! But you—That's—Have you no loyalty?"

"Loyalty?"

"To Galveston," she said angrily. "Are you leaving when we need you the most? I mean to help carry on business and to help build the city back again?"

"Liz. I have no choice, really. Moran bought the luxury liner idea. Ingram wouldn't."

"So you're putting a ship before a city?"

"Galveston isn't dependent on me."

"Oh isn't it? What if every steamship company left Galveston?"

"With Ingram I wasn't a company. With Moran I am."

"Then join Moran, but let *him* go to New York and you

stay in Galveston."

"Conrad's moving the western division to Houston."

"Houston!" For a moment she couldn't speak she was so furious. "Mildred told me that, but I didn't believe her. Houston! That—that cow town? That swampy old infested bayou where they shoot people in the streets?"

"And they aren't doing that here?"

"That's different. We've had a disaster."

Richard wasn't enjoying the exchange. He said, "Beth, let Damon tell his story."

Damon said, "No story to tell. Only what I've just said."

"Two years?" she said.

"Yes."

"And then?"

"Well, I'm a full partner with Moran. If I don't like New York, then I'll move back."

"To Houston."

"Yes."

She folded her arms and said, "You might as well be in Antarctica."

"No, I've been near there when I've sailed around Cape Horn. It's a bit colder than Houston."

After dinner she wasn't about to let them go off to the library and start their drinking spree. No indeed! And there was a bit of reasoning she had to do with Damon. So she took her needlework with her, and once they were all seated—with the men patiently waiting for her to retire—she said to him, "I expected people like Mildred and Frank Crabtree to leave Galveston. Cowards, all of them. But you? Not you, Damon."

"As a matter of fact," Richard put in, "the Crabtrees have decided to stay. Once Frank found out the hurricane tore up Houston a bit, went on up north creating havoc, even sunk small craft on Lake Erie before it died out, he decided it was a once-in-a-lifetime freak and decided the move wasn't worth it."

"Nonetheless, only the cowards left," she said to him; and then to Damon, "How dare you be disloyal to Eric and Max."

"It was Eric's suggestion, Liz."

"Piffle. Why must you build a ship? Why must you try to change Galveston? Why can't you be content?"

"You yourself said that contented people never invent anything, discover anything, or improve anything."

"Well what's wrong with liking life the way it is?"

Richard perceived difficulties if the conversation continued on its present course and said, "An ad in the *Houston Post* offered plasterers four dollars and fifty cents a day, bricklayers five fifty, laborers two dollars a day, and with room and board paid, just to come to Galveston to start rebuilding. That's a great deal of money and is giving quite a few men employment."

"Liz, I'm not leaving forever. I might not like New York. I might move back to Houston, as I said, and that's just across the bay."

"It's not how far away you will be from Galveston, Damon, it's that you will be away at all. You have no loyalty to the city and none to Ingram and Sturgeon who made you what you are."

"I am what I am, Liz, because of what I made myself."

"Repairs are almost finished on the medical school,"

Richard offered. "The board appropriated funds to buy microscopes, new books for the medical library, and have completely equipped my lab. And the dissecting lab has a new—"

"*Two years*, Damon?"

He looked at her, both of them miserably aware of the emotions they must keep in tow, must conceal. And Elizabeth became so uncomfortable that she rose and laid down her needlework. "I'll see you again in the morning, Damon. I must go to bed before I lose my temper with you. And I wouldn't like you to remember me as a shrew."

"It's only two years, for God's sake, Liz. Not forever."

She bustled to the door of the library and turned and said, "Sometimes two years *is* forever." And left the room.

Slowly she undressed, put on her nightgown, brushed out her hair; then went to the window. The fires still burned out there in the city. It had gotten so they were almost a comfort, a symbol of purging, of purifying; for now it was thought that 6,000 people had lost their lives in Galveston during the hurricane, maybe more. She had instructed Shad to open all the storm shutters again but still keep the windows closed against the odor. She stood for a long time watching the fires, and then put out the light and crawled into bed.

But she could not sleep, knowing that Damon was leaving the next day for two years. *Two years.* She turned over on her side, then on her back, then on the other side while the voices of the brothers came floating up the stairs . . . floating up. . . . She dozed with their voices coming up the stairs, up . . . up . . . talking too loudly.

She sat up in bed, hearing them coming up the stairs singing, singing and laughing. "They're drunk," she whispered angrily. Then, "Shut up! Shut up!" she cried. "The neighbors will hear you!"

Richard came into the room glancing at her sheepishly. Damon stuck his head in the door smiling stupidly. "Night Liz."

"You get out!" she cried. "Shame on you! Shame on you both!" And as Richard shut the door, she said, "*You*, John Richard. Look at you! You've no business being drunk when you're apt to get a call in the middle of the night."

He was unbuttoning his vest. "I anticipate getting no calls tonight."

"You could get a call from Mrs. Thornhill."

"She isn't due for two weeks, and she's *always* on time."

"Still, you could be off on your calculations, John Richard. You're not infallible, you know."

"In calculating due dates, I am infabible."

No sooner had he said the words than the telephone rang downstairs. He paused, his shirt half-unbuttoned.

"Well?" she said.

It was Mrs. Thornhill's husband. Her pains had started, he said, and her water had broken. When Richard came up to tell Elizabeth, she threw off the sheet and made him wash his face and helped him get his clothes back on straight. Then ushered him downstairs, made a pot of coffee, and saw that he drank several cups. "I'll be using the Thornhill's bathroom all night," he complained.

"Serves you right, John Richard."

She saw that Shad hitched Little Bit to the buggy and that Richard sobered up enough to drive it, and went back up to bed slamming the bedroom door behind her.

But again she could not sleep. An hour went by. The grandfather clock in the entry struck one. Finally she got up, put on her wrapper, and went to the bathroom.

Because the house had to be shut up with no windows open, and because of the unusually hot weather for October, she was much too warm and stayed in the bathroom washing her face and neck in cool water, removed her wrapper and washed her arms, dallying. Why? What am I doing? she asked herself. What am I waiting for? Why did I put on this silly nightgown which is too tight in the bust and too indecent to wear? Why after having the thing for two years did she put it on tonight? And what was she waiting for?

The answer came easier than she thought. Damon opened the bathroom door.

She turned slowly toward it. There he stood, bare-chested, barefooted, squinting at her in the dim glow of the light coming through the bathroom window. His eyes traveled slowly from her face to her feet and back up again before he said, "Excuse me. I didn't know you were in here."

"Didn't you?"

He stared at her dull-eyed, lids half-closed, hair mussed, and shook his head. "No."

"Then why don't you leave?"

"I'm going," he said, but did not move.

508

"Then go."

He stood a moment more, then turned around and plodded back down the hallway toward the guest bedroom.

She hurried out into the hall, stopped, said, "Damon?"

At his door he turned.

"Richard . . ." she began and faltered.

He waited and when she did not continue, he turned back and went into his room.

She ran to his door and when he heard her there, he turned again. "Richard's gone," she said. "A woman having a baby."

For a long time he looked at her, then said hoarsely, "No."

"Two years, Damon?"

"No, Liz."

"I love you, Damon."

He sat down on his bed, shook his head as if to clear it. "I'm drunk, Liz. I'm not responsible."

"*Two years*, Damon?"

"I'm telling a damn lie. I'm responsible enough. And I say go back to bed, Liz."

"Damon, two years?"

He looked up at her, his eyes flashing in the firelight coming through the window. "Help me, Liz."

"No," she whispered. "No, I won't." She came to him moving noiselessly, her white gown floating as she walked, unreal. But the breasts she pressed his face to were real and in one motion, he brought her down upon the bed and bent over her. He did not speak. He did not have to. His lips, his hands, his body spoke volumes, and slowly, luxuriously carried her to spiritual places she never knew existed. He whispered his love for her again and again, but only once did his voice speak above a whisper to say in the hush of the night, "I never thought you'd allow me, much less encourage me."

Catching her breath she whispered, "Didn't you?"

"You're just too damn much of a lady. . . ."

"Am I?"

The purging fires burned on in the night, but neither of them was certain whether they burned within or without.

Thirty-One

Everybody knew Dr. Kelly's lectures were by far the most interesting of any at the medical school. But every once in a while Richard was reminded of why; and today was one of those times. Will Kelly had what it took to command the attention of young freshmen truly fresh off the farms and ranches; a loud high-pitched voice that discouraged sleeping in class, a Scottish brogue which was different enough to keep their attention, and a fantastic artistic ability that made his lectures more colorful. Today, the anatomy lecture was on the female breast. This, Richard had to see. He had come to show Will his new steam buggy, but saw that he was keeping the class a bit late, something the students didn't seem to mind in this instance, so fixed was their attention to the subject at hand.

Will's dissecting lab was no longer dark. The storm of 1900 had removed the roof directly over the lab, and the Board of Regents had replaced it with a skylight. Not only that, they had dipped down into the funds which had been available all along, and bought new microscopes and lab equipment for the pathology labs, had thoroughly equipped Richard's chemistry lab with new tables, equipment, and ventilation hoods, and appropriated funds for a magnificent new library, complete with a librarian.

Now Will turned from his very colorful drawing of the mammary gland, saw Richard, was reminded of the time, put down his pink pastel chalk, and said, "So! We shall dismiss for now and take up tomorrow where we left off today."

Chairs scraped on the floor, students stood up gathering their notes, and began to file out, greeting Richard as they went. One big bruiser named Kleberg, with Stetson in hand, slapped Will on the back and said, "That was a fine talk, Dr. Kelly. I sure enjoyed it!" Then he said howdy to Richard. "See ya tomorrow, Dr. Morrison."

While Will recovered his dignity and his breath, Richard approached him smiling. Will said, "These Texains! I'll never get used to 'em."

Richard laughed and studied Will's drawing.

"You lascivious professor," Will said. "What are you doing coming here to peer at my female breast at such an hour? You're due at your office, are you not?"

Richard faced him. "Not today. My automobile arrived and my wife and I came out in it for a ride. Would you care to see it?"

"Indeed I would. I've never seen one. Is it a gas buggy?"

"Steam."

"Oh say," said Will. "That's the best kind. She's the first auto in Galveston isn't she?"

"Yes, and I think she's the first one in south Texas."

"Wait till I get my hat."

The auto was a brand-new 1902 Oldsmobile, and Elizabeth felt ridiculous sitting in the thing. It was very small, half the size of a carriage, with baby buggy wheels, bicycle tires, and a whole dashboard of all sorts of gauges and gadgets. Richard said the boiler was under the front seat, and after several blocks of riding in the thing, she believed it.

He came out with Will Kelly in tow. "Oh now," breathed the Scotsman. "Would you look at it? Good afternoon Mrs. Morrison. What do you think of it?"

"Very little," Elizabeth replied. "I hate being stared at, Will."

"Ah but she's a beauty," Kelly said. "How fast does she go, Richard?"

He rared back. "Twenty miles an hour."

"And how much water does she use?"

"Twenty gallons every twenty miles. I'd offer you a ride, Will, but there's no room."

"No, no. I have a conference in a few minutes, Richard, but I'd very much like to take a ride in her soon."

"Good. I'll come by for you tomorrow," Richard said. He got into the automobile and began pulling levers. Steam hissed, needles spun on gauges, and the thing leapt forward with a gasp and began—slowly—to move forward. Richard guided it, holding himself as far away from the steering wheel as possible, as if afraid of it. He turned the automobile around in the street, and they waved goodbye to Will. They had gone a hundred yards when it bogged down in sand in the street and stopped. Richard got out, shrugged for Will's benefit, and pushed the thing out of the sand, got back in, and started the whole process over again, while Will just stood with his hands on his hips in front of the medical hall, shaking his head, no doubt, in awesome wonder.

Down the street toward the beach they went—slowly—with steam puffing behind, the auto hissing and clattering, with Richard looking jaunty in his new straw hat, guiding the thing with great delight, pushing levers, pulling throttles, and Elizabeth holding on to her hat with one hand and to the door of the machine with the other.

"How are you doing?" Richard shouted. "Isn't this an experience?"

"An experience, indeed, John Richard," she shouted. "I'm absolutely embarrassed. I'm being shaken to death and boiled to boot!"

"The seat does get a bit warm, doesn't it?"

"It certainly does and I think this thing has caused Aunt Martha to visit."

He glanced at her. "Oh for heaven's sake, Beth, why don't you say what you mean? This is the twentieth century. Just admit that you're having your monthly visitation. Hold on, dear, here's a—"

The auto dropped into a hole in the street and died. Richard leaped out delightedly and pushed the car out of the hole and jumped back in.

"It seems to me they'd make one of these things with a bit more power," she said.

"It does seem to lack power, but . . ." He pulled levers and flipped switches, and the hissing began again and off they went.

It was bad enough that they were a spectacle riding

down the street like this, but when they approached a horse and buggy, they were a *menace*. Horses reared, causing drivers to fight the reins. Horses backed into buggies, or pranced and snorted and otherwise caused havoc with their rigs and drivers. But Richard seemed oblivious to it.

At last they reached the beach road where workers thronged. In the Gulf, two steamers were dumping giant boulders of granite onto the edge of the beach; and closer to the road, creosoted pilings were being driven into the sand. Pile drivers thundered and drays were rumbling down the beach road laden with steel rods, concrete, and other materials for the building of the sea wall.

Shortly after the hurricane of 1900, Galveston had changed their city management from the old mayor and alderman-type of government to the commission type, because the city fathers believed that the old government had failed. The new board of commissioners had promptly hired engineers to evaluate the cost of a sea wall, and on September 7, 1901, one day short of a year after the great storm, the sea wall proposal was put before the state legislature and passed. There was squabbling because Galveston was virtually bankrupt, but the bond proposal went to the voters. It passed by an overwhelming majority, and in September of 1902, the work on the sea wall had begun.

The sea wall was to be three and one-half miles in length, sixteen feet thick at its base, and seventeen feet high. The huge granite boulders dumped at its base on the Gulf side were meant to break up the waves of the storm tide.

But the thing that seemed insurmountable and impossible, was the proposed raising of the elevation of the island once the sea wall was built. The proposal consisted of jacking up every structure on the island and bringing in dredges to pour sand under every building until the island was raised several feet. There'll go all my shrubs and flowers again, Elizabeth thought. But she was sure such an engineering feat as raising an inhabited island several feet in elevation would be impossible.

The Oldsmobile moved slowly along the road and other Galvestonians out for a ride nodded smiling at the Morrisons, pointing and shouting to each other at the absurd motor car, or waved and shouted to Richard as was the case with the students from the medical school out riding with their girls.

Elizabeth was known by most everybody in Galveston because of her activities and her involvement in community affairs. And now she was certain she would also be known as the wife of that eccentric doctor who owned that awful steam machine. However, in spite of her discomfort, she took notice of the new residences coming up, new frame houses painted white as in the old days. Galveston, these last two years, smelled of new paint and new wood. There was no sign now of those burning pyres that lasted some sixty days back in 1900, but workers digging into the sand still often came across the skeletal remains of animals and human beings.

Richard wanted to take the road that ran by the cemetery because it was paved with macadam and the rest of the streets were still deep in sand, so after a bit, they came to the cemetery road and made their way north.

As they hissed and spewed along, they chanced to come upon a funeral procession and the steam buggy caused the horses pulling the hearse to stamp and rear. The driver fought the reins in desperation as the hearse lurched. People in the procession peered out the windows of their carriages and Elizabeth's face burned with embarrassment.

"Richard, I want to go home," she shouted.

He nodded and tooled the thing down Broadway where new palms stood nodding in the Gulf breeze before the stately brick and stone mansions—which she would never own. Their own neighborhood was as fine as it was in the days before the storm, now newly painted and repaired and with new gardens and trees. He pulled into the shell-paved alley and into their drive. Joe Bob, sitting with Melissa out under the trees of their yard, shouted, "She won't float, Richard."

Richard stopped the car and shouted, "What did you say?"

Joe Bob, with newspaper in hand, stood up and leaned over the oleander hedge. "I say she isn't seaworthy. You'll never get her to float."

Flop bounded out to the car from the house as someone opened the screen door, and Elizabeth waited for Richard to open the door of the steam car so that she could get out of it. And looking up, saw Damon standing in the back door.

Her whole being became paralyzed. She was barely aware of the clamor of Richard greeting his brother and the hullabaloo that accompanied it. She moved as if under water in a warm vacuum of embarrassment and delight so intense she could barely speak. He greeted her like always, a brief, brotherly embrace, took her hand momentarily, but shouting maledictions upon Richard's car all the while. And then the men started going around looking at the steam buggy from all angles.

Melissa knew, and that was all. Only Melissa, and she put her arm around Elizabeth and the two of them went into the house. She sat down trembling in her chair in the back parlor, pressing her hand to her bosom where she could feel her heart thudding. Melissa would not speak about the unspeakable. She would only be there.

Elizabeth rallied, however, in short order, and invited the Swifts to dinner, and they all had a world of things to talk about; the sea wall, the grade-raising to be done when it was finished. There were miracles occurring all over the world, among them the wireless telegraph invented by an Italian named Marconi and which Damon said was fast becoming standard equipment on all ocean-going vessels. They talked about the growing popularity of jazz and ragtime and the king of ragtime, Scott Joplin; of the U.S. Senate having voted on a transoceanic route in Panama. Richard told of the medical school having added histology and embryology to its curriculum, taught by a woman doctor who had graduated from the medical branch in 1900. A new Negro hospital had been constructed.

Damon spoke of the new luxury liner at last. The plans for building the liner and a sister ship were being drawn up by a giant British shipping corporation with which Moran, Morrison and Company would soon merge. From his fine attire, his confident manner, it was apparent that Damon was doing well, which meant to Elizabeth that he was well-to-do. He was the same as always, except that now he had grown a mustache, strikingly becoming to him.

During the evening Damon showed no sign whatever that That Night had ever occurred. Her mind kept going back to it, to the heat of the evening, his embraces, his urgency, of his sleeping afterwards so deeply he was not aware of it when she rose and left the room and went to her own bed. Richard had come in early in the morning and fallen into bed with his clothes on. Damon had left early before either of them awoke, and had left a note on the kitchen table, "Leaving early for New York. My love remains always with you both."

Two years and two months and not another word from him until now. Her coolness toward him at dinner was apparent to everybody, and everybody but Melissa thought it was because she believed Damon should not have abandoned Galveston or her good friends, the Ingrams and Sturgeons. Damon was polite. Only polite.

Later in the parlor, he told Richard he could not stay at the house for the night. "I've rented a room at the Tremont Hotel where I've business to attend to early in the morning. And after that I'll be off again for New York at noon."

"Oh, Damon, you've decided to stay in New York, haven't you?" Elizabeth blurted.

His eyes were sad as he looked at her, and in that instant she read in them all she wanted to know. "Yes."

Melissa went home early, but Damon and Richard and Joe Bob sat up in the parlor for hours talking and smoking and drinking, while Elizabeth sat in the nursery rocking little Richard Damon, letting tears fall on his curly head, weeping and remembering.

But somehow she knew he'd come to her. She knew it. And he did, shortly before noon the next day. Richard had gone to the office that morning as usual, but lingering at the front door, toying with the new doorbell, examining the new etched glass window in the door, letting his eyes rest on her face. At last he was gone.

She was polishing her grandmother's silver teapot, polishing and waiting, and Richard Damon was sitting in his high chair, his sweet face smeared with cookie crumbs, pounding on the tray of his high chair with a spoon, when Prim at last let Damon into the house. After Shad and he exchanged pleasantries and Shad went out to tend his chickens, and she had sent Prim to the grocery store for supplies, he came to stand by the dining table watching her silently as she polished.

All was quiet. The furniture gleamed in its new varnish. The house was spotless with new wallpaper and plaster and paint. There was no evidence left of the destruction of the hurricane of 1900.

When she looked up at him hovering there, his eyes intense upon her, she rose and he held her in his arms. "Liz," he said into her hair, "you understand I tried to get you and That Night out of my mind these past two years. I tried to extinguish the horrible guilt of what I did to Richard and to you and I can't. I want you now as I wanted you then."

"But you didn't write," she said. "It was as if you had made love to me and then left me like they say sailors do to women in every port."

"No, no," he groaned. "You know better than that. I had wronged my brother and I had wronged you. I thought if I broke off all contact for the two years I was away, I might get you out of my mind. But I couldn't. And this town . . . there's something here that draws me back, my thoughts come back to it often, and to you standing on the beach with your hat in hand, on the deck of the *Charlemagne*, in the bedroom that night when the fires from the last of the funeral pyres lit up the room."

"Damon, oh, but you mustn't go back."

He held her from him so that he could look at her. "But I have to. Don't you see? I can't live here, Liz. Because you're here and I can't live near you without having you. Not any more. It was you who caused me to agree to go away for two years in the first place, away from the impossible."

The baby pounded on the tray and Damon looked at him and then at her. "I counted up last night. You said Richard Damon was fifteen months old."

"Yes."

"Then that means he was conceived about the time of the hurricane."

"Give or take a few weeks."

He studied her face. "You'd tell me . . . wouldn't you, Liz? If. . . ."

She shrugged, smiling. "They say the mother always knows who the father is." She shook her head. "But I . . . I'm not sure. I'm not sure at all."

He continued to study her face for a long time to see if she was telling the truth, his eyes reflecting a series of emotions, and finally he said, "I didn't have to come back, Liz. But I came to ask you . . . to come back with me. I've tried to live without you, but I found out my love for you is greater than my shame or my regret. I want you to be my wife. I need you. Richard should shoot me for what I've done . . . and for what I'm about to ask. Will you come back with me?"

She loved him still. But, looking around her at her home and beyond the lacy curtains to her side garden, and back to his face, she said, "Leave Galveston?"

"Yes. We couldn't live here. You know that. There would be scandal. There's my brother . . ."

She shook her head, bewildered. "I don't think I can leave Galveston." Laughing grimly, she said, "As a matter of fact, I don't think I can leave Richard either."

Damon released her slowly, lines deepening on his forehead and around his mouth.

She put her hand on his chest and said, "This town is in me, Damon. It's too much a part of me. It's too late. And I can't leave Richard, he's a part of me too." She shook her head. "No, no I can't leave now, not even for you."

Damon took her hand, raised it to his lips, sending the fires scorching through her body. "I didn't think you could," he said softly, "but I had to try. Remember this. I do love you Liz. Always have."

In that awful moment of decision he lay his hand on the baby's head briefly as if to bless him, and then turned and left the house. From the veranda she watched him climb into the carriage, doff his hat, and cluck to the horse. She watched as he went away from her and out of their lives. She wept watching him go. Her hand went to her abdomen, where the searing heat had never let up since the night he had taken her to him. It was still not too late. She could still go to him. . . .

In his private office over the drugstore, Richard took out his pocket watch. Half-past eleven. Damon's ship would be sailing in thirty minutes. He and whoever was sailing with him should be boarding about now. Morosely, he took the revolver out of his bag, the same revolver Damon had left with Shad the first night he came back after the storm. Left it in order to protect Liz, and Richard had kept it for that purpose ever since. Would to God he'd not find it necessary now to protect her from a fate worse than assault or death—dishonor.

He dared not telephone. Yet, he had to know. He covered his face with his hand and waited, trying to muster his courage. She thought that he was too insensitive to know, but he wasn't insensitive enough not to have felt the thing between them growing, growing until . . . who knows where it might have led? At last he lay the revolver on his desk beside his hat—ready in case she had left—and rose and went to the telephone on the wall, cranked it, waited.

"Hello, Central? Ring me 4621," he shouted. "No, no, 4621!" And he waited again, his world and his very life concentrating on that black object held to his ear, to this moment.

"Dr. Morrison's residence," came her voice on the line.

"Beth?"

"Richard."

They were both silent a moment. Both afraid to trust their voices. It was she who spoke first. "Richard? Please say you'll be home early. Will you?"

"Yes," he said hoarsely.

"When? When are you coming home?"

"Now, Beth," he said, opening his streaming eyes to the expanding world around him. "I'm coming home now."

Epilogue

My earliest memories are of walking on raised wooden boardwalks while mother held my hand to keep me from falling. This was during the incredible grade-raising of the island. There were dredges hovering in the temporary inland canals, pouring sand by the ton under the houses, which were jacked up what seemed to me a great height off the ground. Later, the sea wall was extended another mile down the beach, and the entire adventuresome, protective enterprise proved itself during the hurricanes of 1915 and 1962.

It boggles the imagination what the people of Galveston endured after the hurricane of 1900, and how they recovered and rebuilt the city. To me—especially to me—Galveston is synonymous with *gumption*.

There, to the left, the ships still come and go in the channel, and Galveston has remained an important seaport, while the giant Houston to the north wooed the shipping and oil industries and won, and expanded and

524

grew until it claims to be the third largest city in the United States. Piffle. That's true only area-wise. Chicago has a larger population.

Ah well, if the seigniorial families who they say decided at the turn of the century to keep Galveston a sleepy little resort town could see it now, they would turn over in their graves I think. Not that Galveston has grown, for she's grown very little since the turn of the century. It's the traffic. No, as a matter of fact, it's the *drivers*. I'll wager that Galveston has more dented and battered automobiles on her streets per capita than any other city in the United States. Father would cringe.

I see by his old watch it's time to go. My son, John, is still waiting. But I must look one more time at the medical school, my pride and my first love.

Old Red, they call it now. I made my last tour of it today. Inside, it's dusty and dank and unused except for the storing of building materials and rubbish I couldn't identify. In the basement the wind moaned through the half-buried windows, and on the stairways dead roaches lay, and in the third floor dissecting lab, such a mess of dusty junk stored and scattered. Outside, the old green storm shutters were loose and clattering against the building in the Gulf breeze.

Old Red sits on the edge of an eighty-acre medical complex now, which consists of fifty medical buildings, surrounded by construction which almost dwarfs it but does not surpass it in architectural beauty, for my money. No, never. And yet, incredibly, it sits in danger of being condemned, one of the last of Nicholas Clayton's monuments, that man gone and almost forgotten, dying when on the verge of bankruptcy, his widow unable to afford more than a small, insignificant headstone for his grave. Some say his business never recovered from the storm.

Well, I may never see you again, Galveston, but I'll join your ghosts someday. My mother, my father, old Uncle Shad and Aunt Prim, and the Swifts, and the Hoffmans. Even old Flop. And who knows, maybe even the uncle I never saw who they say had something to do with . . . I think it was Cunard's Lusitania and her sister ship, the Mauretania—though I'm not quite sure—both launched in 1907, the first modern passenger liners of their kind on the high seas. Perhaps his ghost is here too among them.

Well, I can rummage about forever in my memories like all old men do, but I must be going. And I hate crossing the bay to the mainland. Always have. Sometimes I believe Aunt Prim's old tale that tragedies witnessed by a pregnant woman mark the unborn child. Because I was conceived about the time of the hurricane of 1900, and if that old wive's tale is true, it would explain why I've always had this unexplainable, unreasonable hate for the sea.

EXCITING BESTSELLERS FROM ZEBRA

PASSION'S REIGN by Karen Harper   (1177, $3.95)

Golden-haired Mary Bullen was wealthy, lovely and refined—and lusty King Henry VIII's prize gem! But her passion for the handsome Lord William Stafford put her at odds with the Royal Court. Mary and Stafford lived by a lovers' vow: one day they would be ruled by only the crown of PASSION'S REIGN.

HEIRLOOM by Eleanora Brownleigh   (1200, $3.95)

The surge of desire Thea felt for Charles was powerful enough to convince her that, even though they were strangers and their marriage was a fake, fate was playing a most subtle trick on them both: Were they on a mission for President Teddy Roosevelt—or on a crusade to realize their own passionate desire?

LOVESTONE by Deanna James   (1202, $3.50)

After just one night of torrid passion and tender need, the dark-haired, rugged lord could not deny that Moira, with her precious beauty, was born to be a princess. But how could he grant her freedom when he himself was a prisoner of her love?

DEBORAH'S LEGACY by Stephen Marlowe   (1153, $3.75)

Deborah was young and innocent. Benton was worldly and experienced. And while the world rumbled with the thunder of battle, together they rose on a whirlwind of passion—daring fate, fear and fury to keep them apart!

Available wherever paperbacks are sold, or order direct from the Publisher. Send cover price plus 50¢ per copy for mailing and handling to Zebra Books, 475 Park Avenue South, New York, N.Y. 10016 DO NOT SEND CASH.

BESTSELLING ROMANCES BY JANELLE TAYLOR

SAVAGE ECSTASY   **(824, $3.50)**
It was like lightning striking, the first time the Indian brave Gray Eagle looked into the e;es of the beautiful young settler Alisha. And from the moment he saw her, he knew that he must possess her—and make her his slave!

DEFIANT ECSTASY   **(931, $3.50)**
When Gray Eagle returned to Fort Pierre's gates with his hundred warriors behind him, Alisha's heart skipped a beat: would Gray Eagle destroy her—or make his destiny her own?

FORBIDDEN ECSTASY   **(1014, $3.50)**
Gray Eagle had promised Alisha his heart forever—nothing could keep him from her. But when Alisha woke to find her red-skinned lover gone, she felt abandoned and alone. Lost between two worlds, desperate and fearful of betrayal, Alisha hungered for the return of her FORBIDDEN ECSTASY.

BRAZEN ECSTASY   **(1133, $3.50)**
When Alisha is swept down a raging river and out of her savage brave's life, Gray Eagle must rescue his love again. But Alisha has no memory of him at all. And as she fights to recall a past love, another white slave woman in their camp is fighting for Gray Eagle!

TENDER ECSTASY   **(1212, $3.75)**
Bright Arrow is committed to kill every white he sees—until he sets his eyes on ravishing Rebecca. And fate demands that he capture her, torment her . . . and soar with her to the dizzying heights of TENDER ECSTASY!

Available wherever paperbacks are sold, or order direct from the Publisher. Send cover price plus 50¢ per copy for mailing and handling to Zebra Books, 475 Park Avenue South, New York, N.Y. 10016. DO NOT SEND CASH.